"C'mon, lass," Connelly said. "These monsters have had a whiff of you now, they have. They're going to have your scent in their noses. And they're going to know what you are the same as I do."

"What I am," I repeated, not comprehending what he was alluding to.

"You're the Slayer, lass. The Chosen One. The girl who is called to fight the greatest monsters of our time."

I looked at him. One of the vampires had called me Slayer as well, and I hadn't understood why it had spoken to me in English. Perhaps it had gotten a better look at Connelly, seen that he was one of the *guei* and wrongly assumed that I was English or American myself. *Surely* such a term would not be common. I became even more desirous of whatever information Connelly possessed.

"Don't you know what the Slayer is?" Connelly asked.

I considered his question briefly, then shook my head. Astonishment showed on Connelly's soot-blackened face. "Wang never told you of the Slayer . . . ?"

Buffy the Vampire Slayer™

Buffy the Vampire Slayer
  (movie tie-in)
The Harvest
Halloween Rain
Coyote Moon
Night of the Living Rerun
Blooded
Visitors
Unnatural Selection
The Power of Persuasion
Deep Water
Here Be Monsters
Ghoul Trouble
Doomsday Deck
Sweet Sixteen
Crossings
Little Things
These Our Actors
The Cordelia Collection, Vol. 1
The Angel Chronicles, Vol. 1
The Angel Chronicles, Vol. 2
The Angel Chronicles, Vol. 3
The Xander Years, Vol. 1
The Xander Years, Vol. 2
The Willow Files, Vol. 1
The Willow Files, Vol. 2
How I Survived My Summer Vacation, Vol. 1
The Faith Trials, Vol. 1
The Journals of Rupert Giles, Vol. 1
Tales of the Slayer, Vol. 1
Tales of the Slayer, Vol. 2
Tales of the Slayer, Vol. 3

The Lost Slayer serial novel
  Part 1: Prophecies
  Part 2: Dark Times
  Part 3: King of the Dead
  Part 4: Original Sins
  Omnibus Edition

Child of the Hunt
Return to Chaos
The Gatekeeper Trilogy
  Book 1: Out of the Madhouse
  Book 2: Ghost Roads
  Book 3: Sons of Entropy
Obsidian Fate
Immortal
Sins of the Father
Resurrecting Ravana
Prime Evil
The Evil That Men Do
Paleo
Spike and Dru: Pretty Maids All in a Row
Revenant
The Book of Fours
Tempted Champions
Oz: Into the Wild
The Wisdom of War
Blood and Fog
Chosen (tie-in)
Chaos Bleeds
Mortal Fear

The Watcher's Guide, Vol. 1: The Official Companion to the Hit Show
The Watcher's Guide, Vol. 2: The Official Companion to the Hit Show
The Postcards
The Essential Angel
The Sunnydale High Yearbook
Pop Quiz: Buffy the Vampire Slayer
The Quotable Slayer
The Monster Book
The Script Book, Season One, Vol. 1
The Script Book, Season One, Vol. 2
The Script Book, Season Two, Vol. 1
The Script Book, Season Two, Vol. 2
The Script Book, Season Two, Vol. 3
The Script Book, Season Two, Vol. 4
The Script Book, Season Three, Vol. 1
The Script Book, Season Three, Vol. 2
The Musical Script Book: Once More, With Feeling

Available from SIMON PULSE

Buffy the Vampire Slayer™

Tales of the Slayer, vol. 3

A collection of original novellas based
on the hit TV series created by Joss Whedon

SIMON PULSE
NEW YORK LONDON TORONTO SYDNEY SINGAPORE

First Simon Pulse trade paperback edition November 2003

™ and © 2003 Twentieth Century Fox Film Corporation. All rights reserved.

SIMON PULSE
An imprint of Simon & Schuster
Children's Publishing Division
1230 Avenue of the Americas
New York, NY 10020

The text of this book was set in Minion.

Printed in the United States of America
10 9 8 7 6 5 4 3 2 1

Library of Congress Control Number 2003106958

ISBN 0-689-86436-1

Contents

Tales *of the* Slayer, *vol.* 3

Dark of the
Moon

Yvonne Navarro

A.D. 1229

Someday, hundreds of years in the future, the long-gone people of this beautiful desert canyon would first be called the Anasazi—the Navaho word diné or dineh—which, depending upon pronunciation, means either "enemy ancestors" or "ancient people who are not us." In later centuries, their descendants would object to the term and instead use the word hisatsinom, or sometimes moqui or moki—meaning "the dead"—and the region itself would be called Chaco Canyon in New Mexico. At the time of this telling, because this knowledge was not within their reach, the future Anasazi called themselves simply the People, and they lived in harmony with the great Earth beneath them and with all that was upon it. Such had been the way for almost two thousand years and would, they believed, be the way for millennia to come. Mother Earth would provide for them, and they would respect her, and all would live in balance and peace.

But something would come seeking to destroy that prosperity, and someday, in a future place and era beyond their present comprehension, that beast would be called vampire...

Tonight the People watched the Medicine Father walk out of the moon-soaked desert with the infant in his arms.

The Medicine Father was tall and lithe, an uncommon thing among a tribe whose members tended to be no more than ten hands high. Already thirty winters in age, most of the People considered him old, yet his lean, tense muscles were outlined by the cold lunar light, and there was nothing about him that suggested he was aging. In fact, it was quite the opposite—while others among the tribe had padded their bodies with fat in the abundant hunting times of the past several seasons, the Medicine Father had kept his sinewy form by fasting several times a month during private ceremonies in the *kiva*. Still, the bitter winds whipping across the canyon and crawling up the sides of the cliffs seemed to have no effect on his lanky form.

Or, oddly, on the child.

He had been gone for one full season—longer than ever before, long enough so that many had wondered if this time he was dead, perhaps killed by a bear or a dark spirit. But such was not the case, and he stood before them now, thinner but no less imposing. There was a hide draped over one shoulder, and it was beneath this shield that he had placed the child, but the wind break seemed more a thing of obligation than necessity. The babe neither shivered nor tried to burrow against the Medicine Father's shoulder for warmth. The People stared at her as he approached them, and she stared back, unaccountably quiet for a child who would have been expected to squall in hunger and cold. They knew it was a girl child because the Medicine Father had woven cactus flowers into her black hair; that she should have such long hair and be so young was yet another peculiarity.

Her eyes were black and solemn, oversize for her brown, childishly round face. Everything about her was a mystery—she was clearly too old to have been born to the Medicine Father and a woman during his absence, and never had he made an indication of taking a wife. In fact, it was generally accepted that he had spent these last many months in a period of isolation in one of the great *kivas* to the south, and while no one from the pueblo had actual proof of this, word that the tribespeople had from the residents there insisted that the Medicine Father had received no visitors during his seclusion.

So where, indeed, had this girl child come from?

They gathered around him reverently, waiting for his words of wisdom and enlightenment. He was descended from a long line of shamans, and his word would be accepted without question. His mother, White Flower, a wizened and bent woman of more than fifty summers—one of the oldest of their tribe—stepped forward to a place of honor, but she waited with the rest of the People for the Medicine Father to speak. No matter where the child had come from or who she was, if it was in accordance with the Medicine Father's wishes, it would be White Flower who took charge of the girl child and cared for her, who raised her to womanhood and trained her in the ways and traditions of the People.

For a long while the only sound that dared to disturb the silent circle of men and women around the Medicine Father and the child was the sigh of the night wind as it slipped over the rocks of the cliffs and through the bristly bushes that struggled to survive in the crevices between the boulders. Not even a coyote—usually so plentiful—howled across the distant desert, and if somewhere a hawk was ready to hunt, it stayed its flight for just a few more moments. The torches spaced here and there along the walkways cast a warm, orange glow on the waiting faces.

When he was ready, the Medicine Father hefted the girl child high over his head, then turned in a slow circle so that all could see her. "I bring you this child, who shall be called Dark of the Moon." The child hung in his arms without struggling, without smiling. Her gaze was as immeasurable as the sky above her, as impenetrable as the eyes of the Medicine Father himself. "She is born of my loins and the powerful and protective great Grandmother Spider," he continued. All eyes widened in awe and looked upon the girl with new respect. "For many winters I have waited for her birth, for it has been foretold by many of the spirits that someday it will be her duty to save the People—each and every one of us—from an evil which cannot be named." Although it never raised in volume, his voice carried across the desert and echoed against the cliffs, reaching every ear. The words swirled through those who had gathered and seemed to hover in front of them, raising fine bumps of dread along the expanses of skin not covered by leather or cloth.

The Medicine Father lowered Dark of the Moon until he could rest the child upon one hip, then slid the hide from his shoulder and let it fall to the ground. He pushed at it with the toe of one foot until it was straight, then set the girl child down on it and swept the gathered people once more with his gaze. He knelt and placed his wide hand over the quiet babe's head, his fingers long enough to nearly encircle her skull, then pulled his hunting knife free of its beaded sheath. His voice was softer when he spoke again, but no one had any difficulty hearing his words.

"Tonight we place the mark of the protector upon her, one line going down to represent her connection to the great Mother Earth, and another going across it, to signify the balance of Grandmother Spider and the other great spirits."

And as his knife rose and slashed the shallow lines into each side of the down-covered skin of her neck, and as her red, rich blood flowed against its silver blade and onto the thirsty desert soil . . .

Dark of the Moon still never uttered a single cry.

A.D. 1250: TWENTY-ONE YEARS LATER

Far above the *kiva*, the full moon shone bright and strong and big, illuminating the warm desert night like a pale, nighttime sun.

Lying on his back on a mat of woven willow branches, Lone Coyote, a young man of fifteen summers, stared at the moon and contemplated the sky, the world, and all the wonders within it. While he was at it, he gave particular attention to that part of the world which contained a certain young girl named Running Creek.

Smooth brown skin, liquid eyes like a doe's beneath thick, black hair that hung all the way to her hips. Sometimes her grandmother braided it and tied it in loops on each side of Running Creek's head, but Lone Coyote liked it best when she wore it down and let it sway in the breezes. A couple of times the two had met in secret behind one of the ceremonial houses after the new moon harvest blessings, and this last time Running Creek had let him kiss her on the cheek. It was nothing serious, of course, just the prelude to a courtship—

Please.

The two of them, he and Running Creek, were nothing but a fantasy, a dream. Running Creek's father was Destroyer of the

Wolf, one of the most revered hunters in the northeastern part of the pueblo. Running Creek was his oldest daughter, and already of marriageable age, and because of his standing and the dowry she would bring with her, she was a prize indeed. And Lone Coyote . . . what was he? Not much when one considered that his father had died nearly four years before and his mother had not remarried. In truth, she had already been showing her years upon her husband's demise, and there were no takers for someone her age who had a full family—Lone Coyote and his three younger siblings, plus an ancient grandfather and great-aunt—to take care of.

Not only was Running Creek's family not at all interested in him, they had already arranged a marriage between her and another young brave called Red Buck, whose relatives were not only plentiful but wealthy. Red Buck might have no need of Running Creek's dowry, but it would strengthen his family and bring good, strong ancestry into his bloodline, ensuring many fine children. Red Buck himself never even bothered with Lone Coyote, perhaps didn't realize he existed. Life could be so unfair.

Lone Coyote sighed and rolled over onto his stomach, gazing at the fire at the side of the *sipapu* a few feet away. It was supposed to be a sacred thing, that fire, but to Lone Coyote it was nothing more than a few pieces of burning wood and creosote. As it was every seventh sunset, it was his job to keep it going during the darkest hours. He despised the chore, had accepted it only because he'd thought it would somehow bring him some standing within the elite circle of shamans who used it for religious ceremonies. Now he realized the truth—they'd accepted his entreaty only because few of the other unmarried young men were interested in staying up all night to stare at the flames. There was little in the world more boring than having to feed a few thick sticks and a handful of dried creosote bush to this small pyre every hour or so.

And why?

Because it was a *ceremonial* fire, a sacred bunch of burning twigs and brush that supposedly ensured that nothing evil would crawl from the *sipapu*—itself nothing more than a hole in the ground, as far as Lone Coyote was concerned—and invade the village. The *sipapu* was supposed to be the navel of Mother Earth herself, which was crazy—anybody could see that the earth was nothing but dirt and sand and rocks, and all the stuff that grew on it. What could come out of such a small opening, one which, if the truth were told, didn't even go down very far anyway? It was only a small distance across and went into the ground for maybe three or four hands—not even large enough for a rattlesnake den.

Ridiculous. If they knew how Lone Coyote questioned this tradition, the shamans, the medicine men, perhaps even the Medicine Father himself, would sternly talk to him about dangerous evil spirits and dark ghosts and all that, but he didn't believe in any of it. They were just stories, ridiculous old tales spewed and respewed to keep troublesome children in line and control logical-minded men and women, keep them from thinking on their own.

Still, he was careful to keep these opinions to himself. His family and the elders would be appalled, as would his friends and probably everyone else in the settlement—perhaps even Running Creek. Did not anyone think for themselves? Was he the only one who saw how easily they were all manipulated, how they allowed the decisions and power over their own existences, literally over their lives and death, their *futures,* to rest in the hands of a few old men?

Spirits, indeed. Lone Coyote had never seen such a thing, nor did he know anyone else who had. Sure, there were the shamans and medicine men, but no one had ever *seen* them "see" a spirit or whatever it was they supposedly did. The entire system was based on their claims, on *illusion*. If he marched out of the *kiva* at daybreak and announced that he had seen the spirit of the night snake, and that it had spoken to him—surely he could make up some interesting tale—maybe they would make him a shaman too.

A draft slipped down into the *kiva* and the sacred fire sputtered, but Lone Coyote ignored it and flipped once more onto his back to stare at the sky beyond the opening in the roof. That silly fire built up heat in the *kiva* and the breeze felt good against his skin, cooling. It was a small respite in the hours he'd been in here, although it brought little comfort at the thought of the several more that stretched in front of him. He was tired, and sleepy, and did the elders ever consider relieving the night-watchers like him of their daytime duties? Of course not. They thought this was some kind of privilege, an *honor*. More absurdity. The only honor in watching a fire burn was if it was during a battle and you were the victor who'd set it among your enemies' things.

He yawned, thinking that he should add another stick or two to the fire. Maybe he would in a minute, but right now he was feeling kind of bad about how fate was conspiring to keep him and Running Creek forever apart. If he closed his eyes and concentrated, he could relive the sensation of kissing her cheek, how his lips had felt against the warm, velvety softness of her skin and the way she'd smelled like cactus blooms in late summer. The image of her smile, so sweet and bright, floated just behind his eyelids and—

Something crashed behind him.

Lone Coyote woke up with a start, then scrambled to his

knees when he realized the *kiva* was nearly in darkness. Only the light of the stars and the moon, now starting to wan, trickled in through the opening overhead. It wasn't much to see by when he'd been expecting something considerably warmer, like the light of the sacred fire's flames.

But the fire had gone out.

Shadows and darkness surrounded Lone Coyote. Only the area directly below the hole in the roof had any illumination at all, and everything beyond it was saturated with blackness, *heavy.* He could smell the smoke where the last of the embers had burned out, but he couldn't place the fire itself. He knew where it *should* be, but the only thing in front of his straining eyes were spots, like the little dancing flecks that happened when his eyes were tired and he rubbed them too hard. To make things worse, the warmth that he had resented earlier was gone; now the *kiva* was cold and damp, unnaturally so for the height of the desert's growing season, even at night. The chill that crawled across the bare areas of his skin reminded him of early winter and made a shiver course down his spine.

Lone Coyote glanced at the sky nervously, half expecting to see one of the medicine men scowling down at him. So far, so good, but he needed to get this fire going again before they discovered that he'd allowed it to burn out. He had a piece of flint in the leather pouch at his waist, so all he needed was a stone, a few fresh sticks, and some of that dried creosote to get it started again.

But when he moved forward in the darkness, something moved with him.

Lone Coyote froze, his heart beating heavily. "W-Who is there?" he managed. His voice sounded pathetic, weak and frightened as a girl's, and he resolved to make it more forceful. "Show yourself!" he said, more loudly this time.

In response, there was nothing but the faint hiss of the wind. It was the wind, wasn't it?

Thump.

The young man whirled but couldn't pinpoint the sound. Was it behind him? Or off to the side? The sudden movement had left him dizzy and breathless, the blackness around him disturbingly like being in a bottomless pit. He spun his arms in circles, searching for balance, then ended up on his knees anyway, gasping with shock. He couldn't see it—he couldn't see *anything*—but the ground was wrong, far too cold. Once in a great, great while, in the dead of the cold months and after a day of winter rains, the fields would freeze after nightfall. When that happened, the grasses would become like the tips of spears, sharp enough to break through uncovered skin. That's what Lone Coyote thought was happening now—it felt like there were a thousand tiny stings along his kneecaps and shins.

His hands went forward automatically and came down on the same, needlelike surface. He cried out as his skin split and moisture—blood—coated his palms. The thumping noise came again, this time behind him, and Lone Coyote scrambled around like an angry scorpion. It was a useless move, because he still couldn't see anything. But he was now absolutely convinced that he was *not* alone.

"Who's there?" Now he sounded exactly like what he was, a panicked young man on his own in the dark, and terrified. "What do you want?"

Instead of answering, something cut him deeply across the meaty part of his left shoulder.

If he'd cried out before, now Lone Coyote screamed. Having his carelessness with the sacred fire discovered by the elders, being thought of by the others in the village as afraid or even cowardly—none of these things mattered when faced with the agony that ripped across one side of his body. Blood coursed down his arm like too-warm wash water, and he threw himself in the opposite direction, instinctively trying to put distance between himself and the attacker he couldn't see. Surely someone would hear him and come to his aid, one of the male warriors, or the shamans, who were never far from the *kiva* and its holy objects and offerings—it wasn't *that* far underground. His scream stopped only when he ran out of breath, and he sucked in air to start again, fueled by the torturous pain running through his arm and chest.

But he never got the chance.

And in the morning the medicine men would find what was left of what had once been a handsome young man named Lone Coyote. In the cold, damp light of a heavily overcast day, they would look at his remains, and at the black ashes of the sacred fire next to the *sipapu,* and they would mourn. . . .

In the center of their adobe, Dark of the Moon watched White Flower as she hummed to herself and tossed a handful of the small, rare gopher bones across a soft piece of leather she'd placed on the ground. They landed in a pattern, sort of. There was a rib, next to a little leg bone . . . or was that something else, one of the dead creature's forepaws? She just couldn't tell, and it was all the more frustrating for her when the ancient White Flower turned a watery gaze in her direction and waited expectantly. All these years of coaching and hinting and teaching, but Dark of the Moon's mind was as impervious to the arts of prophecy as the cliff walls were to gentle morning breezes. All she could do was look helplessly back at her grandmother and say nothing, and that, of course, told the whole tale.

White Flower didn't say anything, but her head, covered in still-thick hair that the years had turned the color of angry storm clouds, bobbed in disapproval. She swept the bones up and dropped them back into the pouch she'd pulled from the corner, where she kept her most treasured items, then sprinkled them out once more. Her hopeful glance at Dark of the Moon only lasted a moment before she shrugged and gave up on the idea that Dark of the Moon could read the bones; the surrendering was probably what stung the most.

"I am sorry, Grandmother."

White Flower said nothing, and Dark of the Moon fell silent. There wasn't much for her grandmother *to* say that hadn't already been voiced, time and time again, over the past years. Both her father and White Flower believed she should have had the sight long ago, starting with the onset of her body's change to womanhood at fifteen. But that had been seven years ago, nearly twenty-eight full seasons, and . . .

Nothing.

It was a disappointing thing to both elder members of her family, and Dark of the Moon knew it diminished her greatly in their eyes, cast a shroud of doubt over their belief that she would be able to fulfill the prophecies that had been made about her existence. It both frustrated and shamed her . . . and, although she would never dare admit it to either of them, it awakened her own dark seed of unease. When the time came, would she really have the abilities that were needed to battle the . . .

What?

She had no idea, and according to what she could pry out of her father, neither did he. She had *something*, that was certain; that she could feel an unseen power coursing through her was undeniable, that others—her father, the other men and women in the settlement—could discern her strength and distinctly un-womanlike ability to fight could also not be ignored. She could best any of the warrior and hunting males in the village, but that told her nothing more than she could defeat a mortal man. If she listened to her father's soothsaying, the opponent she would someday face was anything but.

How could she be trained to fight something about which they had no knowledge?

Dark of the Moon watched her grandmother as she studied the gopher bones. The years and the harsh summers had not been kind to the old woman; her face and hands were weathered, her fingers were shaky and covered in skin so thin it was nearly transparent. Dark of the Moon could see the delicate line of veins beneath the skin, a pattern of life built from decades of hard work, much of it dedicated to the raising of her granddaughter while her son attended to the daily business of being the medicine man for the village. After all that effort had been put into her, what would she do—how could she live with herself—if she let this woman down?

"The bones say that the time is near," White Flower said suddenly. The line of thought in Dark of the Moon's mind broke apart and fluttered away, and she focused on her grandmother's hushed words. "You should begin to prepare yourself. The Medicine Father will come for you tonight."

White Flower swept up the bones and dropped them into her pouch again, but she did not spill them onto the piece of leather a third time. Sitting cross-legged on a pronghorn hide, Dark of the Moon watched the old woman tuck the pouch back among her pile of belongings in the corner. *The Medicine Father will come for you tonight.* Odd that White Flower should refer to her son that way, as if he were an entity, rather than flesh and blood of her own body and Dark of the Moon's long-dead grandfather.

She looked around the small adobe dwelling and felt a sense of anticipation building on the air. Was she frightened? No, she didn't think so. Excited was probably more accurate, but she wished she had someone to talk to about it. She loved White Flower, of course, but she was old, and often she just didn't seem to understand the way that Dark of the Moon, and the others of her age group, thought about things. If only she had a mother in which she could confide, a woman who most likely would be no more than fourteen or fifteen summers older than she was.

Well, she didn't, and that was the way it was. Had she really been created of the union between her father and the great Grandmother Spider, then carried to full birth in the egg sac of that same hallowed being? Such a thing seemed so strange, especially when she watched the women of the village who were with child, with their bellies distended and their faces glowing in anticipation of the new life soon to be born. She knew her grandmother and her father loved her, but their feelings were not the same as those she saw on the faces of the mothers and fathers in the pueblo. Her father's and grandmother's feelings for her were . . . reserved. *Conditioned.* It was as though they felt affection for her but thought they shouldn't feel too *much,* and they always made her think that those same feelings would somehow diminish if she didn't perform well in the tasks assigned to her.

And those tasks, they were different too. None of the other young women in her community were required to know the same battle skills as those of the male warriors. Instead they learned to weave baskets and prepare food, to tan hides and sew clothing. They fashioned and painted exceptional pottery and Dark of the Moon knew several young women who had learned to make beautiful jewelry from the turquoise that had been traded from the peoples of the distant southern lands. Those lands were rumored to be lush and green and moist, so different from her home, and filled with wild and exotic creatures like the big, multicolored birds that with enough patience learned to mimic some of their owners' words. She wished she could go there and see for herself the forests of which the returning traders spoke, see the strange and wonderful creatures—

"You must prepare yourself." Again White Flower's grating voice broke into Dark of the Moon's thoughts, forcing her back to the present.

"Prepare myself?" Dark of the Moon repeated. "To see my father?"

"Tonight he is not your father," White Flower said. "Tonight he is only the Medicine Father." There was a sharpness in her tone that gave away her impatience and Dark of the Moon felt immediately ashamed for questioning her grandmother's directions.

"What should I do?"

White Flower had already folded up the leather on which she'd spread the gopher bones, and now she replaced it with a scarf of soft, woven animal hair. A colorful pattern had been dyed into it, lines and shapes representing the earth and the elements. On this she carefully arranged a painted pottery bowl into which she poured fresh water, a soft clean cloth, and a bundle of dried herbs made of wild sage, piñon, and creosote. Next to these she placed a packet of clean clothes. "Wash yourself carefully and put these on," White Flower said. "Take your time and pray to the spirits to give you guidance in the times to come. I will prepare a meal for you so you do not go hungry."

"Go hungry?" Dark of the Moon couldn't stop the question from leaving her lips.

"It will be a long night."

She had more questions—many more—but Dark of the Moon wisely kept them to herself as she drew the curtain across the adobe's entrance and tied it in place for privacy. It would do no good to further tax her grandmother's patience, or worse, disappoint her with what the old woman would consider a curious nature that was beneath Dark of the Moon's year and status. She already felt different than the other women her age, isolated by the birthright that her father insisted was hers.

Dark of the Moon wondered at fate, and at the destiny the spirits had decreed for her—what made her different from anyone else? When she shed her clothes and looked down at her body in the light cast by the torches and the cooking fireplace, she did not believe she was different from anyone else . . . except, of course, that now, at twenty-one years, she was an old maid, far past the age where any worthwhile young warrior would want her for a wife. She thought she looked as pleasing as any other woman, and she certainly didn't feel too old for marriage or childbirth, or anything else.

Dark of the Moon wet the cloth and ran it carefully over her skin, knowing she should be praying as White Flower had instructed, but unable to concentrate or find any comfort in the chants she had learned so well through the years. Instead, she wondered—as she had many, many times over the years—why *she* had been chosen, and not someone else. She wasn't sure she *wanted* to be special, because to be "special" had, more than anything else, meant to be *shunned*. She'd grown up without friends among her peers, without siblings, and mostly without *warmth*. And there would be little of that in the future, certainly no husband or children. While she couldn't change it, it was not the life she would have chosen for herself. She wished, again, that she could see the future like White Flower, because what she imagined for herself ten or twenty winters down the line—herself as an unmarried old woman taken into the household of a younger shaman out of pity and obligation, and made to care for his family—was bleak, indeed.

Still washing, being careful to cleanse her skin of desert dust and grime, Dark of the Moon drew in a breath and tried to calm herself. The movement filled her senses with goodness—the smell of White Flower's rabbit-and-blue-cornmeal stew—and Dark of the Moon suddenly felt guilty for not appreciating her life more. There were many in the pueblo whose lives were not so enriched, who struggled in the fields at the height of summer to bring in food for their families. The Medicine Father's standing brought him great plenty, and those same people who worked so diligently were the ones who contributed to the wealth of his—and through him, Dark of the Moon's—household. She should really be more grateful.

Finished with her washing, the young woman took the bundle of dried grasses and rubbed herself down with it, letting the heady smell of the sage in particular fill her nostrils. It was a good scent, the one that reminded her the most of the great Mother Earth and her bounty. That done, she shook out the packet of clothes and inspected each item carefully to make sure they were free of scorpions—the nasty things, bark scorpions in particular, liked to crawl between the folds of leather and fabric and hide. The bigger ones were scary to look upon and gave a painful sting, but they weren't particularly dangerous; as tiny as they were—usually less than the length of a finger joint—the sting of the pale tan bark scorpion sometimes caused death.

She'd never seen this packet of clothing before, and its pieces were strange and wonderful all at the same time, sort of a hybrid of men's and women's garments. There was a soft leather shirt that had thin, decorative strands running vertically down its front. Each strand had been woven with dyed wooden beads in many different colors. Following that was a pair of men's pants made from that same carefully cured leather, and these had a matching line of beaded strands running down each side from waist to ankle. For a moment Dark of the Moon wasn't sure she should put them on—perhaps there'd been a mistake and these were not meant for her. But when she glanced over at White Flower, she saw the old woman watching her and nodding her approval.

Dark of the Moon slid the top piece over her head, then hesitantly pulled on the pants. The leather was soft as any fabric she'd ever felt, lovely against her skin. Still, the pants felt odd on her legs, bulky yet freeing—never again would she have to be concerned about whether or not inappropriate parts of her anatomy were revealed when she did battle training. The thought made her grin a little; had she known men's pants were this convenient, she would have tried to wear them long ago.

There were no new sandals, and for this she was glad. Her much-repaired pair was comfortable and worn, and they fit well to her feet. When she was fully dressed, Dark of the Moon combed her hair and rebraided it with meticulous care—it wouldn't do to look sloppy when her father arrived. To help hold the plaits in place, she wove several long, thin strips of leather within each one, fastened small bright feathers from one of the southland birds at the ends, then tied them securely. That done, she turned to face White Flower.

Her grandmother grunted her approval, then motioned to the eating area. "It is time for your meal."

Obediently Dark of the Moon went over and knelt on the hides spread on the floor. White Flower had arranged a fine meal for her, almost like a celebration feast—spicy rabbit-and-blue-cornmeal stew rich with vegetables and beans (Dark of the Moon's favorite dish), fried squash blossoms with sweet prickly pear relish, and to further the young woman's impression that this was a celebration, White Flower had also apparently baked Feast Day cookies earlier in the day, flavoring them with honey and *piñon* nuts.

Dark of the Moon ate . , . but found she could not fully enjoy the meal. Her thoughts kept turning to the upcoming evening and the arrival of her father. She told herself to be patient—after all, as her grandmother would no doubt tell her, she would find out soon enough—but it did little good. The food had taste but her mouth did not want it; it swallowed as well as any other meal, but her stomach was unsettled and unappreciative of the good bounty. Dark of the Moon felt ashamed at this, knowing how hard her grandmother had worked to prepare the meal; White Flower, however, either didn't notice Dark of the Moon's lack of appetite or excused it because of the circumstances. She saved a small portion for herself, then picked up the remains of the spread, waving away Dark of the Moon's attempt to help.

And then there was nothing to do but wait.

Waiting. It seemed Dark of the Moon had been doing this all her life, and yet tonight that waiting was finally going to come to an end. Now that it was here, she wasn't sure she was ready. The results of her training had been good, but would it be good enough? She had no explanation or description, no *knowledge,* of whatever demon she was to face. Would she be able to defeat it?

And what if she were not?

The minutes stretched by, and for the first time in as long as she could remember, Dark of the Moon actually wished she had more time before having to face her destiny.

And then the curtain to their adobe was drawn aside, and the Medicine Father stepped into view.

In addition to Dark of the Moon and her father, there were at least four dozen medicine men and elders in the main ceremonial *kiva* tonight. She'd never seen so many elders gathered in one *kiva,* and despite its great size, they made it seem small. It wasn't so much their physical presence, although that was considerable; it was the unseen sort of . . . *power* that they radiated, the idea that here was gathered so much of the great history of their people and, perhaps, a good deal of knowledge about the future as well.

The air was close and hot, thanks to the five or six sacred fires that had been lit, again more than Dark of the Moon had ever seen. Everything about this night seemed to be in excess—the costumes the shamans wore (not to mention her own new outfit), the fires, the number of men crowded into the *kiva*. They ringed the walls and watched with solemn, dark eyes as the Medicine Father led her down the ladder and motioned for her to take a seat where places had been saved for them on the stone ledge at one side. The fires flickered and glowed red and yellow as the smoke swirled up and out of the ventilation openings, creating mysterious-looking patterns between Dark of the Moon's eyes and the faces of the older men.

She sat and waited, her wide eyes taking in everything, missing nothing. They had clearly been down here for some time, judging by the water vases and the remains of several meals which had been carefully set aside. A number of the shamans hummed and muttered to themselves, their words too low to be understood. Five of them sat cross-legged before drums, apparently waiting for the right moment. Offerings of fruit, vegetables, and freshly killed small game were positioned just so around the *sipapu* in the center of the room, placed in the best of the village's pottery bowls and adorned with fragrant spices. Again, it almost looked like a celebration.

Except . . .

The expressions on the weathered faces of the men around the *kiva* were anything but joyous. Instead they melded from one expression to another as the minutes crawled past, showing shock, anger, and disbelief; one or two of the most ancient men looked as if they would drown in sorrow.

And even more looked utterly terrified.

The Medicine Father was in full ceremonial dress, but the beads and stones woven into his clothing were an odd color. Black and brown, some dyed indigo, everything about him cast a somber presence, cooling an atmosphere that might have been warmed by all these fires. His gaze was cold as he surveyed the others, and if it held any compassion at all, it was only as he glanced at his daughter. For this Dark of the Moon was glad; she didn't know what she would have felt had the emptiness in her father's eyes extended to her.

"We are ready to begin." The Medicine Father's voice was quiet, but it was still heard in every corner of the *kiva*. Every noise instantly stopped, from the self-murmurings of the shamans to the scrape of a wooden spoon against a bowl as its contents were positioned in a fashion more pleasing to the spirits.

And then, there was the silence.

Her father strode over to where she sat and stood before her expectantly. Dark of the Moon wasn't sure what to do, but when he offered her his hand she took it, instinctively standing. He led her to the center of the *kiva* and stood with her next to the *sipapu;* she couldn't help but notice how black and dark the hole in the earth looked, despite the festively arranged food, trinkets, and cactus flowers surrounding it. She had seen it dozens of times—no, more like hundreds—but never before had it seemed so menacing.

She dragged her gaze away as the Medicine Father put his hands on her shoulders and gently turned her to face the elders. While she had been staring at the *sipapu,* they had moved closer, and now Dark of the Moon and her father were on the inside of a small ring of the pueblo's most respected and power-ful medicine men—only her father held more standing than anyone else in this room. Their eyes were penetrating and deep, soaking in the light of the fires as much as the shadows against the *kiva*'s far walls. Dark of the Moon felt oddly paralyzed, disconnected, as if only her father's presence kept her spirit from being lifted free of Mother Earth by all the mystical strength surrounding them.

One of the shamans, a man who was the most ancient among them and who was called Weeping Antelope, squatted and began to beat softly on a drum. Several more men did the same, ultimately forming a rhythmic pattern that undulated around Dark of the Moon and the Medicine Father. She listened, awed and humbled as always by the echoing beauty of the instruments, wanting it to go on and on. But beauty never lasts, and soon another of the elders, a medicine man who had no drum, added words to the sounds, singing in a low and scratchy voice. Another did the same, then another, and another. Their low, singsong words twined around one another until, with a little patience, Dark of the Moon wove it into a story, one that went on and on, running into and over itself without rhyme or even a pause to breathe. . . .

From the darkness it came
Out of the forgotten bowels of the Earth Mother
Where it had been banned for eons
And imprisoned by the Father of the Stars.
Up and up and up, constantly testing,
Scratching at the boundaries of its prison,
Searching for a way out and into freedom.
But always it was contained by the sacred fire
And the prayers and constant vigilance
Of those who watch over the People.
Finally it began to weaken within itself

And draw away from the People in the light.
But when the younger of the People were born,
A new generation began to question the Great Truths.
Their faith in the Old Ways was tenuous,
Their belief in the ancient rituals illusory.
And the beast in the belly of the Mother
Opened its bloody eyes,
Fed on their doubts,
And began once more to awaken.

Dark of the Moon listened, fascinated, her gaze streaking from one speaker to the next as each holy man picked up the chanting story. The tale flowed, the words pouring like finely ground cornmeal in the warm sun, glittering and smooth, never missing a beat as one man finished speaking and another picked it up.

Up from the deepest crevices of the belly it crawled,
Vile and scrabbling beneath the soil,
Polluting every living thing it touched along the way.
As it neared the navel of the great Mother Earth,
It realized that the time of its dark opportunity was at hand
For the guardian of the sipapu *had been careless*
And he had fallen asleep.
While the guardian dreamed of earthly pleasures
The sacred fire that warmed the opening
Of the Earth Mother's belly died and went out
And there was nothing left to stop the beast
From crawling through her navel,
That sacred spot from where all things
Came and will come,
And it stood ready to poison the world.

In the silence of the unprotected kiva
It found the foolish young guardian
And its hunger was great and consuming
As it tasted the first blood it had found in eons.
And thus it feasted then left the kiva
With neither fire nor guardian to stop it.

The guardian? With a start, Dark of the Moon realized that one of the guardians had been a young man named Lone Coyote, whom she hadn't seen around the village for several days. Thinking about it for a moment, she also hadn't seen Lone Coyote's mother or father, or his younger sister. They must have been sworn to secrecy by the elders, who hadn't wished to panic the pueblo's inhabitants, and rather than hide their grief over losing a son, they had gone into seclusion.

But more important, what had happened to the beast?

As if they could read the questions in her mind, the next words of the elders' song answered her.

Now the beast roams unchecked within the pueblo,
Hiding in the shadows,
Invading the dwellings of the People
Where its only desire is to feed and spread its kind
Across the landscape of the great Mother Earth herself.
One beast begets another, and that beast sires in kind
And they will spread like a plague of summer locusts
Unless the one who has been called steps forward,
Raises her mighty weapons
And slays them once and for all.

The drumming circled around her along with the sweet-smelling sage smoke of the fires. It was all so . . . strange—her father's belief in the spirits of the earth and sky, his claim that her mother was a being other than a flesh and blood woman. Now the elders were saying that something evil had crawled from the *sipapu,* something not at all spiritual, but with physical form. This evil had killed one boy and would continue to kill and spread itself.

But did she believe that? Dark of the Moon wasn't sure. It seemed so much like yet another tall tale that had been formed and elaborated as, at least to her mind, pure entertainment. Why was she, one woman, charged with stopping something such as this? *Could* she even do so?

She who is called must not fail in her duty
Or the People shall surely perish
And disappear from the vista of Mother Earth forever.

Dark of the Moon said nothing, but her mind was racing. If she was hearing the song of the elders correctly, they were saying that the fate of everyone rested on her shoulders alone. What *was* the beast they sang about? Was it a man? An animal? Or a twisted combination of both? Her mind was giving her fantastic pictures of a man with a ringtail's head and a bobcat's extended claws, but that was ridiculous.

The drumming stopped abruptly and there was silence in the *kiva* as they all stared at her. Dark of the Moon wasn't sure what to do now—should she say something? What?

Then her father turned her until she faced him, and he began to speak.

"Daughter, I have long told you of your great birth mother, and of your destiny to defend our home and the People. The time has now come for you to embark upon that sacred task." A few feet away, Weeping Antelope set his drum to the side and got shakily to his feet. He picked up a pouch and carried it reverently over to the Medicine Father.

"These items will help you in the great battles to come," her father told her. "We have only this night to prepare you for the future, so you must take heed and learn quickly, for much responsibility has been given to you by the Great Spirits. We have always been connected to the precious earth and to everything from which we came, and now we can feel the beast that has come from beneath. It insinuates itself into every part of our daily lives, waiting, watching, *wanting*. And you, my daughter, are the One Who Has Been Called to stop it."

Again, Dark of the Moon said nothing, but inside her chest, her heart was beating rapidly. Yes, this was the moment for which she'd been waiting, and training, all her life, but was she really ready for it?

Did she have a choice?

"Take heed," croaked Weeping Antelope from her father's side. His voice was old and scratchy, like an animal hide cracked and dried from too many years in the sun. "You are more than just a girl, even more than the offspring of a mortal and a Great Spirit."

Someone else came and stood on the other side of her father, a man called Flying Hawk, who was about fifty winters in age. "You have been gifted not only with the powers of your mother, great Grandmother Spider, but the strength of her companion gods, the Warrior Twins."

"And you have the quickest abilities of the great horned water serpent," said someone else from behind her. Instinctively, she started to turn, but her father's hand on one shoulder stopped her.

"Tonight," her father said, "we will teach you many things to aide you in your battles, for the way will be hard and victory will not be easily won." Dark of the Moon thought she detected a note of compassion in his usually stern voice. It also didn't escape her that this was the second time he'd referred to *battles,* as in more than one. She'd thought the song of the elders had referred to only one beast, but now they were implying that it had already multiplied. If so, was she expected to fight them all?

Apparently so.

"You will need weapons."

"You must have faith."

"You must keep your spirit strong."

"You must never falter."

Now there were voices all around her, too many for her to identify—all the elders had come to their feet and were surrounding Dark of the Moon and her father, their instructions and counseling flowing around her like the wind, too fast and elusive to pinpoint. Amazingly, everything they said seemed to sink into her brain and stick—

"Never let yourself be trapped in a box canyon."

"Protect your back and your neck at all times."

"You must strike with surety."

"Your opponent can be destroyed if you separate its head from its body, but your killing blow will most likely be to the heart."

"Your death weapon will always be made of Mother Earth's sacred wood."

"The creature is a drinker of humanity's blood."

"You must never taste the blood of the beast itself."

"The beast is neither alive nor dead. It is undead."

"Choose death before allowing the creature to feast on your blood."

"The creature will multiply and spread if you do not stop it. . . ."

"If you do not stop it . . ."

"If you do not stop it!"

Dark of the Moon blinked and opened her eyes. She was stretched out on the floor of the *kiva* on a mat of woven yucca leaves. She couldn't remember lying down, but she didn't think she'd been sleeping. She had the slightest tinge of an ache in her head and realized that the elders had likely put something in the fire, and that she'd inhaled it through the light smoke that always floated on the air down here. It was rumored that they sometimes used dried desert plants to obtain a state of meditation, but she wished they'd allowed her to make her own choice about that—loss of control over herself wasn't something she wanted or enjoyed.

Now they all sat cross-legged in a ring around her, a little farther away than before, and when Dark of the Moon turned her head to the right she saw her father. Between him and her were several objects, things she'd never seen before and which, at least to her knowledge, had no equal in the pueblo. He motioned for her to sit up and she obeyed, at first feeling lethargic and heavy, as though her arms and legs were weighted down by great pouches of creek stones. But the more she moved, the more that languid feeling was replaced by a sort of tingling, an excitement that made her realize somewhere inside her was a great rush of strength and energy, just waiting to be freed. There was fear, yes, but now there was anticipation, too.

"We have meditated and prayed over you to give you extra strength and support in the spiritual realm," her father said. His voice had regained that eerie, echoing quality. "Now we present you with the weapons for battle, and we know that you will use them well and with good intent."

Thankfully, Dark of the Moon's mind had cleared enough for her to concentrate on her father's words and what he was doing. She watched with interest as he ceremoniously offered her a carefully carved *atlatl*. When she took it from him and hefted it curiously, she realized immediately that the wooden throwing stick had been fashioned for her grip alone—the finger loops would fit the hand of no other, and the sight along the spear groove seemed like an extension of her own keen hunting vision. It was a beautiful piece, adorned with bits of obsidian and precious macaw feathers, polished to a high, dark sheen.

But the Medicine Father and the elders were not finished, and her father held up something else. Dark of the Moon placed the *atlatl* across her knees and accepted the next gift. It was a pouch constructed of meticulously woven cactus fibers and decorated with stains in the shapes of spiritual figures; inside were at least five handfuls of thin, sharp-tipped wooden spears. Their edges had been honed so finely that they were dangerous to handle.

"All these items have been blessed by the elders, by me, and by the Great Spirits," her father told her. "As we have sung to you, the beast you seek to kill is a drinker of blood. It has crawled through the *sipapu* from the deepest underbelly of the earth and its evil will multiply unto itself and destroy the People if you do not stop it." He paused to make sure she understood the severity of his instructions, then continued when she nodded. "It will take from many forms and use many features in its efforts to disguise itself—look for it in the eyesight of the bobcat, the cunning of the coyote, the talons of the hawk, the horns of the antelope, the coils of the night snake, and, perhaps, even in the faces of those you might otherwise trust."

This was something she had not anticipated, and Dark of the Moon felt a shiver creep down her spine. "Is it . . . a shape-changer?"

The Medicine Father shook his head. "No, not in the sense of which you speak. It cannot transform itself from human to animal, but it *does* hide its true self beneath a human veil, only revealing its ugly nature at its most brutal of moments."

"What will it look like?" Dark of the Moon asked. She was un-aware that her voice had dropped to a whisper.

For the first time she could remember, her father hesitated. "No one knows for sure. It is held in legend that it looks human much of the time, but no one has ever sung of how it appears in its true form." He looked at the ground for a moment, then con-tinued. "It is a stealer of spirits, my daughter. You must take great care, not only that it takes not of those who live in the pueblo, but also that it takes not of *you*."

Had it not been for the smooth wood of the *atlatl* in one hand and the pouch in the other, Dark of the Moon would have crossed her arms protectively at such ominous words. She had known her responsibility—at least in theory—all her life, but somewhere in her mind she must have believed she would be called to fight something . . . *normal*. A bobcat, perhaps, some-thing supernaturally oversize and gone wild for the taste of human meat. She swallowed, swallowed again, and finally found the courage to voice the most important question.

"When do I face this beast?"

Her father's eyes were penetrating and endless, like pools of black water on a moonless midnight.

"Tonight," he said. For all the fear that Dark of the Moon could feel coursing through her bones, his voice was utterly emotionless. "And every night until you triumph . . .

"Or perish."

And thus, on the first night of her calling, Dark of the Moon's battle for the fate of her people began.

When Dark of the Moon climbed out of the *kiva*, she had no idea how much time had passed. Was it the same night, or had she been in there a full twenty-four hours? There was no way to tell, other than it was far into the night and the inhabitants of the pueblo were asleep, the pathways between the adobes deserted in the wan light of the new moon. She carried her *atlatl* and her pouch of wooden stakes, plus a few other trinkets in smaller pouches tied to the belt at her waist, odds and ends needed for little things she had learned over the years from the Medicine Father. She was, she supposed, as ready as she was ever going to get.

The problem was, she had no earthly idea where to go.

Of all the things the shamans and medicine men, and her father, had told her, they had left out the one thing most critical: Where, exactly, would she find this evil beast?

The countryside around the pueblo was huge, nearly incomprehensible. It was cut by hills that ranged from barely an incline to the size of a small mountain. Valleys filled with scrub, cactus, and rattlesnakes crisscrossed the spaces in between, and a man—or a woman—could very easily fall to a painful and anonymous death in almost any one of them. The pathways that led from the pueblo high on the cliff face to the valley floor were sometimes only as wide as a man's chest, intentionally treacherous to negotiate and meant to keep out enemy invaders. And if a person didn't find the oblivion of death quickly enough should they fall, the desert's natural residents—bobcats, coyotes, foxes, and more—were always willing to help them along.

Not knowing her destination, Dark of the Moon walked aimlessly through the large pueblo, searching the deep shadows of the corridors between the dwellings for something which had no name or face upon which she could focus, no shape she would find familiar. She wished she had the inherent instinct that both her father and grandmother seemed to have about things—they always seemed to know what to do, how to do it, and where to go to get it done. She, on the other hand, had no such sense of inner guidance; while she knew she was supposed to do *something*, it was as though some intrinsic seed of . . . *self* had failed to crack open and sprout.

At the edge of the sprawling pueblo now, Dark of the Moon stared out and over the expanse of the great canyon below. They were well protected here, with their village, which was growing bigger and becoming more crowded at every passing season, set high within the cliff boulders. It was a good place, a *safe* place, and it both angered and terrified her that something threatened it, something more powerful and insidious than the simple vicious-ness of a bobcat or other predator. And here she was, one lone young woman, armed and facing a desert wilderness lit by a sliver of moonlight that allowed her to barely decipher which was bush and which was rock. How frustrating.

After making sure the pouch of sticks and her *atlatl* were se-curely fastened to her belt, Dark of the Moon moved a wooden ladder into place that allowed her to descend from the bottom-most level of the pueblo to the ledge that would ultimately lead to the ground. Here and there she could see young warriors posted on the ledge of the levels above her, watching for any-thing that might threaten the villagers. She knew they were there, and they knew she was too. Now that she had left the pueblo proper, one of them would stand watch by the ladder to make sure that it was she, and not someone else, who returned.

It took her some time, but finally she stood below the cliffs, where the land flattened out for larger spaces at a time, creating miniplains of tall desert grasses. Feathery and plentiful at the height of their growing season, they rustled in the night breezes, and Dark of the Moon knew the sound would mask many others. Again she wondered why she was out here like this, why she had been chosen over someone else—would not a young warrior from her pueblo have been more fitting for this task?

She was still considering this question when the creature attacked her from behind.

Something—perhaps that elusive instinct that most of the time she was convinced she didn't possess—made her spin to face it at the last instant. She had no time to wonder where it had come from, or why it had charged her rather than conceal itself; her spin took her neck out of its reach, but its sharp teeth scraped the skin of her upper arm and left a long, stinging wound covered in foul saliva. She cried out, but more in surprise than pain. When it lunged at her again, she backhanded it hard enough to send it tumbling into the thigh-high grasses.

For a moment—only that—Dark of the Moon simply stood there, letting her brain absorb her first true sighting of the beast she had been born to destroy. It looked as though it had once been a man, although she didn't recognize him from her pueblo or any of the surrounding communities. That might be because the creature looked old—no, beyond that . . . *ancient,* something that had lived for more years than she had ever thought possible or desirable. Dark hair and skin, it jolted her that his origins could be from the People themselves—that he might have once been human—yet she knew in her heart that this was so.

But whatever dark spirit now resided in his body had twisted him both in soul and appearance. When the grasses swayed and whispered, Dark of the Moon knew it was coming for her again, and she braced herself for what she would see: mottled skin covered in dirt and ashen patches stretched over a skeletal face, a scalp upon which stubbornly clung overlong strands of filthy, thin hair, a nearly naked body covered only by a tattered piece of sewn loincloth. Its eyes were red, glowing like embers, while the sparse moonlight glinted off pointed, decaying teeth. And hadn't the thing's mouth been rimmed in fresh blood? She wanted to glance at her arm to see if any residue remained, but she didn't dare.

Because it was coming for her again.

Dark of the Moon stepped to the side as it leaped from the grass, but not quite quickly enough. Another few inches and it would have passed her entirely; instead, the thing's arm linked with hers at the elbow and they spun awkwardly, like badly balanced children trying to twirl each other around. The beast stumbled and went to its knees, dragging her with it, snarling and snapping the entire time. The feel of its skin against hers was nasty—slippery—and it smelled horrible, like the leftover cooking grease from game left to go rancid in the hot sun.

There were few in the pueblo—actually, no one—who would help her train by doing battle with her, so this was Dark of the Moon's first encounter with something in a hand-to-hand situation. And, of course, she'd never dealt with someone—or some*thing*—that really wanted to do her harm. The words of her father and the elders were one thing, but reality was quite another. They were on a slight incline that made them roll, and she was dimly aware of fending off more blows than she'd ever realized could be thrown in such a short time. Some connected, some didn't; she didn't have time to think about any of them or worry about the mounting pain. When their tumbling finally stopped, it was only because their momentum had taken them to a bone-jarring halt against a jagged boulder.

Dark of the Moon yanked herself free of the beast's hold and scrambled to her feet, at the same time fumbling with the tie that held her *atlatl* to her belt. But the knot wouldn't come loose, and the blood-beast was on her again in no time at all. It hissed like a bobcat and tried to claw at her face, and she barely got her hand wrapped around its wrist in time to stop it. Angry now, she yanked it forward and slammed the outer edge of her other hand down on the bridge of the monster's nose. She heard a satisfying *crack* and the thing howled in pain and rage as it fell backward.

It showed no signs of stopping its attack, but Dark of the Moon was ready when it bounded toward her this time. Planting her feet wide, she held one of her wooden stabbing sticks at the ready—

"... *your killing blow will most likely be to the heart.*"

—and plunged it deep into the center of the creature's chest.

She supposed she'd had a preconception about what would happen. A lot of blood, of course—you couldn't stab something in the chest and not have it bleed—more of a fight was a possibility, perhaps a keening death wail that would split the silence of the desert night.

But not this.

Not ever.

The beast burst into red dust.

She'd been going forward, her speed and strength driving her weapon to its target; now Dark of the Moon found herself right in the middle of a thick cloud of fine earth. She gasped and breathed it in, choked and stumbled as it went into her nose and filled her eyes with grit. She waved her arms as if she'd walked into a cloud of flies and was frantically trying to shoo them away, then regained enough of her eyesight just in time to stop herself from taking a tumble down the side of a small wash as she tripped over something in her path. It took a few more moments, but she finally rubbed enough dust out of her eyes so that she could see again.

And she almost wished she hadn't.

First Dark of the Moon had assumed the obstacle in front of her feet was a rock—dark and motionless, a small round hump in the grasses a few feet away. But there had been something off about that belief—a give in the side of the object when she'd hit it with the toe of her sandal. Curious, she knelt to examine it, and discovered it wasn't a rock at all.

It was a child, facedown in the grass.

"Are you all right?" she asked automatically, then immediately felt foolish. She shook the child's shoulder, her stomach knotting when the small figure failed to respond. Rather than ask again, she slid her left hand under its back and turned the youth faceup.

It was a boy. He was perhaps five years old, and his eyes were open, staring at the sliver of new moon above but no longer seeing anything in this world. His face was scraped and smudged with dirt, and his knees and hands were caked with dust and blood, as if he had run from something and fallen repeatedly amid the brush. More blood was splashed on his shoulder and down the front of his thin chest, but no breath made the rib cage rise and fall. When Dark of the Moon gathered him into her arms and stood, his body held no more human warmth.

How foolish she had been to never consider this—of course the beast, newly released from the bowels of the earth and strengthless, would go after someone young and just as weak as it. Such was the way of the predator, and this child had been the perfect prey. What made it even more heartbreaking was that Dark of the Moon *knew* this boy, knew where his adobe was and had talked to his mother and father in passing. The last time had been three or four days before the ceremony in the *kiva*, a simple word or two of greeting on the morning-splashed path. Now she was forced to bring them the worst news of their lives.

Cradling him in her arms as she carried him back to the pueblo, she did not try to brush aside his long, black hair when his head lolled forward. It would spare her the sight of his face, hardly begun in life and once full of childish laughter and energy, now lost forever to death. No, she left his hair to spread itself across his face and neck like a soft black blanket, grateful that it covered the two bite marks that the beast had left on his neck.

And in her grief, with the darkness shrouding the desert in

night tones of black and gray, Dark of the Moon never noticed the blood that washed the white of the dead boy's teeth and trickled out the side of his mouth.

Daylight brought no comfort to Dark of the Moon.

The boy's name had been Deer Tracker, and despite many years of praying and making careful offerings to Kokopelli, he had been his parents' only child. Amid the wails of Morning Sunrise, his mother, Deer Tracker's father speculated that the boy had stolen outside after he had bedded down for the night. Deer Tracker had always been fascinated with whiptail lizards, and perhaps he had chased after one and lost his way; Dark of the Moon thought it more likely that the creature she'd killed had been waiting in the darkness for just such an opportunity: a defenseless boy. Their anguish had been almost unbearable, and she had spent a sleepless night wishing she could have found and destroyed the beast before it had done such terrible damage.

Was it over now? The days passed, but somehow Dark of the Moon thought it was not. The thing she had been destined to kill was gone, yet she felt no peace in her heart and there was a restlessness to her thoughts that could bode nothing but ill. On the surface the days looked bright and clear, drenched with the normal summertime heat. Men and women worked in the growing plots tending to the corn, beans, and squash; the women gathered around the large stone *metates* and ground corn as they always had. Trading took place, households were tended, and life went on.

As often happened when a loved one was lost to a senseless incident, Morning Sunrise and Spirit of the Buffalo, Deer Tracker's parents, went into seclusion; no one saw them, but no one commented on it, preferring to leave the family to their grief. Yet Dark of the Moon could sense that something was wrong. No, she could *see* it. Surely it wasn't her imagination that each sunrise revealed fewer and fewer people in the pueblo, more families sequestered behind the newly blocked doors to their adobes. Every day people no longer stopped to chat, and the laughter of the children was seldom heard. There was, she thought, an aura of fear in the pueblo, a sense of wrongness that made everyone hurry about their business and cut short the ceremonies that had once been regularly held in the *kivas* under the moon's light.

Neither Dark of the Moon nor Grandmother had seen the Medicine Father since the night of Dark of the Moon's big ceremony in the *kiva*. After it had ended, he'd told her he was going into the desert to speak to Grandmother Spider and the great Warrior Twins, to ask their guidance about the beast and also for blessings on the coming fall harvest. He had been gone nearly two weeks when Dark of the Moon decided on her own that it was time to visit Morning Sunrise and Spirit of the Buffalo and pay her respects, and also to offer any help that she could, be it giving a listening ear to the boy's mother or even helping with the small chores that the child used to perform. When no one answered her knock at their adobe, Dark of the Moon thought they had been in seclusion and mourning long enough—surely they needed to replenish their food supplies by now. She pushed open the door and stepped inside without being invited.

The adobe had a . . . *smell* about it, a strange and rather unpleasant scent of rot, freshly turned soil, and dampness, an odd thing in the desert. There were times, infrequent throughout the year, when monsoons would ripple through the canyon and beat at the cliffs; often these would leave the air heavy with the fragrance of water and wet rock. What crept up Dark of the Moon's nose now was vaguely reminiscent of that, but darker somehow, more the way she imagined a hidden cave would be if she were to discover and disturb it after hundreds of years.

It was early evening, a little while before sunset, and the thin light that filtered through the doorway did almost nothing to dissipate the gloomy interior. The man and woman had fastened oiled animal hides tightly over the two windows as part of their mourning and, of course, no one had questioned this; now Dark of the Moon wanted to rip the skins free and let in some light and fresh air. She stifled the urge; it was not her right to do so, and besides, she was actually an uninvited visitor here. She took about six steps inside and stopped, uncertain; her eyesight had always been exceptional and despite the dimness she could see the remains of a meal scattered carelessly across a woven mat on the floor. There were three different kinds of mice in the canyon— deer, grasshopper, and harvest—and there were several of each feeding from pottery bowls filled with drying, half-rotted food that had been left on the mat, as if no one had cared enough to put them away.

Dark of the Moon scowled and cleared her throat. "Hello?"

The adobe had two rooms and someone should have been there, come forward to greet her from the back room. No one did . . . yet she was certain she wasn't truly alone in here. She was reluctant to venture beyond the main room, to invade the privacy of this grieving family, yet it was obvious something was wrong. Perhaps they were sleeping? It didn't make sense that they wouldn't rise to meet someone who had been bold enough to enter without their permission.

"Hello?" she called again.

This time there was *something* in response, she was sure of it. A sort of sliding noise from the other room, as though someone were waking up. If that was the case, then so be it. She was filled with unease, and suddenly Dark of the Moon wanted very much to make sure that Deer Tracker's parents were all right, that they hadn't done something drastic like decide to try to join him in the spirit world. She had barely registered her own concern about that when she heard another noise, this one a more pronounced *thump,* as if something heavy had been knocked over. Still no one said anything or answered her two previous greetings.

The doorway to the back room was covered by more animal hides, these carefully cut and sewn together to form a curtain, evidence of the fine handiwork of Deer Tracker's mother. Dark of the Moon moved cautiously across the floor and reached toward it, but before she could pull the covering aside, something crashed through it and attacked her.

The sewn-together animal hide came down on top of her, and for a heart-stopping moment, she was smothered by both the door's covering and whatever was on the other side. She tasted weathered leather in her mouth and wrenched her head to the side, then realized that whatever was on the other side of the thick curtain was snarling and trying to *bite* her—

The beast!

But she had killed it, she *had.* Still, there was no time to think about what she had or hadn't done. She was unarmed; both her *atlatl* and her wooden stabbing sticks were back at her own adobe, wrapped in oilcloth and packed away—she'd thought her dealings with the darkness were over, and without the Medicine Father to tell her otherwise . . .

A foolish assumption.

Dark of the Moon rolled with the creature clinging to her like a life-size spider. The adobe was spacious but it still didn't have much floor space from one wall to another. She crashed against the entrance wall and felt the edge of the doorway strike her painfully in the middle of her back. Her breath left her in a rush, but she still had the presence of mind to hold on tightly to her attacker, pulling it against her body and using it to hold the protective curtain in place between them.

She felt the creature trying to regain its balance, registered the scrape of its claws across her skin as it struggled to pull the covering aside and reach her flesh. She twisted on the dirt floor and took it with her through the doorway to the pathway outside the adobe, grappling like a sun spider with a beetle. Dimly she realized that the thing was howling now, fighting to get *away* from her. Dark of the Moon hung on, determined not to let this thing go free to spread its death among the People in the pueblo. She finally ended up straddling it with the animal hide draped over its face and upper body. Behind her, the beast's legs beat frantically on the dirt as its wailing increased to a fever pitch. Undeterred, Dark of the Moon yanked the covering free and tossed it aside, exposing the creature to the last, feeble rays of the day's sunlight.

Directly beneath her, the evil thing's body burst into flames.

She cried out and flung herself away before she could get a good look at it, but not quickly enough. With the destruction of the beast—or so she'd thought—Dark of the Moon had gone back to her usual clothing, an overdress of soft leather. The flames seared her thighs for one seemingly eternal moment, then the impossible thing that had occurred the other night happened again.

The creature beneath her burst in a flurry of dust.

Dark of the Moon hit the ground on her rear end, getting a painful jolt up her spine. For a few seconds she simply sat there with her mouth open in shock, feeling the burning along the insides of her thighs and trying to comprehend what had just happened. There was so *much* that the Medicine Father had never told her about—the dust, the creature's strength and speed, the *fire*. Had he even known? Or had it been yet another of the lifelong "lessons" he and her grandmother were always trying to press upon her? If so, this one could have cost Dark of the Moon her life, and she was quite angry about it.

She pushed herself to a standing position and looked around, expecting to see a crowd. But there was no such thing; in fact, very few men and women were scattered up and down the street, and there were no children in sight at all. Those of the People who were present hung back from Dark of the Moon and the large, reddish pile of feathery soil on the ground at her feet. Their eyes were wide and showed just as much surprise as Dark of the Moon had felt, but there was also an obvious aura of suspicion and anxiety, as if they suspected that something terrible was going on and they wanted no part of it. That was likely the reason for the absence of the children—the parents were keeping them safely at home and out of harm's way.

Left on her own, Dark of the Moon ground her teeth against the painful sensation on her legs—she would tend to her wounds later. Right now she had to go back inside Deer Tracker's adobe.

Now that she knew something had gone wrong, horribly wrong, and the evil that had escaped from the *sipapu* had multiplied, it took everything she could dredge up in the way of courage to step back through that doorway. Dark of the Moon did it anyway—this was, as she had been so often told, what she had been born to do. She would not turn her back on her destiny, or her responsibility.

Her tumble through the doorway with the monster had ripped the entrance covering half free, so it was a little brighter inside now. There wasn't much to see that she hadn't glimpsed the first time, except now she could see a bit deeper into the back room of the adobe. Still, the light outside was fading fast, so that wasn't much help—every passing second spread the already numerous patches of darkness on the inside of this small home and put the remainder of it deeper into shadow.

Was that another sound she heard from the back room? Yes, definitely. Someone, or some*thing* else, was back there, and with every step forward she took, Dark of the Moon became more convinced that the absolutely unthinkable had happened: The beast had managed to multiply itself before she had killed it. But how?

Despite the heavy thudding of her pulse, there was no question that she would step into that back room. Still, she did not go unarmed, even if she had left her weapons at her own home. It only took a second to shoo aside the mice and pick up a food tool made of wood. It didn't have much of a sharp end, but with enough pressure, it might be a decent substitute for one of her stabbing sticks. Life was a learning experience; never again would she be caught without those and her *atlatl* at her belt.

Feeling a little more confident, Dark of the Moon stepped through the doorway into the second room of the adobe belonging to Deer Tracker's parents.

And they attacked her from both sides.

Two beasts, one large and one small. She went down under their weight and fury, but she did not go down easily. She felt the smaller one's teeth clamp onto her upper arm and yelled in pain as the skin gave way, but the creature was finding it difficult to search for a life-giving vein when its target refused to stay still. The other one, larger, had grabbed her by the neck and head; to defend herself, the young woman punched at it with her other arm, ignoring the smaller version of the beast still trying to cling to it. The two creatures crashed together and the one biting her let go and fell against the bigger one; both stumbled backward and into the front room, and when she regained her balance, Dark of the Moon got her first solid look at her attackers.

And she at last understood what she was up against.

Crouching in front of her like animals, their faces malformed into visages of evil, were Deer Tracker and his mother, Morning Sunrise. The Medicine Father's words flashed through her mind—

"*. . . hide its true self beneath a human veil, only revealing its ugly nature at its most brutal of moments.*"

And then both of them rushed at her.

Her arm was throbbing, and the wound was sending little warm pulses of blood running down to her elbow. Dark of the Moon realized instantly that it was her bleeding—the smell and the sight of the rich, red blood—that was driving Deer Tracker and Morning Sunrise nearly insane. *These creatures are bloodsuckers!* she thought in amazement. *Like a pallid bat gone through an unnatural transformation by a bad spirit—once human, now twisted into evil monstrosities!*

But there was no more time to think about that as the two of them leaped on her. Dark of the Moon pushed all her logical thoughts from her mind and let her body shift into pure, fighting instinct. She could not step out of range of both, so instead, at the last moment, she dropped to one knee and stretched her arm out on one side. With Dark of the Moon's head curled down protectively and nothing to latch on to, Morning Sunrise tripped and fell clumsily over the sudden obstacle in her path. On the right side, Deer Tracker surely never knew what hit him—the child-beast ran full speed into the shaped piece of wood clutched firmly in Dark of the Moon's hand.

Still balanced on her knee, Dark of the Moon spun through Deer Tracker's dust and grabbed on to one of Morning Sunrise's legs before the bloodsucker could get back to her feet. She yanked as hard as she could and Morning Sunrise flailed for balance, then hit the floor anyway. Upright or down on the ground, it didn't seem to matter to the bloodsucker; she nevertheless tried to attack, snarling and growling the entire time like a trapped coyote.

Dark of the Moon still had the piece of wood in her hand, and she stabbed at Morning Sunrise with it. The creature threw herself out of range, then scuttled backward until she was up against the adobe's rear wall. Dark of the Moon advanced, giving herself a little time to study and learn about her adversary, then was shocked when Morning Sunrise actually spoke to her.

"You cannot win." Once an attractive woman with a clear and lovely voice, now Morning Sunrise's features were twisted and discolored. Her forehead and brow had thickened and were creased with deep wrinkles, and her entire face had sunken in on itself, accenting the newly prominent ridges of bone beneath the skin. Her eyes, once a warm brown, were now a hideous shade of yellow. "Why fight it? It is only a matter of time until we multiply and rule the pueblo."

Morning Sunrise's gaze flicked to where Dark of the Moon's arm was still slowly seeping blood, and she licked her lips. Dark of the Moon's mouth turned down; she distinctly disliked being thought of as *food* by another person, whether or not that person had been transfigured by evil. It dawned on her that the thing she had killed outside by exposing it to daylight had been Spirit of the Buffalo, Deer Tracker's father. "It is you who cannot win," she told Morning Sunrise. "Mother Earth's great spirit will never allow those of your kind to taint her wonderful home."

Morning Sunrise laughed, startling Dark of the Moon. "You think there are only a few of us, you foolish girl? We are many, and you are only one. When you die—and you *will*—maybe one will replace you, but she will also only be one. And after her, one more." The bloodsucker grinned. "Surely you are not so blinded by righteousness that you cannot see this."

"Righteousness? Perhaps," Dark of the Moon said. "Foolish? Not at all."

And before Morning Sunrise could get out of the way, Dark of the Moon lunged across the space that separated them and rammed her piece of wood deep into the center of the woman-creature's chest.

Then Morning Sunrise, the last of Deer Tracker's family, was no more.

Dark of the Moon walked alone on the streets of the pueblo the following nights. Usually someone was around—old men who couldn't sleep would sit next to their front doors and smoke pipes containing tobacco traded from the southland visitors; sometimes women would pace in front of their adobes as they tried to lull cranky infants back to sleep. But if the pueblo contained life tonight it was hidden, driven away by the ghosts of those who had passed away. And she had to wonder how many that really was. Did the blood beasts retain their spirits, swallow them whole as they seemed to do with the body's life fluid? Or when confronted by such overwhelming wickedness, did that precious spiritual essence flee to where the other spirits dwelled among the sun and clouds?

It was a ponderous question, and one she could not answer. The beasts she had killed had seemed to retain much of the original people, yet all goodness had been drained away, replaced only by hunger and, apparently, the desire to reproduce their own kind. Did these monsters act on their own, instinctively? Or did they follow the direction of a lower, darker, and maybe, more powerful spirit?

Again, Dark of the Moon had no answers.

She wished the Medicine Father were here, but many days had passed since she or White Flower had last seen him. Feeling a strange mixture of vindication and guilt, Dark of the Moon had returned home after destroying Morning Sunrise. There she had retrieved her weapons and fastened them to her belt—never again would she be naive enough to venture out without them. Her grandmother, at least, was safe, and while they hadn't talked about what was happening in the pueblo—White Flower had never been a woman prone to speaking much—the old woman seemed quite inclined to follow Dark of the Moon's insistent instructions not to venture outside the adobe.

But Dark of the Moon wondered if that would be enough. What was to stop these creatures from simply going inside at will, just as she had done to the residence belonging to Morning Sunrise and Spirit of the Buffalo? Very little . . . at least, so it seemed. She was severely hampered in her lack of information about the enemy, what they feared, what they could or couldn't do, and her experience was limited. Why had her father not told her of the deadly effect that daylight would have on them? She suspected it was because he hadn't known, and that in itself was a troubling revelation.

In the Medicine Father's absence, early this morning Dark of the Moon had seen the remaining male elders and shamans praying and singing inside each of the smaller *kivas* in turn. Hour after hour had passed, but their vigilance and beseeching chanting had never fluctuated—they were like tireless warriors armed with weapons of words and song and mystical desert herbs. Their faith was admirable, but from the looks of the empty pueblo streets tonight, the results had been less than successful.

It was full dark now, and silent. Split only by a cool desert night breeze, the pueblo was an eerie place, full of shadowed spots where danger might lurk. Where once the window openings had spilled golden light onto the street from small, interior home fires, now most were simply darker shades of ominous black as the residents retreated to the safer, inside rooms. Worse, she saw many had been covered as had the windows in Deer Tracker's home, either by hides or heavy blankets.

With a sinking feeling Dark of the Moon realized that the infestation of the blood drinkers had spread throughout the pueblo right beneath her nose. So many of the adobes were connected by doorways that led into the next one, and the one after that, and for many of these families, getting to their own rooms meant traveling through those belonging to any number of others. In the way that the People lived, it was as if most of the sprawling pueblo was one huge dwelling in which all members lived, rather than separate and distinct living spaces. For most, there would be no place to run or hide—everyone, good or bad, had access to everyone else.

All her life Dark of the Moon had felt alone—during her childhood when few of the other children would play with her, as a girl trying to learn the skills expected for survival, as a young woman watching the others of the pueblo pair off and form lifetime partnerships that resulted in babies and families. Most of all she had felt set apart by her mystical birth heritage, her strength and the constant training that her father had given her.

But she had *never* felt so alone as she did right now.

There was a noise behind her and Dark of the Moon spun, her *atlatl* up and ready. She lowered it when she saw a child standing a few feet away, a tiny girl of about four summers whom in past times she had seen now and then playing around the pueblo. Although Dark of the Moon couldn't place the child's father, she recalled that her mother was a small woman with beautiful hair that hung well below her hips. Behind tangled locks, the little girl's black eyes were wide and terrified in her dust-smudged face, and she clutched at a small straw doll as if it were the only thing left in her world that she could trust. Sadly Dark of the Moon thought that was probably the truth.

"I can't find my mother," the girl said. Her voice was high and sweet, but the words ended in a half hiccup, half sob. "We went to visit her friends and she told me to play outside, and she never came back out." The girl brought her doll up and stroked its head. "It was dark at their house and I didn't go inside. I was scared."

Dark of the Moon said nothing, not sure whether to believe the girl or not. She *looked* normal, but the memory of Deer Tracker's beast-twisted appearance in a child-size body was still vivid and strong. "Will you help me find her?" the girl finally asked.

Instead of answering, Dark of the Moon asked, "What's your name?"

"Dancing Cloud," the girl said softly.

"That's a very good name."

She nodded solemnly. "That's what everyone says. My mother says I'm named after my father's grandmother." Still clutching her doll with one hand, the child reached down and nervously twisted the hem of her shirtdress as she looked around at the empty pueblo. It was a decidedly childlike thing to do, and Dark of the Moon felt her suspicions wavering. The girl's clothes were as dirty as the rest of her; as was often the case with children, Dancing Cloud didn't seem bothered by the coolness of the night or the chilly stones of the paved street beneath her bare feet.

Dark of the Moon lowered herself to one knee so she could talk to Dancing Cloud without looming over her. "So what did you do when your mother didn't come back out?"

"I ran away," the little girl told her. "I hid in the field by the biggest *kiva*."

Dark of the Moon nodded. "And did you see anyone else?"

"There were some men in the *kiva*. They were singing." Yes, that would have been true. But what had happened to them? As if she'd known Dark of the Moon's thoughts, Dancing Cloud continued. "Then some other people came out of some of the adobes and went into the *kiva*. Everyone in there started yelling and crying. So I stayed in the grass."

So there was her answer. While she had wandered to the other side of the pueblo, the elders in the *kiva* had been attacked by a group of blood drinkers. If she understood the way things were happening, this meant that those who had been attacked might become blood drinkers themselves, thus perpetuating the cycle. Was there no end to this evil?

"Will you help me find my mother?" Dancing Cloud repeated. A tear rolled slowly down one dusky-colored cheek, and the sight of it tugged at Dark of the Moon's heart. "I can show you where she was."

She would search for the girl's mother, but if the results were as she believed they would be, she doubted the child should see how that hunt would end. Dark of the Moon made a quick decision. "I will look for her, but first I want to take you somewhere safe."

"Safe?" Dancing Cloud's eyes widened even more. "Why?"

"Because there are . . . bad spirits on the streets tonight," Dark of the Moon explained. "And children your age should not be among them."

She motioned at the girl and started walking, and was pleased when the child obeyed. Trying to be reassuring, she reached down and took Dancing Cloud's free hand in hers. The skin was dry and cold, uncomfortably so, and Dancing Cloud pulled away from her and wrapped her arms around the straw doll. Dark of the Moon frowned. "Why are your hands so cold?"

Dancing Cloud shrugged as she followed. "I always get cold," she answered distantly. "Mother says I should dress warmer but I never remember. It doesn't bother me."

It didn't take long to make it back to Dark of the Moon's own adobe, and she was gratified to see the warm glow of an evening fire coming from beyond the small window opening. The smell of heavily spiced beans and onions drifted on the air just outside the doorway, and Dark of the Moon smiled down at Dancing Cloud. "I'll bet you're hungry," she said. "My grandmother is a wonderful cook."

Dancing Cloud glanced sideways at her. "Yes, I'm very hungry."

Dark of the Moon pushed aside the door covering and saw her grandmother stirring a pot of beans over the cooking fire in the back corner of the room. The old woman looked up and smiled in relief when she realized who it was. "I'm glad you are safe," she said simply.

"I found a child who is separated from her mother," Dark of the Moon said. "I'll leave her in your care. A good meal and a warm fire can only do her good."

"A child?"

At White Flower's quizzical look, Dark of the Moon turned back and realized that Dancing Cloud hadn't followed her into the adobe. Her heart jumped. Had the little girl been snatched from her side without her even noticing?

She rushed outside, then stopped and took a deep breath when she saw Dancing Cloud standing forlornly outside the door. The girl looked reluctant and unsure, frightened of every-thing. "What's the matter?" Dark of the Moon said. "Why are you still out here in the dark?"

But the child hung back. "I don't know," she whispered.

Dark of the Moon took the girl by the elbow and had to fight the urge to snatch her hand away. The girl was freezing; she re-ally needed to be inside. "Come on," she urged. "Come inside. It's all right—no one will hurt you."

Dancing Cloud's mouth stretched wide in an unexpected

smile and she stepped out of reach. "All right." She practically pushed past Dark of the Moon in her hurry to go through the doorway. Dark of the Moon shook her head—she was such a strange child—and followed.

Inside the adobe Dancing Cloud was already sitting by the fire, watching White Flower with an adultlike, intense interest. The old woman said nothing and Dark of the Moon wasn't surprised; her grandmother had never been one to fuss over a child, believing that the young were better served if they made their own way and learned by watching others, receiving guidance only when they were headed astray.

"I have to go back out," Dark of the Moon said. "There is something I need to . . . check on." Dancing Cloud didn't seem to notice, but the tone of Dark of the Moon's voice made White Flower glance at her with a knowing gaze. "I'll be back as soon as I can, but it may be some time."

White Flower looked back at the container of beans she was stirring. "The child and I will be fine together. I'll feed her shortly."

Dark of the Moon nodded, then double-checked her *atlatl* and the pouch of sticks before slipping back outside. Her last backward glance showed her White Flower and Dancing Cloud settled comfortably in front of the small fire and satisfied her that the old woman and child were safe inside her family's own adobe.

It took quite a while, but she found Dancing Cloud's mother at the southeastern end of the pueblo, sitting with four other men and women. They all looked human, but Dark of the Moon had no doubt that every one of them, including Dancing Cloud's mother, was a bloodsucker. The closer she drew to them, the more she could *feel* their collective evil, suffocating and thick, increasing like a vicious, growing dust storm. Still, she felt no fear as she approached them, and whether that was courage or foolishness remained to be seen. Since there were four of them, she took four of the wooden sticks from her pouch and positioned two in each hand so that they protruded up from between her fingers, as if she had fashioned a pair of spiked wooden knuckles for herself. A flick of each hand would release them one at a time, if and when needed. And she had no doubt it would, indeed, be necessary.

The instant they saw her, they broke up and stood, then began first backing away, then trying to circle around behind her. But Dark of the Moon would not be so easily overcome; a few well-placed steps and she had her back safely to the wall of the last adobe. They must have thought they now had her cornered, because the ones who had put the most distance between themselves and her began edging toward her once more, their twisted faces showing more confidence.

Dancing Cloud's mother stepped forward, and Dark of the Moon at last remembered her name—Touch the Night. It suited her, because although transformed by evil's corruption, she was still a beautiful woman. Perhaps her altered existence had even added to her loveliness, deepening the blackness in her eyes and accentuating the slimness of her small-boned body. "We know what you are," she said. "We have heard all the legends." Her voice was husky but clear. "They tell of what you were born to be—a great slayer of our kind."

Dark of the Moon tilted her head to one side. *Slayer*—the Medicine Father had never said as much, but she supposed it was an apt description. "Yes," she agreed. "That is what I am."

Touch the Night spread her hands in a gesture of supplication. "Why must we battle, Dark of the Moon? The great Earth Mother has room for all of us—the earth is a big place."

Dark of the Moon's mouth curved in revulsion. "You have no claim to the great Mother or the good spirits anymore," she told the other woman. "You left all that behind when you chose to become a night beast."

Touch the Night considered this, even as her companions inched closer. "You're wrong," she finally said. "I did not *choose* this. But that matters little now—I am what I am."

"And I am what *I* am," Dark of the Moon responded. There was no mistaking the meaning or the finality within her words, and Touch the Night and her companions didn't try. Instead, she and one other, a man, rushed at Dark of the Moon.

Dark of the Moon stepped forward to meet them, never hesitating. Fists and teeth and fingernails, elbows and knees at every turn, kicks that seemed to come from every direction—it was a hard battle for Dark of the Moon, surprisingly so. When the human part of their spirits died and the evil part took control, the blood beasts had somehow become infused with the sort of knowledge usually reserved for warriors and for which Dark of the Moon herself had trained all her life, an instinctive speed and skill in hand-to-hand battle. Dark of the Moon was so new at this, and never had she faced more than two opponents at one time. . . .

But she would, and did, prevail.

At the end, there was only Dark of the Moon and Touch the Night left, standing and evaluating each other warily. Both were disheveled and bloody, both had withstood countless blows and felt the pain of the conflict. Touch the Night no longer looked exquisite; now she was battered and bruised, with her hair tangled and wild, her clothing dusty and ripped in half a dozen places. Dark of the Moon didn't know how she looked, and didn't care; she'd used up the four stabbing sticks and now held only her *atlatl*. She didn't dare take even a few seconds to remove another wooden stick from her pouch—if she tried, she knew Touch the Night would be on her in an instant.

The other woman circled her, but her movements were more tired than crafty. When Dark of the Moon would have gone for her, Touch the Night skipped backward a few steps and began speaking, clearly hoping the conversation would stall the coming attack long enough to let her recoup her energy.

"You will never win," Touch the Night told her. "This is a battle beyond your comprehension, beyond your *abilities*. Your efforts are futile."

Dark of the Moon raised one eyebrow. "I have heard this same statement from your kind before. I think you use it as a litany to try to convince yourself of something that will never be so."

Touch the Night laughed, the sound floating unpleasantly along the scant desert breeze. "What a fool you are, child. Perhaps it will be your youth that is your downfall. My daughter told me of your gullibility, about how you stupidly invited her into your home."

Dark of the Moon had been creeping forward, but now she froze. "Your daughter." It was a statement rather than a question—already Dark of the Moon knew she had made a terrible, unforgivable error in judgment. It had taken Dark of the Moon so very long to finally locate Touch the Night and her companions, and during that time, she had left the darkest of children alone with White Flower. So long, in fact, that the girl had obviously left White Flower, circled around, and found her way back to her mother before Dark of the Moon could get to her. But what of White Flower?

"Yes," Touch the Night continued, "Dancing Cloud has always been such an obedient child. I would give her a task and she would do exactly as I directed, then come to me for well-deserved praise. Tonight was no different."

"You're lying," Dark of the Moon finally managed to say. Her voice was a shocked whisper, but Touch the Night had no problem hearing it.

The bloodsucker gave her a dark smile. "What would be the point?" That awful grin widened, showing deceptively beautiful teeth. "In this case the truth is much more *delicious.*"

As the enormity of what she had done settled over her, for a moment—one that seemed to stretch into eternity—Dark of the Moon couldn't get any air into her chest. Then she lunged forward, with the butt end of her *atlatl* braced painfully against her hipbone. The beast-woman had thought Dark of the Moon too overwhelmed by her horrid miscalculation to attack, so Dark of the Moon caught Touch the Night totally by surprise. The once beautiful woman had only an instant for her eyes to widen and her mouth to form into an *O*, then—

Dust.

Dark of the Moon stood there, still gripping the *atlatl* in an attack position, staring uncomprehendingly as the brownish-colored dust layered its tip and the front half of the lovingly rubbed length of wood.

Then she whirled and headed back to her family's adobe, hoping against all odds that there was still time to save White Flower.

Everything inside the adobe was shattered.

Dark of the Moon didn't know if it was because her grandmother had put up such a fight, or because the small creature she had mistaken for an innocent child had smashed the pottery and furniture out of reckless, wicked glee. In her heart she wanted to believe nothing but that White Flower had battled, and perhaps bested, Dancing Cloud. But the thoughts in her head, the ones that whispered of reality, would not be silenced.

There was no blood, and for that Dark of the Moon was pathetically grateful—she didn't think she could bear the sight of a bright red splash or puddle that might belong to the old woman who had raised her.

Dark of the Moon allowed herself two minutes—no more— to search amid the rubble for any sign that White Flower might have survived. Finding none, she gripped her *atlatl* and headed back into the darkness.

She could sense the presence of the blood beasts in the pueblo, but she could not find them.

They were there, but always out of sight, always just out of range. Dark of the Moon could hear their footsteps in the silent village, hear the pattering as small pebbles were sent tumbling down the sides of the cliffs by stealthy footsteps. On rare occasions, she caught muffled giggles and murmurings in the blackest of the shadows between the adobes, but the voices always faded into nothingness when she grimly went to investigate. As each quarter hour passed, her frustration built along with her anger, until she didn't know which would surpass the other at any given moment. Her grandmother was surely dead, as were most of the occupants of the pueblo; she had failed in her sacred duties, and that failure had proven she was not worthy of the task which she had been given.

Had she ever been? Dark of the Moon didn't know—she had no one to tell her, or teach her. The Medicine Father had tried, but he had not explained enough, and she could not help but resent him for it. Because of this, she thought he should perhaps take on part of the blame, although she, of course, had been the one chosen to wield the weapons and defeat the beast.

Again she had failed.

It wasn't hard to realize that each night the circle of light from the growing moon revealed more horrors in her pueblo, more blood drinkers roaming the pathways nearly at will, unafraid and defiant of her status as their would-be destroyer. More and more of the People had fallen victim and were now breeding like an evil pestilence. Where would it all end?

Dark of the Moon's search of the pueblo, while as thorough as she could make it, proved fruitless. From one end to the other, beneath a newly formed full moon and only one full cycle from the time when the sacrificial fire had been allowed to burn out by the young and foolish Lone Coyote, the pueblo had seemingly emptied of all human life save hers. She thought there must still be true humans in it, but they were well hidden, their terror making them as impossible to locate as the blood drinkers were to catch.

At the farthest end of the pueblo, standing on the edge of the south mesa, Dark of the Moon had finally exhausted her search. Perhaps it was her fatigue, but the beasts were too crafty, and too quick for her. For every step she took, the creatures seemed to take three; every time she ducked behind a boulder to search, the noises in the darkness told her they had anticipated her coming and already moved elsewhere. Her fury and frustration were still there, yes, but both had become tempered by disillusionment and disappointment; she no longer believed she could best the things of the night, and she *knew* she could not save the People.

"My poor granddaughter, you must be so tired."

Dark of the Moon spun at the familiar voice, then stopped in her tracks as White Flower emerged from the shadows between two huge red boulders. It could not be so, but she looked disturbingly . . . *right,* the same as she always had—dark gray hair pulled into two neat tails and secured at shoulder length with thin strips of leather, not a bit of dust or cooking dirt on the woven shirtdress she had bound at the waist with a hand-beaten silver belt inlaid with turquoise stones. While she'd only seen it a few times over the years, Dark of the Moon recognized that belt as one White Flower saved for the most special of occasions. Even the old woman's leather slippers were clean and free of the stains of the desert pathways, her fingernails scrubbed of any residual cooking mess.

"Grandmother?" The title slipped from between Dark of the Moon's lips in spite of herself. "Is it . . . is it *you*?"

"Of course, child. Who else would it be?"

There was an achingly well-known tone to White Flower's voice, and the speck of doubt Dark of the Moon was already feeling grew larger. Was there really a chance that her grandmother had survived a battle with the child-beast?

"I went to the adobe," Dark of the Moon said. She wanted very badly to touch White Flower as a gesture of reassurance to no one but herself. Still, instinct kept her cautious, and she slipped sideways when her grandmother would have stepped toward her. "I saw the destruction there."

"The girl did that," White Flower said reproachfully. "Such a misbehaving child, throwing temper tantrums for no reason. I tried to stop her, but it was useless. Finally, I just left." She paused, then asked, "Did you see her?"

"No," Dark of the Moon said, then wished she hadn't answered so readily. Her grandmother's eyes flashed in the moonlight, and Dark of the Moon could have sworn she'd seen a shine of satisfaction. Or was that a hint of darkest red?

"Don't concern yourself with naughty children," White Flower said. "Here." She untied a small food pouch at her side, then pulled out one of her special *paselitos* and offered it to Dark of the Moon. The small pie, filled with sweetened and mashed wild berries, was still warm from baking; its aroma drifted across the space between them and brought with it memories of happier times not so long ago, before the night beasts had invaded the pueblo and Dark of the Moon's world. "I pulled these from the cookfire before that dreadful girl broke apart everything in the adobe."

Dark of the Moon nearly reached for the pie out of reflex, but at the last moment she jerked her hand back. A good thing, because just before her fingers would have touched it, the aged face she had known for so long transformed into one of evil and ugliness, and the gnarled hands went to claws that tried to grab at her wrist. Dark of the Moon scrambled out of range and glared at the blood beast that now had control over her grandmother's body.

"Vile thing," she spat. "Abomination!"

White Flower laughed. "You only say such things because you have not experienced what I have." She gestured at herself, then at Dark of the Moon. "Look at you, with your bruises and your battered body. How weary are you from this fight that will never end? There are more of us than you could ever imagine, Dark of the Moon." She thrust out her jaw, emphasizing the long, pointed teeth that now filled her mouth and pushed her lips outward. "You will die and your body will rot into the earth, and no one will remember you. I, on the other hand, will live forever!"

"But you will do so trapped in the body of an ancient one," Dark of the Moon pointed out.

White Flower shrugged. "What difference does it make? I feel as though I am only twenty summers again. I am strong and sure of myself." Her eyes glinted. "And *hungry*."

"I can take care of that for you," said Dark of the Moon, and she threw her *atlatl* with all her strength.

Her aim was straight and true. The weapon buried itself in the center of her grandmother's chest, and for an instant White Flower's twisted expression held that same look of astonishment that Dark of the Moon had seen on Touch the Night's face, that sense of *Surely this can't be happening to me!* Then she—and Dark of the Moon's *atlatl*—blew outward in a spray of lung-choking dust.

It shocked Dark of the Moon that the *atlatl* had been destroyed with the blood drinker—she hadn't expected that. Now that she considered it, the same thing had happened to her wooden sticks; held in her hand as she struck, they remained intact, but if she let go . . . gone, right along with the creature she'd killed. Still, her *atlatl* had been more than just a small wooden stick. It had been a full-size, elaborately carved, decorated, and blessed weapon, and it certainly hadn't been in Dark of the Moon's plans to lose it. In fact—

Someone clapped their hands heartily behind her.

Dark of the Moon spun and went into a crouch without thinking, then nearly went to her knees when she saw who it was.

"Father!"

"A fine attack," he observed. "Even if it remains a futile effort."

For a moment Dark of the Moon couldn't speak. "Futile?" she finally repeated.

Always a handsome man, her father stood there and said nothing. He looked to her as he always had: dignified and mighty, somehow more deserving than others of everything around him by virtue only of his existence. Eventually he raised one dark eyebrow and regarded her sardonically.

"My strong but blind and foolish child." He shook his head. "Do you really think that because you best one old woman, you are worthy?" His mouth turned up at one end in a wry smile. "I suppose I should find it offensive that you would kill one of your own family—my mother—but in truth it matters little. I cannot be concerned with the fate of someone so stupid."

Dark of the Moon's mouth worked, then she found her voice.

"Stupid? You call Grandmother stupid for what she became, yet you are the same! Do you think I do not know? Do you think I cannot sense your evil? That I cannot *smell* you?" She ground her teeth. "You, of all people—*you* should have been stronger, *you* should have been wiser than to let yourself be swayed by the blood drinkers. Yet you become one with them, you embrace their corruption as if it has always been inside you." Her eyes bore into the Medicine Father's. "Is that it, Father? Is that the truth? Has their evil somehow *always* been in your heart?"

The Medicine Father laughed, a sound Dark of the Moon had seldom heard over the course of her lifetime. Now that it was far too late, she wished that circumstances had been different, that somehow she, him, and White Flower could have bonded more firmly and laughed and loved like other families. True, they weren't at all *like* other families, but had that meant they couldn't function like one?

As her father had said, it mattered little now.

"You are evil," she said, as much to make sure he knew how she felt as to convince herself.

"Am I?" He spread his hands, looking strong and confident in the sharp moonlight. "I am what *you* made me, Dark of the Moon. I am what I am because of what *you* allowed to happen."

She shook her head, horrified at the thought. "No. You're lying."

"Not at all," the Medicine Father said agreeably. Dark of the Moon thought she had never heard him sound so serene. "I am *your* victim. *You* allowed this to happen. You were born to do great things for the People, and you failed them. I trained you well, prepared you for the great battle to come, but you failed me, as well. Should a man not be able to safely search in the sweet predawn light for healing herbs?" He regarded her solemnly. "Yes, I have been joined with the creatures from the belly of the earth, but it is because of *you* that this has happened."

Shame coursed through Dark of the Moon, making her dusky skin flush darker in the cool night breeze. Her father was right, of course—she *had* been charged with the massive responsibility of which he spoke, and instead of prevailing, she had fallen under its weight. Now the few of her people who remained bordered on extinction, and she could not hope to save them.

But she could, if nothing else, stop this one creature, this stronghold of malevolence that no doubt walked the streets of her pueblo like the god he'd always held himself up to be. If only he had lived up to his own proclamations and protected the People as he should have.

Dark of the Moon had a stabbing stick in her hand almost without realizing it. She charged without warning, giving no hint whatsoever of her intentions. She took the Medicine Father down to the ground in a tumble that was painful enough to make them both grunt; her air went out in a rush, but she recovered instantly, balled her hand in a fist, and raised it to strike him.

She couldn't.

Her body and mind and spirit would not permit her hand to move, would not allow her fist to find the flesh of his face or thrust her wooden weapon into his heart.

By everything that was sacred on the Mother Earth, this man was her *father*. He had raised her and nurtured her and supported her, had done everything from teaching her to speak in the way of the People to fighting in the way of the beast slayer that Touch the Night had described her as. How could she be expected to *strike* him, no matter what he had become?

But the Medicine Father did not hesitate.

Too late Dark of the Moon realized that the man she was grappling with was no longer her father, and he certainly had no more parental urges to safeguard and nurture. His first punch caught her on the right side of her jaw and snapped her head to the left with enough force to make the bones in her neck creak in protest. Dark of the Moon fell sideways and before she could get to her feet, the Medicine Father delivered a vicious kick to her side, one with all his weight behind it. His leverage and position over her were perfect, and she heard more than felt her ribs as they cracked and caved in; his second kick to the same spot jammed something already cracked and sharp-ended into the soft tissue of her lungs.

Dark of the Moon tried to inhale and couldn't, then coughed and saw blood—black in the last, austere light of the moon—spew out of her mouth and coat the ground in front of her. She rolled onto her side and tried to get away from her father, but he only followed, delivering one kick after another. Finally, when she lay curled into an airless fetal position, the Medicine Father stopped and stood over her, watching as she struggled vainly to pull air into her body beyond the blood filling up her lungs.

"Such a foolish, foolish girl," he murmured. He crouched and watched her for a moment, then reached out a finger and drew it through the spittle and blood leaking down her chin. Dark of the Moon tried to pull away from him but couldn't—she hadn't enough breath to push strength into her muscles, and agony was coursing through her body as it screamed silently for air. Lying there, she didn't know what was worse: the horror of seeing her father thoughtfully lick his finger, or knowing she was going to die at the hands of her own parent.

"Sweet," he said softly, then pushed her hair off her forehead with the same rare tenderness he'd given her a decade and a half ago as a small child. "But now you are in so much pain. You think I am evil, and you're right of course. Still I have feelings for you, leftover shades of . . ." He paused, as if searching for the right word. "Responsibility."

Her father worked his way around behind her, then lifted her to a sitting position in his arms and regarded the old scars cross-cut into each side of her neck. Dark of the Moon wanted to protest, to run and rest and heal and return to fight him—and his kind—another day, but she knew it was not to be. "I will not leave you to die in such pain," he told her. "A parent should never let his child go like that. And I could save you, but I won't. As your father, I will give you this one, last gift . . .

"Death."

And Dark of the Moon had just enough time to be grateful before the Medicine Father twisted her head sharply to the right and the light of the full moon winked away into eternity.

Huddled in a secret *kiva,* a new one anointed and blessed by special rituals and the strength of the great Grandmother Spider, the few remaining elders read the death of their champion in the embers of the new sacred fire that sputtered weakly by the maw of the *sipapu* around which they sat. Their aged faces were grim and lined with the exhaustion of the decisions they had made over the last few weeks, and the harsher ones to come. With their guardian defeated and the battle all but lost, there was no one left to stand between the People and the demons that now freely roamed the night-shadowed pathways of the pueblo high in the cliffs.

As dawn finally broke over the pueblo and the few remaining villagers ventured tentatively forth, they left the guarding fire to die in the *kiva,* gathered as much of their belongings as could be found within the hour . . .

And fled, destined to disappear forever amid the great expanse of a protective Mother Earth.

Ch'ing Shih

Mel Odom

June 10, 1856

I

The serving girl in the Blind Turtle tavern carried a polished knife, which I felt could be her undoing, although clearly she did not. I guessed that she was new to her craft. A practiced thief worked better in concealment, even when he or she stole in the public eye, as she did then. An experienced thief would have dulled the knife's finish with lampblack or charcoal.

"Girl," one of the Englishmen called in his coarse, barbaric tongue. "More wine. Chop-chop."

The girl nodded and placed a fresh pitcher of rice wine on the carved wooden platter she carried. The tavern owner had made the platters himself, carving them from thick sections of trees into likenesses of turtle shells, then lacquering them heavily till they looked like burnished dark red oak shields. Each platter was different, and each had a story, though the foreign patrons that most frequented the Blind Turtle did not know that.

The *guei*, by which we referred to the invaders that had over-run the city twenty-four years earlier in 1842, cared little for our culture or our way of life. They had come with their opium and built warehouses all along the Whangpu River to conduct trade with China. Our language was rewritten on a daily basis, as was our way of life. *Guei*, in the Chinese common tongue, meant "foreign devils."

At that time, I thought the term appropriately fit the white men. But that was before I learned that the *ch'ing shih* was not just a story made up to frighten lazy or rebellious children, and that I had a destiny to be much more than I had ever dreamed of. Or that the destiny that had chosen me guaranteed an early and violent death at the hands of monsters.

The girl wore a long black dress, and her hair was pulled back. She was perhaps twelve or thirteen, old enough to start getting the curves of a woman that would doom her to a singsong house. There she would enter a life of prostitution and she would learn the house rules.

The rules were simple: Don't complain. Don't bite. Don't scratch. Don't steal. Don't avoid abuse, because marks on your face or body mean the house can charge the customer more if those were not agreed to prior to the delivery of service. Don't fight except to save your life. And never, never injure a paying customer.

I knew about that life because I had escaped from it only a few months before. During that escape, I had also killed a man for the first time. There were others I had killed since, but I did not count them. Nor did I take pride in those deaths. I had killed those men only to save my own life or that of someone I had chosen to protect. I did not choose to try to save everyone. I was wise enough, even then, to know that I could not save everyone. There was, however, a price that had been paid for learning that, a cold bleakness in my heart that I am convinced will never go away. The monks at the temple where I was raised always taught that knowledge comes at a price.

That night I was certain I could not save the life of the serving girl if she made a mistake. I was also convinced that she would make that mistake, and I hoped to be gone from the Blind Turtle before that happened because I knew I could not bear to watch her die. I did not leave immediately, though, because I had my own work to do and I had to keep up appearances.

The girl smiled at the Englishman as she approached. She moved well enough that she had potential at her chosen clandestine occupation as a thief. I saw that because she avoided most of the rough handling offered by the other men in the tavern, and I judged her intelligent because she ignored the suggestive and biting vituperation that followed in her wake.

Upon deciding to become a man, I found that vulgar use of the language and single-minded pursuit of mating were the hardest to wield as tools of my disguise. After months on the docks, I had a reputation as a quiet young man. It helped that most of the foreigners believed I had little spoken English and French, though I understood both well enough. I also enjoyed the reputation of being earnest and worth the hiring as a stevedore to ferry goods to and from the cargo ships that lay at anchor out in the river. Despite my size, most boat captains knew I had a strong back and carried no resentment of the work, nor the meager pay that they offered for a hard day spent at it.

After a full day's work at the docks, I stank as badly as any man that stood at the bar. I was covered with fetid river mud from wading ashore and pulling the flat-bottomed skiffs that we used to off-load supplies from the British, American, and French ships. I took no pride in that feat, though I could have because it marked me as a man that had worked as hard as any man around me.

But I was not a man as those around me believed me to be. I was a dockworker because that was the only way I was able to travel around so much of Shanghai during the day. During the evening, as it was now, my smelly clothes, sunburned face, and grimy appearance made me invisible in a crowd of Chinese workers.

Working the city was risky in the evenings, but turned dangerous when full night was upon Shanghai. Evenings summoned Englishmen, Americans, and Frenchmen from the buildings where they counted the money their employers made by the hour, by the day, and by the week. They came with their wives sometimes, but mostly with their mistresses or with women they had hired from the singsong houses.

The girl stopped at the man's table and poured the wine into his cup. She deliberately stepped into the Englishman, molding her body against the man's side and back. He grew more aware of her, more confident in his own manhood.

Her deliberate kowtowing to the man's baser side sickened me. I turned away and looked to the small cup of wine I had paid for but had barely touched during the past hour. The wine was a cover while I studied the other work I had planned for the evening.

I had seen the girl at the Blind Turtle before. She had been working there for only a few days. I didn't know her name, but I knew her features, and I knew the way she moved because I always pay attention to the way people move around me. That devotion to detail had been ingrained in me during the days I spent at the Way of the Tiger Monastery after being orphaned. The Way of the Tiger Monastery had been built to train Shaolin nuns in healing through herbal cures and remedies.

Those days in China in 1866, and even in Shanghai, where religion and the emperor's hand were looser due to the invasion of the *guei*, remained dark for those who wore the robes and colors of their monastic order. The destruction of the Shaolin temples first delivered by the Manchurians in the seventeenth century had not relented, but neither had those acts been completed.

The monks at the temple that shared ground with the one where I had been raised had never left those walls and grounds from the time they were accepted. Chinese merchants as well as the newer Western merchants met their need for trade. After years of caring for themselves, those needs were often frustratingly modest for foreign merchants.

"How old are you, girl?" The man roped an arm around the girl's waist. She didn't fight him, but I alone at that moment seemed to know why.

"Fifteen," she lied gracelessly. "Soon be sixteen." She spoke in broken Pidgin English but I suspected she knew more of the language than she let the man believe. Most of us knew more of the language than we let on; it was a survival skill, a means of letting the invaders believe they had the upper hand over us while we patiently gathered the information we needed to live the meager lives they let us have in Shanghai in those days.

"Well, missy, you're practically a young woman then," the man said.

"Yes." She tried to keep up a brave face, but I saw through her efforts and knew that she was scared. Fear knotted her shoulder blades and drew her body in on itself. But hunger and greed lurked there as well. And the canniness of a wolf, because I saw that she believed herself to be smarter than the half-drunken men that taunted her.

"What's your name, missy?" The man was fat as many Englishmen were. Talk on the docks and in the city suggested that the fatter an Englishman was, the more power he carried in the company he worked for, and the more excesses he indulged in and paid for. Although not always true, the observation was true enough. His round face was red. Great blond whiskers jutted out from his cheeks, making him resemble some forest animal.

"I called Kwan-Sook," the girl said.

"And what does that mean?" the Englishman asked.

I felt more revulsion for the man sweep over me, but I kept my own emotions under control. The *guei* always ask what our names mean but give no thought as to what their own might mean. They think our names are part of our language, without believing that their own names might mean something in their own language that they have forgotten or never knew. That simple act alone, repeated time and again, served to remind my countrymen of their foreign natures and the vast gulf that lay between us.

"My name mean 'moon-kissed petals,'" Kwan-Sook answered.

She lied, but the Englishman had no way of knowing that. She had chosen the name translation, obviously, for the suggestive nature such a name implied.

"That's a pretty name," the Englishman said. But the way he said that and the manner in which his eyes appraised her body told me that he didn't care what she was named. The name was only a label, something to call her, an incantation that gave him power over her.

"Thank you."

"Would you give me a kiss then, Moon-kissed Petals?" The Englishman drew a fat forefinger down the girl's cheek.

Four other men sat at the table with the fat Englishman. All of them were lean, letting me know that they did not wield the power the fat man did.

One of them caught my eye because he wore his hair red and full. I guessed him to be in his mid-twenties, but it was hard to know because so many *guei* looked the same to me with their large features and sunburned skin.

He was tall and thin, though broad of shoulder. In the lamp-lit interior of the Blind Turtle with the dark night lying in abeyance outside the tavern windows, his wide eyes were smoky gray and constantly moving, always taking in the people around him as well as his surroundings. I had the feeling that the man was a hunter or an outlaw. Many of the *guei* that came to China during those days were criminals in their own countries, but they were men that the companies often eagerly hired to use against the resistance to trade maintained by some of the villages and the emperor's guards. The man's jaw jutted like the prow of a ship. He would be, I judged, a very determined man once he chose his course.

I also believed him to be a very dangerous man, and in that I later proved to be right. He carried a saber at his side, as did many of the guards that stood post around the warehouses and protected the lives of the company men. He struck me as no guard, though, but rather an independent sort of man. His clothing was nowhere near as fine as that of his companions. The broadcloth shirt and rough breeches were scarred and faded and much worn, though well cared for. He was no man of means. Yet I had observed that the other men had treated him with respect while he was with them.

I also knew that he was fresh to Shanghai, and to China, for he had many questions that new arrivals constantly ask. The surprising thing about this was that he had a decent command of both the Chinese common tongue and Mandarin, though spoken with a grating accent that I did not recognize. Most new arrivals had none of our language.

"I no can give you kiss," Kwan-Sook said with modesty that I was certain was feigned. I could see through her act, though the men—except for the red-haired one—seemed completely fooled.

Shyness, I believed, was a quality that men of power were drawn to with intent to corrupt and destroy it. In the singsong houses, girls who could act demure and virginal night after night, time after time, were constantly in demand.

Even in the monastery where I was raised, I was never truly given to demureness. Many of the women there had been appalled at my actions because I had—through only quiet rebellion—refused to accept my station in life.

"And why can't you give me a kiss?" the Englishman demanded in mock anger.

Every man at the table knew the Englishman would get what he wanted. Only the red-haired man seemed uncomfortable with that.

"Because then I get into trouble with Kim-Sang."

Bian Kim-Sang owned the Blind Turtle. He did not like the *guei* much, but he loved their money. Many of the foreigners built restaurants that served their dishes, but when they came to drink and to carouse, they came most often to Chinese taverns. Some of them even frequented the opium dens run by Chinese owners. It wasn't that they loved our culture or wanted to get to know our ways; it was because they chose to hide from their compatriots so that their excesses and predilections might not be known and taken advantage of.

"You no get into trouble," the Englishman said, mimicking her broken English like a parent soothing a reluctant child. He placed a beefy hand on her shoulder possessively. "I see you no get into trouble." He raised his voice. "Kim-Sang."

"Yes." Kim-Sang answered from behind the bar. He was short and slight, no larger than myself. A wispy mustache and beard clung to his face like seaweed from a fisherman's net.

"You don't care if this young lady gives me a kiss, do you?" the Englishman asked. He drawled "lady" out sarcastically, as if we were all in on his joke at her expense. His eyes and his hand never left Kwan-Sook. "That way I can tell my countrymen what a fine establishment you have here and that the service is always good."

"No," Kim-Sang answered. He knew that refusal on his part would be ignored anyway, and might even incite the *guei* to leave his establishment before they had spent all their money. He kept no girls and sold no opium, so the only profits he could make came from the barrels of rice wine and imported whiskey.

Besides, Kwan-Sook was only a female, nothing worth any risk to himself or to his profits. That belief was not a personal failing, but one that stemmed from the culture of the land. Even the British and the Americans had their own problems in dealing with women. Especially high-minded and high-spirited ones, as I have since been told.

The Englishman looked at Kwan-Sook. "I can kiss her?"

"Sure," Kim-Sang said. "You kiss if want. I no care. I no kiss. She ugly. Much flat face." He was smarter than he let the men realize. Any Chinese man who made his living around the whites had to be very intelligent and savvy to survive. But they also had to be selfish, unafraid to sacrifice other Chinese men and women for their own gain should the need arise.

The men laughed at Kim-Sang's words, and I knew they had all seen the slim curves that Kwan-Sook was beginning to show. As a woman, she would have been beautiful.

"Come here, missy," the Englishman said, wrapping his other arm around Kwan-Sook and drawing her into his embrace.

The girl struggled against the Englishman and cried out in protest, but she did not break free of his drunken grip as I felt certain that she could have. If you scratched a man's eyes, he would release you. I knew that from experience. The girl knew exactly what she was doing.

The red-haired man shifted at the table uncomfortably. "C'mon, Gresham," he said in a calm manner. "You've had a bit o' sport. Leave go the girl."

Kwan-Sook continued fighting for a bit, but remained limp like a mouse trapped in the paralyzing jaws of a venomous snake. Her eyes peered away from the man, avoiding his gaze. Her hand disappeared into the folds of her long dress and it was then that I first saw the masked shape of the small knife she carried.

I also saw the fat Englishman's equally fat purse, heavy with coin, hanging from inside his jacket. The amount that must have been there filled my mind with larcenous thoughts of my own. My needs then—my responsibilities—were so great that they were never far from my thoughts. So far tonight in the bar, the pickings had appeared small. But the fat Englishman—Gresham, I reminded myself because I wanted to remember the name for future reference—he carried a prize.

"What's the matter with you, Connelly?" Gresham asked. "Don't you like the tender young flesh that's available in this place?"

Distaste showed on the red-haired man's face. "I don't lust after children," he stated baldly.

"Well, now," Gresham said, taking obvious offense at the accusation. "You're the fine one, ain't you? Come to sit at a man's table and drink of his generosity, enjoy his fellowship, and then get all judgmental."

Without a word, Connelly reached into a pocket and dropped coins onto the table. Silver glinted. "I'll pay for me drinks."

Despite my liking for the man for the way he took up for Kwan-Sook, I also marked him as a potential target before I left the Blind Turtle. He parted with his money easily, and such men as that were always targets. My needs were so great that I could not afford to be influenced or swayed by the generosity of those I intended to steal from. I told myself those people could always make more money because they truly owned the city. Other people less able to care for themselves depended on me, and there was never a day that I didn't feel the pressure of that need.

Gresham grimaced. "Look at yourself, then. All full of it, you are."

"I was told that you were a man to come to about the legends and myths of this place, that you had knowledge of this culture." Connelly's eyes took on a hard appearance. "I was also told that you had questionable tastes."

Gresham's face darkened in near apoplexy. "I want the names of the man or men that dared tell you anything of the sort! And if you're lying, by God, sir, I'll see that you do with a sound thrashing!"

Connelly smiled, and even though he sat outnumbered at the table, I knew he had no fear for his life from those men. I did not know if he was that confident of his own prowess or if he was just foolhardy. "That will take more than you've got seated around you, it will."

The other men shifted uneasily, and I knew that they believed his soft-voiced claim. I watched the man with greater interest. If they recognized him as a threat, then so would I.

"Be off with you then," Gresham declared. "And the devil take you for your affront to me." The fat Englishman still didn't release Kwan-Sook, and he sat holding her covetously like a child would a threatened prize.

I don't know what Connelly would have done had events played out differently, nor do I know what Gresham would have ordered. For in that instant, Kwan-Sook bared her knife and went for the fat Englishman's purse.

The sharp edge of the knife sawed through the purse strings in a single slice and the leather pouch dropped almost noiselessly into a hidden pocket sewn into her dress. But the knife blade, keen and polished as it was, also caught the light from one of the lanterns hanging from the soot-stained ceiling.

"Hey!" one of the dockworkers yelled. "She's stealin' from you, guv'ner!"

Maybe if the dockworkers hadn't been drawn to the spectacle, all waiting to see if Connelly got cut up or shot or beaten for daring to speak to Gresham in such a manner, no one would have seen the girl's theft. It was ill luck, and even worse timing. If I had been the girl at that moment, I would have left the purse for later, while Gresham had his mind on anything but me. But she wasn't me, and she wasn't used to thieving in the dark streets and taking advantage of Shanghai's shadows. All I could imagine was that her desperation or greed far outweighed her fear.

Gresham glanced down and spotted the cut purse strings dangling from inside his jacket. He growled a vile oath and released his hold on the girl with one hand, then began searching her skirts frantically.

"Don't just sit there, you lummoxes!" Gresham shouted at the men around the table. "Help me get my money back from this thieving jezebel!"

The men rose to their feet, though most of the Chinese men did so reluctantly. They gave Connelly wide berth, but he stood his ground as if undecided.

Kwan-Sook raked her knife across the Englishman's eyes. Blood wept down his features from the long cut that ran across his forehead. Perhaps she even tried to blind him. Whatever her intent, she succeeded in getting him to let her go.

One of the men sprang from his chair and rushed at her with out-flung arms and loud curses spilling from his crude mouth. In another step, he would have her. But then Connelly's foot was there, catching the man's back foot as if by accident, causing the pursuer to trip himself while his rising foot caught behind the planted one. The man fell, coming down heavily on the back of another man seated at a nearby table, driving them both forward until the table collapsed under their combined weight.

Even as the table crashed to the floor, Gresham rose to his feet and yelled, "After her! After her! A reward to any man that brings her down!"

A pack of howling men arose from the tavern crowd. All of those who got to their feet smelled the promise of bloodshed that was in the air, and they wanted to take part in it. Several of them grabbed the young woman before she reached the tavern's back door.

Kwan-Sook screamed in fear-filled pain as the crowd bore her down to the ground. They pummeled her relentlessly. Gresham's purse surfaced in the morass of moving bodies, and a few bright coins spilled across the floor. The fat Englishman howled more curses and moved swiftly to grab his purse.

I remained where I was at the bar, but my heart pounded in my chest. Involving myself at that time would have been self-destructive and foolhardy. I knew I couldn't do anything for the girl inside the tavern.

"Outside!" Gresham ordered. "Take the thieving little wench outside! We'll deliver her a proper amount of justice then!"

I forced myself to remain calm as the men pulled Kwan-Sook to her feet. She screamed for help and for mercy, but we both knew neither of those would be forthcoming.

Shanghai was divided into two cities. One city housed the whites and those of my people who had chosen to, and could afford to, comfortably fit into their remade world, and the other city was called Chinese City, where the common laborers and fishermen dwelt. Although Chinese City was supposed to enforce its own laws, the British military hunted there freely for any man who had broken their laws or stolen from them.

The crowd took Kwan-Sook through the back door of the

tavern. Behind the bar, Kim-Sang looked sad, and—for a moment—as though he were tempted to do something to interfere. I knew that he kept a fowling piece behind the bar and had killed at least two men during the years he had owned the Blind Turtle. But in the end, he returned to wiping glasses for his prospective customers when they returned.

The reasons were simple: Kwan-Sook was Chinese, and she was female, making her practically worthless in our country in that time and place; and Gresham was an Englishman, powerful and wealthy enough to buy a round of drinks for the house when the men returned after meting out the justice they intended for Kwan-Sook. And if the men were thirsty, profits could be made.

Several other men stood in the bar. A few of them left, obviously certain that the English militia would be called at some point, and that heads would be cracked by those hard-fisted men given the slightest provocation.

I went with those who departed, telling myself that Kwan-Sook's fate was no responsibility of mine. It was not my place, I argued with myself, to try to save those too stupid to save themselves.

As soon as I reached the street outside and watched the silvery curls of fog drifting through the city, I knew I couldn't leave. I heard her screams in the alley behind the tavern. I knew I could not ignore that.

Shanghai was still awake. Music from the singsong houses stained the fetid night air. The voices of men and women echoed around me. Harbor noises, the clank of pulleys and sails luffing as rigging popped and snapped against the masts of the small cargo ships and gunboats lying at anchor in the Whangpu River, rolled through the narrow streets. Outside Chinese City, in the greater area of Shanghai that the *guei* laid claim to, restaurant and entertainment houses would still be doing business by the light of oil lanterns, safe in the protection of street lanterns.

But here in Chinese City, shadows ruled the streets. And one thing I had learned since leaving the monastery and coming to Shanghai to find a new life: Shadows were my friends.

I walked unhurriedly to the nearest alley. I wished that Kwan-Sook would die quickly with the same fervor that I wished I would arrive in time. I also wished that I were not such a fool.

In the alley I quickly shed the mud-stained man's clothing I wore, leaving only the black silk blouse and pants that I wore beneath those things when I knew I would be working at night. I also stepped out of the boots and remained barefooted. My feet bore heavy calluses from the work I did at the monastery, and I preferred to have my toes free to aid in climbing.

I pulled two black silken scarves from the pockets of my blouse, wrapped one around my head above my eyes and the other across my lower face to mask my features and to more readily blend with the night. My heart beat more rapidly, but I knew that part of me relished the coming battle.

At the men's monastery so close to its sister order, I had watched the monks box, and I had learned much of their way of openhanded combat and practiced it in secret until Master Wang had discovered me going through the moves one night. At the women's temple, I had learned some of the fighting skills I now knew, but I learned more from Master Wang.

I don't know how many times he had watched me until he came forward and offered to teach me more. He was drawn, he said, to the wonder that a female could learn so much, could render the moves with such grace and art and power when Wing Chung was usually the chosen art form because nearly all women lacked the necessary upper body strength. He had been near the end of his days then, and his passion for the martial arts practiced at the monastery kept him alive.

For three years we practiced in secret. I was a diligent student. Master Wang came to love me as I came to love him. He told me he had never had a brighter student, and I believed him because in all the time I was given the opportunity to know Master Wang, I never knew him to lie. He also taught me English, how to speak the foreign tongue as well as how to write it. In his heart, I think that he knew I could not stay at the women's temple, though I do not believe he had any clue of the future that lay ahead of me.

Last year, when I was sixteen, Master Wang passed away quietly and peacefully. I mourned him. Respectfully, I cleaned his grave every day, though most of the other monks never knew why I cared so much for him. Five months after that, I left the women's temple and went to Shanghai, hoping only to find my own way in the world and to flee the burden of the strict monastic life. I longed to see as much as I could of the outside world I had heard about from merchants and travelers.

I had not known the greater and more heavy burdens that would be put before me, nor that I would have to endure so much heartbreaking pain.

Dressed in black now, trusting that I would be impossible to identify later, I turned back to the Blind Turtle. I stopped momentarily at the nearby shop where sails were patched and mended, and took one of the six-foot poles that held up an awning. The awning drooped, but by that time I was already gone, racing for the tavern, hearing the shouts and jeers of the men celebrating Kwan-Sook's cries.

I threaded the staff through a tie on the inside of my blouse, then scaled the wall to the peaked rooftop. On the roof I moved quickly and quietly to the side facing the alley behind the tavern.

Seventeen men filled the alley, ringing Kwan-Sook up against the wall. Three of Gresham's companions stood over Connelly, obviously posted there as guard so he wouldn't interfere with the punishment being handed out. Some of those men were Chinese, and it angered me to see that they took pleasure in Kwan-Sook's pain.

The girl cowered against the wall, covering her head with her hands and arms as she screamed for help. Not many animals in the wild toy with prey. Even cats generally do so for the purpose of better learning their skills as hunters.

But those men that night—they handed out pain and fear because they enjoyed it.

I gathered myself, pressed in close against the rooftop so that the moon behind me wouldn't cast my shadow to the ground. Four men held lanterns, obviously carried from inside the tavern. In the space of a drawn breath, I assembled my plan of action.

I freed the staff from my blouse strings and dropped into the alley in the middle of the crowd.

II

I landed in the alley without a sound. The men nearest me turned immediately, recognizing me as a threat. In my hands, the wooden pole became a live thing, lashing out in sweeping blows or thrusting out to slam into faces and other vulnerable areas. Men cried out in agony as bones broke and flesh ripped under my vicious attack. I held nothing back because I judged the men to be sadistic brutes worthy of no kindness, no mercy. Still, I killed none of them. I had been taught to revere all life.

Master Wang's favorite weapon had been the staff, though he had mastered other weapons as well and had taught me in their use. And his favorite weapon had become mine. I whirled and moved, the pole twisting constantly in my hands. My palms rasped and whispered across the unfinished surface, but—thankfully—there were no splinters to throw off my rhythm.

A man reached for me, and I broke his hand. Another man slashed at me, causing me to dodge to the left, and I swept the staff up under my right arm and twisted my body back toward him so the staff caught him in the face and knocked him aside. By that time I was in motion again, sweeping the feet from another man with a long arc of the staff, then coming up to slam the weapon's blunt end between another man's eyes to stretch him prone on the ground.

The men retreated. I feinted toward them, driving them back further still, then altered my blow to shatter the lantern carried by one of the men along the front. Flaming oil spread over the men nearest the lantern bearer. They brushed at the fire that clung to their clothing, yelling curses.

They called me a demon. And not once, I was sure, did the thought that I was a woman cross their minds.

"Kill them!" Gresham screamed. "Kill them both!"

Connelly struggled to rise from the ground but one of the men guarding him kicked him in the head.

I stepped across the unconscious body of one of the men I had felled and reached for Kwan-Sook. "Come," I told her. "Come if you would live."

She looked at me with wide, staring eyes. But she didn't move.

I grabbed her wrist and yanked her from the wall, shoving her toward the street. Two men stood in front of us, blocking the way, but clearly uncertain whether they could stand against me.

"Don't let that thief escape!" Gresham shouted.

One of the men dove for me. I held the staff, hands spread wide apart, and swept his arms to my right. Still moving, I stepped in and kicked the man three times in the ribs and stomach. He crumpled.

The other man tried to grab Kwan-Sook. I thrust the staff between his feet and tripped him, drawing back to tap the blunt end against his temple only hard enough to render him unconscious instead of kill him.

"Look out!"

I recognized Connelly's barbarous accent immediately and turned.

Metal flashed in the air.

I saw the slender shape of a throwing dagger flipping through the air. A quick flick of the staff knocked the knife away, and before the weapon clattered to the ground, I had Kwan-Sook by the wrist and was pulling her toward the mouth of the alley.

Something warned me: an instinct or a feeling that always seemed to hover around me whenever I engaged in battle. Master Wang had never been able to explain the ability, but he thought that the unexplained awareness might have been coupled with my quick mastery of all that he taught me, as well as the extraordinary strength I had. I was stronger than all women I'd ever met, and believed I was stronger than most—if not all—men. At least, I believed I was stronger than *normal* men.

Gresham fought his way to the front of the ragged line of men, slapping and shoving at those who stood in his way. Too late, I saw the small pistol all but hidden in his fat hand. Flame spewed from the muzzle.

I felt Kwan-Sook jerk in my grip. Turning, I saw the neat round blue-black hole that took shape over her right eye, then the crimson ruin that fell across the back of her neck and her shoulders, where the back of her skull had exploded outward from the bullet's impact.

Her eyes turned dull as I watched, and I knew no life remained within her.

I released her hand and let her fall into the alley. Then I ran, knowing the only life I could save at that point was my own. A second bullet struck sparks and stone splinters from the alley corner as I fled. I felt something rip across my cheek, then the warm flow of blood.

I ran and chased the shadows of the city till I was safely one of them again.

"Xiaoqin, why are you crying?"

Ashamed, I turned in the darkness to look at Nah-Mi. I knew her voice was the one that called out to me, just as I knew all the others were asleep.

Nah-Mi was only five years old. She had put on a little weight since I had found her rooting through rotting vegetables in an alley two months ago, but she was still a skinny, frail thing. Her eyes gleamed with yellow luminescence in the pale glow that reflected through the dirty, narrow windows of the potato cellar under the burned-out husk of the hostelry above us.

I did not want to tell Nah-Mi of Kwan-Sook and the way that I had failed to defend her. Nah-Mi's memories were all full of nightmares. I knew she had nightmares because when we shared the pallet on the hard earthen floor, she constantly kicked and fought, and sometimes screamed. I didn't know what she endured or how she survived before I found her and took her in, but I knew that I did not want to add to those terrible times.

"I'm crying because my stomach hurts," I replied. It was the easiest lie I could think of that I felt certain Nah-Mi would understand.

"Oooh, I'm sorry," she said. "Did you eat?"

"Yes, little one."

"Maybe you need to eat again."

I thought of the way that Kwan-Sook's head had exploded. "No, I don't need to eat again."

"Maybe it was something you ate, then."

"Probably," I answered. I wiped away the tears that clung to my cheeks. I knew why I cried, just as I knew that I could not explain the reasons to Nah-Mi. My frustration was great that night, and I felt trapped by so many things that were beyond my control. The anger was intensified because I felt many of those things should have been within my control.

I listened to the rhythmic breathing and snores of the nine other girls around us. The oldest was ten. The youngest was Nah-Mi. During the four months I had been in Shanghai, I had found six other girls living in the gutter or about to be sold to the triads that ran the singsong houses. Two of the girls about to be sold into sexual slavery were put up for sale by their fathers.

Women were not, and are not, prized possessions in China. A farmer did not want a girl child because she was not strong enough to work in the fields. Nor did a master craftsman want to teach his skills to any other than a son or an adopted male apprentice.

Once, while unloading a boat out in the harbor, I spotted the body of a dead girl child floating by. Most of the men I was working with joked about the matter, saying that the only good that came from a woman were her abilities to keep house and produce strong sons to help a man. Even in the monastery, we heard stories of how baby girls were left to die in the forests and on the riverbanks, or drowned outright in the river.

Women had never been respected in China. And then, when the emperor and the *guei* fought each other for trading rights, food was hard to come by. No workingman wanted to waste his hard-won food on a girl child.

"I could rub your stomach for you," Nah-Mi offered.

Her generosity brought more tears to my eyes. I struggled to control my breathing. In the darkness I knew that I could hide my tears even though I couldn't stop them.

"No," I told her. "I will be fine. But thank you." I sat with my back to the earthen wall of the cellar. The damp fetid musk of the mudflats on either side of the Whangpu invaded the small space.

The cellar was tiny, and if it were not nearly buried beneath the burned-out husk of the old hotel, I would not have had even that place for the children. They would have had to sleep in alleys or on rooftops, changing locations every night as so many homeless in those times did.

The number of homeless people had risen since the taipans, the self-appointed guerrilla warriors fighting for a Chinese-controlled China, had risen up against the foreign invaders. Many people in the outlying towns and villages had come to Shanghai because they had been burned out by the British militia and barely escaped with their lives. They didn't want to be caught between the taipans and the British again.

So people fought for food and for jobs and for places to sleep at night. Alleyways controlled by triad gangs or by *guei* bandits charged rent for day or night. Small rooms for let would be packed with people sleeping nearly shoulder to shoulder on the floor, and they were only allowed six- to eight-hour shifts for their money. Those who slept outside Shanghai's walls were prey for beasts as well as roving bands of thieves that would often kill destitute victims.

I had found the cellar for myself, cleared the space, and fought off all those who had shown up to claim it. In the beginning the space had been more than enough for me, and I had traps arranged to warn me if anyone tried to break in. Then, when I first took in Rong-Fang, who still lived with me and was only eight, the space started to dwindle.

I had never intended to become the protector of the girls I took in. When I found them in dire straits, though, I hadn't been able to turn them away. They all needed someone, and they all had no one. I had no one, but I was a fighter and intelligent. At the time, I had thought I had needed no one. But I had come to find out that caring for them filled a need inside me that I had never known I had. Somehow, protecting them made me feel more complete.

Eleven people sleeping on the floor nearly covered all the available space in the basement. We were outgrowing the sanctuary I had found for us. Soon, I knew, I would have to find a new place for them. For *us.*

But I didn't want to think of that then because my mind was already overcrowded with unpleasant thoughts. The thought of moving scared me. While I had dwelt among the Shaolin nuns and worked the fields with the monks, I had known security. But I had never known peace. From birth I had seemed filled with a restless energy, a need to get out and do *something.* But I hadn't ever known what it was.

The price I was to pay for that knowledge was hideous. And then it was almost upon me.

"Xiaoqin," Nah-Mi said in a sleepy voice, "I'm cold."

I held out my arms. "Then come to me, little one. I will warm you."

She crawled through the bedding I had bought or stolen from those who were more fortunate, from those who could afford to replace the things I claimed for us. I took her into my arms and held her.

Nah-Mi's heart beat against her thin ribs and I felt the vibration echo within my own body. Sometimes, when I was working long hard days out in the harbor, or when I crept through the shadows and risked my life against the pistols and swords of men that would kill to protect what I would take from them, I felt self-pity for the predicament I found myself in by taking care of the young girls. It was a tremendous financial burden, and an emotional one.

And I never truly saved them; I was honest with myself about that. But I gave them better chances after a time to save themselves. Three of the girls I had taken into my care had been killed while trying to emulate me and become thieves. Another had been taken by one of the triads and forced to work in a singsong house. Two others had been sold to Englishmen and I hadn't been able to find them. One had died from opium addiction, the cursed disease delivered into our country by the *guei*.

When I was truly honest with myself, I knew that I was only delaying their deaths. Even without the opium, even without the *guei*, Shanghai was no place for girl children.

"Xiaoqin," Nah-Mi said.

"Yes, little one," I replied.

"Tell me a story."

Her breath fell softly against my injured cheek. The Englishman's bullet had torn fragments from the stones that had lacerated my skin. I didn't worry about the wounds because I healed quickly. Lately I had been healing faster than ever, though I had no explanation for that because I never rested or ate properly.

"What story would you like to hear?" I ran my fingers through Nah-Mi's long black hair. I didn't know anything about my family. I didn't know if I had a little sister. But if I did, and if we had been allowed to stay together, I knew I couldn't have loved her any more than I loved Nah-Mi. "Would you like to hear the story of Yah-Shen? Of how her wicked stepmother slew the fish that was her friend? And how the fish's bones granted Yah-Shen's wish to go to the spring festival and find a husband so she could escape her wicked stepmother and half sister?"

"No," Nah-Mi whispered sleepily. "I want to hear the good story. The one about how one day you will buy a boat and sail us away from this place to the biggest castle in the land, where we can all live happily ever after."

Her words cut me to the bone. I didn't know what had ever possessed me to tell them that story. It was just something that I wanted to believe in myself, back when I thought escaping Shanghai was possible. Money came into my hands from my dock work as well as the thieving I did, but the money was spent almost as quickly as it came in. At present, it would take me years to save up for a boat. Even then, everyone would be suspicious of the money I had made and might even guess at how I had made it. I had given up on that dream, but Nah-Mi and some of the others hadn't. They were too young, too helpless, and needed to believe in the story.

"Perhaps another time," I told Nah-Mi.

"Tonight, Xiaoqin," she pleaded. "Please. It is my favorite story."

Tonight, I told myself, *you could not save Kwan-Sook. But you can save Nah-Mi's dreams.* But I also could not help thinking that Nah-Mi would hate me when she finally came to know the truth: that the boat would never be bought and we would never escape the terrible city around us.

So I began the story of how I would someday buy a beautiful boat that would sail us anywhere in the world we wanted to go, and I described the great castle we would all live in. In my mind, though, I vowed vengeance against the Englishman Gresham. For Kwan-Sook, but also for myself, because his actions had reminded me of how little control I had over my own life and how temporary the safe harbor I granted these orphaned children would be.

I discovered who Gresham was the next day. He served as a warehouse overseer for an English shipping franchise called the

Windsor Sails Trading Company. The company shipped a number of things, but mostly they shipped opium up from India and on into China through Shanghai. Secondary companies took over at the docks, reinvesting some of the profits locally to build an army-in-waiting. Their personnel managed two restaurants, an entertainment house, five mercantiles, a singsong house, and took profits from four opium dens that I had learned of while I had searched for information.

During my time spent as a thief, I had learned to acquire such knowledge through observation as well as talking to people who knew those things. The people I bought information from never knew my real name or even why I wanted it, though I am sure they suspected the reason, just as I was certain I was not the only person they sold that information to.

Three nights later I discovered Gresham also did business that his employer didn't know about. Many of the *guei* let their power go to their heads. Money was power in Shanghai, as was position, but mostly money. Each overseer and every worker that found ways to line his pockets did so, and those illicit profits spilled over onto Shanghai's fleshpots and opium dens. Those profits were fueled by the *guei* anger at being marooned in China, and by prejudice against people that did not like those who had invaded their country.

The previous nights I had followed Gresham through the dives and haunts of Chinese City—he seemed to favor those because he could mistreat the women that worked in those places. He was quicker and more able physically than I had at first suspected, so that was a mistake I quickly admitted to myself.

As much as I had learned while on my own in Shanghai, there still remained many other things to learn and no one to teach me except my own experiences. Master Wang had schooled me in that, saying that every man—and women who were able—

would ultimately be made responsible for his, or her, own education. I had learned a lot during the months I had lived in the city. In the streets and shadows of Shanghai, I had become a hunter, but one that was not known.

Gresham acted differently that night. He was more furtive, more quick to make his move once he had chosen a course of action. And he went without his usual coterie of bodyguards. He also carried a small package inside his coat that he appeared very fretful about. During his walk, he kept touching the package through the lining in his coat as if to reassure himself that it was still there.

I had observed other instances of men that acted in such a manner, and I couldn't help being excited by the prospect. Each man I had targeted and tracked that had acted so had always provided me with a larger sum to steal than I had at first believed possible.

I had hopes for Gresham that night, but in my heart I also longed for vengeance for Kwan-Sook. Her only crimes had been in being too greedy and too impatient. The price she had been made to pay had been too high.

During the last three lonely and weary nights with Nah-Mi and the other children, I took on a measure of guilt for myself, as well, in Kwan-Sook's death. I knew there had been a slim chance the men might have let her live after they'd finished with her in the alleyway had I not intervened. But in the bright light of day, I felt certain that my guilt in the matter was false. Those men had not gone there merely to defile Kwan-Sook and give her a beating. They had lusted after her blood because she had been someone weaker than they were, someone whose death no one would have cared about.

I cared about her, though, because she represented so many young girls that were murdered by uncaring hands, or lived, broken in spirit and in body, in remembered terror. And I cared about my part in Kwan-Sook's death. No one could have counted on that.

Instead of the Windsor Sails Trading Company, Gresham went to one of the older Chinese customs houses that had been allowed to stay in business. The shipping warehouse belonged to the Blue Tiger House, one of the oldest establishments in Shanghai.

The Blue Tiger Customs House was at least a hundred years old, though well cared for. It was a place that had stood even while other buildings had been destroyed, first by the British gunboats, then by the taipans as they tried to invade Shanghai to rout the *guei*. The fact that the customs house had remained unharmed through those events spoke of good luck and perhaps respect for—or fear of—the people that conducted business there.

The heavily lacquered tiles on the building's peaked roof gleamed in the moonlight, and by day the deep red stain took on the appearance of fire. The customs house had stood on the dock area when only fishing and weaving had supported the small village that Shanghai had been before the British had come with their opium. A heavy sign hung from the post that jutted out over the customs house entrance. The sign depicted a rearing, snarling tiger etched in blue, though that color looked black in the night. The attached warehouse stood behind.

At that time I didn't know much about the Blue Tiger family that ran the house. The Blue Tigers weren't talked about much, and I had gathered that they had a lot of power and a lot of money. I had never had occasion to work for them because I labored during the day, filling my nights with the children and the thievery necessary to keep us all fed. The Blue Tigers generally did their business in the quieter hours of the evening when most workers had turned their attention to the city's taverns and singsong houses.

Even now, as I hid in the shadows, men worked to unload the small boats that sat at anchor along the Blue Tiger docks. Voices drifted over the lapping water, but the talk was less than was usual among dockworkers. Warehouse foremen moved among the dockhands, yelling instructions and threats over the crates that were being brought to the pier by hand.

I didn't know what business the Blue Tigers were involved with, but I suspected at least some of it was in opium. Few businesses in Shanghai then existed without the benefit of the fruit of the dark poppy.

Gresham waited at the edge of the pier outside the customs house. He looked out of place because he was the only *guei* there. I knew then that the stakes he sought were high, because no Englishman traveled Shanghai's streets unprotected when he could afford that protection. With his position, Gresham could have had men with him. But he didn't. Either he had been commanded not to by whomever he was there to see, or he hadn't wanted to split his profits. He waited, fidgeting restlessly and availing himself of the snuffbox he carried.

I waited as well, keeping myself calm through the breathing techniques Master Wang had trained me in. But my heart hammered and I felt the anger over Kwan-Sook's murder boiling up hot and restless. Waiting never came naturally to me, though I had learned the skill.

I wore black from head to toe and carried a few throwing knives, a small short sword, and a proper staff that had been stained with charcoal and given a good finish. My original plan had been to attack Gresham when he was vulnerable and break the Englishman's knees as soon as the chance presented itself. I had promised myself that I wouldn't take his life because the

Windsor Sails Trading Company was big enough to avenge the murder of one of their important employees, and because of the way Master Wang had trained me. The British never allowed much in the way of trespasses against them without speedy retaliation.

I hadn't taken the man, though, and that proved to be a mistake. Gresham's furtiveness had alerted me to the possibility of greater fortune, and I had let my judgment be swayed. I should have taken the Englishman earlier. Then things might have gone differently and so many people might not have died.

But I didn't. I was young and overconfident. In my defense, I didn't know the true nature of the enemy I faced. Their deaths would haunt me forever.

A few minutes later a Chinese man strode from inside the customs house. Three men followed him, but they all moved like guards, staying close and letting their eyes rove constantly. They kept their hands close to their weapons. These men were trained and careful about their business. They wore swords, not ornate things that denoted station or only served as ornamentation, but true fighting blades. And they carried British or American revolvers.

I had only seen those kinds of repeating pistols twice up close. Their invention was new, although gunpowder was a centuries-old creation of my people. Chinese generals had first thought of building cannon as well, but the British had become the masters of the seas and waterways by thinking to mount them on their great ships. In the end, even though they had fewer ships, the British had returned to China and captured Shanghai and other ports in my country. Master Wang had taught me considerable history, and I had listened politely even though I did not know how any lessons of the past would help me with my uncertain future.

The man from the customs house wore a formal silk robe. The garment glowed green in the light of the lanterns strung along the pier. He moved smoothly and evenly, and his gait looked almost unnatural. He kept his hands laced over his stomach. Long scarlet nails glinted like knives, each of them over six inches long. He looked middle aged and handsome. He wore a fierce mustache and thin beard, and his hair was tied back in a queue.

Gresham followed the other man, dwarfing him by his height and girth. I judged that the man was only a little taller than I. But the Englishman acted afraid of the customs house man.

The dockworkers gave the Blue Tiger man a lot of room, moving back fearfully. I had witnessed that kind of behavior along the docks before because there was no shortage of manpower to be had by the shipping companies.

When the inspection of the crates was completed to the customs house man's satisfaction, he gave a few final orders regarding the handling of the cargo and returned to the customs house. Gresham followed.

I too followed. But I raced through the shadows to the rear of the warehouse. I should have waited. I knew that then. My target was Gresham and the fat purse he carried. But since he had carried the small package to the customs house where buying and selling was done, I felt certain that his fat purse would grow fatter still.

Greed, especially when fired by need, makes fools of everyone. I was greedy that night, to my later sorrow, and my needs were great.

I could have waited in an alley for Gresham to leave, but I chose to investigate the possibilities presented by the Blue Tiger Customs House. No matter how fat Gresham's purse was that night, I knew the amount would not last forever. Hiding and feeding the girls I was trying to save drained every resource I could lay hands to. I felt constantly on the edge of ruin, and there were still nights that we all went to sleep hungry no matter what I did.

During that time, I resented the burden I had somehow been unable to avoid, but if there were a way to have it back, I would. So many things were taken from me that night. For all that I had been through, for all that I had done, I had still been a child in so many ways.

At the back of the warehouse, I hid in the shadows till the guards passed. The presence of the guards did not alarm me. Most warehouses kept them. If honest thieves did not steal from the warehouses, there were also employees and rival warehouses to worry about.

When a thick black cloud scudded over the half-hidden face of the moon, I took out a padded grapple and a length of knotted silken cord. During my career as a thief, I had chanced upon the grapple and found it useful many times.

Whirling the grapple at my side, I tossed it over one of the beams holding the peaked roof. The grapple landed with only a muffled *thunk*. Bracing myself, feet against the warehouse wall, I ran up the side of the building as quickly as if I'd been on level ground. Master Wang had taught me the art of ropes, just as he had taught me how to fight while clinging to one or using one like a whip.

Balanced on my toes across one of the roof's support beams, my back pressed into the slanted roof above, I hauled up the silken line only a heartbeat before the two warehouse guards came around the corner again. I hunkered on the beam and watched as they continued.

Behind the warehouse the other storage buildings appeared dark and inert. A few lone night watchmen went about their rounds, but I felt certain they had not seen me in the darkness.

The lanterns they carried blinded them to the night even as light ripped away the immediate shadows.

I wrapped the grapple and line around my waist again. The padded handle of the sword I carried in a sheath down my back rasped along the slanted roof as I crept forward on the beam. Three quick steps brought me up against the warehouse wall. The ventilation window I was after was only an arm's reach down.

I hung upside down, my knees bent to hold my weight on the beam. Blood rushed to my head, but I was also intoxicated by the challenge I had laid before myself. Sometimes I wonder if I had not come by thievery honestly—by trying to care for the children—if I would have found my way into that line of work anyway. I had such an affinity for those feats, and always felt the excitement of the moment. I was never altruistic, but perhaps I would never have been desperate enough to steal had I not gone to Shanghai.

Taking a knife from among those that I carried, I opened the clever latch in a matter of moments. The latch was not much of a challenge because a ladder would have been necessary to reach the window from the inside or outside. I put the knife away, waited till another cloud covered the face of the moon, then pulled the window open and slithered inside as quickly as a lizard.

III

The beam I had alighted on under the roof outside the warehouse continued on inside the structure. I leaped from the window frame to the beam and hauled myself up.

The bit of cloth I left on the window frame to muffle the thud of the window slamming back into place worked well. Hardly any noise came from the window, and the cloth blended into the shadows on the wall. Even with me knowing the cloth was there, I could not see it.

I scuttled along the beam like a crab, always placing one foot firmly ahead before trying to move the one behind. I rolled my weight, testing each foothold before trusting it completely.

At the other end of the building, a door opened and light from a lantern flooded the warehouse.

I froze, becoming still as water at rest in a pond, occupying only the space I needed. I breathed in through my nose and out through my mouth, willing my heart to cease thundering against my ribs.

A guard carrying the lantern led the way into the warehouse. The yellow light carved a path through the maze of crates and rolled materials. The robed man followed the lantern bearer. Gresham trailed the man. Three more guards brought up the rear.

"That isn't the amount we agreed on, Jae-Chol," Gresham protested. He held a purse, and from the size of it I gathered that whatever was in the package he had delivered to the customs house had considerable worth.

The robed man, Jae-Chol, turned smoothly, catching the Englishman in mid-stride so that he stumbled forward. Quick as a snake, Jae-Chol's hand flicked out. The polished nails rested lightly against Gresham's throat.

Gresham froze, twisting his head up like a mongrel dog submitting to a more powerful opponent. Lantern light splintered from the long, curved talons. I knew that men who wore their nails long in that fashion did not usually even feed themselves. Servants always stood close at hand to feed them and clean them, aiding with clothing as well as hygiene. But I was certain that Jae-Chol could use his nails, and even inflict dire damage with them.

"Would you have me tell my master that you chose not to conclude our arrangement?" Jae-Chol demanded in a fierce voice.

Gresham's answer was a short while in coming. His voice hung in his threatened throat. "N-Nnn-Nno, Jae-Chol. Of course not."

"I want Master Fang-Chou to be happy," Jae-Chol said.

"Yes," the Englishman said. "So do I."

"Then this price that I have here is adequate?"

Gresham swallowed hard. "Yes."

"Good." Jae-Chol caressed the fat Englishman's face, but even in the poor lamplight I saw the red marks that were left against his pallid flesh.

Released and practically dismissed from Jae-Chol's attention, Gresham stepped back. Greed showed in his face. He would never be satisfied with his treatment at the other man's hands, but he wouldn't argue the point any further. Perhaps, if circumstances were to change and put Jae-Chol at his mercy, Gresham would remember the rough manner in which he was handled, but I doubted that. Gresham was the kind of man that would always put profit above honor or face.

Jae-Chol took a small box from the package that Gresham had given him. Carefully he placed the box on the ground. No larger than a grown man's closed fist, its wood was green, slick, and as wet as seaweed fresh plucked from the ocean. But the polished surface held a golden luster as well. Either the color had been worked into the final polish, or whatever the contents of the box were glowed with an inner fire.

Stepping back, Jae-Chol spoke words that I couldn't understand. They weren't in Chinese or Mandarin, nor did they sound anything like English or French.

When he finished, his hands drew intricate patterns in the air. Fiery symbols glowed briefly, like the last gleam of dying embers in a forgotten campfire, but the colors were blue and red.

The box glowed brighter, giving off more light than the lanterns carried by the nearby men.

The power of the box passed over me like the tingling that sometimes filled the air during monsoon season when the lightning flashed. If a scarf had not covered my hair, I felt certain that it would have stood on end.

With a brittle snap that reminded me of chicken bones breaking in a dog's powerful jaws, the lid to the small box sprang open. A light blue cloud of vapor, the same color of blue that showed around the edges of a white-hot streak of lightning, boiled up from the box.

A moment later the vapor stopped moving and calmed. Then it became the glowing blue figure of a young man not much older than I was. Below the waist, his body was just blue vapor, with only a faint suggestion of legs.

I stared at the young man's handsome face, hypnotized by the otherworldly beauty he possessed. But at the same time, I felt a cold chill race down my spine at the magic I saw revealed before me. All my life I had heard stories of such things, but I had never before seen them. If I had not been afraid of dying before I took my next breath, I felt certain I would have panicked. But I was already afraid. The young man was not Chinese, nor was he American, French, or British. He was unlike anything I had ever seen before. His face was clean shaven and sharp featured, but even more sharp featured than the *guei*.

A normal person could not fit into that box. But I could not guess what manner of being Jae-Chol had called forth from the enclosure. I watched, my attention mixed with fear and anticipation to see what next transpired.

Gresham stepped backward even farther, pressing into a stack of crates. The fat Englishman wasn't prepared for this occurrence. A canny wariness shaped his features as he watched the events unfold, like a merchant at market spotting a gullible buyer.

Jae-Chol continued speaking. The blue vapor figure stared

around the warehouse as if he could see through the darkness that the lanterns merely held back. I crouched in the L of crossed support beams, hidden in the thickest shadows I could find.

The blue vapor figure ignored Jae-Chol. The Blue Tiger man spoke more loudly and with an edge in his voice. Still, I could not understand the words that he spoke, but each syllable hammered into my heart, stirring deep and primitive anxiety that I had never before felt.

The creature—I could not think of him as a young man anymore—turned its head and glanced up. His voice was deep and sonorous, a sharp bite of warning and irritation.

Jae-Chol ceased speaking. If he had been trying to control the creature, he had failed, for the creature showed a mind of its own.

Then the beautifully evil face turned up toward me. Blue fire glinted in the hollows of the creature's eyes.

I cowered on the beam, feeling the fetid heat of the air gathered in the roof area of the warehouse. Standing in the mouth of a gasping dog could have been no worse at that moment. At least being in the dog's mouth would have been safer.

The creature lifted an arm and pointed to me.

I pressed back against the beam, wishing that I could seep into the wood as the darkness did.

The creature spoke harshly.

"An intruder!" Jae-Chol snarled. "We are being spied upon!"

Lanterns swung up in my direction. The light tore away the protective embrace of the shadows.

"There!" Jae-Chol cried in savage triumph. "I see him there!" He pointed at me.

The guards pulled their revolvers and fired at me. Bullets gouged divots from the wooden beams, tearing away the old dust- and soot-covered surfaces to reveal the white wood beneath. The thunderous reports swelled and filled the warehouse.

I ran, staying low as I raced across the narrow beam. I left the lantern beams behind me for the moment because the men could not hold me in the light and shoot at me at the same time.

From the corner of my eye, I watched as the blue vapor creature shot at me. The beautiful male body changed in midflight, becoming that of a great hooded snake with gleaming blue fangs. The snake creature twisted through the air and came at me with incredible speed.

Knowing I could not outrun the creature, I jumped from the crossbeam to the top of a stack of crates. My bare feet thudded into the crate and I performed a roll to get to my feet. Spotting the creature flying through the air and striking at me, I lunged to one side.

The creature slammed into the stack of crates as the flat cracks of the guards' revolvers split the air. I felt the center of gravity shift beneath me, then the crates started to topple. I ran, two quick strides, and leaped for the next stack of crates. I rolled and got to my feet again, already moving into a sprint. My only thoughts were of the window where I had entered the warehouse. If I could reach it, with all of Shanghai lying outside, I felt I had a chance to escape with my life. I held no further hopes of getting the fat purses I knew Gresham carried.

The maze of crates, barrels, and bolts of cloth boiled with activity as the snake-thing continued pursuit and Jae-Chol's guards tried to catch up to me. However, they also feared the creature that hunted me, and that worked in my favor. But the edge was slight. If the snake-creature caught me, I might not have to fear the untender mercies of the guards' pistols.

Three jumps later, all of them taking me closer to the window at the back of the warehouse, the snake-creature anticipated me and struck the next stack of crates I had chosen just before I landed. Unable to make a graceful landing, I slipped and fell to my hands and knees, and could only ride out the tumble of crates as the stack overturned beneath the savage power of the impossible creature.

When I hit the ground, the wind went out of me. For a moment I thought I would lose consciousness. But I knew from past experience that I could take more physical damage than most men I had ever met, and that ability had grown even greater over the past few weeks.

I pushed myself up as the snake-creature wound over the top of the alley of crates. Reaching over my shoulder, I whipped my sword free. I took the weapon in both hands, balancing my body behind it as Master Wang had taught me at the monastery. But those practices in the woods beyond the monastery fields and orchards, and even the swift, desperate battles I had fought in the shadows of Shanghai did not prepare me for the sight of the monstrous hooded snakehead that shot toward me now.

Wild flames danced in the creature's eyes. The huge fangs, as long as my arm, glinted as the huge mouth popped open. I smelled its breath then, acrid and revolting, like the musk of a freshly opened grave.

I dodged to the left, knowing that even if I hit the creature, its momentum would send it into me. I'd seen the force with which it struck the crates. If it did the same to me, I'd more than likely be crippled if I wasn't killed outright.

The creature passed within inches of me. Only then did I realize that the monstrous head was at least eight or nine feet across. I swung the sword. At that distance, I couldn't miss.

The blade passed through the creature with incredible ease, then bit into the wooden warehouse floor. At first, even though I felt it was impossible to do so, I thought I had missed the creature.

Then I saw the gaping wound in the creature's side. Where my blade had touched the thing, the reptilian hide became marred and turned back into vapor that drifted aimlessly and began to dissipate, like blood in the water. Floating in the air in obvious agony, the snake body—at least thirty feet long, I now saw—coiled restlessly in on itself.

"Don't stand there, girl!" a man's voice barked. "Run for your bloody life! Steel will hurt the *draumach,* but it won't kill it!"

Instantly I drew back into a nearby alley between stacks of crates and bolts of cloth. The *draumach,* for so it was as I later learned, concerned itself with reconstituting its form.

The man from the Blind Turtle, Connelly, stepped out of the shadows to my right. The fact that he had recognized me as a girl surprised me. I had underestimated him, or I had underestimated my own ability of disguise. If he proved to be the danger, I knew I would never see him again and everything would be fine. But if my disguise was the problem, I was risking exposure as well as death every time I stepped out into the dark streets. I got a good look at Connelly as one of the Blue Tiger guards came around the corner and the light from the lantern he carried smashed over Connelly.

Connelly was dressed for the night in dark clothes and his face obviously blacked by lamp soot. He wore crossed shoulder holsters that carried revolvers and carried a big-bore shotgun. He pulled the shotgun to his shoulder and aimed at the warehouse guard.

The shotgun blast cracked and the lantern exploded into a thousand flaming pieces, most of which winked out before they hit the ground. However, a pool of fiery liquid dropped to the warehouse floor and spread into a river that lapped against the crates, barrels, and bolts of cloth. The cloth caught fire at once. The guard slammed backward, his face a mask of crimson ruin and broken white bones.

Connelly broke open the double-barreled shotgun. He plucked the spent cartridges from the weapon and replaced them with fresh rounds from a bandolier that crossed his chest. "Run, girl! Now is definitely the bloody time!"

My mind careened with a thousand questions. I wondered what he was doing there, if he too had followed Gresham. And I wondered how he knew what the thing was.

I started toward the other end of the alley. Sudden light invaded the darkness just ahead of the man that turned the corner and confronted me from less than a dozen feet away. A pistol came up in his other fist as he held the swaying lantern up.

I gripped my sword with one hand as I stopped, turned sideways to present my profile and seize less chance of being hit, and slipped out a throwing knife from those concealed in my clothing. I flicked the blade at him. The knife turned once and took him in the shoulder, below his bearded chin and above the pistol that suddenly spat flame in his fist.

The bullet cut the wind by my ear and I knew that I had avoided death by only inches. I turned to run as the guard fell backward. His lantern smashed against the barrels behind him. The barrels sat carefully stacked. For a brief instant I saw the lettering and the warning on the side.

I threw myself forward. I didn't know how long the oil-fueled fire from the lantern's reservoir would take to burn through the sides of the barrels, or even if that was necessary to set off the contents.

Connelly stood in the alley where the writhing *draumach* had nearly recovered its snake form. He pulled the shotgun to his shoulder again, but I slapped the barrel away with my sword before he could fire.

My instinctive urge was to follow the block with a slash that would have disemboweled him. Perhaps he had saved my life, but his appearance at the Blue Tiger warehouse was no testimony to his true intentions. For all I knew, he wanted me alive to use as a diversion while he accomplished whatever he had set out to do there.

"You're alive." He said it like he was surprised. I thought I spotted relief in there as well, but the lighting was poor and I had no reason to think that he would be relieved at my continued good health.

"Gunpowder!" I told him in his rough tongue.

A question formed in his light eyes, then I saw that he understood what my gasped warning meant. He cursed.

Movement to my left alerted me that the *draumach* attacked once more. I stepped forward suddenly and slid my right leg behind Connelly's as I slammed the palm of my right hand into his chest with all of my weight behind the blow.

He tried to fight me, and his larger size was almost enough to tilt the scales in his favor. But, as I have said, I was uncommonly strong for my size and gender. The breath went out of Connelly in one last fevered curse, and he went backward to the floor just as the *draumach*'s head narrowly missed him.

Instinctively I put out a hand to the *draumach*'s body to steady myself. Frost covered my flesh at once, and I felt the intense and terrible cold only an instant before numbness set in. I withdrew, but set myself and whirled the sword, cleaving through the vaporous creature and once again breaking the form it had chosen for itself.

The *draumach* writhed and howled in an inhuman voice. The terrible eyes blazed with insane fury. I knew then that it had chosen to hate me forever.

But that thought was a fleeting one because in the next instant the barrels of gunpowder detonated. Blinding bright light flashed through the warehouse. Waves of concussive force, each triggered by a barrel of exploding gunpowder following on the heels of the last, toppled stacks of crates in staggered disarray. I heard nothing, but I felt horrible pain in my ears with each explosion.

The *draumach* ripped into a cloud of blue fog that swirled and drew in on itself among the upper rafters of the warehouse roof.

Filled with sheer terror, certain that I had lived by luck alone, I pushed myself to my feet from under the smaller crates and barrels that had landed on me. I found my sword only a few feet away. Fisting the weapon's leather-wrapped handle, I gazed in disbelief at the destruction that had filled the building.

Fires spread everywhere, tendrils of flames dancing on the goods, the warehouse floor and walls, and even, in some places, the rafters and the roof. No longer did the narrow alleys stand to allow passage of cargo handlers and warehousemen. Debris lay strewn where ready investments and probable profits had been neatly organized only a short time before.

Broken boards and skeins of loose cloth moved to my right. I could still not hear.

Connelly stood only a few feet away. He brushed smoldering embers from his clothing and hair. His mouth opened. He shouted.

I could not hear the words that he used, but I felt certain he was telling me to do what I had already planned to do. I ran for the back of the warehouse. The window there was open. If they had not been knocked down, there were still stacks of crates I could use to get up to the window or possibly to the rafter.

I ran, fleet as a deer, avoiding flames and the stacks of crates and barrels that continued to fall as their foundations gave way. I could not guess at the amount of money the Blue Tiger owners lost in the warehouse, but they were an old house and probably did not wrap all their money up in ongoing ventures as many new trading houses did.

When I reached the back wall, I leaped atop a pile of crates and raced for the window. Thankfully, many of the stacks against the back wall had survived the string of explosions. I went up quick as a seasoned sailor climbing a ship's rigging.

I opened the window and felt the cool air of the alley wash over my face. Without the use of the grapple, trusting my strength and training, I dropped to the ground and rolled. Even as I came to my feet, three men stepped from the shadows of the Blue Tiger warehouse.

They wore robes much as Jae-Chol did, and I recognized the mark of the Blue Tiger upon them. They wore their nails long. Their hair trailed nearly to their waists. Two of them had their hair bound back in leather ties, but the other let his hair whip free, and it danced in the seemingly cool wind streaming in from the harbor till the strands looked enough like tiny snakes that the experience made me ill at ease.

They filled the alleyway in front of me.

I wanted only to escape. I turned to flee in the other direction. But before I could take more than a step, the guard with the unbound hair suddenly stepped in front of me.

The back of my neck prickled. Nothing human moved that fast. Nothing I had ever seen had ever moved that fast.

I lifted my sword, holding the hilt high in both hands and twisted so that the blade slanted down across my left side. In that position I could both defend myself and instantly strike back.

The three men closed at once. Desperate, I ducked and moved, avoiding grasping hands filled with cruel black talons, and managed to disembowel one of the men. His intestines spilled out onto the alley floor before him.

I expected him to fall to his knees in shock. I could not imagine a worse fate than to be disemboweled in combat. The shock alone usually brought most victims to their knees.

Instead the man stood there as though he were only inconvenienced. I watched transfixed when I should have been running for my life, but I had been through a lot in the past few minutes.

The wounded man bent down and picked up his own intestines and replaced them within his stomach. I noted then that there was not as much blood as there should have been. Usually, as long as a man's heart beat within his chest, blood pumped in copious amounts from any grievous wound. But this man did not bleed as much as I would have expected. It was as if his heart did not pump.

Grinning, the man sliced the hem from his robe with his talons more easily than a tailor cutting silk. Using the swath of cloth, he bound his stomach with practiced skill to hold his intestines in. I had heard that the Japanese warriors did that before they ever stepped into battle, so that a man could take even killing blows without losing his footing in his own entrails.

They came at me again like a pack of predators. If I had not been so much smaller and they so eager to spill my blood, I might not have survived. Still, with the skills Master Wang had given me, along with the unnatural speed and strength I had always had, I managed to stay alive. Even so, I doubted my ability to do so for long.

The blows I delivered unto those three men should have been deathblows. I pierced the hearts of two of them and slashed the neck of the third. Mortal men would have fallen. Mortal men would have died. But with these men, not even much blood wept from the harsh wounds I dealt.

This all passed in seconds. I felt my breath grow ragged in my throat, felt my arms and legs start to flag. I no longer fell into offensive and defensive postures naturally, no longer knew each move ahead of time or at the same time that one of my opponents moved.

As I watched, their faces changed. Before, they had been men of middle years, men of average looks, men that I would never have given a second glance out on the streets.

They became monsters. Their teeth elongated into fangs. Hard lines twisted their features. Their eyes turned red and their hair took on a green-white cast. They snarled and snapped like mongrel curs, and the bloodlust that fired them seemed to grow stronger.

I recognized them then from all the old stories I had heard. Master Wang had dealt in many such legends and tales in his works. They were undead, vampires that rose from the grave for vengeance or were transformed by older vampires of great power.

"Now, Slayer," one of them snarled in English, "now you will feel our true wrath!"

I battled them with renewed desperation, but I didn't know what to do. Flames leaped from the window in back of the warehouse. Shadows twisted and scurried on the alley floor as we fought, shifting with the changing light. Slowly, inexorably, they began to wear me down, trapping me with my back to the warehouse. I felt the heat inside the structure through the wooden wall close behind me.

Then a flaming ghost seemed to drop to the alley behind the vampires. I parried a flailing hand and stepped in to kick one of my attackers in the chest to momentarily drive him back.

The "ghost" shed the flaming cloth that had been used for protection. Connelly attacked at once, meeting one of the vampires as the evil creature turned toward him. Connelly lifted the shotgun and fired from point-blank range. The buckshot drove the vampire back a step or two, but the foul thing only smiled and wiped a hand across its chest to smear the small amount of blood that appeared there.

Connelly dropped the shotgun and pulled a short piece of wood from one of his boots. He shoved the wood through the vampire's heart and I watched the creature turn to dust.

Then I remembered the other parts of the vampire legend. They drank blood from the living, but they could be killed by sunlight, wood piercing their hearts, or their heads sliced whole from their bodies.

I dodged a fistful of talons and moved to my left. Parrying the next vampire's sweeping blow with my sword, I stepped beside the creature. I drew my right foot up and stamped the side of its knee. Supernatural creature or not, immortal or not, the knee was one of a man's—or a manlike creature's—most vulnerable areas.

Bones shattered in the thing's knee. Pain soured its features. Before it could recover, I swept my sword back in a short arc with all my remaining strength. The keen blade sheared through the vampire's throat and spine. The gruesome head leaped from its shoulders, then the body and the decapitated head turned to dust before hitting the alley floor.

The third vampire hesitated, obviously surprised to see its two comrades eliminated so quickly. Connelly circled the creature, and I took that moment of distraction to pierce its throat with my sword so that it could not turn its head. Connelly wasted no time in sheathing his piece of jagged wood in the vampire's heart. The creature turned to dust and dropped to the alley floor.

We ran, and I was surprised at how Connelly kept up with me. Then, when at last he began to falter and I knew that I could outrun him if I wished, I slowed, and we stopped in an alley several blocks from the Blue Tiger warehouse. The shadows closed around us, but the fire burned in the distance. We stared at each other, gasping for breath, safely out of each other's easy reach.

Perhaps he distrusted me as much as I distrusted him then.

Crowds gathered from the taverns and singsong houses along the docks. Alarm bells rang out in the harbor, from buildings and ships, calling men to save what could be saved of the burning warehouse. Some of those people that answered the call for help, I knew from experience, would be drawn to the opportunity for theft. I had gone for that opportunity when chance presented itself.

I breathed raggedly as I watched Connelly try to recover from his exertions. My throat and lungs burned from the smoke pouring from the Blue Tiger warehouse. I felt bruised all over my body from the debris that had fallen on me in the warehouse, and from the blows I had suffered at the hands of my undead opponents.

Connelly put his hand on my shoulder.

I almost took his arm off with my sword.

He must have sensed the way that I moved, though I was trained to move fluidly and strike without warning. He took his hand back.

"Easy, lass," he told me in his offensive tongue. Then he switched to Chinese, which he had obviously not had much experience in. "We need to get out of here."

I remained mute. I could not believe he gave voice to something that was so plainly obvious. I could barely hear him over the strident ringing in my ears from the explosions that had ripped the warehouse apart.

"Can you hear me?" he asked.

"Yes," I said.

"Do you understand me?"

I stood there with my sword in hand, ready to battle him and the monsters that I had thought were only childhood stories. "I understand you."

"Is there someplace we can go?" Connelly asked. "Someplace that you will feel safe?"

The question was an odd one. I had never felt safe in Shanghai. Knowing that my life was always forfeit if it was discovered that I was a girl and had been part of the armor that I had put on every morning, just as I had wound cloth around my upper body to disguise my woman's curves.

There was no place I felt safe. And I certainly wouldn't feel safe with him. Also, I didn't want to take him to the basement where Nah-Mi and the other girls slept.

"Not with you," I told him.

"I have a room," Connelly offered. He looked uncomfortable with the suggestion, and I liked him for that. Not many *guei* would act reticent about the implications of such an offer. For all his confidence and prowess, he still remained innocent in some ways. "I promise you, I mean you no harm, and I will offer you no disrespect. But I think we should talk."

I said nothing.

"I need to talk to you," he went on. "Please."

Perhaps I might have gone with him in any event, because I was curious about the vampires and about what he was doing there. I was also curious about why he seemed determined to seek me out. And if I had taken on new enemies in Shanghai— the vampires or the Blue Tigers—I was experienced enough then to know that the more I knew about them the better off I would be. If only to avoid them more carefully in the future.

Perhaps I would not have joined him under any circumstances, for he scared me—he was different and I had trusted no man since Master Wang. Connelly had gone to the Blue Tiger warehouse seeking the vampires for his own reasons. How safe could anyone have been around such a man so foolish?

In the end, I had no choice.

He reached for me and caught my right arm.

I had my blade at his throat.

IV

Connelly made an effort to block my sword but we both knew it was wasted. "Please," he said with pleading eyes. "Allow me this indiscretion. Were it not necessary, lass, I would not act so familiar."

I nodded.

He held my arm and pushed the sleeve back. "Your name is Xiaoqin. You have a birthmark here." He touched the discolored flesh. "I saw it in the alley behind the Blind Turtle that night when you tried to save the serving wench from Gresham and his cronies."

In the future, I decided, I would take pains to conceal the birthmark. If Connelly had seen it, then others might, and such a mark was sometimes hard to conceal when working on the docks. Once it was known, I would never again know any semblance of safety in Shanghai.

"When you were a child," Connelly said, still speaking softly, "you were always embarrassed by this mark. You thought it was ugly, and that it disfigured you."

I felt uncomfortable that he would know so much about me.

"A friend of yours told you that you should wear the mark with pride," Connelly went on. "He told you that the mark looked like a bird in flight. A dove."

I pulled my arm from him and backed him off with my sword. Despite the fact that he wore the heavy revolvers in twin shoulder holsters, he stepped back and held his hands up at his sides, offering no resistance.

"It's okay, lass," he whispered. "Let's just go gently here, shall we?"

"Who are you?" I demanded.

"My name's Sean Connelly. That probably doesn't mean anything to you."

It didn't.

"How did you know about my arm?" I asked.

"Wang told me."

I narrowed my eyes at him in disbelief.

"It's true," Connelly insisted. "We . . ." He hesitated, thinking. "We *worked* together."

"I never saw you at the monastery."

"You did. Maybe you don't remember me, but I was there."

I didn't believe him.

Impatience showed in Connelly's gray eyes. "C'mon, lass. Wang had a lot of friends. You didn't get to meet any number of people that came and went while you studied with that old monk. Most of the people that came to that monastery came to see Wang."

That was true. I remembered the occasions I had gotten jealous of the time Master Wang was spending with several guests. I had been curious about his visitors, but I had always assumed those visits had to do with monastery business, with the trade that was carried on there, with the work he did. He'd never mentioned to me that he had told anyone of me. And I couldn't think of a reason why he would.

"Master Wang copied books," Connelly said. "He had a large library, and not all of those volumes were materials that were on a Shaolin monk's required reading list. He copied those books for others. For a price. Other books he copied so that he might have a copy of his own."

I didn't know the truth of that, but I did know that Master Wang kept several books that I wasn't allowed access to. They were in foreign languages that I didn't understand, though I knew he did. He worked laboriously at his desk and outside the monastery in his quiet places when he could. He had a fine, neat hand, and the lines he put on paper were exact.

"Perhaps," I said.

"C'mon, lass," Connelly said. "These monsters have had a whiff of you now, they have. They're going to have your scent in their noses. And they're going to know what you are the same as I do."

"What I am," I repeated, not comprehending what he was alluding to.

"You're the Slayer, lass. The Chosen One. The girl who is called to fight the greatest monsters of our time."

I looked at him. One of the vampires had called me Slayer as well, and I hadn't understood why it had spoken to me in English. Perhaps it had gotten a better look at Connelly, seen that he was one of the *guei* and wrongly assumed that I was English or American myself. *Surely* such a term would not be common. I became even more desirous of whatever information Connelly possessed.

"Don't you know what the Slayer is?" Connelly asked.

I considered his question briefly, then shook my head. His exposition sounded familiar, but I knew it couldn't be true. Those had only been encouraging stories Master Wang had given to a poor orphaned girl who needed something more in her life.

Astonishment showed on Connelly's soot-blackened face. "Wang never told you of the Slayer?" Then he used a Chinese word, which meant "divine executioner." It was then that I realized that Master Wang had never told me the stories of the Divine Executioner in English. We had always spoken in Chinese when he told me of those things. We had practiced English often, but those were exercises in conversation and in business.

"You mean the Divine Executioner," I said, translating the Chinese word more precisely. "He told me of a girl who would be given the power to fight monsters. Power that was handed down through the girl before her." I spoke the Chinese word that he had used. For a moment, I suppose, both of us were amazed at how much had been lost in such a simple translation.

"Yes," Connelly said, understanding. "Wang did tell you of her."

I nodded. Those had only been stories—wondrous fables, I had thought—meant to encourage me to follow my own spirit rather than be a woman as my culture would have me be.

The Shaolin believed differently than the emperor of China. The monks had fought the emperor several times in the past until the military destroyed several Shaolin temples and drove the order into hiding. Many of the nuns that served the Shaolin sisterhood had suffered having their feet bound so that they would not grow and would remain childlike. Small feet are a sign of great beauty for women in my birth country. When those women so afflicted were grown, they had deformed feet so tiny they were practically useless, crippling them so that they had to be carried or could not long remain on them without pain. I always cut the restraints from the feet of the girls that I took under my protection. The practice was growing out of favor, but many women had been left crippled by those cruel bindings.

"What did Wang tell you of the Slayer?" Connelly asked.

I remembered the stories and almost smiled. I had sat across from Master Wang as he told me the beautiful tales of past Slayers who had challenged monsters, stories of the greatest triumphs, and tales of heartbreaking sorrow. The Slayers burned mostly as brief candles against the unrelenting night of evil that at times rose up and tried to swallow the world. Only the Slayer stood for the chance to balance the scales so that the evil things could not run rampant.

"Stories," I said.

Connelly shook his head. "Did Wang ever mention that you might become the Slayer one day?"

"No." I looked at him. Even as unbelievable as the vampires had been at the Blue Tiger warehouse, Connelly's question was even more unbelievable. I could not be the Slayer. If anyone would know, surely it would be me. And such a thing did not truly exist.

Connelly cursed. "He should have told you! By God, he should have told you! He was the one that identified you and named you for the council." He turned and paced in the alley.

For a moment I considered breaking from Connelly, running and leaving him there in order to escape the madness of the night. But I couldn't. I remembered everything Master Wang had told me about the . . . *Slayer.* I tried to become accustomed to the English term as Connelly paced. I knew that the legend had grown from the earliest of times when demons were first said to walk the earth, that the first Slayer had been given the power to fight those demons.

As a younger girl, I had dreamed of being the Slayer, so that my life could be given purpose. I thought Master Wang had told me those stories to give me something to cling to, some idea that my life might hold more than it did. That I might have hope. That was the reason the girls I protected talked of the fine ship that I would one day own and use to sail them to the gigantic castle they envisioned. Everyone had to have dreams. Even while I still lived as a cargo handler and a thief in Shanghai, I sometimes thought about Master Wang's stories and wished that I might be her. Perhaps that was why I took in the orphaned girls and tried to protect them.

But the price paid by those who became the Slayer . . .

Such a price I never wished to pay. Death was the Slayer's only constant companion, and from the time that she came into her power, she owed her own violent death at the hands of monsters so that another girl might rise and become the Slayer anew. In that moment I wondered—if Connelly were right, and I had no proof that he was—who the girl was that had last been the Slayer. The one who had died before me.

"Well, then," Connelly said, returning to me. "That's it, then. That's where we'll begin." He appeared to be trying to reconcile himself to whatever task he pictured in his mind. "This is not unheard of. There have been Slayers before that have lived out their lives and never even knew what they were. At least you know something of the Slayer. I can teach you the lot of what you need to know. After all, this isn't my first time to train a Slayer."

"What are you talking about?" I asked. His attitude that only his agenda mattered was beginning to irritate me.

"I'm talking about you and me, lass." Connelly stared at me. "I'm talking about you picking up the mantle of your destiny, of course, for there's nothing else to be done for it."

"No," I said, taking a step back from him.

Without thinking, he moved in pursuit of me. "Xiaoqin."

His use of my name unnerved me more. I lifted my sword and placed it between us, point down. I fell into the ready stance Master Wang had trained in me for years. The sword's edge was turned up, ready to rip and destroy. If he had tried to touch me in that moment, I would have killed him. I believe he knew that then, though we never talked of it later.

His features softened. "Xiaoqin, you must listen to me."

I shook my head. My heart exploded in my chest, drumming faster than the ringing in my ears.

"You've got to come away with me," Connelly said.

"Why?" I asked.

"You're not safe here. Fang-Chou's men recognized you tonight. They know who you are. They know what you are."

Connelly cursed again. "They knew before you did because the *draumach* told them. I heard it tell them."

"You speak that monster's language?"

"It's a demon tongue," Connelly said. "And yes, I speak a fair bit of a few of them. That *draumach* spoke one of the languages I was familiar with." He smiled. "That was a bit of luck, eh? But it couldn't all go against us tonight, could it?"

"How would the *draumach* be so certain about me?" I still wasn't convinced of Connelly's assertions.

"Because the *draumach* is mystical in nature. Just as there is a certain mysticism about the Slayer."

"It has to be mistaken," I said. "Just as you are mistaken."

Connelly shook his head. "I've made no mistake, lass. And were it a mistake, it would have been Wang's. Not mine."

I held my sword between us, denying him the ability to get any closer. My mind swam, trying to catch all the errant thoughts and confusions that sped like a school of minnows. I could not concentrate. Focus remained elusive.

"I can hide," I said.

"And they will find you."

"You don't know that," I accused.

"I know Fang-Chou," Connelly insisted. "He is one of the oldest vampires in China. Perhaps in the world. You call them *ch'ing shih*."

"*Ch'ing* Shih," I corrected. I hated the way the man corrupted my native tongue. I detested the manner in which he had stepped into my life and turned so many things around. If he and Master Wang carried on conversations about me that I did not know of, and I was certain that they did due to everything Connelly knew, then I felt terribly betrayed by the one person that I had believed truly cared about me.

How could Master Wang fool himself into believing that I was the Slayer? Why didn't he tell me? Or was he only delusional, hoping to gain some acknowledgment or praise by passing me off as the Slayer? The questions chased themselves in my mind. Even though I wanted to discredit Master Wang because it would have been the easiest thing to do, I could not disrespect his memory. I had loved him for being a father to me, and I was certain that—in his own way—he had loved me as the daughter he had never had.

"Fang-Chou will come after you," Connelly declared. "Once he knows the Slayer is in this city, close to his nest, he won't rest until you are dead. He can ill afford the threat that you represent."

"He won't find me," I said stubbornly.

"He *will*," Connelly argued. "The Blue Tiger triad is old and it is powerful. Even before they organized, Fang-Chou ruled this place. I learned that in just the past few weeks before I met Gresham."

I remained unswayed.

"Wang is the one who told me about Fang-Chou," Connelly said. "In the past, we had put agents into the field here, lass, following up stories we had heard. But we never located Fang-Chou. He has successfully remained in hiding."

"Who is the 'we' you refer to?" I asked.

"The Council of Watchers."

I shook my head. "I do not know of them."

Connelly gaped. "You've never heard of the Council of Watchers, but you've heard of the Slayer?"

Embarrassment flamed my cheeks. I was already aware that there were many things I didn't know. Despite Master Wang's best efforts to give me a good education, I lacked. But then, when I realized that Master Wang hadn't taught me everything he could have, I felt insecure about the knowledge he *had* given me.

"No," I whispered. Obviously, Master Wang had chosen what he wanted to tell me of the legend of the Slayer. Perhaps he had judged that I wouldn't have been as enamored of the idea of the Slayer if I had thought she was powerful and independent, yet subjugated by a gathering of men. Especially Western men. If he had lived longer, Master Wang might some day have told me everything.

Or perhaps he had thought I would never become the Slayer after all. As I later learned, not every girl who has the potential to become the Slayer does.

Men walked by the mouth of the alley, but none of them looked in our direction. That time of night in Shanghai, only death and trouble could lie in the shadows, and no man wanted to trouble himself with seeking out that which was all too likely to find him itself.

"Watchers are men who guide and instruct the Slayers in their care," Connelly said. "They are teachers, mentors, weapons masters, and sources of knowledge about the hellbeasts and all things magickal in nature that the Slayers are called on to battle."

"And you are a Watcher?" I asked, certain of the answer but still wanting to hear it from him.

Connelly nodded. "As was Master Wang."

I tried to think about that, but I couldn't see Master Wang as anything other than a monk. He had lived, and he had died, strong in his beliefs. He was a man of peace, and he was a warrior. That was the dichotomy of the yin and yang that the Shaolin monks recognized in all of nature. A man could not truly stand for one thing if he did not have intimate knowledge of what he stood against.

"You didn't know that, did you, lass?" Connelly's voice sounded soft and sincere.

"I did not know what a Watcher was," I said, trying to keep the helplessness from my voice. "Now I have only your word that such men even exist."

Sorrow stood out on Connelly's soot-blackened face. "They do exist, Xiaoqin. That's why I'm here."

I looked at him.

"Wang died nine months ago," Connelly said.

I released pent-up air from my lungs, surprised that I had been so tense. I still remembered the morning Master Wang had been buried. His body, wrapped in funeral shrouds as it had been handed down into the open grave, looked more small and frail than he had ever seemed in life. He had been ninety-eight years old. Everyone at the monastery had expected his death—everyone but me. And I had needed him most of all.

"I didn't learn of his death until six months ago," Connelly went on. "The letter found me while I was in South America. It had to pass through my ancestral home in Dublin, Ireland."

I was amazed at how quickly the names of those exotic foreign places came from his lips. How many places had Connelly seen? Even scared as I was in that alley that night, I remember wondering how much Sean Connelly had seen and done. All my life, since opening the books Master Wang had given me to read, I had wanted to see the places mentioned in those pages.

"I came to Shanghai two months after that," Connelly continued. "As soon as I could get ship's passage. It took me time to get up to the Way of the Tiger Monastery, because the way is hard. Evidently I arrived there just days after you had left."

I remained silent.

"I stayed at the monastery for a while," Connelly said. "I thought, like some of the other monks believed, that you were probably grieving over Wang's death and would come back after you'd made your peace. They, and the sisters at the other temple, told me that they didn't know you well."

"They didn't," I agreed. Maybe if they had, leaving wouldn't have felt like the only thing I could have done.

Connelly waited for a while, then realized I wasn't going to speak any more. He said, "When I finally realized that you weren't coming back, I traveled here to Shanghai."

"Were you looking for me?"

Connelly hesitated, then shook his head. "While I was in the monastery, news arrived of Gresham from one of the people Wang regularly employed as spies in Shanghai. The merchant had learned that I was at the monastery, and he knew that I would pay as Wang had paid for any information about the vampires and other demons that live in this city and this country. Watchers spend their whole lives watching, gathering information, and hoping they live long enough to make sense of it all before the demons become too powerful. Slayers can't fix everything, and it's best if they're used as judiciously as possible. The informant told me about the package that Gresham was supposed to deliver to Fang-Chou."

"Did you know what was in the package?"

"No. Only that it was supposed to be magical in nature."

I looked at him, hoping I could discern a lie in the midst of all the fantastical things I was being told. "You knew I was in Shanghai."

"Not until I saw you in the alley behind the Blind Turtle four days ago." Connelly studied me, then grinned. "If you didn't come back to the monastery, there weren't many places for you to go, were there?"

I remained silent.

"In the alley," Connelly said, "I recognized the moves that you used, and I knew that Wang had trained you. His style is indelible."

That was true, and I took pride in the compliment he paid my master and me. Master Wang had marked in body and in spirit every student he had chosen to teach. Only then, as I watched Connelly carefully, did I realize that I recognized the moves he had used back at the warehouse.

"Master Wang taught you," I said.

Connelly nodded. "I was never a good student, but I was accomplished enough to satisfy him."

"My master's satisfaction never came easily," I said, wanting to set the record straight. "If he was satisfied with you, then you were a good enough student. Perhaps not excellent, but good enough."

"And that, lass, is a backhanded compliment if ever I've heard one."

It was strange how I felt I had to reassure him. Perhaps it was because we had shared something more than the battle in the warehouse, which was not enough to build a friendship on. Perhaps I only wanted the kind remembrance of my master to meet my own needs. I didn't know.

"Perhaps," Connelly said. "Perhaps I was good enough. Wang told me I could have used another thirty or so years of instruction, though."

"He always told his students that," I said. "Even when he knew he wasn't going to be there to give it." The admission pained me for a moment, reawakening the dull ache that had been with me since the day Master Wang had died.

"At any rate," Connelly said, "when I saw you in that alley that night, recognized the birthmark for what it was, I knew that you had made your way to Shanghai, although I didn't know why."

"To live," I said, making that a challenge to whatever he had in his mind that might involve me. "To live unfettered and free." But that hadn't been what had happened. I had taken in Nah-Mi and the other girls, burdened myself as I had never been burdened before, and I had worked hard at survival every day I had been in Shanghai. I had taken pride in every one of those days, though I had no one to share that accomplishment with. Master Wang would have told me that the pride I took was too much, that I only did what I had to do.

Connelly looked at me. "When I saw you around Gresham, I thought perhaps you had been drawn into battle with him and the Blue Tiger vampires."

I returned his stare. Part of me did not want to disappoint Connelly, but I determined not to lie. If he became dissuaded, maybe he would go away and leave me alone. I sensed that even if we parted that night, he would be troublesome in the future. He believed in the legends of the Slayer and I did not. I still had so much to learn.

"Until tonight," I stated clearly, "I had never seen a vampire. Nor had I believed they truly existed."

Displeasure showed on Connelly's face. "Well, lass, that's changed sure enough, now hasn't it?"

I made no reply. He already knew the answer.

Connelly paced restlessly again. The alarms still rang through the night. Torches and lanterns gathered down at the harbor, but the twisting flames that lapped at the dark night sky above the Blue Tiger warehouse and customs house testified that all efforts would be in vain. If the warehouse had belonged to the *guei*, there might have been more rescuers that would have tried harder.

"We have to go, Xiaoqin," Connelly said.

"Where?" I asked.

"Away from this place. For now. The vampires will be hunting you." He looked to the harbor. "We can catch a ship somewhere. Make new plans."

"I will hide," I said.

"Damn it, lass!" Connelly wheeled on me. "This city is no safe place for you! Can't you hear a word I'm tellin' you?"

The rough tone in his voice caused me to lift the sword instinctively to protect myself. Before he could take another step, the point hovered just below his chin.

He spread his hands and he made the anger fade from his face. "Easy does it now."

"Don't threaten me," I told him. I felt the tightness in my voice and I knew it almost cracked.

"Well, now, it's not me threatening you, lass. That's what you don't seem to understand. It's Fang-Chou and his boyos. They'll track you through this city, they will. And they'll find you."

"How?"

"Those bloodsuckers can trail like hunting hounds," Connelly said. "They can catch your scent in the wind. Even if they can't hunt you up, the *draumach* will. It will ferret you out right enough. Find you. Find places you've been. Trust me when I say that you can't hide from that thing. That's what a *draumach* does, you see. It finds things. Though I don't know what Fang-Chou would want with one and that causes me considerable consternation."

Places you've been.

My heart ran cold. I thought of the basement beneath the burned-out remnants of the old hotel where Nah-Mi and the others would be. Doubtless they would be up talking or playing games as they sometimes did, eating the food that I had brought in earlier that day, so that the cupboard would be empty again on the morrow and all the work I had done to provide that sustenance would need doing again.

But they were there alone. I wasn't there to protect them.

I turned and I ran, sticking to the alleys and the shadows I knew best.

V

The basement sanctuary wasn't far from the harbor. The hotel had been located in the no-man's-land that occupied the area between the warehouses and the more affluent buildings and homes that lay farther inland.

Back when Shanghai had been primarily a fishing village, the people who had lived there hadn't cared about the proximity to the water. But the *guei* had, and the Chinese that came to want to be like them had learned to care as well.

The dockyards earned money, first by the transport of cargo into and out of the city. They also earned money in the taverns and singsong houses established to take a sailor or fisherman's money more quickly than he had made it.

Behind those areas, where the hotel had stood, lay the barrens. Those places had fallen in disarray and ruin, and no one had rebuilt them. Renting those places made no money that any investor was interested in making. In those days in Shanghai, only large profits interested anyone. Sailors and fishermen all had their own hovels or ships that they lived on, and those who had become wealthy—or at least wanted to appear that way—would not live so close to the dockyards and odorous mudflats.

Vampires can't enter a dwelling, I reminded myself as I ran. Master Wang's books had taught me that. But I took no comfort in that. I didn't know if the cellar below a burned-out hotel counted as a dwelling. It was not a proper home.

By the time I arrived, the massacre was already taking place. Flames danced in the ground-level windows of the old hotel's basement. In the back, the cellar door was flung open wide and flames crackled and spat there, reaching out toward the sides of the stairwell, as if to pull the entrance down into their fiery embrace.

The girls screamed in fear, and—if there was anyone in those abandoned buildings to hear—no one came to their aid.

Vampires fed on the young orphans I had taken as my sisters. Those lives that I had worked so hard to save were extinguished in seconds as the monsters feasted on their blood.

Nah-Mi screamed and tried to break free of the circle. A vampire in front of me laughed and cursed at her as he caught her and pushed her back.

Coldness filled my heart, pushing away the fear and uncertainty that had tried to claim me. I took a fresh grip on my sword and struck without warning. His head leaped from his shoulders and he turned to dust.

Another vampire shoved a pistol toward me. I took his arm off at the elbow then slashed his throat before he could turn away or even truly realize I had crippled him. He also turned to dust.

The other vampires threw down their dead and dying prey and turned to me.

"Xiaoqin!" Nah-Mi shrilled. She got to her feet and raced toward me. She had been cowering beside the building, lost in the shadows pooled there, or perhaps left to be tormented later. Tears reflected silver on her face as her little legs flashed, and she ran toward me.

The vampire closest to Nah-Mi moved in a blur and caught Nah-Mi up in a twinkling. Impulsively I started for her, listening to her fear-filled cries for help. She screamed my name over and over.

The three remaining vampires took up positions between us, becoming a wall of undead flesh and flashing talons. I cut, thrust, parried, and blocked with all the skill Master Wang had given me. But it wasn't enough. I wasn't skilled enough and I wasn't truly prepared. My sword only killed them if I decapitated them, and they knew that. All other wounds would quickly heal.

They came for me, giving me no quarter as they drove me backward over the bodies of the girls I had tried to save from starvation and abuse along the dockyards and in the alleys of Chinese City and greater Shanghai. Despite my concentration on saving my own life that I might save Nah-Mi's, I saw the blood-smeared features of those girls. They had been given no chance. They had been killed because the monsters that had been looking for me had decided to kill them for sport. Or, maybe when confronted, one of the girls had told them I was their protector.

One of the vampires thrust a fistful of talons at my face. I brought my sword forward to meet its blow, and the keen edge slipped between its fingers and cleaved its hand all the way deep into its forearm. It howled with pain and murderous rage. I whirled and lopped its head off, feeling a stirring of satisfaction as the creature turned to dust. I yanked the blade back and set myself to swing again.

From the corner of my eye, I saw another vampire move out of the shadows with a revolver in his fist. The muzzle flash flared bright yellow in the darkness, almost as bright as the flames that consumed what was left of the ruin of the old hotel. I felt a sledgehammer strike my right side and I partially spun around.

Glancing down, I saw the blood trickling from the wound. Surprisingly I felt no pain, though I felt certain it would come. If I lived so long. In all the months that I had lived and worked and thieved in Shanghai, I had never been so grievously wounded. I had always been so careful, never risked too much. In that moment of crystal revelation, I remembered the stories of the Slayer, of how the girl was always fated to die in her fight against the monsters that roamed the world.

I did not want to die. It was not cowardice, because I did not fear death. I had seen how peaceful Master Wang had looked when he died. I simply wanted to live to see those places I had always heard sailors and merchants talk of. Especially Gold Mountain, which was what my people called California because of the gold mines that had been found there. Many men had shipped out to work in those growing American cities and on the railroads that were going to cross the United States. I wished to live long enough to see those things.

Connelly and Master Wang had to be wrong. I could not be the girl next slated to be the Slayer. I was Xiaoqin, an orphan only. Nothing special or magical or noble. And I felt guilty because I so desperately wanted to live.

The man fired again, and only then did I even think to take cover. But it was too late. The bullet struck my stomach and knocked me from my feet. My sword slid from my hand when I hit the ground.

Vampires closed in at once, while the third held Nah-Mi. Malevolent hunger and triumph gleamed in their eyes.

Struggling weakly, the breath gone from my body because of the double impact of both the bullet and the smashing against the ground, I tried to reach my sword and get to my feet. Failing both of those, I concentrated instead on getting my blade. My vision blurred and agony ripped through my body, but my fingertips grazed the sword's hilt.

One of the vampires stepped on the blade, trapping it. I looked helplessly up at the thing, knowing there would be no mercy in its dead heart.

"No, girl," the vampire said.

I knew then that I was going to die, that I would never see any of those far-off places that I had often thought of.

The vampire bared its fangs in a horrible rictus as it leaned down. Its scaly tongue tracked across my cheek, rough enough, I was certain, to tear flesh. I turned my head away and closed my eyes, certain I would have felt sick to my stomach if my stomach were not numb. I wanted to kick him off me, but my legs would not work.

"I'll have your blood, Slayer," the thing said. It opened its jaws wide and leaned in to do just that.

Then it turned to dust as a length of wood pierced its heart and Sean Connelly was there.

"Easy, lass," he said gruffly. "I'm going to get you out of here."

I tried to move and still couldn't. Nothing seemed connected, like I was a bag of loose bones. I couldn't feel my feet. I tried to tell him to see to the girls, but I couldn't. Nah-Mi's screams still rang in the alley over the crackling fire that raged within the ruined hotel.

More of the vampires fired at us, but their shots were hurried. Connelly pulled both his pistols from his shoulder holsters. He fisted the weapons with grim determination and drew their hammers back. He fired with deliberation, knocking down three men with five shots. One of the vampires rushed him while the other held on to Nah-Mi, but Connelly turned quickly and blew the top of the creature's head off.

The vampire did not die, but it did grope blindly for Connelly.

Wheeling, Connelly smashed the pistol barrel against the back of the vampire's neck. The creature fell to its knees. Before it could rise again, Connelly grabbed the stake he had dropped to pull his pistols, then he rammed the wood into the creature's back and pierced the heart. The vampire turned to dust and blew away in the heated air.

Connelly turned back to me. Anxiety showed on his face. He cursed. "Oh God, lass, but those bloodsuckers done for you, didn't they?"

"Nah-Mi," I said, but my voice came out so hoarse and so hollow that I couldn't hear myself over the rasp of the burning building.

Gently Connelly knelt and pulled his shirt off, baring his upper body. He pressed the shirt against my stomach, trying to staunch the flow of blood. "Hold this, lass," he entreated.

I tried, but I had no strength left in me.

He cursed again, but I knew the invective was not directed at me, but at the situation that we both were in. I couldn't believe he stayed and tried to help me. Every man I had met while in Shanghai would have left me there and seen to his own safety. Others might have risked their lives a little only to rob me before they abandoned me.

He tied the sleeves of the shirt around my middle, wadding the loose cloth up to increase the pressure. I felt none of the pain. He gathered me up in his arms. I couldn't feel his arm under my legs, but from the way that he held me, I knew his arm had to be there. He lifted me easily because I was less than half his size and he was fierce and strong.

I caught a last glimpse of Nah-Mi as the remaining vampire ran off with her. She screamed my name, and her screams grew more faint. Then, thankfully, I passed out and knew no more.

I learned of the boat ride out of Shanghai days later when I came out of the dark sleep that claimed me for almost a week. Connelly told me later that I had almost died and he'd had to bring me back by breathing air back into me the way he had seen pearl divers in the South Pacific do. During his travels he had seen many places, and in the days that followed that night when all my adopted sisters had been taken from me, he told me stories of many of those places as he nursed me back to health.

Only one true memory remained mine during that boat ride

down the Whangpu River under the hidden moon. A man named MacReady, a fellow Irishman as Connelly called him, owned the boat. MacReady had brought Connelly into Shanghai as a favor and for the gold that Connelly had paid, but MacReady was also there to do business of his own. He was a short, squat man with a florid face, long side whiskers, a mustache, and a gold tooth.

I remember lying on the deck on my back, brought out into the fresh air from the cloistered confines of the cargo area belowdecks. Connelly leaned forward to breathe air into me, pressing his mouth against mine so that I felt his chin stubble against my cheek where the vampire had abraded the skin with its rough tongue. I felt repulsed at Connelly's touch in some small corner of my mind that yet remained mine. No man had ever been so familiar with me.

I couldn't move. Not just from the waist down, but not at all. I felt as though I were wrapped in the bandages that the Egyptians were said to use to bury their dead. In his last days, Master Wang had been fascinated by the new science of Egyptology, as the British were coming to call those studies.

"Sean," MacReady said from somewhere behind Connelly as he put his face in mine again. "Give it up, lad. She's done fer. An' from the looks of her, she's gonna be the better fer it. I ain't never seen nobody live through bein' gutshot like that."

"No," Connelly gasped. Desperation rang in his voice. "She's still alive. She's the Slayer. She can live through this. These girls, Mac, they're not like you and me. They're not frail."

"Aye. I know that, lad. I've seen 'em me own self, an' I've heard tell of ye talkin' about 'em. But this poor girl, she's done fer, lad. Even if she lives, why I'm willin' to bet she's a cripple. That bullet went through her, Sean, but only after it bounced off her spine. I could see that plain enough when we dressed those wounds."

I was aware that I was naked beneath the blanket Connelly

had covered me with. I felt bandages on my stomach and side, but I did not feel my legs.

"I've lost a Slayer before," Connelly growled. "By God, Mac, I'll not lose another one. I promised Wang that I would look after her if she outlived him."

My chest was still. I did not breathe. Strangely, I remained somehow fully alert.

Connelly leaned forward again and breathed for me. Pain fired through my upper body, carried up from the wounds I suffered.

"Let her go, Sean," MacReady begged. "She's all busted up inside. Think about it, lad. The power of the Slayer belongs to a girl capable of bein' a warrior, not to a cripple. Better to let her die and let the power pass on to the next girl."

"No," Connelly argued. "She's not dead yet. I'm not going to let her die." He bent forward and breathed into me again, but I could tell that he was on his last legs. He couldn't continue much longer.

Then I looked forward to that moment of death. I knew that his efforts were the only things keeping me alive. When he stopped, the darkness would cover me and take me away from the pain and from the haunting guilt of seeing Nah-Mi taken from me.

"Is it fer yer own self that ye're a-workin' so hard?" MacReady asked in a soft, quiet voice. "Or is it fer the girl?"

Connelly cursed his friend with ragged breath. His chest heaved as he struggled to find the strength to go on.

"Let her go, Sean," MacReady said. "I'm beggin' ye. Ye're doin' her no good, an' ye're doin' yer own self no good while ye're at it."

"No," Connelly growled.

I felt the gentle rise and fall of the boat beneath me. I was at peace, I remember that. It would have been so easy to simply let go and drift off to sleep to never awaken.

Connelly breathed for me again, and I saw tears in his eyes as he drew back. I knew he was giving up.

"Don't you die on me, lass," he growled. "You're a fighter. Wang always wrote to me and told me that you were a fighter. Now don't you go and prove him wrong."

His words stung me. I stared at him but couldn't speak. Then, deep in my chest, I felt my heart flutter and reach for its first beat. Then it beat again and again, and I found the strength to take my first breath on my own even though I was determined not to try.

"She's breathing, Mac!" Connelly said in joyous disbelief. "She's breathing!"

I was. Then darkness descended on me and consumed me.

Days later, I awoke in the Way of the Tiger Monastery. I recognized the room as the one that Master Wang chose to work in. His prized possessions, books he had both traded for and had laboriously copied, filled shelves against the walls and sat in stacks on the floor. Owning the books broke none of the vows of poverty Master Wang had made.

Even if the books were valuable, I never knew it because I never saw him sell one for monetary gain. He only traded books and copies of books so that he might acquire more. Even after his death, none of the other monks had elected to remove his belongings. No one at the monastery had known the true worth of the books, or to whom they might be valuable.

I remained bedfast till my wounds healed, which they did under the careful ministrations of the sisters that were brought to the monastery to nurse me back to health. During those days, I was unkind to the sisters, ignoring them and disregarding their medicines. When Connelly found out I was doing that, he took it upon himself to see that I followed their instructions.

I healed quickly. Only a small amount of surgery had been required. Everyone seemed surprised that I was alive and had not bled out. Both bullets had passed through my body, leaving holes in my flesh that had required sutures. Damage to my intestines had to be mended as well. I was in a great deal of pain, and that added to the discomfort I had at being alive.

I wished I were dead. Any time I slept, Nah-Mi's frightened shrieks rang in my ears.

Even surviving as I had, I was only half alive. The bullet that had struck me squarely in the stomach had damaged my spine. I was paralyzed from the waist down. I was worthless and I knew it.

When I left the monastery after Master Wang's death, I had gone only so that I might live my own life. I did not want to be a burden to anyone. That was why I had disguised the fact that I was a girl, so that I could work to support myself.

Sometimes as I lay abed, I heard some of the monks and the sisters whispering among themselves when they thought I was asleep. They said that I was selfish for leaving the monastery after they had each worked to see that I was fed and had a bed. After all, I had been an orphan, and a useless girl at that. Of course, the sisters did not remark upon my gender, but they agreed that I had been selfish to desert them so handily four months ago.

None of them spoke about me whenever Connelly was around, which was most of the time. Occasionally, he had business that took him away with MacReady, whom I seldom saw and had reason to be grateful for such a thing. MacReady thought I was a waste of time, that it would have been better if I had died in Shanghai so that he and Connelly might start out on whatever other adventures lay ahead of them.

I often heard MacReady comment on how lying about the monastery was costing him money, that a ship didn't stay afloat anywhere without considerable steady investment and a working captain. When he bothered to respond, Connelly told MacReady that he was already wealthy enough to live ten lifetimes even as extravagantly as he did. MacReady would tell him that given the present state of the world, a man could never tell when enough was enough. And anyway, MacReady wanted more than enough.

Connelly was there when I woke for breakfast. He served me at noon. And he nearly always took his supper with me. He made certain I drank the potions that the sisters left.

Most of all, Connelly talked. He told me of the Slayer, of the girl Margaret Madden, whom he had called Maggie, the girl he had been assigned to and had trained. I tried not to be interested, but his stories of their adventures told in exotic detail and with crispness, caught my attention time and time again. Although he did not say so, I could tell that he had been in love with her, and that her death some four years ago had left him scarred.

Death, according to all the legends Master Wang had told me, as well as the stories Connelly told me, should have been no surprise. Connelly should have known that one day she would die. She had, and it had been in his arms.

"I almost gave up then," he told me in a somber voice that late evening as the stars became visible through the room's small northern window. Master Wang had valued northern light because it was the best for an artist or a writer to work by.

"Why didn't you?" I asked before I could stop myself.

He showed me a grim smile, and I realized then how young he still was. Surely he was no more than ten years older than my seventeen years.

"Because giving up isn't in me, lass," he said. "Why, if it was,

I'd have given up when I was just a wee lad. Even younger than you."

"Why?"

He scowled. "My dad was a rough-and-tumble man. A man who showed no kindness to his wife and children and believed not in love, except as a weakness to be exploited in another man. I couldn't find it in me to kill him, and me knowing I'd probably be doing my dear mother a favor, so one day I left. I traveled on ships and ended up in Shanghai, which was how I met Wang all those years ago. He was the one that got me on with the Council of Watchers because I developed an interest in all these books." He pointed at the packed shelves around us. "Wang taught me most of the languages I know. I picked up the others on my own."

I tried to act like I was bored, to get him to shut up and go away. But he wouldn't. When I went into my act, he would bring up tales of other lands, other people, and their ways, and I would become entranced.

He knew it. He knew exactly how to bait my interest. I listened in spite of myself, and in listening, grew hungry and ate the food he put in front of me before I realized it.

VI

"You've got to get up. You can't lie abed for the rest of your life."

That morning, three weeks after the events in Shanghai when I had been shot and all the girls in my care had been slaughtered by Fang-Chou's creatures, I stared at Connelly and felt angry with him.

"I can't get up," I told him. "I'm a cripple."

He glared at me. "You're paralyzed from the waist down, Xiaoqin, not useless. I've seen men who had lost their legs that learned to dress themselves and even hold down jobs."

I waved at my dead legs. "I can't be the Slayer like this."

"No," he agreed.

"That was the job you had in mind for me, wasn't it?"

He sighed, and I could tell that part of him felt sorry for me. I hated that. It was one thing for me to pity myself, but I did not want to see it on someone else's face. They did not have the right.

"Yes," he said. "That was the job I had in mind for you."

"That was also what Master Wang wanted," I accused.

"*No!* By God, lass, I'll not hear disservice to that man from your lips!" Connelly suddenly thrust his face into mine. "Wang was a good man. A good teacher. And he loved you. Your only misfortunes lay in the fact that he died and you were destined to become the Slayer."

Shame blanketed my face in heat. I looked away from him.

His hand caught my face to pull it toward him. I fought him then, flailing my hands and slapping him before he could prevent the blow. Even crippled, I was too fast for him.

Standing back, he smiled at me and rubbed his face. "So you can fight, eh, lassie?"

"Do not dare presume to touch me again," I ordered. "If you do, I will kill you."

"You will, eh? Well, I consider that a challenge."

My hands came up before me automatically.

He grinned. "If you're well enough to fight, you're well enough to work is what I'm thinking."

With that, he reached down to the foot of the bed and flipped the blankets up over me. Before I could fight my way free, he wrapped his strong arms around me and lifted me from the bed. I stopped fighting somewhat. First of all, I didn't truly want to hurt him, and—now that I had been lifted from the bed—I didn't want to be dropped so that I would be forced to lie squirming upon the stone floor like some slug until someone helped me back to my bed. I knew that over the past weeks I had offended everyone in the monastery and no one would feel much compassion to help me if I ended up in that inglorious position. I felt certain I had exhausted the monks' patience.

Connelly placed me in a chair and tied me into place with the blankets. Again, I did not fight him. When he was satisfied with the knots, he dragged me in the chair to the table where Master Wang had worked.

"If you can fight," Connelly said, "then you can catalog." He pointed at the stacks of books on the desk. "Start with these. I want to know what's in them, who wrote them, and if Wang left any notes in them."

"You can't make me do this," I protested.

He shoved his face into mine. I almost hit him.

"Nobody eats for free, princess," he said.

Then I did hit him, a good punch that ached all the way up my arm.

He drew back and cursed in a loud voice that I felt certain would offend any monks that overheard. I also felt certain that even the monks working the fields could hear him.

"Get to work," he commanded, one hand clasped over his eye. Then he stalked from the room.

For three days we repeated the ordeal. By that time Connelly's injured eye had turned magnificent colors like those of a spectacular sunset. Once, he came upon me and trapped me while I was still sleeping. The second morning I pretended to be asleep until he was close enough to hit. I almost got him.

On the third morning he brought up a bucket of ice-cold water from the monastery's well and threw it on me. The cold took my breath away. I sat up by pushing myself up with my arms. I was soaked and chilled to the bone.

"Fight with me this morning, lass," he said, "and I'll bring up a bucket of water every hour and heave it on you. Trust me when I say I'll be after doing it tonight as well. You won't have a dry moment again till I get some work out of you."

I felt so helpless and frustrated that I wanted to cry. I did not. I refused to let him see me like that no matter how hard he bullied me.

"All right," I said. "And for my part, I promise never to attack you again until I can rip off both of your ears."

Connelly cursed and shook his head. "God, but aren't you the spoiled child." Then he threw the waterlogged blankets over my head and trapped me while he carried me to the chair again.

I worked on Master Wang's books for two weeks before I found the flower pressed neatly between the pages of a journal he had kept.

For the first few days I had sat tied in the chair but I hadn't worked. My rebellion did not find much of an audience. I was out of the bed, which Connelly evidently considered such an improvement that he didn't expect much more. Finally, out of boredom and curiosity—which was fostered by the hints of stories and legends and myths Connelly would talk about enough to whet my interest, only to tell me the full tale was in one of the books on the desk—I picked up the books and started reading.

The cataloging went slowly because I read voraciously. Several of the books were tomes that I had already read at Master Wang's insistence. Those I cataloged quickly. Many others concerned demon lore, and I found myself interested even though I didn't want to be. Before, all of these stories had simply been fabrications, tales meant to teach and inspire and entertain.

Now I knew they were the truth.

The flower was in one of Master Wang's journals about the garden he kept outside the monastery walls. Several of the monks secretly thought that the garden was Master Wang's personal weakness, a tribute to his own ego. Even the monks couldn't resist some petty jealousies among themselves. Master Wang had commanded respect from most of the order, other monasteries, emissaries of the emperor, the taipans, and the *guei*. He was not a man who had to beat his own drum.

I took the flower gently from the pages of the book and looked at it. The blossom was a lily, bright yellow with a dark red heart that shot veins of fading color along the petals. Even flattened as it was, the lily remained beautiful, but my mind's eye opened the flower up again through my memory, till I could once more see the full and fragrant blossom that I had pinched from the plant at Master Wang's direction.

"Find something special there then, did you, lass?"

I looked back over my shoulder and saw Connelly standing in the doorway with the noonday tray. Despite our ongoing enmity over my work, he still ate with me. I looked forward to his stories every day. And sometimes I regaled him with legends and myths I had discovered in my own reading. I learned to capture his interest as well.

Connelly sat the tray on the desk. He nodded at the flower. "What is that then?"

"A lily," I told him.

"What of it?"

I shook my head. "I didn't know Master Wang had kept this."

He sat in the chair that he had found somewhere else in the monastery and brought into my room. An expectant look filled his face.

"This was taken the last summer of Master Wang's life," I said. My voice thickened. "Master Wang asked me to take it."

"A lesson?"

I nodded. "You knew about his garden?"

"Of course. I miss it. I can't believe no one at the monastery has stood up to see that the garden continued."

From my window I had been able to see the now barren ground where the garden had been for years. A few volunteer plants had come up, but I could tell no one had worked there.

"I asked him about his garden one day," I said. "I told him that some of the other monks thought his hobby was a weakness, an egotistical extravagance."

"It probably was," Connelly said.

I shook my head. "No. If you believe that, then you didn't understand the reasons he gardened."

"Then you tell me."

His face was so bland I didn't know if he really didn't know or was only getting me to talk.

"He gardened because he could," I said, holding the dry, fragile flower. "Not many people saw the garden because there were so few visitors to the monastery. But he was convinced everyone that saw it talked of it."

"They did," Connelly said. "I've mentioned that garden hundreds—no, thousands—of times. From here to Ireland to the United States to Brazil." He smiled and shook his head. "I'm sure I wasn't the only one."

"No," I assured him, and I remembered how I had talked about the garden to Nah-Mi and the other girls. Sometimes I had heard them telling some of the new girls that I brought in before I was able to speak of the garden myself. "That day in the garden, I asked Master Wang why he bothered with the planting and tending when so few people saw it. He said that it was for the people who did notice it, that they might feel moved to make a garden of their own. In turn, their gardens would be seen by others that might also strive to bring gardens into the world that might be seen. He said that such an act could be like the ripple of a pebble dropped into a pool, that it would spread far from its point of origin."

"Not me," Connelly said. "I liked to look at what he did with that patch of ground, but I had no hankering to be digging worms and planting posies."

"The garden wasn't just about the shrubs and flowers," I said. "Master Wang told me that the garden represented a person's life. Most people live quiet and sheltered lives. Other people never see them when they blossom, never notice the difference when they struggle or when they are tended and loved. But when those people are noticed by others, especially when they live lives filled with inspiration, they unknowingly inspire others to be stronger or more clear of vision."

Connelly gazed at the dried flower in my hand.

"The day that I plucked this flower, Master Wang told me I could take the flower out of the garden," I said, "and I would still see the garden in my mind's eye when I looked at the flower." I closed my fist tenderly around the flower, then closed my eyes. "And I can. The fragrance yet lingers in this blossom, and I can see the garden as it was that summer." Sweet sadness ached within me at the beauty that I saw. In the vision Master Wang was at my side and I stood on my own two legs.

When I opened my eyes again, regretting to let go of the memory, Connelly was looking at me thoughtfully.

"You know," Connelly said, "Wang might have known that you intended to leave the monastery."

"I never told him."

"You wouldn't have had to, lass. You can see it in you clear as day. You don't fit in here. Maybe part of that is because you're the Slayer, and maybe part of it is the wanderlust that you were born with." Connelly was quiet for a moment. "Wang was always one to say that things couldn't get too far from their original natures."

I knew that. Master Wang had told me that several times. I put the flower back in the book, carefully pressed between the pages as I had found it, then joined Connelly for the meal.

Master Wang had known I would leave the monastery one day. Had he also known I would be back and go through his books? At the moment, I felt like the flower had been a special message, from him to me. No matter what happened to the garden, he had told me, I would always remember what it was like. Even gone, the garden would make a difference.

And I understood then that he was talking about himself and about me, possibly even hinting at the legacy of the Slayer that lay before me.

VII

Six days later, feeling returned to the big toe of my left foot. Connelly was excited and held out great expectations, which I did not join in because I did not know what to believe. I did not dare get my hopes up.

After another five days, more and more feeling returned to my legs and I was able to stand. By the end of that week, I was taking small steps while Connelly and even MacReady cheered me on. In the beginning there was a lot of pain. But I wanted to walk again so badly that I endured the agony until I started walking without pain.

At the end of a month I started training again, also at Connelly's insistence. I went slowly, gathering my strength, not believing my good fortune, more than a little afraid that the paralysis would return at any time. MacReady said that he had never seen anything like my recovery, and Connelly attributed it to further proof that I was the Slayer. According to Connelly, and the books that I read, slayers healed quickly, and from wounds that might have killed normal men and women.

I didn't know, and I didn't examine the occurrence too closely. If a magician's trick was understood, some of the magic of the experience went away. Master Wang had taught me acceptance as well as curiosity. Some things, he had told me on more than one occasion, just *were*. I was grateful to be free of the room where I had spent so many weeks as an invalid, to once more stand in the sunlight and feel the wind in my face.

At Connelly's urging, and my own recognition of the need if I was to regain my full health, I began working with him. Under his eyes, I returned to the exercises that Master Wang had insisted on to keep me at the top of my abilities, adding in sessions with the sword and the staff as well as open-hand combat.

Connelly was a harsh taskmaster, but he asked no more of me than Master Wang. In only days I was able to equal Connelly's efforts. In another week he could not keep up with me, and I saw that the fact gave him pride and relief, though my prowess clearly irked him as well.

When I was not working at conditioning or with the weapons, I toiled in Master Wang's garden. I cultivated the plants that had grown there in his absence, tied them up and cared for them so they would flourish, and tore out all the weeds that had taken root. I also sowed seeds so that other annual flowers might rise again.

The additional hoeing, raking, and planting aided my recovery. No longer did I lie restless in the bed as I had when I did not have the use of my legs, and Connelly had freed me from the cataloging and the desk. Now I slept, deep and almost dreamless except for the nightmares of the vampires.

My strength and speed more than came back. I knew I was stronger and faster than I had ever been. And I began to truly believe I was the Slayer, as Connelly had insisted and as some of Master Wang's journals had offered testimony to.

One day, while I was in the garden, Connelly came to me. "We need to talk," he said. His face was serious, stone, and I knew that he had chosen to be irritated with me as he sometimes was when I didn't simply know what he had on his mind.

I continued hoeing. Several of the rows I had planted showed the first green leaves that would drag the plants up toward the sun. I knew what he had come to say. I had seen the thoughts in his mind as he watched me, practiced the forms with me, and battled me with sword and staff and knife and the other weapons he selected. I had defeated him with all of them, and I knew that was hard for him to accept.

"Are you listening to me?" he demanded.

"Yes," I replied. "With you raising your voice like that, I have no choice but to hear you."

"You can't stay here forever, lass."

"I know." I continued hoeing. I knew already that I could not stay at the monastery. I had chosen my time of leaving. When I was certain that Master Wang's garden was once more set to flourish, I intended to pack what the monks would give me to see me on my way and be gone.

Connelly sighed. "Will you come with me to Shanghai?"

"Only to catch a ship," I told him, for I wanted there to be no confusion between us. I determined that his hopes for me would not rise because of something I said—or something that I didn't say.

"You can't do that."

I stood there with him in Master Wang's garden, remembering the willful child that I had been, so given to my own survival and my own freedom that I did not see to the needs of others. "I can do exactly that," I told him in a flat voice.

As we had exercised and dueled, I had thought of nothing else save my own future. I wanted no part of the Slayer's legacy. That brief instance that night when I had lost the children had been more than enough for me. I knew I could not endure a life of such hardship. Even if that life was to be only a short one.

I could not. And I would not.

"You are the Slayer," Connelly said.

"I did not choose to be," I told him.

"Doesn't matter," he said.

"It is my life," I said. I turned from him then, letting him know the conversation was over.

"They will hunt you, you know," Connelly called after me.

"Then I will kill them when they find me. Or I will die trying. But I choose not to willingly go find an end to my life."

"Damn it, lass, you can't just walk away from this."

I turned on him, and I heard the fire in my voice. Part of it was there because of the fear I still felt. In several of my dreams, the vampires succeeded where they had not in Shanghai. They tore my flesh, drank my blood, and turned me into one of them. Through it all, I had heard little Nah-Mi's cries for help echoing in that small alley as she was carried away from me.

"You are wrong, Connelly," I told him. "I *can* just walk away. Don't you remember Margaret Madden? Is it truly your wish to see one more slayer brought down by the monsters? Do you need yet another martyr?"

My words hurt him. I saw the pain strike deeply within him. He tried to speak but couldn't.

I turned away and started down the hillside where the forest began.

"I know where Fang-Chou is," Connelly said.

"I don't care." I kept walking on the two legs that a few weeks ago I thought I might never use again.

"I will go with you, Xiaoqin. You don't have to do this thing alone, but it has to be done."

"It doesn't have to be done by me."

"He will hunt you once you leave the protection of this monastery. There are spells here that blind even the *draumach*'s powers. Once you leave these walls, he will know where you are."

I kept walking.

"The little girl is still alive, Xiaoqin."

I stumbled, then straightened my steps and forced myself to keep walking.

"Nah-Mi," Connelly said. "Isn't that what you said her name was?"

I tried to push his voice and his words from my mind. *He's lying to you,* I told myself. *He's just trying to bend you to his will with guilt.*

Connelly knew he had my attention. "She's alive, Xiaoqin. Nah-Mi is alive. I swear that to you on my mother's grave."

I studied his face. Even after all these weeks spent in close association with him, I didn't know if I could tell when Sean Connelly told me a lie. I did, however, know that he would tell me a lie if doing so suited his purposes.

"How do you know that Nah-Mi is alive?" My voice was dry and brittle.

"She's been seen."

"Where?"

"In Shanghai," Connelly answered.

"By whom?"

"By spies Mac and I have hired."

"These men," I said cautiously, "they would know Nah-Mi if they saw her?" I didn't know how that was possible.

"I drew a picture of her when they first described her to me. I made copies and handed them out."

I considered that. I knew Connelly possessed a fair hand with charcoal and paper. During our time together cataloging Master Wang's books, he had shown me a number of drawings of places he had seen and people he had met. The sketches, some of them loose and some of them finely detailed, could have hung in art studios or sold for handsome prices to tourists.

"Is she still human?" I asked. I could imagine that Fang-Chou or one of his underlings might have turned Nah-Mi, converting her into a ravening beast as sport.

"She was," Connelly replied, "when she was last seen nine days ago."

"Why didn't you tell me this sooner?"

"If I had, what would you have done?"

I answered without hesitation. "I would have gone after her."

"Exactly."

"Now might be too late."

He nodded. "And now might be too early. I don't know if you're ready to confront Fang-Chou, Xiaoqin. But you're giving me no choice here. For all I know, you could have been gone in the morning if I didn't tell you this."

I stood silent for a time, thinking about my life and the twists and turns it had taken. For all my healing, for all the strength and speed that I knew I possessed, I didn't feel much different than I had always felt. But I was the Slayer for this moment in time. Connelly's discussions of the ways of the Watchers and how they knew their charges had convinced me of that.

But I had to go after Nah-Mi. I knew that as well. It wasn't because I was the Slayer; it was in spite of that unhappy happenstance. Nah-Mi was my friend and my responsibility; I could not desert her.

"Where is she?" I asked.

VIII

The next morning Connelly and I made our way from the monastery on foot and under the guard of several armed men the Watcher had hired for the trip. The monks were politely indifferent, and I had the feeling that they were glad to see us go.

From the base of the mountain where the temple had been constructed, we crossed through heavily forested lands for two days until we reached one of the tributaries that led down to the Whangpu River. Most of the lands in those areas were swamps. The floods that had consumed the land time and time again had shaped China's history.

MacReady met our party at the prearranged point. He wasn't happy after having been in place for three days prior to our arrival. However, Connelly told him he was lucky he hadn't been there the full week he'd first told him he might have to wait.

MacReady glared at me, as if everything that had gone wrong in his life had somehow been a nefarious plot on my part. I ignored him, thinking that course of action was best. Instead my behavior only seemed to aggravate him more.

The vessel was a flat-bottomed fifty-foot cargo boat, rigged with two square sails and rowing banks. Luck favored us, though I wasn't sure at the time whether it was good luck or bad, and we seldom had to resort to the oars as we traveled farther inland. There was barely any room aboard the vessel with MacReady and his crew of cutthroats, but I practiced every day, working forms to keep my skills sharp and in an attempt not to think about all that Nah-Mi had to have suffered under the cruel ministrations of the vampires.

"Fang-Chou lives in a hole in the ground?" I asked as Connelly tried to explain things to me again. We sailed with the wind that day, and the boat cleaved through the sluggish press of the tributary, rocking slightly because it was flat-bottomed and was meant for shallow water, which allowed no ballast and no overloading.

"Not a hole in the ground per se," Connelly said, drawing on the pad of paper he had brought out from his personal kit. "Three or four hundred years ago—it's difficult to pinpoint the exact date because the records we have access to are somewhat unclear, you see—a village existed in the area where we are headed. There was a disease, at least that's what the journal keeper thought, that struck the villagers down and left their blood-drained bodies behind."

"Vampires," I said. I sat on the deck under the shadowy canopy of tree limbs that interlocked above me. The golden sun shot patches of light through the emerald-leafed branches. Diamonds of sunlight reflected against the turgid brown stream we traveled.

"Yes," Connelly agreed. "The journal keeper never knew that. And from the abrupt way the entries ended, we can only believe that he fell victim to the predators himself. The journal was discovered much later."

"The vampires devoured the whole town," I said, trying to get around the enormity of that statement.

"It wasn't the first city vampires have done that to," Connelly replied. "It probably won't be the last. Vampires, for the most part, are urban feeders. They like large communities because they can walk about relatively certain no one will ever catch on to what they are doing. But large groups of them have cornered small villages and towns and drank it dry over a matter of a few nights before the general population knew something was amiss."

I nodded. "Was Fang-Chou one of the vampires that attacked this town?"

"Possibly. There are a couple of descriptions from victims that escaped the vampires that could be Fang-Chou. It doesn't matter, really, because Fang-Chou is there now."

"No one believed the villagers when they said they were attacked by a vampire?" I asked.

"No," Connelly said. "Most of the villagers were convinced that the deaths were somehow due to a malady they hadn't yet identified." He took a breath, listening for a moment to the shrill whistle of a hunting hawk. "Shortly after this time, one of the floods rose to storm the city and the surrounding lands. After days of raining, the ground softened up and swallowed the stone building that was the center of the village."

"That's where Fang-Chou is?"

Connelly nodded. "Keeping Nah-Mi was his undoing, Xiaoqin. She makes him easier to notice, easier to track. The witch I hired to ferret out Fang-Chou could not see him in her blood bowl, but she could see Nah-Mi." He looked out at the marshlands around us. "They're there."

We reached the site of the village the next morning after lying at anchor a mile distant during the shallow hours of the night. None of us slept. We couldn't.

I spent the night sitting on the deck, all of my senses alert. I heard the hunters prowling the marshlands, but all of them were natural things: foxes and owls, for the most part.

We left the boat with the dawning sun, an armed party carrying stakes and holy water, sharp swords and axes. I carried a short staff as my lead weapon, both ends sharpened to more easily plunge through a vampire's chest to pierce the undead heart beneath. I wore a brown robe like the one Master Wang had trained me in.

During that long walk, no one really talked. Connelly stayed at my side, festooned with pistols as well as stakes because there was every likelihood Fang-Chou would have human underlings with him as well. I hadn't asked where he had gotten the small army of men that came with us. I hadn't thought to. They were white men and black men, and even two North American Indians I identified by their war paint and breechcloths. All of them, Connelly told me, were experienced vampire fighters.

My stride was loose and limber, and I felt good, as if senses I had never before used were suddenly coming to life. Probably it was only my imagination, but that was how it felt. I had to work hard not to outdistance Connelly and the others.

The Indians led the way. An hour later, they waved us to the ground.

Connelly lay beside me, the musk of him strong in my nose from all the exertions we'd undergone. "There," he whispered hoarsely. "Do you see it?"

I followed the line of his pointing arm and spotted the mound in the middle of a fetid swamp. Clouds of mosquitoes hung above the turgid water. Turtles lay in the mud and I spotted a few ripples where small fish touched the surface of the water from underneath. Little sunlight touched the area, leaving it mostly cloaked in a wet nether light that resembled the darkness that hangs in a room lit only by a fireplace.

After an hour of watching, we spotted the four men that guarded the entrance to the hole in the ground that Connelly believed led to the building the swampland had engulfed. Another hour passed before those four men were relieved.

We waited an additional fifteen minutes for the new guards to settle into their routine. They talked among themselves, but the conversation was mostly listless and intermittent. Despite the fact that they were vampires, they were bored men given a boring job and with little to share among themselves. Mostly the talk was of women and what they would do with riches if they ever came into them. They also faulted each other in rib-ald voices, rejoicing in past indiscretions at one another's expense.

I could tell that Connelly didn't like the rough-mouthed men or their bragging ways. I think he felt embarrassed for me at hearing all of their comments and the foul language they spewed. I didn't remind him that I had worked on the docks of Shanghai and had heard much worse every day.

Connelly called the Indians to him. It was decided that the four of us would take out the guards. One of the vampires sat on a platform in the fork of a tree. I said that I would kill him, and quickly strung the short bow I carried with me.

Looking at me, Connelly said, "That vampire can't make any noise, lass."

"It won't." I took a single arrow from the quiver on my back, then crept into the tree-filled marshland. Long minutes passed. The buzzing mosquitoes made more noise than we did.

I lay in wait in a stand of tall brush less than fifty paces from the vampire I was going to kill. Minutes passed, and I marked them with the slow, rhythmic beating of my heart. I tried not to think of Nah-Mi, telling myself that I would see her soon enough.

Then Connelly gave the signal, a bird whistle, and we rose up from our spots. I pulled the arrow back till the fletchings brushed my cheeks, breathed slowly out, and took aim. The vampire saw me just as I released the string. His mouth opened and he reached for the rifle at his side.

The arrow caught him in the throat, blocking any noise he might have made. He toppled backward and crashed through the brush. My second shaft pierced his heart and he turned to dust.

I turned, another arrow already nocked to bowstring, and saw Connelly and the Indians stand above the dust of the vampires they had killed. Their knives glinted red with blood.

Connelly waved and the other fifteen men came to join us at the opening in the wet ground. At the edge of the ten-foot hole, the stench of decay and rot—the normal stink of the swampland accompanied by the animal smells of a predator that brought its kills home—was overpowering. My nose wrinkled and I breathed shallowly.

Peering through the darkness, Connelly said, "They've got lights inside. You can make out the glow. Just the same, we'll carry our own torches."

As far as Connelly had been able to discover, no one except Fang-Chou's underlings had ever been inside the marsh cavern. They weren't talking. The brief glimpse of the sanctuary gotten by the witch Connelly had hired wasn't overly informative. The witch had seen a great room where Nah-Mi had been held captive.

Connelly and I took the lead. He carried a torch in one hand and a revolver in the other. I walked to his right with the staff in both my hands.

"Stay sharp, lass," Connelly whispered as we went. "Stay sharp and we'll see this thing through right enough."

"Yes," I whispered back. I wanted desperately to believe him, but I didn't. I knew many of us weren't coming back, but we had to believe that we would or we would never have been able to go down into that demon's throat.

The tunnel drove through the earth at least three hundred yards, whipping back and forth. Lanterns lighted the tunnel every fifteen or twenty paces, usually at each curve. The grade told me that we were going down rather steeply, and it was hard not to remember the water sitting so close by. In several places gnarled tree roots protruded from the earth, many of them roughly hacked off to leave sharp ends. Twice we had to ford pools of water that were nearly two feet deep.

As we went, I thought of the Blue Tiger Customs House that had looked so fine before it had burned. I thought of the ships the triad owned, of the trade that it had conducted. Connelly had also shown me drawings of the fine houses Fang-Chou owned in Shanghai and in Chinese City.

Fang-Chou was a man of wealth, and Connelly had discovered that the vampire lord was using the *draumach* to seek out the secrets of his enemies and competitors. Slowly and quietly Fang-Chou was consolidating a power base among the more illicit businesses in Shanghai. Within a few years, Connelly felt certain, the vampire would become the city's undisputed master. I didn't think that Fang-Chou was doing the acquisition purely for profit. I believed that the vampire saw conquering the rival businesses as another means of being a predator. He was already wealthy.

But he chose to spend most of his days here, in a hole in the wet earth far from Shanghai. I tried to fathom why Fang-Chou would do such a thing. I couldn't. The only thing that I could reason was that Fang-Chou was more animal than man, more given to his creature's instincts than a veneer of civilization.

Connelly and I stepped around another turn and came upon the main chamber in the underground area. Several lanterns hung around the earthen walls that were shored up by wooden beams and stone columns. The two-story stone building sat at the far end.

Perhaps the swamplands had sucked the building down into its embrace all those centuries ago, but considerable work had gone into increasing the chamber. A hundred feet lay between us and the stone building, mired in the earth on all sides save the front of the structure and part of the corners around it. The building looked like nothing more than a partially unearthed stone coffin.

It was plain and simple, a place where people had gathered in fellowship and to talk business among themselves. Mortar held together odd-size rocks that had never known a stonecutter's skills. In places, a few of the rocks had fallen out, leaving gaping holes.

Lantern light caught the white and yellow gleam of ivory. I stared at the skeletons that lay in heaped disarray across the open ground of the chamber. The vampires had fed on hundreds of victims and never bothered to clean out the refuse. Fresh bones and partially decomposed bodies lay among the cracked yellow skeletons of older victims.

Cold fury descended on me. I realized then that the monument of bones was as much of a statement by Fang-Chou as Master Wang's flower garden had been. Where Master Wang had hoped to incite others to better their own lives in some way, though, Fang-Chou had built a monument to fear. I felt compelled to destroy the cavern and everything in it.

"Easy, lass," Connelly advised. He started to say something else, but then a shout went up from the building. Shadowy figures moved in the windows and doors.

"Someone is here!" a vampire shouted. "Get up! Get up!"

Connelly took aim with his pistol and fired. One of the figures in the window fell backward. The detonation rolled like thunder in the enclosed chamber.

"Skirmish line!" Connelly bellowed, then fired again and again. "Quickly, damn you all, or they'll be among us before we're ready!"

I shoved my staff into the soft ground in front of me, swept my bow from my shoulder, and fitted an arrow to string in one fluid motion. I targeted the men that came at us from the building. They boiled over like ants whose nest had been disturbed.

I shot arrow after arrow into their midst. The rapid bark of pistols and rifles cannonaded around me. My arrows pierced flesh. Vampires whose hearts were pierced turned to dust, but those that I had missed killing were only transfixed by the arrows and hardly slowed at all.

Then Fang-Chou's creatures were upon us and the fighting turned into hand-to-hand melee. I cast my bow aside and took up my staff. I prayed that Master Wang would look over me from the Celestial Heavens, because he was the closest thing to an ancestor I had.

I met the first attacker with one of the staff's pointed ends. The staff crashed through his breastbone and into his heart. The vampire turned to dust with a shrill cry of disbelief. Avoiding a sword blow, I swung around and whirled the staff, catching my next opponent full on his cheek. The skin split from the impact and his neck broke. One of the Indians hacked the vampire's head off and he turned to dust.

Catching sight of a vampire—obvious because its face was inhuman—bearing down on one of Connelly's men, I spun again and thrust the staff through its back. It turned to dust, leaving the man gasping for air, now that the undead thing's hands had been released from his throat. He lifted his pistol and sent a bullet into the brain of the vampire coming up behind me. I had known the vampire was coming because I had sensed it, though I didn't know how.

We fought to hold our ground, but we were forced back. We stepped over the bodies of our dead, watching in helpless horror as the things that pursued us grabbed up the fresh corpses or the dying men and drank their blood. Connelly and his men bought us temporary respite when they slung holy water over the vampires, burning their flesh and driving them back. But the holy water was quickly used up and the vampires were only angrier than they had been.

I was afraid, but I thought of Nah-Mi and I forced myself to go on. Still, I could not help thinking of all the Slayers that had gone on before me. How had any of them stood up to the test of knowing she would combat monsters until the day she died at the hands of things that would ill use her and then kill her.

It seemed too much to ask.

My breath burned raggedly in my throat. I knew Connelly and the men around me fared no better. I saw Master Wang's garden in my mind again, as it had been and as I had left it. The newly planted garden was only an echo of the beauty that had been, but the ground and the seedlings carried the promise of a bounty that would one day flourish anew.

And it was then that I understood the lesson of the garden. It wasn't about the season or the time. The garden represented the hope that would always be. Perhaps, in time, even Master Wang's beautiful garden would one day wither and no one would come to reclaim it from the parched and wild earth. But there were others who had seen the garden, who took from it the hope and dream of starting gardens of their own. Lives, like landscape, were changed by the dreams of one—the promise of one—who was brave enough to stand for those dreams.

The Slayer stood for the dream that humans would be able to endure, and even triumph against, the monsters that came for them.

In that moment I understood completely. I *was* the Slayer. I *was* the Chosen One. The skills and gifts that had come to me through birth and been made greater by whatever it was that passed on from slayer to slayer had come to me because I had been deemed worthy. Master Wang had trained me because he too had seen my worth. Connelly had stayed with me when I was crippled, and I believed that he would have stayed or at least seen to my care even if I had not regained the use of my legs.

I stopped falling back. I stood my ground. I fought and I slew.

Vampires turned to dust at my feet. When the pile of maimed vampires at my feet grew too high and too close, I leaped over them, gaining more ground toward the building the earth had sucked down.

I released everything, even thinking, only fought as I had been trained and was able to do. I kicked and punched and thrust with the staff.

Then I heard Connelly roaring at the men that were left to regroup. In seconds I had them at my back and our forward momentum rolled over the line of flagging Blue Tigers. We fought them and we killed them, and sometimes we left our own dead and wounded behind.

Then the line broke in front of us and the vampires turned and ran. I pursued them, watching as they broke again to either side of someone standing in front of me.

Fang-Chou was there with blazing red eyes. His green-white hair hung to his knees. He curled the talons of his left hand across Nah-Mi's head.

My heart leaped to see the little girl. She looked pale and emaciated. And afraid, so, so afraid. I knew that I would never get that look out of my mind no matter how long I lived.

"Xiaoqin," she whispered, and I had to read her lips because her voice was too weak to hear.

"Cowards!" Fang-Chou shouted at the remaining Blue Tigers. "You will stand by me, or I will hunt you down myself when I am done with these peasants!"

The Blue Tiger vampires halted their flight. With evident reluctance, they formed a line on either side of their leader.

I stood ten feet from Fang-Chou. I gasped for breath, but I felt ready. The staff was sure and strong in my hands.

"Slayer," Fang-Chou said in the silence that descended throughout the cavern. "When Jae-Chol's underlings told me they had confronted you in Shanghai, I did not believe them."

I did not speak. I did not know what to say to a monster.

"Then," Fang-Chou continued, "when I heard of this one, this *Watcher*"—he stated the word with derisive sarcasm—"I knew that perhaps you might be who Jae-Chol's men said you were." His red eyes bored into mine. "Now I see that those men spoke truly."

I only waited.

"I have killed a Slayer before," Fang-Chou said. "Did your Watcher tell you that?"

The vampire lord's words surprised me. Before I could stop myself, I looked at Connelly.

The expression on Connelly's face told me Fang-Chou's words were true.

I faced the vampire lord. "I didn't come here to die, Fang-Chou."

The monster smiled at me. "Yes, you did, girl."

His acknowledgment of my sex was meant as an insult. Our culture had never looked upon females as having any worth. Even the emperors' wives had held no real station in China as the queens of the *guei* countries did.

His hand tightened on Nah-Mi's head and made her cry out.

I stepped forward.

"No," the vampire lord barked.

I stopped.

"Give me your weapon," Fang-Chou commanded. He reached out with his other hand. The long talons gleamed like razors.

I hesitated.

Fang-Chou squeezed Nah-Mi's head again, making her scream. "Do it," the vampire lord ordered. "Or I will kill her while you watch."

"And if I give you my weapon?" I asked.

"Then I will kill you first, and I promise the child's death will be just as quick."

With reluctance, I held my staff up before me.

"Xiaoqin," Connelly said.

"We don't have a choice," I told him. "We shouldn't have come here. I can't let him kill Nah-Mi."

"He's going to kill her anyway," Connelly said.

Fang-Chou waited. I could tell waiting was something that he did well. His hand never moved from Nah-Mi's head. "Give me the weapon," he said. He held his hand out. "Throw it over to me."

I looked at him, certain he would kill Nah-Mi in an instant if I didn't do what he said.

"Xiaoqin," Connelly said.

I tossed the staff toward Fang-Chou. It started to fall short and the vampire lord reached for it. I moved as quickly as I could, knowing Nah-Mi's life hung in the balance. Taking one long step forward, I kicked the end of the staff with my left foot and spun it around, catching the other end in my hand, then lunged forward with the staff as if it were a spear.

As desperately as I'd had to move, I knew my aim was off. Still, I caught Fang-Chou in the throat with the pointed end of the staff, and I followed through with all the forward momentum I'd mustered, as well as the weight of my body.

The sharpened wooden point tore through the vampire lord's neck, and I shoved him backward. His hand slipped from Nah-Mi's head. I shoved her to the ground as I passed her by.

Connelly and his men joined the fray, and life and death balanced on a knife blade in the underground chamber.

Fang-Chou set himself, ignoring the staff stuck into his throat. With the weapon lodged there, he knew I couldn't withdraw it and strike again. He came at me, and his greater strength pushed me backward. I tried to hold him back, but I couldn't. I felt my feet failing as his speed overcame me.

Desperate, I pulled the other end of the staff down. It was only four and a half feet long, just barely enough to keep Fang-Chou from my face. As I planted the staff on the ground, his talons cut my hair and locks flew away. But the staff held and I used it to lever him up and over as Connelly and his men fought the Blue Tiger men with sword, pistol, and stake.

Fang-Chou arced overhead, and I thought he would crash to the floor and be stunned for a moment. Instead he gripped the staff and pulled himself free, landing on his feet and one hand, only a short distance away. He ran at me, his red eyes blazing hate and pain. I ran at him as well, holding the staff again in both hands. He reached for me, but I ducked to one side and swept his feet from under him with the staff.

Before I could turn, he rolled and was up again, coming at me with slashing talons. I blocked his attacks with the staff and by dodging away. His talons slashed my hair and left cuts on my cheeks. I kicked him and used my elbows to fight him off. Fang-Chou was not a true martial arts fighter; he was a brawler, but a very experienced one.

I ducked and thrust, penetrating his body again and again with both pointed ends of the staff. Blood trickled from several dozen wounds on his body, but I kept missing his heart. Even after all the damage I had inflicted, he showed no signs of slowing.

His leg swept out and he tripped me, on me almost before I could raise the staff to defend myself. He brought his right hand down against the staff. The wood snapped and the blow nearly tore my shoulders from their sockets. He grinned at me, but I was already moving.

Despite the fact that I was scared, I fought on. I was the Slayer, and I would be the champion of whatever unknown force had decided to make me that. I was not worthless. I would stand for something.

And Fang-Chou would pay for killing those girls that I had protected.

"Give up, girl," the vampire lord snarled. "Give up and welcome the quick death I am willing to give you."

"No," I told him, gasping because my lungs strained for air.

He raked his claws at me, and he would have torn me in half had he touched me. I ducked beneath his outstretched arms and thrust one of the broken halves of the staff into his chest. Unfortunately I was hurried, and I missed his heart. I threw myself to the side, rolling as he slashed at me again, feeling his talons bite deeply into my shoulder.

Then I was once more on my feet and I gripped the remaining half of the staff in both hands as I came up behind him. I measured my blow, knowing that it would be my last, certain that he would kill me if I missed. But I trusted my instincts and Master Wang's instruction.

The wood cored easily through his body as he turned, going in under his left arm.

He kept turning, and for a moment I was afraid I had missed again. I knew I would not get another chance and would not be able to escape.

"Xiaoqin!" Connelly yelled.

Fang-Chou rose in front of me. He bared his fangs, his face inhuman. Then he reached for me so quickly I could not get away. Just before his talons touched me, he turned to dust. My aim had been true.

I saw Connelly rushing toward me through the dusty haze left by the defeated vampire. Nah-Mi was running toward me as well.

I stood, surprised that I had found the strength to do so after everything I had been through. Nah-Mi threw her arms around me and cried. I held her tightly and wiped away her tears, telling her that everything was going to be all right and hoping that it would be.

Fang-Chou's hidden sanctuary held rooms of gold and silver and gems, which made MacReady happy. But there were also books, tomes on arcane demons and demonology, that Connelly had never seen before. Some of them, he was certain, were not in the archives held by the Watchers.

We returned to Shanghai and slew the rest of the Blue Tigers over the span of a few nights.

Then I began writing this journal. There are other journals written by past slayers, each of them detailing aspects of her life, private fears, and things she has learned. Each of them—as I feel certain Master Wang would have pointed out to me—gardens in their own right.

But each of those gardens, as does my own, springs from the First, the one who went before and became the First Slayer. As yet, no one seems to know much about her. I wish that I might learn more at some future date, that I might know how she dealt with the powers and the responsibilities she was given to fight the monsters.

Until then, though, I will pass on my journals of the places I go and the monsters I fight. I have agreed with Connelly that we will next go to Gold Mountain, that I might see California for myself. Something draws me there, but I know not what it is. That place, I am certain, has been a special place in slayer lore. Or perhaps it will yet be.

To you readers who are slayers, know that it is all right to feel angry and scared as you are called. Your emotions are justified.

This life was not asked for, and no quarter will be given you by the enemies you will face. But remember that you are the light in the darkness that keeps the monsters at bay.

You are my sisters. Someday, the gods willing, perhaps we shall all meet.

Voodoo Lounge

Christopher Golden

December 12, 1940

I

Los Angeles sparkled at night. Sleek black sedans gleamed as they whispered along Sunset and Sepulveda, rolling from the majestic gates of film studios to the well-guarded entryways of glittering clubs. The doors of those nightspots would open only to permit the vibrant Hollywood elite—the dashing men in razor-tailored suits and the precious, elegant starlets they wore upon their arms. Those doors were the veil that separated a magical place the world called Hollywood from the lives of ordinary people, and each time one of those doors opened it was as though the veil had, just for a moment, been pulled aside to spill out the strains of music to swell the heart, the sounds of champagne glasses clinking and the giddy laughter of youth in full bloom.

Eleanor Boudreau was breathless.

Truth be told, she had barely been able to catch her breath since arriving in Los Angeles two nights before. This was not her world. She could no more pretend to know how to behave in this atmosphere than she could have claimed to know the etiquette required when dining with royalty. And yet . . . and yet . . .

When she stepped from the car—the driver holding her door open—she felt a strange calm descend upon her. A flutter of dove's wings in her heart made her smile, and the way her new gown fell across her body teased her flesh so that she stood up straighter and walked with more grace than she had ever before felt capable of. She wasn't a little girl anymore.

A handful of other people in evening wear made for the door as well, and Eleanor smiled softly at a handsome, square-jawed man who paused to allow her to go ahead of him. The steps that led up to the door of the Shangri-La were adorned with flowers, but many of them had been trampled by photographers who elbowed one another, hoping to get the best picture of each new arrival. There were pops and bursts of light and her eyes stung, and after a moment she realized that as she went up the steps, several of the photographers were taking pictures of her.

Eleanor blushed deeply and though her natural instinct was to drop her gaze, she remembered Miss Fontaine's instructions. *Behave as though you belong there,* she had said. So Eleanor lifted her chin and donned a little half smile that she hoped conveyed her amusement with the attention. Her hair was perfectly styled and she tried not to think about the borrowed jewels she wore.

Then she had run the gauntlet and the flashbulbs were behind her. She stepped into the foyer of the club. The doorman raised an eyebrow as he studied her but she ignored him, feigning a hauteur that she prayed was not as transparent as it felt. Miss Fontaine had told her that she had little to concern her, that the simple fact that she was young and beautiful might well get her inside the Shangri-La.

She swept into the club as though she were late for an appointment with someone she did not want to keep waiting, but once inside she was brought up short by the sheer glamour of it all. The waiters in their smart jackets, the trumpet crying out above the rhythm of the band, the familiar faces that all seemed to meld into one as she glanced about. Faces she knew, yes, but impossible faces, imaginary faces, faces from the silver screen.

"Evening, miss," came a pleasant voice just off to her right.

Startled, Eleanor looked up abruptly. "Oh," she said, "pardon me." Though precisely for what crime she was begging pardon she could not imagine. Still, it seemed the best thing to say.

"Not at all," the man replied. "I'm the one who should be asking for your pardon. It was me interrupting your train of thought, after all, not the other way around."

Then he smiled and suddenly she knew him. The moment of recognition made her take a step back and she nearly collided with a waiter who was speeding by with a tray upon which steaks sizzled. She wanted to tell him, felt an urge to reveal that she recognized him, that she had seen his handsome face so large on that screen at the Palace Theater back home.

Eleanor said nothing, but she was certain he saw it in her eyes just the same. There was a sadness about his smile then, and a certain acceptance. After all, the man could not expect to go about unrecognized, particularly here. Now, though, he was studying her closely.

"What picture did I see you in recently?" he asked. "Was it that Moreland picture, the one about the girl in love with her professor? That was it, wasn't it?"

This time Eleanor could not help but drop her gaze. She was grateful for the poor lighting in the club and the shroud of smoke that drifted through the room. "I'm afraid not," she replied.

Yet he continued to study her. "Well, if it wasn't you, it ought to've been," he said at last. "Were you looking for someone?" He glanced about them with a curious expression, not giving her time to respond to the compliment he had dashed off.

She blinked, pleased he had asked. Anything to loosen the words that seemed to have clogged her throat when he had suggested that she might have been an actress. A movie star. The idea of it made her quiver with both its absurdity and the secret pleasure that anyone would think her capable of such a thing.

"I am indeed, sir," she replied. "A friend. He's a writer and I was told—"

"Ah, now I see," he said, a glimmer in his eye. "You're just arrived in town, aren't you?"

Eleanor took a short breath, upset with herself for failing to keep up appearances. He must have seen how crestfallen she was, for he smiled in sympathy.

"It was the accent. The 'sir,' actually. Or 'suh.' Alabama, is it?"

"Louisiana," she confessed. Much as she had tried to speak without falling back into the cadence of her upbringing—and the months she had spent in England had helped—obviously Eleanor had not yet reached the point where she could speak the English of Hollywood.

"I think it's adorable," he assured her, and there was such warmth in his words that she could not help but be swayed. "Now, your friend . . . he's a writer, you say? We do our best to keep the writers out of here, but—" He paused and chuckled. "You do know that's a joke? In any case, does your friend have a name?"

"Martin Goss."

His smile crumbled, to be replaced by something else entirely. It might have been mistaken for a smile if she had not already seen his real one. He shook his head.

"If you don't mind my saying, miss, you have interesting taste in friends."

"Then you know him?"

"Know of him, at least." With a tilt of his head, he gestured around the room. "But you won't find Marty Goss in this crowd. Not at the Shangri-La. You'll have to go underground if you want to locate your friend."

He told her the name of a place she might inquire about Goss, and Eleanor stared at him. "And it's underground?"

He laughed. "Oh, not literally. Just the sort of clubs he frequents. For a certain element it's the trendiest spot in town. If you're trying to find Martin Goss, that's where you should start. Just be careful what you wish for. This city's made up of layers. Like diamonds and rubies on the top, but every layer you peel back reveals a little more tarnish, and when you get down to the bottom, there are all sorts of ugly things."

It was as though a wind blew through the room then. Eleanor shuddered, but she stood straighter and met his gaze levelly, her chin lifted higher. So enchanted had she been by the music and the glitter that she had allowed herself to forget who she was. What she was.

"That isn't just this city," the Slayer told him. "That's the story of the world."

As Eleanor left Shangri-La the flashbulbs were popping in rapid staccato bursts, but the cameras were not trained on her. Claudette Colbert was coming up the stairs toward the doors of the club, her gown glittering in the onslaught of flashing lights. For a moment Eleanor was frozen, mouth partway open, having forgotten how to breathe. Claudette Colbert was her all-time favorite movie star.

Then a photographer slid in front of Eleanor, flash popping so brightly that she had to blink several times. The Slayer raised a hand to shield her eyes and pushed past the photographer.

"Honey, what's your name? What picture are you in?" the photographer shouted after her.

It was possible she would have to come back here, would have to continue this masquerade, and so Eleanor raised her chin and tried to summon that certain dignity again. As she hurried down the steps she passed Claudette Colbert, who gave her a knowing smile. Eleanor nearly tripped over her own feet and was amazed when a moment later she realized that she had made it all the way to the sidewalk. She had only just begun to look around for her car when the dark sedan rolled up to the curb. The lights from Shangri-La were reflected on the auto's exterior.

She didn't wait for the driver to open the door for her. Eleanor climbed into the backseat. "Let's go," she said. And then she gazed out the window at the club, a longing in her heart as the car pulled away from the Shangri-La. Claudette Colbert had smiled at her. And inside the club, in the midst of all of that sparkle, she had spoken to *him*. Indeed, she had crossed over into a fantastical world she had only ever dreamed of before. Eleanor felt like Dorothy in Oz.

Yet though she had left so much behind, both in Louisiana and in London, she was not at all certain that she wanted to click her heels together. Eleanor wasn't sure she wanted to go home.

Beside her on the backseat of the car, Marie-Christine Fontaine gazed at the Slayer intently. "Well, that was fast. Don't tell me you've already found Martin and convinced him to return to the Council?"

Eleanor raised her eyebrows and studied her Watcher, never quite certain when Miss Fontaine was pulling her leg. It was that dry English humor.

"No, ma'am," she replied, deciding to treat the question as genuine. "But I met someone who knows him."

When she told Miss Fontaine who it was she had spoken with about Martin, the Watcher seemed suitably impressed. "He's a bit young for me, and too old for you," Marie-Christine said archly, "but my, he's handsome, isn't he?"

Eleanor nodded, but her thoughts were drifting back to the Shangri-La. It had been extraordinary—breathtaking, really—but already she found herself stunned and appalled at the thoughts she had had only a minute earlier. Los Angeles was not the place for her. These clothes, the lights of the city, the rarified air shared by these people who were so much more than ordinary—this wasn't her place. Eleanor was a Louisiana girl. When the Council of Watchers had first sent someone to explain her destiny to her, she had been torn. Deep within her she had been thrilled by the idea that she had a fate, that she was special in some way, and yet she had insisted that they train her there, at home in Louisiana. She had been intimidated by the idea of exploring the world.

So much had happened since then. A pair of notorious vampires had stolen the Council's list of potential slayers, then traveled the world, slaughtering them. The Council had gathered all the surviving slayers-in-waiting, unaware that the vampires were working for a demon called Skrymir who *wanted* them all together so that he could eliminate them more easily.

Eleanor had been one of those girls. In her brief time in England she had befriended several of the other potential slayers, particularly Ariana de la Croix. The Council's London headquarters had been invaded and many watchers, Council operatives, and slayers-in-waiting had lost their lives before the demon was at last destroyed. Some of those killed had been Eleanor's friends, and yet she had survived.

Ariana, too, had lived, but it had been Eleanor who had been Chosen when the previous Slayer lost her life. Now Ariana had decided she wanted to become a watcher.

Eleanor had often wondered how her life had come to this,

how an ordinary Louisiana girl had been chosen to combat the forces of darkness. But, then, from what she knew of being a slayer, the power and responsibility very often fell to an ordinary girl. She was torn, now, her heart tugged in so many different directions. Eleanor wanted to stay in London to further train with Miss Fontaine, a member of the Council's board of directors who had been appointed as her Watcher, and to spend time with Ariana. Her heart ached being away, and she marveled at how she could come to be so close to anyone in such a short time. Ariana was already the closest friend she had ever had.

Yet another part of her wanted to go home, back to Louisiana. She had family there and she wanted to see them. It was nearly Christmas and the air itself seemed to shimmer with the magic of the season. More than that, however, there was the presence back home of an ancient vampire who had taken an entire town as his slaves. Kakistos, his name was, and he was building a bayou kingdom all for himself. As soon as she was ready, Eleanor wanted to return to Louisiana and tear that kingdom down, to destroy Kakistos.

London. Lafayette. Both cities called to her. Instead, so soon after she had been told she would remain at the Council's headquarters for the foreseeable future, they had sent her here, to Los Angeles. The Council was vulnerable now, their numbers greatly depleted. All efforts were devoted now to moving personnel up in the ranks, to bringing the next generation of operatives and watchers into play much sooner than anticipated, to locating as many new potential slayers as possible. But it was not merely about new blood. From time to time, a watcher would leave the ranks, sometimes in shame and other times in anger.

Martin Goss was reputedly the only person ever to quit the Council of Watchers out of boredom. The notes Eleanor had read in the bits of his file she had been authorized to read made it clear that, though gifted, Goss was not well loved by his superiors. The man from Nottingham had difficulty with authority and after a particular mission with a group of operatives in which he had patently ignored the instructions of the mission commander, Goss had been restricted to research and administrative work.

Permanently.

Upon his departure Goss had stunned his former employers even further by moving to Los Angeles and seeking out a career as a Hollywood screenwriter . . . and succeeding.

After the horrors of recent months, however, those men who had balked at Goss's independent streak could no longer afford to be quite so judgmental. The man was a brilliant researcher and strategist and an expert in hand-to-hand and armed combat. When John Travers had been chosen to lead the effort to restore the ranks of watchers, retrieving Martin Goss had been at the top of his list. But Goss wasn't going to listen to anyone from the Council.

So they had sent the Slayer.

The engine hummed and lights flashed across the window beside her and Eleanor was lulled by it, her mind sifting through so many images, her heart struggling with so many yearnings.

"Eleanor," Miss Fontaine said.

The Slayer blinked and turned to her. "Hmm? I'm sorry. There's just so much to take in."

"It is an extraordinary place," Miss Fontaine agreed. "But back to business, my dear. When you spoke to your new acquaintance about Mr. Goss, did he mention where we might be able to find the object of our quest?"

It was clear to Eleanor that Miss Fontaine had known Goss when he worked for the Council, but the Slayer could not tell if her Watcher had liked the man or not. She did not want to upset her mentor, but she only knew one way to tell the truth.

"I got the idea that Mr. Goss doesn't like places like Shangri-La very much. With all the glamour and the photographers. There's another place, an underground club. We might not find him there, but it's supposed to be the right place to start looking."

Miss Fontaine's eyebrows shot up. "And this place? Does it have a name?"

Eleanor nodded gravely. "It's called the Voodoo Lounge."

Less than an hour later the driver turned slowly off Santa Monica Boulevard. His name was Walter and he wanted to be an actor. He had been driving a hired car in Los Angeles for less than a year, but already he seemed jaded. In spite of that, or perhaps because of it, Walter had volunteered to help as soon as the name of the underground club was out of Eleanor's mouth.

"Every city in the world has places like the Voodoo Lounge," Walter had told them, his tone weary though he appeared to be only a couple of years older than Eleanor. "If you don't know how to find it, nobody's going to tell you."

But Walter had discovered in his tenure as a driver that the one subculture in the Hollywood caste system that could always be relied upon to know the location of the best parties, the most deviant clubs, and the trendiest underground nightspots were the men behind the wheel. Taxi and limousine drivers and chauffeurs of hired cars. It had taken him less than ten minutes of quizzing his comrades-in-livery to discover the address of the Voodoo Lounge.

As he pulled up to the curb in front of the club, Walter removed his cap and looked back over the seat at them. Eleanor smiled appreciatively. He wasn't conventionally handsome, but there was something about him, a rugged quality, that she thought was attractive. Perhaps he had no talent, and that was what had kept him from becoming an actor. Or perhaps it was simply that luck was not on his side.

Walter pushed a hand through his thick, dark hair and studied her in such a way that Eleanor squirmed a bit in her seat, unused to the brazen attention of American men after months out of the country. She was grateful when he shifted his gaze to Miss Fontaine.

"Ma'am, my job is to take you wherever you want to go," Walter said, brown eyes narrowing as he studied her. "But I figure I've also got a kind of obligation to look out for the people I drive. You oughta know some of the things I've heard about this club. It's . . . ," and he paused there, obviously searching for some way to put his concern into words.

Walter sighed. "Lots of folks from the picture business come here. Actors. Directors. Producers. They get some of the best music, too. Jazz acts that aren't allowed to play in some of the other clubs."

"They sound . . . progressive," Miss Fontaine said.

The driver glanced out the window at the face of the club. There were no photographers here on this poorly lit side street. The Voodoo Lounge did not even have a sign; nothing to identify it save for the two broad-shouldered men who stood on either side of the door.

"You don't understand," Walter said, running a hand through his hair again. "And I'm not sure how to explain it to you. The club's strange, is all. Some of the people who come to this joint . . . they're monsters." His gaze shifted to Eleanor. "Freaks, y'know?"

The Slayer smiled shyly. "Don't trouble yourself, Walter. I've dealt with my share of monsters."

She grabbed the door handle and clicked it open, letting

herself out. Walter muttered a soft curse that he had failed to observe this courtesy. He jumped out of the car to come around to her side, but Eleanor was already closing the door. For a long moment he stared at her gown and then raised his eyes.

"When I say monsters, I'm not just talking about cruel men," Walter told her. "I'm talking about . . . look, I've heard that there are—"

Eleanor smiled again. "I'll be all right. Just don't leave without me."

"Of course not," he said, obviously offended by the suggestion.

As she walked away from the car Eleanor could hear Walter and Miss Fontaine speaking behind her. But already her focus was on the job at hand, and she was examining the front door of the Voodoo Lounge. The club was situated between a textile warehouse and an import/export office building. Its exterior was featureless, with windows shuttered from the inside. Only as she approached the two doormen, who were studying her with a mixture of doubt and curiosity, could she hear muffled jazz music coming from within.

The larger of the two doormen shifted, standing straighter, and moved into her path. His nose was crooked and there was a small scar below his left eye. The man had the unmistakable carriage of a boxer. Eleanor had known a few pugilists in her life, friends of her Uncle Joe, and such men rolled when they walked, their arms just a bit too far away from their bodies so as to be prepared if an attack might come.

"Are you lost, sweetheart? Looking for directions?" the doorman asked.

Once more Eleanor attempted to submerge herself in the role she was playing. She lifted her chin and offered a thin smile of amusement.

"Do I look lost to you, gentlemen?" she asked.

The boxer stiffened and narrowed his eyes. "This is a private club, ma'am."

A trickle of sweat ran down the back of her neck. Eleanor was more nervous than even she had realized, but she refused to let it show.

"That's all very well, then, because I'm looking for some privacy," she told the man with the crooked nose. Eleanor stepped a bit closer to him, and saw the way he reacted to her presence. His eyes studied her face as though trying to figure out if he was supposed to recognize her from the pictures. "I'm supposed to meet a friend here tonight. Martin Goss."

"Look, honey—," the other doorman began.

But the boxer chuckled softly and shook his head, holding up a hand to forestall his partner's intervention. "You're a friend of Marty's, huh?"

Eleanor nodded.

The boxer stood aside with an almost courtly bow. "Then go right in, doll. I'm sure there's nothing in here that's going to surprise you."

"Nothing ever does," the Slayer said, favoring him with a wink before walking between the two men.

The boxer stepped over to open the door for her and he held it as she passed within. There was no foyer, but to both left and right a corridor ran the length of the building and a second door was just ahead. The music was even louder now, jazz with a sprightly piano and a whining trumpet. Cigarette smoke wafted out around the doorframe. Eleanor opened the door and blinked back the multicolored lights that shone in her eyes as she took several steps into the room.

The door swung closed behind her.

The Voodoo Lounge was far smaller than the Shangri-La, and

not nearly so well lit. The orange tips of cigarettes burned in the semidarkness of the club. Pure white tablecloths appeared gray. On the far side of the club the jazz band played, hot lights glistening on their dark skin. But despite the way the music reached inside her, reminding her of home, the band held Eleanor's attention for only the slightest fraction of a moment. Though she tried to hold her astonishment in check, she could not stop herself from gazing around at the tables as she strode farther into the club, searching for the face of Martin Goss in the crowd.

And oh, such a crowd.

She had only seen a photograph of Goss but thought she would recognize him, if not for the fact that every face in the crowd seemed a distraction to her. So many familiar profiles, misted in cigarette smoke or half lost in shadow, silhouetted by the lights from the stage. Hedy and Jean, Ty and Edward G. It was overwhelming to try to put names to the faces, but if she could have made a game of it, Eleanor suspected she would have done quite well.

Yet there were other faces as well, many of them far less elegant, some ugly, even hideous. *Freaks,* Walter had called them. But the Council of Watchers had another name for them.

Demons.

Eleanor shook herself, forced her feet to carry her through the club and her eyes to avert themselves from the terrible visages that mingled among the beautiful around her. On either side of the club was a bar and she listed to the left, hoping to find an empty seat there. That had been the plan to begin with, to ask the bartender about Goss. Bartenders were meant to know such things, or so American lore would have it. When Walter had spoken of monsters she had had images in her mind of mobsters, the enemies of Elliot Ness and his ilk.

But demons here? She passed a table where a needle-faced

brachen demon and a kailiff, its skin the color of rotten limes, sat with a pair of actors who had been in *Gone with the Wind* a year before. The actors she knew from the screen, the demons only from drawings she had been required to study and memorize.

Stunned, she made her way to the single empty seat she found at the bar. In a haze of smoke and laughter and the clinking of ice into glasses, she stared at the smooth, gleaming surface of the bar. For a time it seemed she stared at nothing, her mind lost in wondering what Martin Goss was doing frequenting a club where demons mingled with humans, and why the humans were still alive. The way the lights behind the bar and over on the stage struck the wooden surface, she could see her own reflection and the profiles of the man on her left and the statuesque woman on her right.

"What can I get you?"

The voice came from nowhere. Startled, Eleanor looked up to find yellow eyes gazing at her across the bar. No wonder he had surprised her. No wonder she had not seen his reflection.

The bartender was a vampire.

"What'll it be, sister? I haven't got all night," he said, all business.

"Actually," she said hesitantly, "I'm . . . I'm looking for someone."

Beside her, the statuesque woman laughed. "Aren't we all, sweetie? Aren't we all?"

The bartender raised an eyebrow, which only made his hideously ridged features appear more cruel. He sighed. "Give me a name. I've got drinks to make."

"Martin Goss."

The vampire smiled, fangs bared. Then he glanced at the tall woman with the silky voice. "Hear that, Grace? Marty's hooked another one." The bartender chuckled in derision and shot a pitying look at Eleanor. "Don't worry, honey. You hang around long enough, Marty'll be in."

The bartender turned and went down the bar, attending to his customers. Eleanor had a moment of uncertainty. She knew she ought to have continued prodding this bartender, then asked the one on the other side of the club. If that did not pan out, she could speak to the waitresses. But it occurred to her that it might be best to find out more about the Voodoo Lounge before she pushed her luck any further.

Eleanor began to slide off the seat. Which was when she at last got a good look at the woman beside her. Her breath caught in her chest.

"Grace McCandless," she said before she was even aware the words were being born from her lips.

That perfect face sparkled, full lips parting in a lazy smile. Grace McCandless blinked once, slowly and luxuriously, the same as they had done in half a dozen pictures that had played in the theater back home in the past few years. One of them, *Tears in Rain,* Eleanor had seen five times.

The actress did not even respond to Eleanor's recognition. The two stared at each other, Grace wearing an expression of weary benevolence.

"You really looking for Marty Goss?" the actress inquired at last.

Eleanor nodded. "It's pretty important that I find him, Miss McCandless," she said, forgetting completely that she was meant to be masquerading as an actress herself.

"Poor thing," Grace replied. She took a cigarette from a silver case before her on the bar and the bartender raced back to light it for her. She nodded in thanks and then waited for the vampire to go away before turning to Eleanor again. Grace took a long drag on the cigarette, its tip blazing brightly.

"Marty hasn't come around in a while. But if he does, you should run the other way. I can tell you're new in town, but are you so green you don't know sleeping with the writer isn't going to help your career? And Marty has a reputation, dear. You think this place is strange? He's always the weirdest fellow in the room."

"I don't plan to sleep with him, Miss McCandless. I just need to find him."

Grace shrugged, and even that she did with style. "Suit yourself, honey. Don't say I didn't warn—"

The trumpet blew a sour note and the jazz screeched to a stop. Silence descended on the club. Eleanor saw the way Grace McCandless's gaze ticked past her, over her shoulder, and the fear welled up in the actress's eyes in that moment, all the veneer of her glamour stripped away.

The Slayer spun around, dropping from the chair and instinctively drawing herself up into a battle stance.

A few feet inside the door of the Voodoo Lounge stood a creature more than seven feet tall, with enormous curving horns and a face that seemed little more than blue skin stretched across a huge skull. Over its shoulder the creature carried a second, but his burden was silent and unmoving. Both wore long, dark coats, but the one who staggered into the club under the weight of the other had stains across the front of his coat. The demon being carried was missing a horn and there was a hole in its skull where it had been torn away. Bits of tissue and gristle hung from that wound. It took Eleanor a moment to see that one of its arms was also gone.

"Virgil!" the skull-faced, blue demon bellowed into the silence of the club. Then his face tightened, grief making it all the more frightening, and the creature dumped his burden, the corpse of what was clearly his kinsman, on the floor.

"Virgil!" the demon called again into the silence of the club. "They've done it again!" He fell to his knees, bone colliding loudly with the wooden floor. "They've done it again."

II

A susurrus of gasps and whispers floated through the Voodoo Lounge like the fog of cigarette smoke that swirled around the ceiling fans. Eleanor pushed away from the bar, starting toward the grieving, wounded demon who knelt before the corpse of his kinsman just inside the doors of the club. Dapper men and glamorous women gazed on, more in fascination than in horror, but they never set down their martinis or their cigarettes.

A hand clasped her arm. Eleanor spun to find Grace McCandless giving her a sympathetic yet cautionary look.

"Stay out of it, honey. This isn't your town."

Eleanor frowned. "As I understand it, ma'am, this isn't anybody's town."

She tugged her arm out of the actress's grasp and quickly made her way through the ring of spectators that had begun to gather. There was a strange jostling and shuffling in the crowd and she glanced around, realizing that a wordless segregation had begun to occur among them. With few exceptions, the humans and demons in the Voodoo Lounge were shying away from one another. Their faces were filled with anger, resentment, sadness, and fear, and yet so very few of them seemed at all surprised.

That disturbed her the most. *Why is no one shocked by this?*

The circle of onlookers had left a respectful distance between themselves and the dead demon. Eleanor crossed her hands almost demurely as she approached the cerulean-skinned demon who knelt by the corpse. Its ramlike horns seemed to drag its head downward so that its chin was on its chest, but she knew it was the monster's grief to blame.

Slowly, so as not to alarm the demon, she knelt by the corpse as well. Standing, the grieving creature was at least seven feet tall. Even with both of them kneeling it towered over her, and when she got down next to the corpse of its kinsman, its nostrils flared, stretching the thin blue skin farther across its skull. Its eyes flashed an unnatural red and it sniffed at the air. After a moment, however, the hostile aspect of its countenance disappeared and those eyes only seemed sad. Eleanor thought it must have learned from her scent that her intentions were not malicious.

"What do you want, girl?" it asked, voice racing up her spine and making her shiver.

"To help, if I can."

The demon snorted. Its breath plumed from its mouth with the odor of rotting garbage. Eleanor tried not to inhale close by it, and not to think about what it had eaten to produce such a stench. It narrowed its eyes to slits.

"Your humor is ill timed," it told her.

The Slayer met the thing's gaze and she felt that it saw the truth in her eyes. "What happened? Who did this? You said 'they've done it again.' Who has?"

Its eyes fluttered closed and its lips peeled back to reveal fangs. For a moment she thought it was enraged, but then she heard the groan that came from the demon's chest and she realized that the monster had simply sighed. A shudder went through it and it returned its attention to the corpse. Eleanor noticed so many things about the creature in that moment, curious as to its species. There were ridges all along its horns, and the horns themselves seemed covered with a leathery skin, save for the tips, which protruded like fangs at the end of each horn.

The spectators had been chattering throughout this exchange and the music still played in the background, for in spite of the unsettling arrival of the demon and its dead kin, most of the club's patrons had paused only a moment before returning to their revelry. Whatever this was, it did not concern them. They were aloof, certain that the management would handle it with expediency.

It grunted and glanced up to glare at her again. "Who are you, girl? You have a scent unlike anything I've ever—"

The demon was interrupted by the arrival of a dapper, fiftyish man whose tanned features and silver hair and mustache gave him the air of a film star, though there was not even a flicker of recognition in Eleanor's mind. If the man was an actor, she had never seen him before.

"Obrigor?" the silver-haired man said, his tone curt and businesslike, though his face revealed sympathy. "Arkonis, is he . . ?"

The demon, Obrigor, was clearly relieved by the man's arrival. Obrigor gazed at him with deep sadness and nodded. "My brother is dead. I thought it was over. But it isn't." The blue skin pulled more tautly across his skull structure and Obrigor gazed down at the corpse. "They're still at it, Virgil. They're still at it."

"Who are *they*?" Eleanor asked quietly.

Obrigor stared at her and the Slayer felt upon her the gazes of the many spectators who still ringed the scene. For just a moment she glanced around, but when she saw that Virgil also was staring at her, his brows knitted in suspicion, she grew very still.

The silver-haired man seemed about to interrogate her, but then he became aware again of the crowd around him. He turned, blocking Obrigor and his dead brother—and Eleanor as well—from most of the spectators, and held up his hands in a placating gesture.

"Folks, listen, there's nothing more to see here. Give Obrigor some breathing room. A tragedy has taken place. Please, Mr. Selznick, Mr. Fleming, go back to your seats. Yes, David, I'll be over in a few minutes. The whole club will get a round on the house. I'm going to speak with Obrigor and we'll take care of all this."

Reluctantly, people began to return to their seats. It seemed to Eleanor that the musicians were playing a bit louder, the horns bleating a bit more jauntily than before, as if taking their signal from Virgil out of instinct. Several people hung back, pausing to whisper quietly to Virgil. All the breath went out of Eleanor and her chest hurt as she caught sight, for the first time, of one of the men stealing a moment of Virgil's time. She had loved Gable since *It Happened One Night*.

A moment later Grace McCandless took Gable by the hand and led him toward the bar, giving Eleanor a reproachful glance.

Virgil shooed away the others who had hung back and at last turned to Obrigor and Eleanor. The Slayer hesitated a moment but he made no attempt to send her away so she remained.

"What can I do for you, Obrigor?" Virgil asked. "Is there someone I can call?"

Obrigor shook his head. "If there is a place I can lay my brother down, I will contact others of my kin and they will come. We will have Arkonis's . . . remains . . . away from here as quickly as possible."

Virgil nodded, then turned and beckoned a waiter, who responded immediately. "Jason, is it? Show Obrigor to one of the private rooms in back."

The waiter, who might have been called Jason, nodded. Obrigor stood at last, reaching down to hoist up his brother's corpse. The waiter was off in an instant, leading Obrigor from the room. The dancing and socializing clubgoers parted to make way for them, and then with a single ripple the path closed behind them. No one seemed to have paid any attention at all to the funereal procession that had weaved among them.

Virgil rounded on Eleanor. "Now you, honey." His eyes were narrowed dangerously. "What's your story?"

She was hesitant, unsure how much she ought to share. "I . . . just wanted to help."

He waved a finger at her. "No, see, that would mean you were just nosy. And I've got a sense there's more to you than that. Nosy southern girls don't walk into a Hollywood nightclub with film stars and demons and offer their condolences when somebody dumps a dead cyxiff bluetip on the floor."

Eleanor could feel upon her the surreptitious eyes of a number of clubgoers who were attempting to pick up bits of this exchange as inconspicuously as possible. She glanced around her. Virgil caught what she was doing and he also looked about, a scowl on his face.

"It's none of my business," she told him. "I wanted to help. That was all. I came here looking for a friend—"

"What friend?" Virgil demanded.

"May I assume you're the manager here?"

He laughed softly and rolled his eyes. "Would this crowd pay any attention to me if I wasn't? Yes, I'm the manager. Virgil Moncuse."

Eleanor allowed one corner of her mouth to creep up into the semblance of a smile as she offered her hand to him. "Eleanor Boudreau."

"Pleased to meet you, miss," Virgil replied, completing the ritual. "Now, who's the friend you were looking for?"

"Martin Goss."

Virgil stared at her, then sighed, reaching up to massage his eyes and the bridge of his nose. When he opened his eyes again it was with an expression that suggested he had hoped Eleanor would disappear while they were closed. He shook his head and took her hand.

"Come with me."

But when Virgil turned around several people were blocking his way. One was an actor, Darrell something, whom she recognized but could not recall from where. The other faces weren't familiar, though one of the men, a tall fellow with sparkling eyes and thin, hawklike features, was striking.

"Not now, boys," Virgil told them. "I'll be with you in a minute."

The tall man held up a hand. "I hope so, Virgil. If things like this keep happening, there won't be much of a crowd left for you to deal with. I understand that the riffraff are among your clientele, but I wasn't aware this was their morgue."

Virgil took a deep breath, as though steadying his temper. "Mr. Sackett . . . Lew . . . in a minute. I swear to you."

Eleanor recognized the name. Lew Sackett had directed some of the most popular movies RKO had ever produced. But Virgil Moncuse was surrounded by powerful people every night and he was not about to be intimidated. He waved Sackett away and pulled Eleanor across the club.

Though the idea of being tugged along like a schoolgirl brought up within her the urge to pummel Moncuse within an inch of his life, Eleanor allowed herself to be led on a seemingly circuitous route to the far end of the left-side bar, not far from the stage where the jazzmen played. A large man with a saxophone caught sight of her and raised his eyebrows suggestively. Though she would normally have been offended, there was something playful about him and Eleanor smiled.

In that rear corner of the club there were only a handful of people at the bar. The music was too loud for most people who hoped to have a conversation, but the Voodoo Lounge's manager was obviously more concerned about finding a bit of privacy. He signaled the young, blandly handsome bartender, who finished serving a glass of wine to a woman and then joined them at the end of the bar.

"Darien, I don't want to be disturbed. Got it?"

Though Eleanor could not decide if Darien was the man's first name or his last, the bartender nodded and took a few steps back along the bar, turned his back to them and stood with his arms crossed like a bodyguard. Anyone who bothered to even look in this direction would realize that the conversation she was about to have with Virgil Moncuse was off limits.

The manager narrowed his gaze and stared at her, the lights glinting off his silver hair and mustache.

"You'd be the Slayer, then?" Virgil asked.

Eleanor blinked in surprise. "I don't know what that is."

The man sniffed impatiently. "Don't be coy with me, sweetheart. You're the right age. You're looking for Marty Goss, who used to be one of those damned watchers. Look around you. I run the Voodoo Lounge. It's my business to know this kind of thing. And Marty was always good for a story or two when he'd been drinking." He leaned in closer to her and she caught the scent of cloves on his breath. "What I want to know is, are you here about the killings?"

"I told you. I'm looking for Martin Goss."

He looked at her a long moment and then nodded, satisfied with the answer. "You've really stepped into the middle of something, Ellie."

She winced. Only her grandmother had ever called her Ellie and she was not at all fond of the nickname. Eleanor gazed at Virgil, waiting for him to continue. He seemed reluctant, but then he forged ahead.

"We get all kinds in here," the manager said, gesturing to indicate the club. "Live and let live, you know? The reason this place is so hot is that it gives normal humans the chance to brush up against the darkness. It gives them a thrill. As for the demons, well, they like movies as much as anyone. Makes some of them feel like celebrities to be able to rub shoulders with the film people. Most of the demons who come in here are harmless."

Eleanor frowned. "I saw vampires—"

Virgil nodded. "They're scum. But as long as they don't start any trouble, we're not going to turn them away. Part of the allure of the place. Anyway, I'm getting off track here. The point is, someone's been killing demons in the neighborhood. All of them have been my customers. All of the attacks have been at night, not too far from here."

Like the tumblers of a lock clicking into place, bits of the puzzle fell together in her mind. "Someone following them from the club," the Slayer said, her gaze sliding around the room, thoughts processing this new information. "That's what happened to Obrigor's brother."

Eleanor looked at Virgil closely. "Nobody's seen Martin Goss for a while. He's a former watcher. You think he's responsible?"

Virgil was pensive. After a moment he tilted his head slightly and regarded her. "Honestly, I don't know what to believe. I will tell you this much, though. There are a bunch of demons who have decided to hunt this killer themselves, a kind of lynch mob. If they caught wind of what Marty used to do for a living, they'd be looking at him very closely. Which brings me to my point."

The manager glanced around then leaned in even closer. His eyes were steely and cold. "You're the Slayer, Ellie. This mob finds out you're in town, chances are they're going to take a close look at you, too."

But Virgil Moncuse did not need to explain this to her. Eleanor had made that cognitive leap the moment he had revealed the presence of this so-called lynch mob. It was entirely possible Martin Goss was hunting demons in Los Angeles. His history of erratic behavior was well documented. And if it *wasn't* Martin, he could be in grave danger. Her job was to find Goss and bring him back to London, and that was precisely what she planned to do. But the club manager was right; she was going to have to be very careful.

"Can I speak to Obrigor?"

For a long moment it seemed almost as if Virgil had not understood the question. Then he sighed and nodded. "If he'll talk to you. I'll take you back there."

Virgil headed for a door at the left of the stage. Eleanor stepped away from the bar to follow, but as she did she noticed the bartender, Darien, watching her. Caught looking, he turned quickly away. For a moment Eleanor watched him as he began wiping down the bar, jittery, purposefully avoiding her gaze. Darien had been eavesdropping. Eleanor could not help wondering how much the bartender had heard, and how much of it would have made any sense to him.

In the back of the club the jazz was only a dull thumping in the walls. Virgil led her down a corridor. There were a number of rooms here that were clearly meant for private parties. High, girlish laughter erupted from several. Others were silent and at their doors Virgil knocked and then ducked his head in, in search of Obrigor. Behind a red door in the second corridor they tried—not far from what was obviously the rear exit of the Voodoo Lounge—they found the creature Virgil had called a cyxiff bluetip. Eleanor mentally cataloged the species name for later research, presuming that the second word was merely a reference to the exposed tips of the demon's horns.

When Virgil rapped on the door and pushed it open, Eleanor caught sight of Obrigor. He was kneeling beside his brother's corpse with his entire upper body extended forward, his arms stretched out, palms and forehead touching the ground. *Some sort of ritual prayer*, Eleanor surmised.

At their intrusion the cyxiff raised his heavy head and narrowed those red eyes. His gaze shifted from Virgil to the Slayer and back.

"Who is she?"

Virgil met the demon's gaze firmly. "She said she wanted to help. She meant it. I think maybe she can, if you'll answer a couple of questions."

Obrigor rose to his feet, unfolding until he stood at his full height, towering over them. He moved up to Eleanor and once again he breathed in her scent. A curious expression crossed his grim features.

"Not an ordinary girl," Obrigor noted.

"No. No, I'm not," Eleanor agreed, raising her chin to meet his gaze.

Obrigor grunted, as if in satisfaction. "Ask your questions."

"Only two," she said, not wanting to disturb him any more than necessary. "Did you discover your brother like this, or were you there when it happened?"

Azure lips peeled back from ice-blue fangs and a strange gray tongue danced in the demon's mouth as he spoke. "We were on our way here, across the rooftops. Arkonis caught the scent of something in an alley and descended. He was easily distracted, my brother." Obrigor paused to glance at the corpse with regret. "He glided into the alley and I went on, frustrated with yet another delay. Moments later I felt his pain—it is a bond my kin share—and I returned to the alley. He was wounded, unconscious. Dying."

Eleanor stared at him. A foolish question rose to her lips— *You can fly?*—but obviously the demon had just said as much.

Fly, or glide at least. She wondered if this was some magical power or if the cyxiff could grow some kind of wings. Instead she examined what he had told her. She had not learned much at all. All the Slayer could do was ask her second question.

"Can you show me where it happened?"

Obrigor shook his head ruefully. "I will not ever return to that place. Not in all my lives. But I will tell you how to find it."

Their driver, Walter, found the alley with little difficulty. It ran behind a row of shops and offices and a grand old hotel called the Hyperion. Miss Fontaine instructed the driver to park just a short way from the hotel and Eleanor got out of the car.

"Aren't you coming?" the Slayer asked her Watcher.

Marie-Christine Fontaine deliberated this for a moment. Eleanor wanted her to come along, not for protection or strength in numbers or anything like that—she could take care of herself—but because she did not trust herself to analyze the scene of the crime the way Miss Fontaine might. The woman had been a watcher for decades.

But Miss Fontaine shook her head. "I think not. You've been doing quite well on your own thus far, and if you are to skulk around an alleyway, you'll likely be less conspicuous on your own than with an old woman such as myself in tow. Skulking is work best done solo."

Eleanor was disappointed, but she agreed. It probably was for the best. "You'll be right here, though?"

The driver turned around in his seat. "We won't move, miss. Not an inch," he said, though he seemed troubled. He hesitated only a moment before going on. "Look, you two will forgive me, I hope. I don't usually poke my nose into the client's business, but are you sure this is a good idea? Drivers are supposed to pretend to be deaf, but I couldn't help overhearing. If someone was killed back there and—well, if you're dead set on going back there, you shouldn't go alone."

Miss Fontaine had seemed charmed by Walter previously, but now she gave him a hard look. "Perhaps you ought to rely upon the wisdom of your profession, sir. Your concern is noted and appreciated, but it is also, I must inform you, unwelcome."

Walter looked properly chagrined, his mouth twisting into a sour expression. Eleanor smiled at him.

"It's sweet of you to worry. But I'll be right as rain," she promised.

The driver did not look convinced but wisely chose to say no more on the subject. Miss Fontaine nodded to Eleanor and the Slayer left the car. She strode quickly the half a block to the hotel, then turned right and walked briskly alongside it until she came to the service alley in back. That narrow, paved path would allow deliveries and garbage pickup and repair trucks to visit the hotel and the other buildings here without blocking traffic on the main road.

But it was dark and remote, with a high wooden fence separating it from a similar alley that ran behind the buildings on the parallel block. The shadows seemed to whisper back here, though Eleanor knew it was likely just the wind. Sometimes it was difficult to know the difference. Ever since she had become the Slayer, Eleanor had looked at every shadow with new eyes, realizing that it was possible that there was more to it than mere darkness. Sometimes the shadows were just shadows. But now that she knew there was more than one kind of darkness, there were threats everywhere.

The Slayer was always on guard.

A comforting glow surrounded the hotel, emanating from the Hyperion's windows. Now, though, she turned right again and headed along the alleyway, moving away from that glow and deeper into the darkness. Her eyes adjusted easily—one of the benefits she had discovered comes with being Chosen—and she picked up the pace.

With only the dim illumination of the moon and stars and the distant, diffuse lights of the city to save her from total darkness, Eleanor peered carefully at everything she passed. Trash cans, piles of wooden slats, oil cans, an abandoned, stripped-down bicycle, the recessed doorways of half a dozen buildings.

But it was the scent of blood that told her she had arrived at her destination. The air was redolent with the rich, copper tang of it. A tremor of sadness passed through her, an isolated moment in which she was aware that there was something tragic about a girl her age being familiar with the smell of blood.

Then it was gone and Eleanor was purely the Slayer, prowling that alley. All her senses were finely tuned. She heard every nuance of sound, the rustle of loose newspaper blowing along the pavement, the distant noise of car engines, and the drip of a leaking pipe nearby. Her eyes were wide, taking in all the available light, attempting to make sense of the darkness. The pavement. The rear wall of the brick building to her right, the fence to her left.

On the ground, a glint of metal.

Eleanor paused. Her throat was dry, her heart beating wildly in her chest. Her fingers were curved as though they were claws, a strange involuntary twitch that unnerved her. She shook her hands out, flexed her fingers, and glanced up and down the alley, then up at the windows of the darkened building above her.

She had fought demons, slain creatures of myth and, under controlled circumstances, killed a vampire. But in truth she had been the Slayer only a very short time and investigating dark alleys in which the presence of evil could be tasted on the very air was still new to her.

Eleanor Boudreau was afraid.

Cautiously she crouched by the metal object that lay on the pavement. Its razor edges gleamed in the starlight, and her fingers traced the ornate, heavy metal handle of the thing. *Of the weapon.* Eleanor picked it up and turned it so that it caught more light, and her initial impression was confirmed. It was a katar, a punching dagger of Indian origin. From her studies she knew that it had been developed for use in stabbing through chain mail, but it could also be helpful in piercing the tough hide many demons had.

There was dark blood crusted on the triangular blade, but where the edges were clean she could make out symbols etched in the metal. *Probably magickal,* she thought. *A ritual weapon.* Miss Fontaine would be able to tell her for certain.

Eleanor held the katar loosely in her right hand and stood up. Carefully she studied the scene of the assault again. The Slayer tilted back her head and looked up at the rooftop above. Obrigor had said that his brother had been flying and had been drawn down into the alley by something that caught his attention. Someone bearing a weapon with special properties to aid in its effectiveness in killing demons had lured Arkonis here. It all fit what Virgil Moncuse had told her: someone hunting demons.

That was the Slayer's job, of course, but Eleanor had no interest in killing benevolent creatures, no matter their dimensional origin or the presumptions about their species. Demons were disgusting things. They made her skin crawl. But they weren't all evil.

Someone was hunting them for sport.

Martin Goss? she wondered. But that question was for later.

With a final glance around, she turned to retrace her steps.

Something made her stop, some stimulus niggling at the back of her mind. Eleanor paused, eyes closing for a moment as she tried to figure out what was bothering her, what had stood out for her.

The scent of blood. That familiar smell.

But cyxiff blood wasn't like human blood. She wouldn't be familiar with the odor of cyxiff blood. That copper, meaty smell . . . it wasn't from the murder of a demon. It could have been an animal, but . . .

The dripping sound. A leaking pipe.

Or perhaps not.

Eleanor turned, katar now held in her hand not as an artifact or piece of evidence, but as a weapon, and started to move farther along the alley. There was a narrow gap no more than eight feet wide between the brick building to her right and the bank next door. Inside that gap was a wrought iron fire escape that connected the two structures.

The corpse dangled from the fire escape. A man. His shirt was open, stomach torn apart, and he had been strangled and hanged with his own intestines. Starlight shone on his dead eyes and on his blood, which had pooled on the ground beneath him. The drip-drip-dripping sound was no leaking pipe.

Bile burned the back of Eleanor's throat and it was all she could do not to vomit. Tears stung the corners of her eyes, but she forced herself not to cry as she clapped her free hand over her mouth and took a step backward.

On the brick wall someone had painted six enormous letters in the dead man's blood. It glinted almost as brightly as the edge of the katar blade in the light from the stars and the glow of the city of Los Angeles.

The message was one word: KILLER.

Eleanor took another step back, then was startled as a bright white light shone down the alley. Someone shouted at her. A car engine roared and a red light splashed like blood on the walls.

The police. Someone had called the police.

"You there! Stay where you are!"

The Slayer ran.

III

Despite their penchant for clandestine behavior, Eleanor had been very pleased to discover that the Council of Watchers were not averse to comfort. Her previous experience with them had consisted of a violently bloody train journey and an airplane ride that had clearly been arranged at the last minute, and during which she often felt like imported fruit rather than a human being. Fortunately, in the aftermath of events earlier in the year, her journey back to the United States had been far more comfortable. The greatest surprise of all had been the Pacific Paradise Hotel, a small, luxurious Santa Monica inn that overlooked the ocean.

Tonight, however, her ability to take pleasure in the comforts offered by the hotel had been obliterated. The memory of the man who had been eviscerated in that alley was still burned into her mind. The image of him dangling there lingered in her head and she did not think she would ever be able to erase it. Eleanor had barely managed to elude the police. If not for the enhanced strength, speed, and agility that were her gifts as the Chosen One, they would have found her in front of the corpse with a bloody, antique blade in her hand. The police would not likely have been able to identify the katar, but that would not have kept them from putting her in a jail cell.

"You'll be all right," Miss Fontaine told her.

Eleanor glanced tiredly at her Watcher as they walked up the stairs at the back of the hotel lobby together. Marie-Christine was quite an enigma, as tough a woman as God had ever created and yet capable of extraordinary tenderness as well. In that way, the Slayer aspired to follow her example.

"I know," Eleanor replied with a sigh, hand gliding up the banister as she ascended the stairs. "Sleep. Sunshine. If I can just get a little of both, I'll be all right. Y'all ought to get some sleep as well. Seems like Mr. Goss is involved in this mess somehow. I haven't figured out exactly how just yet. But I will."

Miss Fontaine smiled. "I know you will."

Eleanor thought that perhaps she had underestimated the power of the hotel's comforts after all. As they reached their floor—the long hallway with deep red floral patterns on the wallpaper—she could almost feel the siren call of the soft bed in her room. With the window open she would be able to hear the gentle shush of the Pacific Ocean on the shore just across the street.

"I'm going to fall asleep before we reach the door." The Slayer released a long breath and let herself be led to their room. Miss Fontaine opened the door. From the darkness within that chamber their came a strong, cool breeze, laden with the salt of the ocean. Ghostly curtains billowed in what little light slipped in from the street, a gossamer veil shimmering in the dark.

Holding the door open, Miss Fontaine favored the Slayer with a look of abiding fondness. They had been thrown together in the aftermath of catastrophe, and other than training sessions and an initial supervised field excursion, this was really their first assignment together.

"You did well tonight," the Watcher said as Eleanor entered the room.

The Slayer froze, barely noting the words. Adrenaline surged through her, all her exhaustion purged from her body by the sudden rush of blood in her veins and by the instinctive alertness of her senses. The air in the room was redolent with other odors than that of the sea. Something shifted in the deeper shadows. She heard it. Saw just the slightest striations of dark on dark off to her right.

Eleanor held up one hand to indicate that Miss Fontaine should wait at the door. The Watcher narrowed her eyes, studying the shadowy interior. With a fluid motion, the Slayer settled into a combat position, eyes slitted as she peered into the corner.

"You've made a mistake, coming here," she said, noting the hint of danger in her own voice and strangely startled by it. "Show yourself."

The darkness in the corner seemed almost to convulse and then a figure emerged from it, blacker than the shadows, and yet limned with the dim illumination that came in through the windows. Its eyes were a gleaming emerald green and as it stood, its body seemed to unfold until it stood so tall that it stooped to look down upon them. Its lower body was serpentine, its torso and arms hideously reminiscent of a praying mantis, and there were flat black leathery things that lay on its back and could only have been wings.

"Eleanor—," Miss Fontaine began, alarm in her voice.

The Slayer held up a hand, glaring at the intruder. It had entered their room, but it seemed in no hurry to attack, only to present itself. Slowly she reached inside the long coat that her Watcher had put around her and withdrew the bloodstained katar she had retrieved from the alley.

It sniffed the air and flinched, its back scraping the ceiling as part of its body recoiled from her. "You will not need that, Slayer," it said, each word a kind of snort or grunt, summoned from deep inside the demon's gullet. "Vosen comes to help."

She held the katar tightly in her right hand, the left held up in defensive posture. "Explain."

Its lower body uncoiled further, its torso sliding across the ceiling, and its emerald eyes locked hypnotically upon hers as it loomed nearer. Eleanor was forced to gaze up at it, all the while keenly aware of how exposed her body was to attack. A thin rivulet of ropy saliva dribbled from its mouth and slapped the floor.

"Gossss," it groaned. "There are whispers on the street that say you seek Goss."

A shiver went through the Slayer. Most demons she had dealt with were at least humanoid, but she was unnerved by how unnatural this creature—*Vosen?*—was.

"And you know how to find him?" Eleanor asked.

Vosen hissed, the air whistling as it breathed in. "He is a . . . curious man, Goss. When he wants to know something, he asks me, and I help. I can do the same for you."

The Slayer took several cautious steps backward and glanced at Miss Fontaine.

"And we're to pay you, is that it?" the Watcher demanded.

The mantis creature withdrew slightly, its head ticking back and forth as it regarded each of them in turn. "When you find Goss. I come back here. You pay when you find Goss. Or Goss pay."

Eleanor glanced once more at Miss Fontaine, saw the resolve in her Watcher's eyes, and then turned to the demon again. Unconsciously her grip tightened on the katar.

"Deal."

Once upon a time the Imperial had been among the grandest theaters on the West Coast, one of the oldest in Los Angeles, and one of the very first to show moving pictures, never mind "talkies." Times had changed. Though she was still a grand old Hollywood dame, the Imperial had boards over her box office windows and the posters out in front were faded and torn from years of neglect. Heavy chains secured the doors and the only things that lurked within were the haunting memories of an earlier age.

The Great Depression had come and gone. America had moved on. The industrial revitalization that had come as a result of the war in Europe had given the entire nation the opportunity to pick itself up by its bootstraps. But there were those who had never risen out of the depression, those who had never gotten a chance to see the light at the end of that long tunnel.

Frank Marlowe had been one of those unfortunates. The Imperial had been his baby. Marlowe had kept the theater up wonderfully, bought the most beautiful red velvet curtains, the most up-to-date equipment, the most comfortable seats . . . which were also very heavy seats. Some called it luck that only seven people were killed when the balcony collapsed. Frank Marlowe wasn't one of them.

Already in debt beyond reason, Marlowe could not afford to repair the balcony. He could not afford to pay his employees, or the studios for that matter. The Great Depression was a burden all of America had to bear together, but Frank Marlowe had a whole slew of his own burdens to go on top of it. The Imperial was shuttered and chained and by the time the economy had turned around so that there were interested buyers, the red velvet curtains were moldy, the equipment had been stolen or ruined by vandals, and there had been wind damage to the roof that let the rain in, rotting wood and cloth and those luxuriously heavy seats.

Frank Marlowe had gone bankrupt and hanged himself from the remains of the Imperial's balcony. The property had been taken by the bank. Once a sparkling jewel in the Hollywood crown, the Imperial Theater was now a blemish on its alabaster skin.

All of this Eleanor and Miss Fontaine had learned from Walter during their drive from Santa Monica. The last thing the young Slayer and her Watcher had wanted was to rouse the driver after an already long evening, but the man had already been involved in their intrigue and proven trustworthy. It seemed unwise to risk involving anyone else at this point. Thus, Walter was summoned and appeared at around midnight. Though he claimed not to have been sleeping, his hair was attractively mussed and his eyes had a red tinge.

All things considered, Eleanor thought he looked fine, though she wouldn't have put voice to this opinion.

"You know a great deal about this city," Miss Fontaine said.

His amiable expression faltered, revealing a weariness that had nothing to do with the lateness of the hour and everything to do with the hopes he had had with him when he first came to Los Angeles.

"You spend enough time driving people with money around this city—actors, producers, real estate men—you hear almost every story there is. And the ones they don't know, you hear from hookers and cabbies when you hit the coffee shop on the corner."

Walter blinked, as though only now remembering who he was speaking to. He glanced in the rearview mirror. "Sorry, ladies. I hope I didn't offend you."

"Not at all," Miss Fontaine said thoughtfully. "Not at all."

They rode in a companionable silence for several minutes after that, and then Walter drew the car up to the curb in front of the Imperial Theater. It was everything he had described, and just looking at it made Eleanor's heart ache. Once upon a time it had obviously been grand indeed. Now it was an eyesore, with shattered lights on the marquee and broken glass jutting from behind boards hastily hammered in place.

Eleanor stepped out of the car and ducked her head down to glance in the window at Walter. "Pull down the street a little way. Be prepared to leave in a hurry if necessary. Otherwise, stay in the car. Keep an eye out. If you see something out of the ordinary, use the horn."

The corner of his mouth lifted in quiet amusement at the irony of taking instructions from a teenaged girl, but then Walter nodded. The passenger door opened and Miss Fontaine stepped out. Together they walked to the front of the theater. It was late at night and while some areas of Los Angeles were still quite lively, this block was nearly deserted. There were offices and shops and probably apartments above many of them, but very few lights were on. Most of the people in this neighborhood were asleep by now.

As Walter pulled the Bentley away from the curb, Eleanor went to the front of the Imperial and began tearing boards off the double doors. Nails shrieked as they were ripped free, rusty metal against wood, and she tossed them aside. Miss Fontaine said nothing, only silently urged the Slayer on with a dark look in her eyes. If Martin Goss was here, he must have entered a different way. That much was obvious. But searching for his convenient entrance would eat up valuable time, and they both felt that a more direct approach was preferable.

When the boards had been removed, only the heavy chains remained, looped through the brass handles on the double doors. Eleanor stepped backward, took a breath, and then shot a sideways kick at the doors. Most of the time, though she knew her true destiny, she felt like an ordinary girl. But the power, the raw strength, flowed through her. It felt good to use it. The brass door handles tore right out of the wood and the weight of the chains hauled them to the ground with a clank.

Gently Eleanor pushed the doors open.

The hinges squealed with disuse. The moonlight splashed through the open doors, illuminating a dance of swirling dust as a breeze stole into the theater lobby. The Slayer entered without hesitation, eyes narrowed and focused on every shadow as she slipped into the lobby. Miss Fontaine followed just as quickly, her hand slipping inside her jacket and withdrawing a long, thin, ornate dagger with a whisper of cloth.

"Will you be able to see well enough?" Eleanor asked, her voice low.

The Watcher nodded, standing just inside the lobby, letting her eyes adjust.

They moved swiftly after that. Working on opposite sides of the theater, they checked each nook and peered through the doors that led into the rest-rooms. Eleanor shot an inquisitive glance at Miss Fontaine, wondering if they should search the rest-rooms, but the Watcher shook her head and crooked a finger forward to indicate that they should move along.

On either side of the lobby was a grand staircase covered with moldy red carpet, apparently leading up to the ill-fated balcony. Given Walter's assertion that it had been destroyed, however, Eleanor thought they should search the rest of the theater before climbing those stairs. There were two sets of double doors leading into the theater proper, but as Eleanor tried the one nearest her she discovered it had been blocked by the collapse of the balcony. Thus the Slayer and her Watcher went in together through the only available entrance.

A dozen feet into the Imperial Theater, Eleanor had to pause, a pang of sadness and regret making her take a breath. Whatever stories Walter had heard about the Imperial were inadequate to describe the tragedy that had occurred here. In addition to the wreckage of the balcony off to their right, entire sections of seating had been crushed beneath a partial collapse of the roof. One

of the beams had given way, apparently rotted from water damage, and chunks of ceiling had fallen down into the theater. The
place was open to the sky, a victim of the elements. Years of sun
and wind and rain had had their way with the Imperial Theater.
The place stank of mold, the curtains were sodden and sagging
and one of them had been torn halfway down.

Slayer and Watcher exchanged a glance and a nod, and then
they parted, spreading out to continue their search of the theater. Miss Fontaine went to the aisle at the far left and started
down, glancing into each row for any hidden threat. Eleanor
used the central aisle, the back rows to her right covered by the
wreckage of the collapsed balcony. They started down toward
what had once been the main stage but now held the tattered
remnants of the movie screen. The two of them moved in silence, only the wind through the rotted roof to accompany
them.

The wind . . .

Eleanor froze, tensed, and closed her eyes to listen. There was
another sound in the abandoned theater and it wasn't merely the
settling of damp wood or the whisper of the wind through the
seats. It was a slow and rhythmic creak, an eerie metronome.
Cautiously Eleanor turned and glanced up at the portion of the
balcony that remained. Even in the dim light she could make out
more than she would have liked of the shape above her.

The hanging man's eyes were open and bulging, face a round
gasp for air that would never come. Like the victim in the alley
across town, the dead man's shirt was torn open and so was his
abdomen. This corpse, however, had been hanged not with his
own viscera but more traditionally, with heavy rope.

For only a moment Eleanor thought perhaps what she was
seeing was the ghost of Marlowe, the theater owner, whom legend said had hanged himself in precisely this spot. But then a

flicker of recognition went through her mind, in spite of the swollen, bruise-blue face of the corpse.

A tiny gasp drew her attention and Eleanor glanced over to find that Miss Fontaine had seen the dead man as well. "Martin," the Watcher whispered, and the pain in her eyes was terrible to see.

The Slayer felt an icy tingle along the back of her neck. They had found Martin Goss at last, but so had the demonic lynch mob that had taken matters into its own hands to avenge the murders of its kin. Even as this thought entered her mind, however, Eleanor knew she was wrong. There were pieces of the puzzle that did not fit so neatly once she examined them. One look at Goss and she knew he had been dead for days. The man in the alley earlier this evening had been a fresh kill.

Goss had been a suspect. But something had killed him *before* the murder of the cyxiff bluetip that had been murdered earlier tonight. Martin Goss could not have been the one sport-hunting for demons in Los Angeles. The rest of the pieces clicked into place then. If their serpentine informant, Vosen, knew Goss had been here, he probably also knew Goss was dead. There was only one way it all made sense.

The lynch mob was thirsty for vengeance. They still did not think they had caught their hunter, but were determined to keep killing until they were certain it was over. Now the Slayer was in town, looking for Martin Goss . . . and what was the Slayer's job description?

Of course they would jump to conclusions, she thought. *And of course they'd do something about it.*

"Damn it," Eleanor whispered, shooting a quick glance over at her Watcher and then moving swiftly into the row of seats that separated them. "Miss Fontaine," the Slayer said, "we've been set up."

A loud hiss filled the cavernous ruins of the theater. In the midst of the sodden, moldy seats, Eleanor twisted around to see Vosen slithering out from behind the crimson, half-torn curtain. A chittering noise came from above and she glanced up to see a trio of gnarled, yellow-skinned demons with deadly sharp talons crouching on the edges of the massive hole in the roof. Something shifted in the balcony above and the surviving cyxiff, Obrigor, jutted his horned head out to glare down at her.

"Slayer," Obrigor grunted. "It's time to put an end to the hunt."

There were grunts from the shadows on the far side of the theater and talons began to tear the movie screen up on the stage to tatters. Glass shattered somewhere and Eleanor could picture windows breaking, demons crashing in. They had waited for the Slayer and her Watcher to get into their snare, and now it was closing.

Adrenaline surged through Eleanor and it felt to her as though her blood burned through her veins. She could hear her own breathing, far too loud in her ears, but slow, measured, and for the first time in her life it was as though she had complete and utter control over every muscle, every motion. She had been Slayer for months, had fought and trained, done it all. But now all that training was being put to the test in a way it never had been before, and now she was all strength, all instinct.

Obrigor let out a roar, a kind of strange, unintelligible war cry, and leaped out from the ruined balcony, claws reaching for her even as he fell. Eleanor raced along between two rows of theater seats, running for Miss Fontaine. The Slayer sprang forward, grabbed hold of the arm of one of the seats, and launched herself into an aerial forward somersault, tucking her legs tightly and hoping her gown was not too much of a hindrance. The cyxiff demon crashed into the very same chair she had used to propel herself, shattering the seat. Obrigor was up instantly, but by then the Slayer had reached the aisle.

"Eleanor, what the hell are you doing?" Miss Fontaine demanded brusquely.

The Slayer did not face her, but rather turned to Obrigor and dropped into a defensive posture. "Protecting you, of course."

"Well, don't," the Watcher snapped, sniffing dismissively. "That's a fine way to get yourself killed. I'm not a young woman, Miss Boudreau, but I'm bloody well capable of protecting myself, thank you very much."

Obrigor was perhaps twenty feet away. His blue, leathery skin seemed almost black in the shadows of the theater and his face looked more like a skull than ever. Crimson eyes burned like embers in that skull and he lowered his head so that the vicious tips of his ram horns protruded toward her. Suddenly, though, the demon threw back his head and howled, a sound of rage and grief that echoed through the ruins of the theater.

Upon that signal, the others began to move. The bent, misshapen yellow demons that had perched on the edges of the hole in the roof now dropped down into the theater and began to scramble, capering sometimes on two limbs, sometimes on all fours, toward Eleanor. A tall monstrosity with only a smooth carapace where its face ought to have been emerged through the door from the foyer, and several hideously shaggy beasts ripped the rest of the way through the onstage screen and started for her.

Eleanor glanced at her Watcher, but the woman was already on the move. The Slayer was torn. All the confidence of a few moments before began to evaporate as she worried for Marie-Christine. Despite her assertions, she was too old for this. *And she has to know that her little dagger is not going to be much—*

From a distance of perhaps fifty feet, Miss Fontaine hurled her dagger at Vosen, even as the massive, serpentine demon began to slither over the tops of rows of seats, darting swiftly toward her. The dagger plunged into the demon's forehead with a crack of bone and a wet, sucking sound. Vosen flopped into a chair, head lolling back, dead.

Then, more quickly than Eleanor would ever have imagined, the Watcher reached into her coat again and from behind her back, as if by magick, she withdrew a *kau sin ke*. The weapon was Chinese in origin, a metal whip or flail constructed of five lengths of iron, with the topmost a heavy, deadly weight. Eleanor had trained briefly with it at Miss Fontaine's urging, but had only managed to hurt herself with the unwieldy instrument.

The Watcher swung the *kau sin ke* through the air and ran toward the bestial, hirsute demons that even now leaped from the stage.

"Nooo!" Obrigor screamed.

Eleanor twisted around, cursing herself for becoming distracted. The cyxiff was almost upon her, but was so enraged that it was not attempting to strike her or grab her, but instead had bent down to ram her with its blue-tipped horns, to eviscerate her. . . . Images flashed through her mind of the dead man in the alley, strangled with his own intestines, and of Martin Goss hanging from the balcony above.

Those horns, she thought.

But she wasn't about to let Obrigor do to her what he had done to the others. Her blood burned again, her body reacting to peril almost without interference between instinct and action. The Slayer reached out and grabbed hold of Obrigor's horns with both hands even as he charged at her. She flipped up and over him, holding on tight, her mind already gauging the angle and the strength needed to break the cyxiff's neck.

Obrigor bucked, his horns slid free. Eleanor twisted around in the air and barely managed to land in a crouch, her gown tearing along her left leg. Already Obrigor was charging her again, but he was not her sole concern. The trio of capering, yellow-skinned demons and the no-face beast were closing in as well, though they moved with caution.

Past Obrigor she spotted Miss Fontaine even as the shaggy beasts attacked her. The *kau sin ke* whickered through the air and there was the crack of bone as she caved in the skull of a demon and it slumped to the ground. But then the cyxiff was nearly upon her again, and Eleanor had to focus just to stay alive.

Its skull-face with that stretched, leathery skin was hideous, a nightmare come to life. Every urge within her was to kill Obrigor. Yet even as she leaped away, dodging the demon so that his horns cracked the wall behind her, other thoughts were in Eleanor's mind. Obrigor roared with fury as he discovered his horns were stuck in the wood of the wall. He rocked back and forth but they held fast.

The gnarled, grinning, jaundiced trio moved in on her then.

"Obrigor, listen!" the Slayer called.

She pulled the katar out from inside her jacket. The yellow-skinned demons danced in closer to her and Eleanor attacked. With more freedom to move now that her gown was torn, she snapped out a side kick and caught one of them in the chest, sending it crashing over ruined seats, even as she swung the katar, neatly slicing off the arm of a second. It shrieked in agony and astonishment, clutched a stump that spurted bright orange blood, and staggered back. Eleanor took that moment to move on the third one. It tried to attack, its talons raked her shoulder, but in the next moment she drove her right fist forward, clutching the katar. The wide blade punched through the demon's chest and its tip protruded from the monster's spine in back.

Orange blood spattered her face and the Slayer wiped it off.

The one-armed demon was on the ground, twitching, barely conscious from blood loss. The one she had kicked into the seats was crawling over them, moving toward her even more warily than before. Behind her, the faceless thing with the armor-like carapace covering its head came toward her and it opened a tiny mouth to let out a chittering noise, like a million screaming crickets.

Eleanor put her back to the wall, keeping the insectoid, faceless thing to her right, the capering demon in front of her, and Obrigor to her left. The cyxiff gave a final roar and tore his horns from the wall. He rounded on the Slayer and snarled at her, spitting in rage, crimson eyes blazing in that skull face.

"I'll string the walls with your guts, girl!"

All three demons paused, looking for an opening. Eleanor crouched, katar clutched in her hand, gaze shifting to watch for any attack.

"You're a damn fool, Obrigor," the Slayer snapped. "So you heard the Slayer was in town, asking around about Martin Goss. Well, Goss was my only reason for being there. You think I'm your killer just 'cause that's my job? I don't kill peaceful demons. That's not what being the Slayer is about. If you're not a threat to humanity . . ."

"None of that matters. Listen to me. It would be easy for you to verify that I wasn't here. I couldn't be the killer. We only just arrived in this country. I could show you my travel papers. I want to stop this killer just as badly as you do."

Obrigor snorted, began to crouch, lowering his horns for a run at her. "So what do you expect us to do? Believe you? Believe the Slayer? Work together? Do you think we're that foolish?"

The yellow-skinned creeper clambered across the last of the seats and dropped into the aisle in front of her, hissing. To her right the chittering, insectoid, faceless demon took a step nearer and she saw its long tongue dart into the air in front of her, sharp and swift, possibly deadly.

"No," the Slayer said, her gaze ticking toward Obrigor. "Not that it matters. I *couldn't* work with you. You're murderers, just as bad in your way as the killer you're hunting. He's killing for sport and in your way, so are you. You've made a mistake. But it isn't your first one. Now it's my turn to hunt."

With a sweeping glare that took all of them in, Eleanor Boudreau scowled. "Feel free to run."

Obrigor laughed. "Kill her."

The creeper and the faceless one attacked simultaneously. Eleanor moved fluidly, dodging the creeper's talons and ducking behind it. She grabbed the yellow-skinned demon in a choke hold with her left arm and spun it around to use it as a shield. The faceless insectoid impaled the creeper with its tongue. Eleanor knew its carapace was like armor, that it might protect the demon from her blade. But she had waited for that opening. When it opened its mouth to chitter loudly, furious that its attack had failed, she rammed her fist forward and punched the katar into its mouth at an upward angle, shearing off the top of its head and spilling dark, fetid brain along her fingers.

The Slayer whirled, still holding the creeper's corpse, to face Obrigor.

But the cyxiff was gone.

The sound of applause filled the ruined theater. Eleanor twisted around to find Marie-Christine Fontaine sitting on the edge of the stage, clapping softly, and catching her breath. At her feet were strewn the corpses of a trio of stinking, hairy bestial demons.

Eleanor wanted to smile but found she could not.

Not until this was over.

IV

Most of the city had shut down, but the Voodoo Lounge was still swinging. As Walter drove them up to the front of the club Eleanor spotted an elegantly dressed woman staggering toward a

Bentley with a man on either arm. The woman was clearly drunk and had to pause a moment and bend slightly, one hand to her mouth, prepared to vomit on the sidewalk. Fortunately the urge seemed to pass, for a moment later her male companions poured her into the Bentley, then gave each other a conspiratorial smile before climbing into the car.

As the Bentley pulled away, Walter slid their own car up to the curb in its place. He put the car in park and then paused a moment, not looking around at them. All through this ride back to the Voodoo Lounge in the wee hours of the morning he had been silent, nothing like the amiable Walter they had known. Eleanor had so much on her mind that she had barely noticed at first. Now, however, she reached for the door handle and then paused to glance into the rearview mirror, catching his eye there.

"You have something to say?"

He turned in the seat, even more handsome now that he was so obviously troubled. Walter nodded at the gashes on her arm. "I've been pretty good about keeping my mouth shut. That's what drivers are paid for. You wouldn't believe the things I've seen in my mirror up here."

The driver's features softened and he glanced away a moment before focusing on her eyes again. "I could get fired just for suggesting it, but I was thinking after we've all had some sleep, that maybe I could buy you a cup of coffee tomorrow. And now I see you come out of the Imperial with those cuts, the two of you looking like you've been in a prizefight, and I'm thinking if you go back into the Voodoo Lounge tonight, I might never get the chance to have that coffee with you. I think I should come with you."

A delicious thrill danced across her belly and Eleanor felt her face flush. She allowed herself a tiny smile. "Why, sir, I do believe that's the oddest bit of courting I've ever come across," she said, letting her Louisiana accent come into full bloom. "You're sweet, Walter. I'd love to have coffee with you tomorrow."

Her eyes hardened. "But for the moment, you stay right here. I have one last question I need answered."

The Slayer popped open her door and started to climb out of the car. She paused with one foot on the sidewalk, and turned to smile at her Watcher, whose hand she had held for the entire drive from the Imperial Theater to the Voodoo Lounge.

"Miss Fontaine?" she asked.

The woman lifted her eyebrows, her expression filled with a sense of decorum that somehow belied the bloodshed they had just engaged in. "We've been at this together long enough, Eleanor," the Watcher said. "Please. Call me Marie-Christine."

Once again a rush of warmth went through the Slayer. She smiled and nodded. "I just . . . I wanted you to know that I've always thought you were something. *Really* something, you know? But even with that, I underestimated you. It won't happen again. You're a remarkable woman and I'm proud to know you."

Miss Fontaine smiled. "Thank you, dear. Now, why not finish this business so we can get some sleep?"

"Yes, ma'am," Eleanor replied. "And . . . I'm sorry about Mr. Goss."

The Watcher's smile disappeared and her gaze seemed suddenly very far away. "As am I, Ellie. As am I."

Eleanor slammed the car door and headed for the Voodoo Lounge. Other people were leaving the club now, many of them glassy-eyed and staggering, their minds flying on booze or something more insidious. There were faces she recognized, famous faces she had once admired, but Eleanor could not look at them now. She feared that her enjoyment of motion pictures would be forever soiled by her brief visit to Los Angeles and by the blood and cruelty that she had found here.

On that dark side street in Santa Monica, the city would be waking up in a few hours. Workers would arrive soon enough at the warehouse and the office building on either side of the club. But there was still some time for the creatures of the night—both human and otherwise—to thrive at the Voodoo Lounge.

As she strode up to the featureless door in the middle building with the darkened windows shuttered from the inside, the sound of jazz horns and rhythmic drums whispered out into the street. The same two broad-shouldered goons who had accosted her earlier stepped away from their posts by the door and blocked her path. It was obvious in their faces that they recognized her, and she wondered if Virgil Moncuse, the club's manager, had warned them not to let her in.

"Sorry, miss, the club's closed."

Eleanor smiled. "I can still hear the music."

"Yeah?" one of the goons replied, puffing up his chest. "Well, maybe it's making it hard for you to hear us. The club's closed."

The Slayer narrowed her eyes. So swiftly neither of the men even raised a hand to defend himself, she slammed a fist into the face of the one on her left, then swung her elbow back, shattering the other's nose. Both of them were reeling, clutching their hands to their faces. Blood dripped between the fingers of the one whose nose she had broken.

Eleanor let herself in.

The joint was still jumping. Though there were far fewer people than had been there earlier, a cloud of smoke remained in the air. Burning embers from lit cigarettes punctuated the shadows. Eleanor knew that her hair and makeup must be a mess but she doubted that in the darkened club anyone would really notice that, or her torn gown, particularly not those patrons who were still here at this hour. As she strode across the room, weaving in among small clusters of people who laughed and whispered together, a demon wagged its tongue lasciviously at her, a vampire tried to beckon her nearer and several men smiled at her. Once upon a time she might have been flattered, but at the moment she could feel only revulsion.

A familiar, girlish giggle rose above the chatter and Eleanor paused. At a nearby table, Grace McCandless held a wineglass with such delicacy it was almost as though she thought it might explode. The way she swung that glass as she smiled and laughed and leaned over to flirt with the handsome man beside her, it was a miracle the wine did not splash all over her. It gave Eleanor pause, seeing Grace like that. The actress was still stunning, despite the lateness of the hour and the ruin that most of the other patrons were in. She had been kind to Eleanor, in her way. The Slayer considered for just a moment going over and suggesting to her that she go home now. Then the absurdity of this struck her—why would Grace McCandless listen even for a moment to a teenaged girl from Louisiana?—and she refocused on her reason for coming back here in the first place.

A waiter maneuvered between two tables with a tray of drinks balanced precariously on his fingertips. Grim-faced, Eleanor moved to intercept him. Someone touched her as she passed a group of women and demons, a hand caressing her back and bottom. Any other night she would have broken that hand. Tonight she ignored it.

"Excuse me," she said, still polite as she snagged the waiter's sleeve. "I need to see Mr. Moncuse."

He barely glanced at her. "Yeah, honey, give me a minute."

Her fingers closed around the wrist of his free hand and she squeezed tightly. He gave a sharp intake of breath and the tray began to slide out of his other hand. The waiter was barely able to keep it from toppling.

"Where is he?" Eleanor demanded.

"Ah, hell," the waiter said, staring first at her fingers around his wrist and then at her face. "I just saw him at the back of the club, right by the door that leads to the private rooms."

The Slayer spun away from him and the waiter grunted as she released his wrist. Then he was forgotten and she made her way toward the back of the club, ignoring the looks and the touches and the cigarette smoke, the laughter and the clinking of glasses. Moments later she spotted Virgil Moncuse in the same corner where he had spoken with her earlier, at the far end of the bar, near the door that led into the back rooms of the club. He was in the midst of a heated, hushed discussion with a lanky, leather-clad creature whose mouth was a red slash across its face, fangs jutting like razor blades from its maw.

As she drew nearer, Eleanor saw that this hideous, nightmarish creature was weeping.

Virgil Moncuse shook his head in disgust and laid a comforting hand on the demon's shoulder. Then they parted ways, the demon slipping through the door that led to the private rooms. Virgil pushed both hands through his silver hair and glanced across his club. When Eleanor had met the man much earlier this evening he had seemed confident and collected, in spite of the terrible things that had been going on. He was a dapper dresser, and adding the tan and the mustache to that, he had the air of a film star himself. Now, though, the Voodoo Lounge's manager only looked weary.

The Slayer emerged from a small cluster of patrons who were gathered near the bar. The manager saw her and instantly he looked even wearier, shaking his head and rubbing the back of his neck.

"Why me?" he asked as she approached him. His eyes seemed to penetrate her with accusation. "Don't you think we have enough trouble around here without adding you to the mix, honey?"

Eleanor glanced pointedly the way the slash-mouthed demon had gone. "What's going on, Mr. Moncuse?"

Conflicting emotions washed over the man's features. For a moment he seemed angry, then confused, but he could not seem to summon the words to express these feelings. At last Eleanor saw surrender in his eyes.

"I didn't sign on for this sort of thing," Virgil sighed. He shook his head and moved closer to the bar, leaning against it, taking his weight off his feet as though at any moment he might just lie down on the floor. A dry, humorless chuckle escaped his lips and he regarded her disdainfully. "There's been another killing. A jui-bhat demon. One of my waiters."

Eleanor felt a strange prickle on the back of her neck, like eyes on her, and she turned to cast a quick glance across the club. There were too many faces and too many shadows to see anything clearly.

"I'm sorry about your employee, sir," she said, brows knitted in consternation. Eleanor caught his gaze now and held it. "There's a lot of killing going on in this city tonight. I had nothing to do with the jui-bhat's death, and I plan to stop whoever is murdering these demons so indiscriminately. Whether you want my help or not."

The handsome, fiftyish man sighed and nodded, his gaze seeming to refocus, to see her differently. "All right. What can I do?"

"I need to see Obrigor again. Where would I find him?"

Virgil glanced beyond her. "He left for a while, but I think I saw him come back in."

Eleanor frowned. "He's here? In the club?"

Her tone gave something away. The manager stiffened. "What do you want with him?"

The Slayer reached into her jacket, fingers closing on the

handle of the katar. "I have something to return to him." Her gaze ticked toward Virgil. "Some of your customers have decided to eliminate this killer on their own. But so far, all they've done is murder innocents they suspected were capable of the crime. Including Martin Goss. A little while ago, they decided I was their number one suspect, and they came after me."

Virgil was so crestfallen his expression was almost comical. He sighed heavily and massaged his temples. "That's why you want Obrigor?"

"He was part of it. In his way he's just as bad as whoever's hunting these demons. I'm going to stop them both."

Virgil rolled his eyes heavenward, then focused on Eleanor again. "Here? Right now? Can't you just wait till he's out of the club? Business has been bad enough with all this violence around. Things get any worse I'm going to be out of a job."

Eleanor softened. Despite his sophisticated appearance, Virgil Moncuse was a working man. He was responsible for the Voodoo Lounge. As far as the Slayer knew, he had not been involved either with the demon hunter or with the lynch mob. She fixed him with an appraising stare.

"You won't tip him off?"

The manager had been tense. With this indication that she might be willing to be reasonable, he perked up, eyes brightening. "Not a chance. Obrigor's always been well-behaved in here, but my only concern is the club. I just don't want anything—"

After the night she'd had, the Slayer was alert, on guard for anything out of the ordinary. Obrigor was the only survivor of the attack at the Imperial Theater, but that did not mean there weren't other demons who might target her. As Virgil spoke to her, she glanced about every few seconds, on guard for any threat. But it was only now, as the manager promised his cooperation, that she noticed the bartender.

It wasn't the vampire who had wanted to serve her a drink earlier, but the boy-next-door type who had ensured the privacy of her initial conversation with the manager. Earlier, Virgil had asked the man—*Darien, his name's Darien*—to keep others away to allow them some privacy. He'd had a reason to stick close by then, but even at that time, Eleanor had thought he was listening.

Now, however, he'd had no such instruction or invitation.

Eleanor twisted away from Virgil and glared at the blue-eyed bartender. Darien was too close to them, too far away from the patrons, to actually be doing his job. When the Slayer shot him that withering look he turned abruptly and started back up the bar toward a flirting couple. Darien grabbed a white rag and started to dry wineglasses.

So much of the time, despite who and what she was, Eleanor felt ordinary. When she was training or fighting, and the times she had had to fight for her life, every nerve ending seemed to tingle with heightened sensation. There seemed a kind of membrane that separated the little girl she had been when growing up in Louisiana from the Slayer she was now, as if they were two entirely different personalities. There was a simple courtesy that had been bred into her all her life that would prevent her from indulging in the more rash actions and attitudes of the Slayer in a public place like this, even with the presence of demons.

In the moment when Darien started drying wineglasses, that membrane was pierced. The sense of courtesy, of decorum, that governed her actions was shattered.

With a scowl, Eleanor spun on one heel and started down the bar, nostrils flaring and face flushing with heat. She had released the handle of the katar, but its weight was a constant reminder of its presence. Her fingers flexed as she marched toward the bartender. Behind her Virgil Moncuse called after her, but she ignored him. A moment later he began to follow, but he made no attempt to stop her.

Darien looked as though he had insects crawling under his skin, as though at any moment he might break and run. It was warm in the club, but not warm enough to explain the small trickle of sweat that ran down over his temple, past his ear and down his neck. Though Eleanor stood at the bar immediately in front of him, Darien stared down at the glass in his hand, wiping it intently.

The glass broke. He sliced the pad of flesh just under his thumb and fresh blood welled up, red and bright. Carefully, hands shaking, he set the broken wineglass on the bar and held the white rag to his cut, eyes still downcast.

"Who did you tell?"

Eleanor's voice was barely a whisper. The jazz band had been playing all along, but now the music was slow and sultry, just a piano and a woman singing with the occasional saxophone riff thrown in. But Darien twitched when she spoke, so she knew he had heard the question.

The bartender pretended she wasn't even there.

"Darien," she said, a bit louder. "Who did you tell?"

He lifted his gaze, but not his chin, so that he was looking up at her with his head still lowered. A red flower had begun to blossom on the bar rag he clutched so tightly. He cleared his throat before replying.

"I don't know what you—"

She slapped him openhanded with a crack that resounded through the club and had enough force to send him crashing into the line of liquor bottles behind the bar. Several of them shattered and the sticky sweet smell of liqueur filled the air.

Eleanor leaped onto the bar, broken wineglasses crunching beneath her shoes. The terrified young man with the handsome features and the cool blue eyes gazed up at her, shaking, and the Slayer did not have to ask again.

"F-Freak," he stammered. "You're just as bad as them." On that last word he gestured out at the patrons of the club. "Monsters. Scum. M-My mother . . . if you'd seen what they did to her . . ."

The Slayer flinched back in surprise. "You're the one who's been killing them. But you were here, at work. How could you—"

Darien snorted, regaining some of his composure now that it seemed doubtful that she would hit him again. "Nah. Not me. But if somebody wants to have a little fun hunting them, I'll be the first one to stand up and cheer. They're not human. They're *evil*, girl, or maybe that part escaped you?"

The music had stopped in the Voodoo Lounge. The Slayer could feel hundreds of pairs of eyes on her as she was surrounded by whispers. The whole club had come to a standstill as everyone waited to see what she would do next.

Virgil Moncuse reached up to touch her hand. "Please, Miss Boudreau. No more of this. Not here."

All of a sudden Eleanor felt foolish standing up there on the bar in her ripped dress, menacing the pitiful Darien. His loyalties, his attitudes, made sense to her. Demons had killed his mother and now he had to work among them. He was ignorant at worst, too stubborn or too stupid to allow that not all demons were evil. He was—

"Hold on." Ignoring the rapt attention and the whispers of the clubgoers, the Slayer dropped down behind the bar. Her lip curled in anger as she grabbed the front of Darien's shirt and hauled him to her. "Sometimes," she said, voice trembling with frustration and anger, "sometimes I'm just too nice. Here I was trying to understand your attitude, you sick, demented little man. For just a second I forgot why I wanted to break your nose to begin with.

"You were eavesdropping. Someone told Obrigor and his cronies I was the Slayer. It had to be you. You nearly got me killed, sir. I don't take kindly to that sort of thing. What I don't understand is, you hate them so much, why would you want to put them on to me in the first place?"

In the midst of his fear, though he was still shaking and sweating, Darien allowed the tiniest smile to lift the corners of his mouth. It was gone an instant later and his gaze darted about, avoiding her eyes.

"I think you must be—"

It was as though her fury sent its signals directly to her body, bypassing her mind entirely. Her fingers clutched his face and Eleanor rammed Darien's head into the mirror behind the bar. The glass shattered, showering reflective shards onto the floor. His face and her fingers and lower arm were cut and scratched, drawing tiny blood lines on their skin.

"I'm through being polite to you, sir," Eleanor whispered. The silence in the club was so complete that her words carried all the way across the room.

Darien hissed in pain, winced, and when he spoke again it was in a snarl. "You were gonna poke your nose in, try to stop the demon murders. The filth were looking for a suspect. I didn't do it for them. I did it to protect *him* from all of you."

Rage unlike anything she had ever felt filled Eleanor then. This lowlife bastard was a bystander, but he was so pleased with the murders of these demons, regardless of whether or not they were evil, that he was willing to sacrifice her life to let them go on just a little longer.

She squeezed her eyes shut, fighting the urge to beat him further because she was not sure she would be able to stop. When she opened her eyes, Darien flinched.

"You know. Tell me."

The bartender's eyes widened. "What?"

"You know who it is. Give me his name."

Darien hesitated only a moment this time, but his response was not to name the killer. Instead, his eyes tracked to the right, searching the crowd of silent, gaping onlookers.

You've got to be kidding, Eleanor thought. *He's here? Right now, he's here?* But a moment later she realized she should not be so stunned. All of his prey had come from this place. So had his information. He would have had to slip out to do this latest killing, but it only made sense that the killer would be here.

The Slayer turned. The entire crowd stared at her but in their midst was one man whose eyes widened at her attention and who took a step backward. The man was tall and his eyes, thin face, and hawk nose gave him a predatory air. Eleanor had seen him before and she knew his name. It was the film director, Lew Sackett, who had seemed so dismissive of Arkonis's murder.

And why not? Since he had committed that murder.

Eleanor let go of Darien and vaulted over the top of the bar. Walter Moncuse tried to take hold of her arm, tried to speak to her, to plead with her not to cause any more trouble in the club. She shook him off and started for Sackett, and the murderer turned to flee.

Voices were raised in shock now, breaking the silence. Some people called after the director but he swore and shoved others out of the way. Eleanor pursued him. Someone else grabbed at her and she shoved the man to the ground, then leaped up on top of a table, shattering plates and knocking glasses off. She jumped easily from one table to the next, closing the distance between herself and the murderer without having to shove through the other patrons.

Sackett ran for the door, but from this height the Slayer could see a number of the demons in the club beginning to force their way through the crowd to intercept him. Her mind whirled with conflict in that moment. She had to stop them from killing Sackett because that was not the way human justice worked. Demons dealt with things very differently, and far more permanently. Eleanor wanted the killer to pay, but not to be torn apart in the middle of a nightclub.

From the shadows near the front door of the club stepped a tall, skeletal figure. In the semidark his blue skin looked black, but Obrigor's horns gave him away.

"He's mine!" the cyxiff bellowed so fiercely that the humans near him hurried away, pushing deeper into the club, moving from his path as he strode toward Sackett.

The director—the murderer—froze. The Slayer was behind him, Obrigor in front, and other demons were encircling him now on all sides.

"You . . . you can't do this! Do you have any idea who I am? This isn't some back alley. Look around you, creatures! You're in a room filled with witnesses."

The demons had slowed but their circle still tightened, corralling the killer to await Obrigor, who pushed through them now, baring his teeth in a horrifying grimace. "You'd know all about back alleys, wouldn't you, Sackett?"

Obrigor grabbed Lew Sackett's face in one massive hand and his arm in the other. Eleanor leaped to the table nearest them, adrenaline racing through her, moving with the swift sureness of instinct. She drew the katar out of her jacket and brandished its blood-encrusted blade.

The cyxiff demon lifted Sackett from the ground and lowered his head, preparing to eviscerate the man with his blue-tipped horns.

"No!" Eleanor launched herself into a somersault that carried her above the heads of the demons encircling Sackett, and as she twisted her body out of the somersault, she bared her teeth and brought the katar down with all the strength and ferocity of the Slayer.

With a crunch of bone and a spray of gore, she hacked off Obrigor's head. Weighted with those horns it slammed to the floor with a loud clack. Lew Sackett tumbled to the ground with the headless corpse of his would-be killer.

There was an outcry of fury and venom from the demons. Several of them started for her immediately. She dropped into a crouching battle stance, the crimson-dripping katar in her hand and blood spattered on her face and hair and clothes.

"My name is Eleanor Boudreau. I'm the Slayer," she said. "That's the only warning you get."

As he began to drag himself to his feet, Lew Sackett let out a whoop of pleasure and approbation. "You tell 'em, honey. I like your style."

Eleanor spun into a roundhouse kick that snapped his head back and Sackett plummeted back to the floor, unconscious, a large red welt forming instantly on his cheek.

"Slayer . . . ," one of the demons began, inching toward her.

She raised the katar defensively. Her gaze ticked from one hideous face to the next and she saw in their eyes that they had no malign intention toward her. They only wanted justice. There was a part of her that wanted very badly to just give Sackett over to them. But much as she knew she might regret it later, Eleanor couldn't do that.

"You want him to pay," she said, scanning their horrid faces. "So do I. I swear to you that he will. I'll see to it."

For several long seconds in which the entire club seemed to hold its breath, they glared at her, debating, breath rasping, and jaws gnashing. Then the one who had spoken took yet another step closer and slowly nodded his head.

"You'd better."

When Lew Sackett regained consciousness he immediately wished he had not. His head felt as though someone had driven nails into it and his body was stiff. The taste of blood filled his mouth and before he even opened his eyes his tongue searched for its source. One of his teeth was broken and jagged and another was missing entirely. He wondered if he had swallowed it. There was a terrible smell and he wondered if it came from him.

He felt dazed, the night's events all mixed up in his head. As he tried to reconstruct them, to make sense of what had happened to him, he at last opened his eyes. The roof above him had an enormous hole in it and sunlight streamed in. His immediate reaction was relief. The night was over. The morning was here.

Then he blinked and stared at the ruined ceiling. "Where the hell am I?"

Carefully, wincing with every ache and bruise, he rose to his feet and surveyed his surroundings. Once it had been a theater, and a lovely one at that. But the collapse of the ceiling and part of the balcony had combined with the elements and now it was just a ruin, a dead piece of Hollywood history. He took a step and kicked something metal and heavy.

Lew looked down and his eyes widened as he saw the strange, wide-bladed weapon the girl had used to kill Obrigor. It was a sort of dagger, made to be clenched in the fist. Though it pained him, he bent and picked the thing up, admiring it. A slow smile moved across his face as he thought what he could do with a blade like this.

Which was when he noticed the sound, the slow, swaying creak coming from just above his head. Lew Sackett raised his eyes and stared at the hanging corpse of Martin Goss, whose abdomen had been ripped open and whose organs dangled from the wound like so much rotting fruit.

In that very same moment the theater door burst open and two men with guns stepped into the room, training their pistols on him and shouting at him so loudly that with the agony of his headache he barely heard them. Behind them came several other men with guns, these in uniform.

The police.

Lew glanced from the police to the hanging corpse and then down at the strange weapon in his hand.

"Drop the blade, Mr. Sackett," one of the detectives ordered.

A weary grin split his features and he let the blade fall from his fingers. This was Hollywood. He was an important man here. But this time he didn't have to ask if these people knew who he was. It was clear that they did. And equally clear that they cared not at all. They only cared *what* he was.

A killer.

They were parked just down the street from the Imperial Theater. Walter was behind the wheel and though he yawned several times, he seemed wide awake. Eleanor and Marie-Christine had carried Sackett into the theater, the Slayer still spattered with blood, both of them exhausted, but they were not going to go home until they were certain the police had responded to their anonymous tip.

Now it was all over. The police were inside. They would find Sackett and the katar and they would find the corpse of Martin Goss. It was possible they would link Goss's murder—and Sackett—to other suspects Obrigor had murdered, but it was unnecessary. The Council of Watchers would press the local authorities on Goss's murder and, eventually, Sackett would be convicted.

Eleanor yawned and it started a chain reaction, causing first Miss Fontaine and then Walter to yawn as well.

"That's that, then," the Watcher said. "Sackett's in for it now. Well done."

"It feels sort of odd, though, letting the guy take the fall for things he didn't do," Walter said tiredly, gazing out the windshield at the theater.

"Actually," Eleanor said, "it feels like justice to me."

Walter turned to face her. "Don't get me wrong. I understand it. I just wish there was a cleaner way to do this." Then he chuckled softly at his own words. "As if there's anything clean in this town."

Marie-Christine cleared her throat. "Let's get some rest, shall we? After all, you two are meeting for coffee later, aren't you?"

Eleanor flushed and glanced into the rearview mirror, where she caught Walter watching her. "Yes," she said. "Coffee." She glanced at her Watcher. "Then back to Louisiana tomorrow? Back home?"

Miss Fontaine frowned. "Kakistos has been entrenched in the bayou for decades, Eleanor. He'll still be there if you take a few days to rest. You've earned it."

Walter put the car into gear and pulled away from the curb, driving them back toward their hotel. Eleanor watched the rearview mirror for a minute or so but he did not glance back again.

"The demons never rest," said the Slayer. "So neither can I. Not until it's over for me. Not until the end."

The Code of the
Samurai

Nancy Holder

Dead spring blossoms fall,
Winter snow in the fortress,
Blood on white petals.

—Death poem of Lord Asano, retrieved from his corpse by Kohan, his concubine, and presented to his widow, Lady Asano, upon the first anniversary of his death.

TOKYO, DECEMBER 1, 1993

"Lord Asano! It is snowing!" Jun Asano shouted to the vampires in the shadows. "Blood shows best on pure white snow!"

As snowflakes sprinkled his shoulders, Jun stood straight and fearless on the stone wall of Sengaku-ji Temple. Moonlight glowed on the stone tomb of Oishi, Lord Asano's chief retainer, which was covered with a simple wooden awning on which the grave-cold snow continued to fall. The pale ghostly beams lovingly caressed the surrounding graves of the forty-seven *Ronin*, fingers of translucent light prowling up and down the rows in search of memories of honor, plucking away, like weeds, the reality of the horrors those loyal-men-turned-vampire had visited upon the population of Tokyo.

Though Japanese had revered these fallen *samurai* for years, honoring them with prayers, *kabuki* and *noh* plays, movies, novels, and TV series, the truth was that the *Ronin* had become savage vampires three hundred years before; and they were responsible for the most gruesome deaths in all of Asia.

The surviving members of the historic Asano family had sworn to destroy them. But despite three centuries of attempts, they had still failed to bring down more than a dozen minions, and those demons had been new and, therefore, inexperienced. The mere thought of killing vampires as savage as the Terminator was daunting; but with their long lifespans, they added to their arsenal of self-protective maneuvers, while the human Asanos continually reinvented the wheel.

Now the task of annihilating their foes had fallen to Jun, although he was only twenty. And he was only human.

He was what was called a "dark" Japanese, his complexion approaching a tanned appearance, and he had bleached his hair red. He had also lightened his eyebrows, and some of his cousins claimed he looked like a tawny lion. All that he knew was that, as leader, he must fight like a tiger, and carry inside himself the heart of a true warrior. He had no choice. It was his destiny.

In his right hand he gripped his *bokken* training sword, made entirely of oak. The stronger sword, called the *shinai,* used in traditional Japanese *kendo* swordfighting against actual combatants, was useless against vampires, as it was made of bamboo. In matters of true death, Japanese vampires were the same as European, American, Australian, African vampires—all were fanged demons of the international shadow world. It was a wooden stake plunged through the heart that dusted them to ash. Bamboo just made them angry.

Angry vampires were even more dangerous than those who hid, waiting for their prey to come to them.

"Lord Asano! I am your descendant, Jun, and I am here to kill you! It's snowing, just like the day your vassals avenged your death. So I now take my revenge on you!"

Crouching in relative safety behind the bushes and trees on the hill behind the temple wall, Jun's fifteen companions gripped their stakes and silently urged Jun on. These were the core team members of the Asano Living Clan. Moonlight splashed on nervous faces, tight lips, a tear of anxiety here and there. All were dressed in black, and some wore traditional headbands tied across their foreheads, reminiscent of World War II *kamikaze* pilots, though these were emblazoned with the blue-and-white Asano crest in a large blue circle on white. All were fully prepared to die . . . or so they asserted. In modern-day Japan it was more difficult to die for someone else than it had been back in the 1700s, when Lord Asano had died his own first death.

Times had changed.

The vampires had not.

Though Jun threw back his head with contempt as he brandished his *bokken* in his *kote,* the thick, padded *kendo* glove, the truth was that he was terrified. Yet he would rather die—literally—than reveal his fear to anyone. Leadership had been thrust upon him three days ago through the brutal murder of his little sister, Mariko. He had thrown himself into grief and rage; and now it was his job to stop the savagery. *Now.*

Jun's cousin Ichiro had been the leader until six months ago; during a fruitless raid, he had died an agonizing death at the hands of one of Lord Asano's vampiric descendants, who were collectively known as the Vampire Clan. It was the mutilation and sadism involved in Ichiro's death, and not the death itself, that had paralyzed the members of the Living Clan into inaction for half a year. Although Ichiro's brother, Yoshi, took on the leadership role, he never managed to rally their side to action, and they had paid dearly for that cowardice.

In that time, sensing that there was no human force overseeing them, the Vampire Clan had ripped out the throats of a dozen Asano family members. The survivors panicked; some fled to condos in Hawaii, and others to timeshares in San Francisco and Seattle. Jun's paternal grandfather, Akira, moved to Korea.

Akira Asano was killed in Seoul shortly after his arrival. Next, three of Jun's aunts were killed on the Hawaiian beach of

Waikiki, their mangled bodies left for German tourists to find.

After Mariko's death, Jun had finally stepped forward and demanded to be made the new leader—a title he would hold until death claimed him, as well. As such, he had immediately called for a revenge raiding party—and though their ranks had been whittled down, the warriors among the Asanos had stepped forward to join him on his mission.

"Lord Asano! Don't be a coward!" he shouted as he dropped from the wall, landing near one of the long rows of stone graves. He was clad in black like a ninja, except that his pants were buttery black leather imported from Milan, and he had ordered his black angora sweater through the Japanese men's fashion magazine, *Men's Club*. The Asanos were a very wealthy family, and there were progressively fewer of them to share their fortune.

However fashionably dressed he was, he melted into and moved with the shadows with the practiced grace of a trained assassin. Jun had studied *kendo*—Japanese swordfighting—for all but three of his eighteen years. He had known since his first baby steps in martial arts that his family battled real enemies, not simply those constructed from straw, and that at any moment, he might be called upon to fight against the notorious Asano vampires of Tokyo.

Now, as leader, his job was to guard the Living Clan—all the descendants of Lord Asano, whether in Tokyo or elsewhere—twenty-four/seven, as they liked to say in America.

Twenty-four/seven, until I die . . .

As he crept past the grave of Oishi, Lord Asano's chief retainer, Jun couldn't help a low bow of respect. Behind him, he heard the others inhale their breath, surprised; but Jun held his ground and bowed again. He wanted his respect to be duly noted by the monsters who haunted the temple. No matter what form their *samurai* loyalty had taken, the forty-seven *Ronin* had obeyed *Bushido,* the rigorous *samurai* code of honor.

He thought of little Mariko, only six years old; he knew the others were thinking of the terrible way that Ichiro had died as well. The horrors of those deaths, all the others, were real. But so was honor.

"Lord Asano, it is snowing," he whispered. "My blood will show best now. Come to me; come for my blood."

Ahead, behind another row of *samurai* graves, something moved with wicked stealth. There was a scrape of stone on stone—a gravestone being moved, perhaps. Jun swallowed hard and raised his *bokken.*

He thought, not for the first time, *American Vampire Slayer, where are you? We need your help. We will all die without you.*

He sent out his spirit—in case that helped—and called to her, as he had on the Internet, reaching out to public forums where people in other countries—especially America—had laughed at him for believing in a legend. Vampire Slayer? Wasn't there a low-budget Hong Kong movie by that title?

But vampires had been regarded as legend, had they not? And the forty-seven *Ronin,* so fantastic and fabulous in their loyalty, had truly lived. Truly died.

Truly risen again.

YOKOSUKA, DECEMBER 1, 1993

"You're not going to die," Odette Cohen said to her daughter, India, and it was not a question. It was an order.

"Absolutely," India replied, as she and her mother watched the sailor load the back of the staff car with Odette's beautifully matched luggage. The trunk was already brimming. Odette had a full day before her flight from Narita Airport in Tokyo to Manila, but she had decided to spend the night at the Tokyo Prince Hotel, near the airport.

India knew that Odette couldn't wait to get the hell out of Japan.

"Don't be such a little drama queen. I'll be back before you know it," Odette added, softening a little. She smiled wistfully at India, who was, after all, her only child. Somewhere in her cold, ambitious heart, she did truly love the daughter who had nearly ruined her figure.

Or so India's father asserted.

She wondered if she, India, would still be alive when her mother decided to return to Yokosuka. India Cohen was the Vampire Slayer, and eventually she would die in the line of duty. It was a fact she had accepted along with the job, which had been thrust upon her five months ago.

She had accepted it, but not learned how to live with it. The very idea that her days were numbered had never occurred to her until Christopher—Kit—Bothwell had appeared in her life and told her who she was. She had been fifteen. She was still fifteen now. Like any other girl her age, she was supposed to live forever.

Mommy, India wanted to say, *don't leave me. I'm scared.*

The words hung in the air unspoken, as her mother reached out to tuck an errant wisp of hair from India's ponytail, tsking at her unkempt appearance and shaking her head.

India and her mother stood in their house in Nimitz Court, which was not, frankly, appropriate quarters for the commanding officer of a submarine. But there had been a fire on the base shortly before Captain Cohen, his wife, and daughter had arrived in Japan, and most of the topnotch housing in Halsey

Terrace had been destroyed. The Cohens had had to live in the nurses' quarters for three months until billeting could locate something approaching Captain Cohen's rank. Nimitz Court wasn't, and these things mattered in the military. It was the same as in the film industry, or so India's mother insisted.

Odette had complained long and loud about just how unsuitable their new quarters were. Too small, too ordinary, and not enough room for all the live-in help she required: maid, sewing girl, cook, and house boy.

"I am the most famous actress in my country," she reminded India's father on a nearly daily basis, prodding him to demand something better. She would toss her shiny black hair, cut like Juliette Lewis's in *What's Eating Gilbert Grape,* and glare at him through heavy makeup. She wore enormous tourmalines in her ears, gifts from the former Marcos regime that had ruled the Philippines. "If the newspapers saw me living in such squalor—"

"Want to talk squalor?" her father would interrupt her bitterly, taking a gulp of booze. "Then go back to Manila."

They both drank a lot. Odette's favorite was sloe gin fizzes; India's father drank gallons of single malt whiskey, which he had learned to love while stationed in London. It was not good for his career that he loved alcohol so much; he was the commanding officer of a very expensive nuclear vessel, and a steady hand was required for the tiller.

So it had been with a mixture of relief and sadness that India had said good-bye at the dock last month, when her father had left for a six-month cruise.

Now, less than three weeks later, her mother was escaping, just as Kit, India's Watcher, had predicted.

"It's all for the best, India," he had reminded her when she'd run to him with the devastating news. "We can work much more freely with both your parents gone."

She and Kit would be alone, almost as if they were together . . . in another way. . . .

"It's getting late. You'll hit traffic," India said to her mother, hiding her misery.

"Yes." Her mother checked her lipstick in the hallway mirror. A statue of Kwan Yen stood beside it on a small gilt table, not because either of her parents had any fondness for the Chinese goddess of mercy, but because it had been a wedding gift from a Chinese fan of Odette's many films.

"Well." Odette blew an air kiss at India, then turned on her very high heels and lifted one finger at her driver, who was standing beside the sleek black town car. He wore tropical whites, and his cheeks were pink. He looked thrilled to be driving Odette Cohen to Tokyo.

Flags—U.S. Navy, flag officer with four stars, the Stars and Stripes—fluttered from the sides of the car. Both India's parents were very important people, and they had the hood ornaments to prove it.

India trudged to the curb, outfitted in a black down jacket, black T-shirt, and black jeans. Her mother hated the way she dressed, hated that she didn't wear makeup. India kept her hair in a ponytail. Odette hated that, too.

"I'll call you from Grandmama's tomorrow night," Odette promised. Her eyes were glittering. "Or the next morning if we get in too late." High color gleamed in her cheeks.

We? I'm sure she means everyone in the airplane. Not . . . anyone else in a special "we" sense. She's traveling alone.

"Say hi to her," India requested. "To Grandmama."

"Of course." Her mother looked mildly insulted. But India hardly ever saw her Philippine relatives, and sometimes she wasn't sure if they remembered she was alive.

Odette's driver opened the car door and Odette slid in with

the grace and elegance that had won an American sea captain's heart. She sat squarely in the middle of the leather backseat. In Japan, the position of honor was behind the driver, but Odette loved to remind everyone she knew that she didn't "really" live in Japan. She lived in Japan on an American military base. So she never curtseyed to Japanese custom.

She rolled down the window and said, "Mind Mama-*san*. Show her respect. I don't want her quitting on us."

Most of the servants Odette hired eventually quit. India knew it had never been because of her.

The car pulled away, India waving halfheartedly after it. As if on cue, thunder rolled; then there was a flash across the horizon as cold rain began to fall. She trudged back to the house, where Mama-*san,* their maid, was already stripping her mother's bed, balling up the sheets and throwing them angrily into the laundry basket. India was both grateful and embarrassed by Mama-*san*'s fury at her mother, and avoided her by going into her room and locking the door.

"India," Kit greeted her.

He was sitting on her bed, which she had partitioned off from her doorway with a large carved wood screen her mother had had shipped from Manila, then decreed that she didn't like. India's heart thudded at the sight of him, and that he was in her bedroom. She could never get over how handsome he was— dark hair like hers, but blue eyes, three-cornered, as they were called. He looked very English, and he was magnificently built. Not all watchers trained alongside their slayers, but Kit did— and she knew a lot about his body, and the way he could move it.

He, of course, would have been shocked at what she was thinking.

"You could have just knocked," she accused him, though she couldn't hide her delighted smile.

She wanted to run to him and throw her arms around him. But though he knew she loved him, they hadn't ever talked of it. More unspoken words: Her life contained great gaps of silence. "Instead you break in, all Mrs. Doubtfire."

"Mrs. Doubtfire?" He looked incredulous as he indicated his black turtleneck and wool pants. "Surely you can see that I'm not dressed like a woman?"

Then they both looked at what India was wearing—she was nearly his twin—and she burst out laughing.

"We've got to go to Tokyo," he said, rising to take her hands in his. It was his way; he often held her hand, he occasionally put his arm around her. But it was because he was a warm man, a caring watcher, and not because he wanted to be her boyfriend or anything like that. She knew that. She really did.

"More deaths?" she asked. "More bad deaths?"

He nodded, and she sighed. Tokyo was being hard hit by vampiric activity. The police were trying to keep it quiet, but Kit had spies in the police department; they were helpful because they believed he was some kind of British secret agent disguised as a British naval officer who was commissioned to help them with "strange occurrences." A combination of James Bond and Fox Mulder with a little bit of Captain Ramius thrown in.

It was almost true.

"We've got a meeting with someone who's trying to do something about it." He looked thoughtful. "He claims he's related to the vampires."

India made a face. "*Gomenasai*, Watcher-*san*. I thought you said 'related to the vampires.'"

Kit let go of her hand. She was very sorry but she didn't let him know it.

"He says he's from the same clan."

"Clan." She let that sink in. "And this is some American

wacko who has seen *Rising Sun* way too many times."

Before he could reply, there was a noise in the hall—it had to be Mama-*san*—and Kit put his finger to his lips. "We'll talk about it tonight. In the car. On the way to Tokyo, to meet with this person," he said firmly.

"We could have gone with my mother. You wouldn't have had to drive." She didn't want to go to Tokyo in the icy rain. She wanted to sit down with some good videos and a bowl of popcorn, like the other girls on base.

With him . . .

"I know it's not your favorite thing to do on a rainy night," he whispered, as if he had read her mind. *But what's to read?* "And I am sorry about that." He eyed her. "I am truly sorry about your mum, too. But as I said, with her visiting your family, it'll be easier for us to conduct business."

Business. The business of killing, or being killed.

"It won't be all that much easier," she argued. "I'll practically be under house arrest. Mama-*san*'s a total power-tripper. She's going to make sure I eat all my veggies, do all my homework, and have no fun whatsoever until Mom and Dad get home."

"Not tonight." His eyes twinkling, Kit nodded and pulled a small glass vial from the pocket of his pants. "Latest thing," he announced. "Very strong. It would drop a rhino in its tracks."

She hesitated, studying the amber liquid. Kit was very handy with herbs and a few basic magicks, and this was not the first time she had taken some kind of potion from him to make the people in her house sleep a little heavier.

It wasn't very advanced, and it certainly wasn't anything that sprung from him. He used magicks, but he wasn't magickal himself. So to speak. But back in the States—back before she knew she was the Slayer—she had never met anyone who could detect the presence of a demon from a hundred feet away. Actually, she had never even known that demons existed before she'd met him.

"It'll just make her sleep, right?" she asked, trying not to insult him. "No fancy stuff?"

"It's just a sleeping draft from an old druggist's shop in Bloomsbury, near the British Museum. Perhaps she'll stop worrying about her charge and have a nice dream or two."

His face was soft, kind. He was so different from her father; he was a strong man who had enough self-confidence to be able to really care about other people. He didn't think it was going to take something away from him to look outside himself.

"Heck, I'll drink it myself, then." She took the vial and turned it over in her hand. Amber liquid sloshed in the glass container, which was about two inches long and made of very thick glass. She liked the heft of it. It wasn't like something you could buy at the base exchange.

"Have you been having a lot of nightmares again?" he asked her.

She nodded, feeling tired and wan, thinking that he must surely see the dark circles under her eyes. She had not had a good night's sleep in nearly a week.

"Perhaps it means something," Kit observed. "Your nightmares. I'll check into it."

With the Watchers Council, she mentally filled in. He did a lot of checking into things. Kit was new as a watcher, unseasoned and untested—and very young, and very cute. He admitted to her that it had come as a bit of a surprise that "his" girl had been the new Chosen One. Watchers Council bets had been on a different girl, but that particular person had, well, died.

In a very stupid car accident, shortly before the previous Slayer had herself been killed by a congara demon. She wondered if somewhere up in heaven, the unlucky Slayer—whose name had not been revealed to her—was going, "Damn it!"

"Thanks," she said, closing her hand around the potion. And then, "So. Tokyo."

"I'll drive us up," he informed her, going all business. "We've got a good store of weapons in the trunk of my car, yes? What about your weapons bag? Are you well stocked with crossbow bolts and stakes?"

"Yeppers," she said cheerily. "Fully loaded and ready to rumble. Got a lot of all that cool junk that makes me, me."

He touched her hair. "You're brilliant," he said fondly.

His touch set her on fire. She wanted to grasp those fingers, press the tips against her lips and kiss them. But she dare not. That kind of relationship was not allowed. If she ever made that kind of move, he would be duty-bound to request a transfer. The Watchers Council was already watching them—*ha ha, pun there*—to make sure nothing like that happened. High spirits, youthful passions—it had happened before, according to the annals of watcher-slayer history. It could never happen again.

She knew this because someone in the Council had privately written her, explaining the ways of the world to her, and warning her to steer clear of "romantic entanglements" with Kit. Whoever had written the letter had signed it, "A friend," and India half believed it was some other woman who had a crush on Kit.

Not that I'm a woman, exactly. I'm only fifteen. But I probably don't have all that long to live, which means I'll probably grow up faster than most girls.

Betraying none of her thoughts, she crossed to her closet to get her weapons satchel. She smelled the sandalwood soap Kit used and closed her eyes against the reactions it elicited in her. Kit smelled better than any other guy she had ever known, exotic, sensual. Grown-up. They were going to be alone together on a round-trip to Tokyo, and she was going to be smelling him for hours.

Stick to business. Killing. Death.

"So," Kit continued. "Let's make a plan. You eat your dinner, give Mama-*san* the potion, wait, oh, a good forty-five minutes, then meet me on Mamushi Trail and we'll leave from there. Good?"

"Mamushi Trail. Why always Mamushi Trail?" she grumbled. *Mamushi* were highly poisonous indigenous snakes. Their venom would probably not kill her, but it could do a job on Kit.

"Cover of darkness," he replied, as he always did. He raised his brows expectantly as he smiled at her. "Good?" he said again, in his clipped, British way.

"Yes, Mr. Bond," she answered soberly. "Veddy good."

"Brilliant." He flashed her a set of stunning white teeth. She didn't smile back.

With a flash, he was out the window . . . and India was finally, truly, all alone.

Mama-*san* succumbed easily to the sleeping potion, and India was out the door with her black leather jacket and her weaponry by eight o' clock. Snow had not fallen in Yokosuka, but rain had, and the streets were wet and slick. There was a possibility that the chilly night would render them icy. Recalling the death of the potential Slayer who had died in the car accident, India walked carefully in her boots. She kept to the curbs and crossed at the crosswalks—making sure, however, that no one who could recognize her saw her heading for Mamushi Trail.

The trail was cut into a mountain that led from one part of navy housing to another. Kids went there on occasion to smoke or take drugs, but it was generally avoided after dark. The dense growth could hide more than just slithering serpents—that were, she reminded herself, hibernating at this time of year.

It was good that normal kids had the sense to stay away, because the local vampires liked to party there too. India and Kit had gotten rid of more than one batch of fangy Japanese demons while rendezvousing on the trail for an entirely different mission.

Black on black on black—Slayer and Watcher and the dark of the sticker on Kit's large, black BMW announced him as a British naval attaché to Admiral Simmons's command. The Watchers Council of Britain had been able to pull a few strings. It had been quite difficult to figure out a way to put Kit together with India once she had been Chosen. Fingers were crossed that the next Slayer wouldn't be so . . . mobile.

But it wasn't up to the Council. Just as India's being Called had not been their decision. Powers far stronger than a group of men and women in London arranged these things. India wasn't sure who those powers were, and she wondered if they also decreed when slayers died, and how. But again, that was not information anyone had shared with her. She might go to her grave never knowing these things.

They drove slowly through the base, obeying the speed limit. Rain began to fall again as Kit drove past the Marine guardhouse; the young man on duty saluted sharply as he noted Kit's officer's decal on the BMW. Then they were off the base—"in town," was the military parlance—amid the shiny streets of Yokosuka.

"Listen to this," Kit said. He held up a CD jewel case; the cover read HARAJUKU EVILS. About a dozen young Japanese kids glared back at her, all made up like Elvis Presley, down to his greasy ducktail haircut—even the girls.

"'Evils'? Typo?" she asked.

"Don't you hope that it's not a typo?" he replied, grinning. He had a mischievous side that she loved. They had spent many an hour devising traps for particularly inept vampires, their gallows' humor version of slayer practical jokes.

"With Harajuku groups, it's hard to tell," he reminded her.

"*Hai-hai*," she said in Japanese. *Yes, yes.*

They'd been to the Sunday gatherings of Harajuku street bands, where hundreds of Japanese singers and dancers dressed in heavily themed outfits, from 1950s greasers to goths to elaborate glitter rock, performed to the strolling crowds on the grounds of the Olympic stadium. Extremity was the name of that game, and the Japanese kids really got into it. They expended incredible amounts of energy preparing for Sundays, working out precision dances, practicing their songs, and living the rock star dream.

They both chuckled, and Kit slid the CD into the player. India settled back to listen, watching the raindrops, wondering where her father was on the high seas, wondering if her mother's driver had run into the bad weather yet.

Tears spilled down her cheeks.

"Hello, what's this?" Kit asked, and he sounded so British that India had to laugh.

She wiped her eyes and said, "Mom and Dad stuff. As usual." She added, a bit forlornly, "I haven't got much other stuff."

"Nonsense. You've got your friends and you've got the slaying."

"Not much to cry over on those fronts," she replied, giving him her patented Look of Evil. "Unless you count facing death on a nightly basis a reason for tears."

He reached over and patted her leg. She knew that he meant it as a supportive gesture, but his touch weakened her defenses—she loved him so, and it was so stupid of her to love him at all—and she cried harder.

"I hate my parents," she said simply, then took a deep breath and reached for the pack of tissues in her weapons bag. "There. All done."

"Want to talk about it?" he queried, but she knew he wasn't much for that kind of thing. She was a girl, into emotions. He was a guy—and a Brit—into fixing problems with a stiff upper lip.

"Nah." She looked out the window. "Do we really have to do this in the rain?"

He shook his head. "I do believe we will be doing it in the snow."

She frowned. "You're kidding, right?"

A few more kilometers on the highway proved the accuracy of Kit's observation. The rain became sleet, and then snow; he kept the Harajuku CD cranked up high the way she liked it, and as they listened and watched the snowflakes, she grumbled about not having brought a heavy enough coat. But Kit always kept some of her things in the trunk, and sure enough, he told her he had brought her black down jacket.

We sound like an old married couple, she thought, then amended that. *At least, like an old married couple on TV.*

They for sure didn't sound like her parents, and they were the only married couple she got to observe at close range. With so many hails and farewells among the military officer fathers of her friends, having a mom and dad in the same house was an oddity.

Their headlights caught the flurries of snow as they sped northward and diffused the other cars on the road into blurry shadows. India listened to the Harajuku Evils, who were apparently singing in English although she couldn't make out any of the words. She liked their sound—wall to wall—and she tapped her boot toes together as they whizzed past Yokohama.

By then, enough time had passed to move from personal meltdown to professional slayer-watcher conversation, so she went first.

"What's the info that you have on this antivampire clan?"

"I'll start with the vampiric side of the equation. There's been increased activity around the Sengaku-ji Temple. The legendary forty-seven *Ronin* are buried there," he filled her in. "Apparently some young man is claiming to be the descendant of Lord Asano, the one whose death ignited his masterless *samurai* to disobey the shogun and seek vengeance on Lord Kira."

"I don't know the story."

Kit frowned at her. "You should. It's one of the most famous in Japanese history. I don't know how it ties in with our contact. But I rather think this descendant has happened upon a nest of vampires, and has absolutely no idea what he's come up against. He's bothering them, and they're retaliating."

India whistled. "And he's still alive?"

"One assumes." Kit gave her a semi-amused look through his dark, heavy lashes. "But of course in our business, one can never be certain of such things."

"No, one can't." She bobbed her head in time to the pounding backbeat of the Evils. "For all we know, this guy is a vampire. Your contact guy."

"The thought had crossed my mind as well."

Six months ago, if someone had told her she'd be driving around Japan with a British naval officer who helped her kill vampires and other forces of darkness, she would have asked him what he was on. Now, it all seemed like normal life. It *was* normal life.

Scary.

"How'd he contact you?" she asked. "Flashed the bat signal on the side of Mt. Fuji?"

"Apparently he didn't actually contact me or the Watchers Council," Kit replied. "He sent out a global e-mail to a list of organizations known for their interest in the occult. We have a watcher on staff who acts as a lookout for those sorts of things. It has to do with something called routers, and I hesitate to guess what they are."

"You mean, there's an Internet watcher-spy checking for keywords like Death to All Vampires."

"Not at all. That is, not a spy." Kit straightened his shoulders on behalf of the entire Watchers Council of Britain. "Granted, they don't realize we're monitoring them—"

"*Spying* on them—"

He huffed. "This young man is looking for you, India. He's not sure you really exist. But he says he needs your help."

That made sense. Most people—and things—assumed she was a myth. And a lot of people needed help of mythic proportions. The forces of evil crossed all lines—national borders, international waters, time zones and time lines. They attacked innocent bystanders as well as those who had declared themselves the enemies of darkness.

It made sense to hope that there was such a thing as a vampire slayer.

"This guy's name? . . ." she asked.

"Jun Asano. He's been sending out an SOS for about three days. And it's getting more impatient."

"And things in Tokyo are getting worse." She ran a finger down the side of the CD case. "He's got to be the real deal, Kit. On the side of the good or the bad, who can say? But I'm thinking we're on duty here."

"As you say, Slayer," he concurred.

They reached Tokyo about twenty minutes later, all skyscrapers and enormous neon billboards; despite the fact that it was almost nine-thirty, and snowing, the streets were clogged with traffic. Kit was an able and practiced driver, however, and he and India were soon turning onto a street near the temple entrance without her untimely death in a car accident.

"Why are we meeting him here?" she asked.

He scanned the street for a place to put the car—in Tokyo, one did not so much locate a legitimate space as double- or triple-park, and hope for the best—and pulled around a Dumpster and turned off the engine. India was a little taken aback—it was such a haphazard job—but he looked at her soberly and said, "We're meeting him here because this is where he comes to fight the vampires, night after night."

"Couldn't he wait in a nice coffee house for us?" she muttered.

He reached down and popped the latch for the trunk, indicating with his head that she should climb out of the car. "Not when people are being eviscerated," he answered. "He feels it is his responsibility to put an end to it as quickly as he can."

Her cheeks burned as if he had smacked her. She knew that demons and vampires preyed on the innocent all the time. Hundreds, if not thousands, of people died in a month whom she could have saved, if she'd been around to do her bit for good. But she couldn't be everywhere at once; and if she thought about that too hard, she would go crazy. Oh, she made noises about not wanting to go out in the cold, and staying home and goofing around—*okay, messing around, as in making out, which I have never, ever done*—but she knew her duty. And she didn't need some man who was not Chosen to remind her of it.

She opened the back door to retrieve her weapons satchel while Kit got the things out of the trunk. She waited for him to lead the way and then, as she turned, he touched her elbow.

"I'm sorry, India." He looked troubled. "That was an unconscionably cruel thing to say."

"Oh, that's . . . true," she finished. Every part of her being was focused on the place where he'd touched her.

The moment was over, though, and Kit was already leading the way toward the temple entrance.

"We're just going to stroll in?" she whispered loudly.

"No," said an accented voice. "I bought you tickets."

A figure stepped from the shadows and into the watery light of a streetlamp. He was unnerving, like some *manga* superhero in a Japanese comic book; tall, hulking, and muscular, he wore a knit cap and black clothes. Concealed as he was from scrutiny, she saw a pair of dark eyes and that was about it. With his boots, the prototypical Gen-X young Japanese *animé*-style man. All he lacked was a duster.

He looked tense; he said to her, "Are you the American Slayer?"

She thought about retorting, "I've never killed an American in my life," but instead she said, "India Cohen. *Hajimei-mash'te*," and gave him a regal bob of her head. Kit looked impressed with her Japanese-style manners, and that made her warm inside.

"*Ah, so*," he said, sucking in his breath and bowing low. "Asano. Jun. *Hajimei-mash'te*. How ya doin'." His inflection was all off, but she didn't insult him by giggling.

Then he bowed to Kit and said, "You are her helper?"

"Her Watcher," Kit replied mildly. "Yes, her helper. Bothwell is my last name. How do you do?"

"We are dying in Tokyo," Jun replied. "That is how we are."

"We came as quickly as we could," Kit told him. "We saw your call for help on the Internet."

The man nodded. "As they say in the song by the Police, 'sending out an SOS.'"

"Indeed. It was most effective," Kit told him. "You are to be congratulated on your resourcefulness."

Jun lowered his head and murmured, "My English . . ."

"You did a good job. Where are your vampires?" India asked.

He looked pained. "They're playing with us. They haven't come back to their graves since I became leader."

India considered. "Maybe they're afraid of you."

His brows furrowed beneath the cap. "Don't make a joke," he snapped. "They killed my sister three nights ago." His voice broke.

"I'm so sorry." She bowed again, more deeply. He bowed back, also more deeply.

They began to walk toward the entrance, Kit on one side of India, Jun Asano on the other. Kit won out in the smell-good contest, but she liked Jun's swagger. He walked like a gunslinger about to take over the town.

Kit ventured, "It's a myth about their having to return to their place of rest. Their graves. They don't have to do that, ever. Just stay out of the sun."

"Ah." Jun sighed. "That would explain it then. What a drag."

"Your English is amazing," India said sincerely.

All she could see was his eyes, assessing to see if she was making fun of him. *This is a guy who's been brought low,* she thought, feeling a kinship with him. No one in her family had died, but no real warmth had grown there either. That was a loss of sorts.

She said, "So, you have a blood feud going on? With your, ah, vampiric ancestors?"

"Chushingura?" Kit asked.

"Yes. The legend is true," Jun replied, speaking to Kit. Then, seeing the blank expression on India's face, he added, "Let me tell you my family's story, Slayer-*san.*"

EDO, 1701
IN THE PALACE OF THE SHOGUN, MARTIAL LEADER OF ALL JAPAN

Takumi no kami Naganori, Lord Asano, could bear it no longer. The insults heaped upon him by the master of protocol, Lord Kira, were more than a nobleman should be forced to endure, no matter how pressing his obligation to the shogun.

Newly installed as the leader of his clan, Asano had been selected to entertain the imperial envoys from the emperor himself, with the knowledge that Kira would mentor him. But the cretinous old devil had done nothing but mock and humiliate him since his arrival, and Asano had just discovered the reason why.

"You didn't give him enough presents," said his concubine, as she lounged on brilliant orange and red pillows of fine silk. "All the palace is talking of it."

Her skin was snowy white, her hair the dramatic lacquered upsweep of a highly favored courtesan. Kohana was the name he gave her, Child of Flowers. She was absolutely the most beautiful woman in all of Nippon, including his wife, whom he adored with all his heart. Kohana was his for pillowing and conversation here in Edo; when his obligation was complete, he would probably never see her again.

"I gave him plenty of presents," Asano argued as he paced. They were resting in his private rooms, the scent of fresh straw mats a testament to the incredible labor he had supervised in order to prepare the shogun's palace for the envoys. He had spared no expense. The mat makers of Edo had worked through the night, when, on a whim, Kira had ordered him to change all five hundred mats . . . overnight.

"I brought silk, and spring water *sake*. He took my valet's maidservant for a plaything. He has been more than richly compensated for a job he must perform, by right of duty to the shogun." Asano touched the long *katana*, the *samurai* sword that hung in its scabbard around his waist. "He is a *samurai*, but he is behaving like a common peasant."

"True enough," Kohana said. She held a length of silk against her supple form, and smiled beckoningly at the man who would be her love for as long as he was in Edo.

"I am a young noble," he continued. "My clan will take my lead. The *samurai* code demands that I take a stand against corruption. Should I weaken my family's fortunes to please the greed of a shriveled old man?"

"No," Kohana said reasonably. "But you must please the envoys regardless of your personal feelings, my lord. That is *your* duty."

He was not insulted by her frank conversation. Asano loved bright, clever women. His wife was such a woman. She was a *samurai*'s wife. And Kohana was a *samurai*'s concubine.

"Asano-*san*! Lord Asano!" bellowed a brittle voice. It was Lord Kira, screaming at him like a village woman at her daughter. "Come here at once!"

Asano raised his eyes to heaven and whirled on his heel, clenching his fists. "You see how he treats me!"

"It is all a political show," Kohana soothed. "You have manly vigor. He does not. Go to him, my handsome lord, and then come back to me."

He paced. He was in a fury. "If I go to him now, I will kill him."

Kohana paled. "You mustn't even say such a thing," she admonished him. "If you so much as expose the blade of your sword in the shogun's palace, you could be executed."

He said nothing. He stomped toward her and grabbed the silk from her; it fluttered to the fresh, clean mats and lay there like a pool of blood.

Kohana lay back and smiled invitingly, opening her arms. "Expel your feelings in me," she murmured. "Then you may face him with more serenity. He will not know that you refused to come. He will assume you didn't hear him."

Asano hesitated. As if on cue, the rich strains of court music—*gagaku*—rent the air. *Sho* and *hichiriki* wailed alone, then joined each other, rising like two slender iris stalks toward the moon; in the background, as if on a riverbank, a drum sounded, and then a *biwa*. The effect was stirring, warming Asano's already-heated blood; he mentally tossed aside his resentments and his frustrations, and prepared to take his pleasure with his woman.

The reedy *sho* ascended, the flutelike *hichiriki* lifting toward it—cranes in a dance, a swan in flight . . . Kohana.

"Asano!" the brittle voice querulously commanded. "I require your presence *now!"*

Kohana paled. Asano's eyes bulged.

"Did you hear that? No honorific! He has dropped the *san* from my title! He addresses me like a serf!"

"Perhaps he forgot," Kohana ventured. Nervously she gathered up the scarf, gliding a distance away from her lord. Asano was humiliated before her, a mere woman, and though *samurai* had a code of honor that included no violence toward females, the cut of the insult was so deep that there was no telling how the infuriated victim would react.

"Call out to him. Let him know you're on your way," she half suggested, half begged. She lifted up an exquisite *yukata* of indigo and slipped it on, loosely belting it at the waist. "It will placate him, and he will remember his manners."

"I will not bellow like some fishwife," Asano insisted proudly. "I am a *daimyo* from an important clan. Kira has nothing to teach me about manners, nor I him."

"But he has a lot to teach you about protocol," Kohana reminded him steadily. "You need his advice. Please, my lord, don't push him. He is far more powerful than you."

"The code of the *samurai* states that we must fight to prevent bureaucratic corruption," he insisted again. "This man is nothing but corrupt."

Kohana was now truly frightened. Tears welled in her eyes as she extended her arms beseechingly and sank to her knees.

"I beg of you, Asano-*sama*, let this insult pass. Be practical. I would die if harm came to you."

"Don't you dare order me around!" Asano shouted at her. "You are for pillowing, not matters of state! Don't forget your place!"

Kohana lowered her gaze, terrified for him. She had not known him long, but she had seen that he had quite a temper. If he rushed out of these rooms to confront the odious but influential old man, only tragedy would come of it.

"Stop crying!" Asano yelled at her.

She bowed her head to hide her tears. She closed her eyes and listened to the rustle of his long silk trousers as he made his way out of the room.

As he stomped down the corridor, Asano knew that Kohana was right. For all her being a woman, she played court games with a special depth and brilliance that inspired him. If he approached Kira in anything but a restrained, respectful manner, his own reputation would pay for it. He was the leader of his clan, and everything he did reflected on all his people. Though he was new to such responsibility, it made perfect sense to him. It was the way of the world.

But his own world had shrunk to this single palace, and to the nobles dwelling inside it. Lord Daté had found greater favor with Kira—no doubt he had bribed him with richer gifts, currying his good word with false sincerity, and Kira had withheld nothing from him in return. Daté knew all the rules of etiquette they were expected to follow, and had received detailed written instructions from Kira outlining the expectations both young nobles, Daté and Asano, were required to fulfill. He had made a dozen excuses regarding why Asano did not yet have his own copy of the instructions. Time was growing short; the envoys would soon be here; and Asano may as well hang himself if he could not perform his part in the ceremonies as well as Lord Daté.

Perhaps this was what this was about—one more opportunity to bribe the doddering senile old fool, one more chance to abase his own honor in order to receive what was rightfully his.

No! I will not fall down to that old man, he thought fiercely.

The *gagaku* rose to a steady high note as he swung around the corner and walked on the nightingale floors—so named because the wood made sweet notes as one walked upon it, an alarm cloaked in cultural discretion. The surrounding guards were instantly on alert, for the sound of the floors signaled that someone was approaching the inner sanctum of the shogun.

All six of them bowed as they caught sight of Asano. From his lofty station in life, Asano barely inclined his head. He knew they would not be insulted; in the sophisticated setting of the shogun's palace, one appreciated that others knew about matters of rank and respect; it was well that others maintained the ethical standards of behavior.

As his feet played the floors, Asano's hand fell toward his blade. One of the guards caught his eye; Asano saw the warning there—*Good sir, calm down!*—and he lowered his arm to his side.

Across the interior rock garden in the forecourt, his nemesis stood in his ceremonial black *kimono* with Lord Daté, who looked very uncomfortable when he spotted Asano.

"Finally you deign to arrive," Kira said harshly to Asano.

As was required, Asano dropped to his knees and made obeisance. "I apologize, Lord Kira. I did not hear you."

"Is that what you would tell our august shogun, if he called for you? Your ears must be full of wax. Clean them."

Asano clenched his jaw.

"Lord Daté's sword has a nick in it. I ordered him to take it to the shogun's private sword master. Lend him yours," the man flung at him.

Asano stared at the man in utter disbelief. What Kira was telling him to do was unthinkable. One never, ever lent his sword to another *samurai.* To even suggest it was an intolerable insult.

"The nick is slight," Lord Daté said anxiously. "I am sure the sword master will return it fully repaired in a very short time."

Lord Kira glared at Asano. The old man wore his gray topknot braided and pinned in place, lending him an effeminate appearance. His face was slack with age and drinking. His eyes appeared to be closed, the lids were so heavy and wrinkled.

"Lend him yours," he repeated, gesturing from Asano to Daté.

"Please, such an offering," Daté blurted, swallowing hard. "It is so generous of you, Lord Asano, but I cannot possibly accept."

A decent man would have allowed the matter to end there. But Kira was no decent man.

"Asano!" Kira snapped. "Do as I say!"

This time, there was no way to ignore the fact that Kira had not used the honorific *san* after Asano's name. It was a deliberate insult to his personal honor and to his clan's honor.

It could not be permitted to stand.

"Kira-*sama*, Lord Kira," he began, exalting the man by using *sama*.

"What, *Asano*?"

A third time, his name was uttered without proper respect.

Asano put his hand to his blade. The old man's gaze dropped to Asano's trembling fingers, and he took a single step backward.

"Asano," he said again, like a child daring another.

Asano narrowed his eyes. He knew in his heart that it was against the law to pull his sword loose in this place. He knew that losing his temper was a violation of his *samurai* upbringing.

Perhaps seeing the second thoughts in his expression, Kira smiled evilly and said, "You really are a country bumpkin, aren't you?"

The *gagaku* soared; *sho* and *hichiriki* together. Musical voices shot toward heaven, so many arrows loosing the threads of destiny. Asano could almost feel the wheel of his karmic destiny turning, shifting . . . all of it glittering to a point at the end of his sword.

The *gagaku* wailed, and Asano slid his sword free. Then, as if its spirit had grabbed hold of him, he lunged toward Kira in a fluid motion, a fantastic dance of *samurai* grace and indomitable spirit. No one could so insult a *samurai*, and live. It was not only Asano's honor at stake, but that of all *samurai* everywhere.

And so he swung his sword at Kira; and only by seeing in his mind the face of his beautiful wife, waiting for him back in his country castle, did he avoid slicing open Kira's head. Instead, he cut a thin slice into Kira's forehead, which immediately streamed with blood. Head wounds were like that.

The old man shrieked; the guards ran forward to subdue Asano; and watching Kira's show of terror, Asano's hatred boiled over. He threw off the shogun's guards as if they were toys and raced after the aged devil, who shrieked again and began to run. His overlong trouser legs balled him up and he fell.

Lord Daté threw himself into Asano's path, raising one hand and crying aloud, "Asano-*sama*! Please stop! This is the shogun's palace!"

But Asano couldn't stop. He was too angry. He leaped over the other *daimyo* and tore after Kira.

More guards raced toward him; all was a blur of color and the melodious cries of the *sho* as it played alone. He was thrown to the ground and swords and lances thrust at his neck and along his back.

Even then, he could not give up his fury. He shouted, "I would have killed you, old bastard! One more arc of my sword, and I would have your head in my hands!"

Shocked, the guards pretended not to hear as they trussed the great Lord Asano like an animal and spirited him away.

. . .

Asano's inquisitors likewise did not hear anything he might have wanted to say, in order to defend himself and possibly save his own life, as well as the lives of his entire clan. A town had built up around the castle; there were villages on his lands. All would starve, now that his lands would be confiscated and his name reviled.

He thought of his exquisite wife, who had not yet borne him any children; and at that moment he was glad of it. His sons would have become untouchable by any other noble house; the shogun might have even ordered their deaths.

He wondered what would become of his younger brother, who stood to lead the clan now that he, Asano, was in custody. It was possible that he would die as well.

The sentence came down swiftly: death through ritual *seppuku,* sometimes more rudely called *hara-kiri.*

Asano was to take his shorter knife, his *wakizashi,* and disembowel himself with it. It was an agonizing way to die. If he was lucky, he would be allowed a skilled second, who would behead him as soon as his ritual cut through his abdomen was completed.

Kira, he learned, had taken to his bed, claiming that the flesh wound Asano had dealt him was infected and likely to kill him. Surrounded by his beautiful women and mewling sycophants, he made the most of his opportunity to seal Asano's fate, stating to a scribe that he had no idea what had so provoked the ignorant country squire to such an uncontrolled rage.

For her part, the concubine, Kohana, was frantic. For the time that he was in Edo, she belonged in her soul to the fine young lord, whose hot blood and high passions had inflamed her. Life for her did not exist past each moment that she was to please him, and protect him. In every discrete moment of time, it was her duty, and she was proud that such an honor had befallen her.

Thus it was that she devised a plan for saving him, and as soon as it was dark, she put it into action.

Dressing for a stroll, a veil over her hair, she put on her lacquered *geta*—her beautiful platform shoes—and minced her way across the gravel of the castle grounds to the tiny cave set in a cliff wall. Many might have simply paid homage to the Buddha there and gone on their way. But Kohana had learned from the other courtesans of the witch who lived there . . . and who had made many dreams come true.

The cave entrance was dark, save for the statue of the seated Buddha, stone snails covering his head to symbolize his patience and compassion; a few votive candles flickered before him. There were three persimmons as well, and a small handful of flowers.

"Come to call?" a voice wobbled.

It was the witch. Her long white hair draped over her shoulders; she wore fabulous robes of burgundy silk, and an *obi* of brilliant copper and gold. Her face was long, distended, and half rotted away. Her hands were little more than skeletal fingers that clacked when she moved them.

"Come in, my poor daughter," the witch said in greeting when Kohana approached. She had been stirring something in a pot. She took a taste of it from a lacquered spoon, grimaced, and stirred some more. "Your tears break my heart."

The courtesan abased herself, stretching out on the stonework in front of the Buddha, and the witch chuckled deep in her throat.

"Rise," she said. "You were unable to help your young lord lying down, were you not? What makes you think it will help now?"

Kohana was mildly shocked at this ribald comment. She

raised her head, to see that the witch had lit a torch and held it out. The old woman's eyes gleamed a milky blue. There was no brown in them, and no black.

"You are said to be a powerful witch," Kohana said without preamble as she got to her feet. "Save him, and all my riches will be yours."

"Riches. I am wealthier than the emperor himself. You have nothing that I need," the crone retorted contemptuously, snickering to herself.

"Save him," Kohana pleaded.

"You have something that can be used, however." She beckoned for Kohana to come forward into her cave. Slowly Kohana got to her feet and did as she was urged.

"Show me your neck." The witch raised her bony fingers and tugged at the folds of Kohana's *kimono*.

Kohana obeyed. The witch examined her neck, running her sharp fingernails along the delicate skin. The concubine shuddered, and then screamed as the witch sliced deep into her skin with her nail.

The witch held her while she struggled, then said, "Stop this at once, or I won't help you." Then she jerked her head and said, "My son, come. Taste this fine lady."

Frightened, Kohana's gaze moved from the woman to a movement behind the witch's shoulder. Her eyes widened and she tried to scream again, but this time she was so unnerved that no sound at all would come out.

The thing that glided toward her wore the face of a malignant creature, white and grotesque, the mouth drawn up and back like the parody of a smile. Its eyes glittered and glowed a brilliant crimson . . . or was it gold? She thought giddily of her silk, lying on the straw mat in Asano's quarters.

The creature said, "How beautiful. How wonderful."

"This is my son," the witch said. "Unlike yourself, he hasn't had many lovers." She chuckled. "You see, he is a vampire, my dear."

"No," Kohana murmured, struggling, though she had no idea what a vampire was. "Please. I beg of you."

"You made the offer. I will accept it," the witch said firmly. "Now, after he has dined, you will take my son to Asano-*sama*'s place of confinement. You will get him inside, into my lord's cell. And he will change your love into a creature that will not die to-morrow."

A creature?

"Please, no. That's not what I had intended." Kohana struggled in her steady grasp. "I wanted you to *rescue* him!"

"We *are* rescuing him."

The witch's monstrous son glided toward her. Her skin prickled; she trembled from head to foot.

"Not like this!"

"My son will take his pleasure," the witch insisted. "And then, you may return to your life, you lovely, highborn whore," she said to Kohana. She smiled beatifically, as if she had not spoken so rudely.

As if in a nightmare, Kohana touched the wound at her throat. She was weak from loss of blood, but she knew that the vampire moved closely behind her, ready to carry her to Asano's cell, if need be.

Dazed, she draped herself once again with her veil, concealing the jagged cuts. She could smell the demon on her skin, wrapping her in the stench of the grave like a finely embroidered coat.

They reached the stone guardhouse about half a kilometer away from the palace itself. The witch had told her that the back cell was where Asano was being held. The little structure was not heavily fortified; Asano was a *samurai* and would not try to escape. He had no particular allies in the palace who would dare death themselves to save him.

She knocked, and her summons was answered by the jailer, a squat man whose lips parted at the sight of a beautiful courtesan presenting herself for his inspection. Kohana had been handsomely paid for her ability to stimulate and enthrall; she was able to give the jailer a large silk sack of gold, and made so many other promises that he eventually surrendered his honor and let her into the corridor leading to Asano's cell. Her heart was beating hard. The man turned to go and it was then that the vampire attacked him, breaking his neck and dropping his body to the floor.

Kohana wondered at the stir his murder would cause, but gave the man no more thought than that. He had disobeyed his orders and he deserved his death.

The vampire dragged him into the guardhouse's small storage room and slammed shut the wooden door.

And then the demon pulled the wood-slatted door off Asano's cell.

"My lord," Kohana murmured, sinking low in obeisance.

"Kohana," Asano said hoarsely. Then he looked past her to the vampire and said, "What have you brought here? My death in a more odious form?"

"No, your life," she murmured, hiding her tears. The fresh scab on her wound broke, and blood streamed from her neck onto her exquisite *kimono*.

Your life in a more odious form.

There was no decision to be made. Before Asano could consent or refuse, the vampire advanced on him and tore his fangs into the *samurai*'s muscular neck. Asano struggled in his grasp, but the creature was much stronger than he. Kohana watched as the vampire drained Asano of blood. Then the monster sliced open his own chest and forced Asano to drink. The *samurai* seemed eager for the coppery liquid, and Kohana was sickened by the sight of his eager slurping.

The vampire smiled over Asano's head at her, then laid him on the *futon* bedroll that had been made for the convicted man.

Kohana fainted; when she came to, Asano's prone body bolted upright. His eyes opened, and they were ablaze with the fires of hell.

She despaired; he was her love no longer.

Without a word to her, he set upon her as the other vampire looked on. Finding the wound, he set to nourishing himself.

He allowed her to live, a flicker of humanity remaining in him for a few hours. Then it was entirely extinguished by the evil that unfolded like cherry blossoms in his unbeating heart.

The vampire coached Asano in the rest of the plan; he was to demand to die before sunrise, without the aid of a second, insisting that he wished to show his remorse for his actions by suffering an ignoble death. The former *daimyo* would have refused such a humiliation, but the demon who now inhabited Asano's body was only too pleased to assure his continued existence by avoiding a beheading.

There were a few witnesses, mostly for form; the emperor's envoys had arrived and the matter of a disobedient *samurai* was an embarrassment to everyone. In another place, another time, Asano's death would have been observed by every noble in Edo. But he was to die in obscurity, his lack of honor thus assured.

To fulfill his last request, Asano's execution was set for midnight. It fell to Lord Daté to escort him to the execution site. There stood the small lacquered platform, set with his knife wrapped in paper. There, the cord for him to tie his thighs together, so that he would not jerk and flap like a fish as his body reeled with agony.

Prior to his change, Asano had written a death poem, which he recited. Several of the witnesses—*samurai* all—wept at the thought of such a fine specimen of their code, ripped so untimely from their ranks. He placed it in the folds of his robe, and then he exposed his abdomen. Without hesitation, he took his knife, and cut deeply and firmly into his own flesh.

The death was a good one; the vampire inside Asano found it excruciating but endurable. Once he was declared dead, his concubine took his death poem from his body, preserving it for his wife, and he nearly grabbed her hand when she moved away from him as quickly as possible, obviously terrified of him. The love she had carried for the doomed *samurai* had changed to horror, and it amused him, nothing more. Gone were any tender feelings, any weakness. Now he could become in death what he had failed to be in life—a warrior without equal, a *samurai* feared and respected by all.

In the distance, the wailing of the *sho* overlaid the lamentation of Kohana, the exquisite concubine, as she lay upon her silken pillows and wept for the fine young lord who would never see her beauty again. There was no chance that she would consent to be the consort of a demon, if indeed such desires still raged inside his body. She wished she had allowed him to die with the modicum of honor left to him; whatever he had become, there was no honor attendant upon his condition. He was ruined.

She heard the gossip later that his body had been spirited away before he could be cremated. She knew the truth—that as a vampire, he was walking the earth once more.

Kohana did not then know that after Asano was changed, he approached his vassals and demanded that they allow him to change them, too. Forty-seven of them consented to become vampires, and one by one, he drove their souls out of their bodies while he drank their blood, and offered them his.

Two years later he himself led the attack on Kira's castle, and the greedy old man was beheaded—after Asano taunted and tortured him, leaving bite marks on his neck and chest, drawing out his death. The legend was told that Asano's loyal retainers had done the deed, planning the attack for two years. But the truth was that Asano had instigated it himself. As all of Kira's guards were killed during the raid, there was no one to accurately detail what really happened.

Three hundred years later, the legend continued. . . .

TOKYO, DECEMBER 2, 1993

"And so Asano lives on, with forty-three of the forty-seven," Jun finished. "We have only four confirmed kills in all of that time.

"Long ago they pledged to kill or change all members of the Living Clan." He pulled a key from his trouser pocket and began to open up the guard gate in front of the temple entrance. "He sees us who are still living as disloyal for not willingly becoming vampires and serving him."

"Lotta that going around," India said. "Immortality gives guys big egos."

Jun grinned at her. "I think I understood what you said. You speak very quickly."

India grinned back. "Eviscerate yourself when you say that."

He cocked his head. "You're not as I expected," he said frankly. "You are very much an American girl."

"Perky," she suggested dryly.

He was enthusiastic about that adjective. "Very."

They had a little moment, Vampire Slayer and vampire slayer, and then India broke it by moving a little closer to Kit, basically declaring her intentions. Which were to help, and not get any further involved than that.

"They are ravaging Tokyo. Something has happened to anger them. They are more . . . determined than before."

Before she had a chance to respond, he got the guard gate open. It was an old metal contraption that she could have crushed in a microsecond, but he seemed proud of himself for having a key and being able to let them in on the sly.

She pulled her jacket more closely around her shoulders as the snow tumbled over the three of them. They slipped quietly onto the temple grounds.

It was another world, compared to the crowded Tokyo street scene just a few feet away. Pristine snow glistened on large stone lanterns, on manicured evergreen trees, on a towering statue of a *samurai*. Despite the turmoil Kit had told her about, there was an undercurrent of goodness here. She was no Buddhist, but she knew holy ground when she felt it. Maybe it was all the hopes and dreams that the Japanese had poured into their prayers as they paid homage to fallen heroes. Continuing the tradition of ancestor worship, the Japanese people had revered Asano and his vassals for centuries, never dreaming that they were praying to incarnate, soulless evil.

Adding that to the list of Easter Bunny, tooth fairy, happy parents . . .

Still, something in their prayers seemed to have soaked into ground. *What did they used to call it? Good vibrations.*

She sensed something in the darkness and whirled in its direction, instantly dropping her weapons satchel and whipping a stake from inside her jacket. Jun laid a cautionary hand on her shoulder and whistled once, sharply.

The whistle was answered by another, and two tall guys stepped into view with their hands raised like unarmed cowboys. They were quite tall, like Jun, and when they saw India, they glanced at each other in an almost comical exaggeration of astonishment. They blinked at one another and then at her.

Jun said under his breath, "Many of them do not believe in you. They did not think you would really come to help us."

And we're back to the Easter Bunny . . . and the Vampire Slayer . . .

He spoke to the two in rapid Japanese. One nodded; the other murmured something that sounded very like "We are not worthy," then bowed to India. Astonished, but knowing something of Japanese customs, she returned the bow with a slight edge of authority.

The taller of the two newcomers whistled again, and more people stepped from the shadows. There were about a dozen of them, guys and girls, most very young, maybe a couple even younger than she. They all wore black; their faces were a mixture of hopeful, wary, and just plain freaked out.

These people really need help.

Jun spoke to the group, pacing back and forth, gesticulating and making stabbing motions. They listened intently, casting their gazes toward her. One of the girls smiled very shyly and gave India a little wave, then spoke very softly to Jun, adding her two *yen* worth to the conversation.

After a few minutes, Jun announced, "We have all agreed to make you our leader. We want you to help us destroy the Vampire Clan once and for all. And we want Lord Asano to turn to dust."

India glanced at Kit. "You want to make me your leader?" she repeated.

"Hai." Jun looked hopeful. "I will gladly step aside."

I'll bet.

"Ah, well, I do have school . . . ," India began. Then she realized how ridiculous that must sound to them—a supernatural vampire fighter who worried more about grades than killing bad guys. Not that that was true; it was just that she had to make her way in the world, and where she came from, that didn't happen without a high school diploma. Weird, but true: even the Slayer had to think about her future.

She said to Kit, "Can we make it work?"

"Of course," he replied smoothly. She couldn't tell if he was saying that to be nice around the freaked-out Japanese guys or if he really meant it. She had such a strange life, the mundane all mixed up with matters of life and death. It was mind-boggling, really. Sometimes she didn't know how she and Kit kept it all straight.

"You can say yes," he added, not so much telling her what to do as providing some guidance. His handsome face was alight with both pride and concern for her, and she was thrilled.

"All right then," she said, turning to the group. "I'm your leader. Take me to your bad guys."

They all heaved a collective sigh of relief. Jun shook her hand, then they filed in a row, like a receiving line at a wedding. Each one came up to her, murmured his or her name, bowed, and shook hands. They had all worn gloves against the cold, and a number of them made a point of taking them off to shake with her. She took hers off as well. Their skin was warm, their grips strong.

She said to a girl who looked vaguely like one of the girls on the cover of Kit's new CD, "Are you the Harajuku Evils?"

The girl looked at her blankly, blushing seven shades of scarlet. "Pardon?"

"Never mind. Off topic." She rubbed her hands together. "Okay, a few questions first. If you're from this big family whose entire mission in life is to kill dangerous vampires, how come there aren't more of you?"

High color rose in Jun's cheeks as he walked behind a large stone square set in the ground and came back with a *kendo* shortsword in his fist. She and Kit had worked with several of them in varying lengths.

As he rested the sheathed blade in his hand, he said, "This is a raiding party. I didn't want to risk everyone."

He spoke to the others; several of them went behind the large stone cube and retrieved weapons. She saw two crossbows and a long wooden lance. Distance weapons. That was good; she wasn't sure all of the Living Clan would be able to withstand hand-to-hand combat. A number of the girls looked quite fragile.

Jun's reply caused a stir in the group. India had no means to translate their reaction until a girl dressed in black jeans and a big black sweatshirt and overcoat frowned at him.

"We have to be honest, Jun-*san*." She looked at India and moved her shoulders just like an American. "Our relatives are afraid. Many have moved out of Tokyo. Many have died recently. Mariko-*chan*, Jun's sister, was killed only three days before."

"'Ago,'" another Living Clan member corrected her. He was poked in the ribs by a shorter, squatter guy for being so obviously tacky.

"We'll try to make sure no one else dies," India assured her.

Another girl half raised her hand and said, "Why is there only one of you?"

India held out her hands. "I've often wondered the same thing," she replied. "If I'm the only thing standing between the forces of evil and the world, why don't I at least have some backup?" She glanced at Kit. "No offense. You know what I mean."

"I do," he said. "I've wondered that myself."

"You have?" She was surprised.

"Of course. We all wonder why there's only one Chosen. We being the Watchers," he added. "No one's got a jolly good answer."

"Tut tut," she quipped, teasing him for using Britspeak. Amused, she turned back to her new followers, to see that none of them had followed a word of their conversation.

"Any other questions?" *Such as why this job doesn't come accessorized with a rocket launcher?*

"Have you ever killed a vampire?" one of the older guys asked. He might have been as old as thirty.

"Yes. Several," she told him. "And lots of other kinds of demons."

"Have you ever killed a dragon?" he continued.

"Dragon . . . I've never seen one," she said, intrigued. She hadn't known that dragons were real.

"Let's go look at the tombs," she suggested. "See if we can figure anything out. Like if *they* think they have to sleep near them. If they don't know they can sleep just about anywhere—and that they don't even really have to sleep, just stay out of the sun— they might be trying to get back to their graves. You folks might be making them nervous. And nervous is good. Nervous is not paying good attention."

"*Honto desu,* Slayer-*sama,*" Dragon Boy said. "That's very true."

"*Hai-hai,*" Jun chimed in. He gestured for her to follow him. As she reached for her weapons satchel, Jun grabbed it and slung the handles over his shoulder.

"I was going to do that," Kit grumbled. India glanced at him, wondering if he could actually be jealous. *That would be so incredible. . . .*

They shuffled through the snow, their footfalls loosening the icy crust so that their movements sounded as if they were walking over cornstarch, the way they used to do it in the movies to sound like people were walking over snow. India reflected on that circular reality for a moment, then pulled herself back to the moment. She was more stressed out than she had realized—first her mom leaving, then waiting for Mama-*san* to fall asleep, then the ride alone in the car with Kit, plus, she was cold and tired. She wasn't used to evil things lurking and popping out at her whenever they felt like it, and the way Jun and the others were glancing nervously around did not make her feel any better.

I shouldn't let them know I'm scared, she realized. *They're into all that macho Japanese leader stuff.*

Walking tall, she kept herself poised for battle, quelling her anxiety, staying focused but not fearful. Kit must have sensed the change in her attitude, for he flashed her a brief smile and a discreet nod.

She warmed inside, beginning in her lower abdomen and fanning outward. She wished they could hold hands. But that would be completely wrong, on so many levels.

They walked along a pathway punctuated by occasional buildings and small shrines. She had no idea what they were used for or what they signified, but now was not the time to play tourist. They were on a deadly errand, and everyone needed to keep their wits about them.

After a few minutes they turned right into a walled square, and everyone froze to stare at the row upon row of Japanese-style graves, each with a small, simple obelisk atop a slab of granite. The moonlight glowed down on the nearly fifty graves, which had for so long served as a moving symbol of fidelity and honor.

Highlighted by moonbeams, a shadow rose from among the gravestones and flitted across the back row, scrabbling out of sight. India craned her neck in its direction.

It was followed by another, this one a more distinctly human-like figure. There was a hiss like a cat, followed by the clang of metal on stone.

Jun sucked in his breath. "Their swords are hitting their gravestones," he said quietly.

An apprehensive murmur ran through the group. The tension level among them mushroomed. One of the girls began to cry and another girl put her arm around her and spoke to her soothingly. They touched cheeks, and India wondered briefly if they were sweeties. She didn't know any girls who liked other girls in that way, and she was fascinated.

Then she was back to business, gesturing for Jun to get something out of her bag with which to arm himself. He held up his arm and flexed back his wrist; she guessed he had something up his sleeve, and gave him a signal that she was fine with it.

As she surveyed her little band, she noted that each one carried a stake. They seemed pitifully underequipped, although she knew from experience that hand-to-hand combat with a stake in one's hand generally produced the best results. That, and crossbows.

She moved to Jun and rummaged in the bag, keeping an eye out for more moving shadows. She withdrew her favorite crossbow and a quiver of bolts, and handed them to the girl who had begun to cry.

"Do you know how to use this?" she asked her in English.

The girl looked unsure.

India was about to repeat the question when the shadows exploded and launched at them like black rockets.

Dozens of vampires attacked en masse, a roiling, dark horde unleashed on a handful of humans. A few were dressed in medieval *samurai* battle gear—thick leather armor, gauntlets, and helmets topped with scimitar-shaped blades. Others wore more modern dress. She saw that many were tattooed. Tatts were big in Japan. Always had been.

As they took in their predicament—so many vampires, so little them—pandemonium erupted among the Living Clan members. The two guys who hadn't been able to believe that India was the Slayer assumed battle stance; one with a stake in his fist, the other with a *samurai* sword in his left hand and a stake in his right.

The girl with the crossbow screamed and dropped it, running and stumbling through the snow. A vampire leaped after her, and Kit raced after him, stake at the ready. Then the vampire slipped on an icy patch and went down on his knees, and Kit seized the advantage. He grabbed the vampire's shoulder, threw him onto his back, and slammed his stake through the monster's heart as he dropped to his knees in the thickets of snow.

With perfect form, Jun held his wooden short sword firmly against his lower abdomen—the Japanese center of *ki,* or life energy—and deftly stepped aside as a fierce-looking vampire with a long, black mustache rushed him. Then he rammed the sword into the vampire's arm. Enraged, the monster turned toward him, and in that moment, Jun plunged the sword through the devil's heart.

The vampire exploded.

The merest whisper of a satisfied smile crossed Jun's face as he glanced India's way, and then he was on to the next combatant.

Good fighter, India thought approvingly, as she handily staked the first of a trio of vampires to reach her. She dusted, her debris mixing with snow to make a grimy paste. Since the vamp was female, India knew that she had not killed one of the original forty-seven *samurai* or their master, Lord Asano. No girl *samurai* back then.

As she managed a sharp kick to the shin of her second assailant, she wondered if any of the oldest vampires were even present in the melee, or if newer, lower-ranking demons had been sent to pick off the raiding party while their elders lounged around, aristocrats preserving their safety while their underlings did their dirty work.

Jun may have been wise to limit his presence here tonight, she thought. *There are an amazing number of vampires here. This might be one of those famous Japanese suicide missions, so best not to send everyone out to die all at once.*

That's my life—sooner or later, I'm going to go on a suicide mission, and that'll be the end of my slaying days. Then the next girl will go in. I wish I could warn her; I wish I could live forever so there'd never been another girl who had to face dying at the hands of some freaky monster. It's like some horrible, tragic relay race or something . . . more like switching in a fresh player at a soccer game.

But as the watchers know, you can't play if you can't field a team . . . and you can't field a team if all your slayers die together.

Beside her, one of the human fighters leaped into the air, let out a bloodcurdling yell, and slammed his open hand down the center of a vampire's skull. The vampire's head cracked open like a walnut, exposing its brain, and while it was reeling from the damage, the warrior took two very precise lunges forward and staked the sucker through the heart. It dusted.

"Banzai!" India yelled in congratulation, and the guy flashed her a huge, prideful grin before he went on to the next one.

The wind blew; the snow fell. Drifts whipped up and all around her, as when a skier shushes up next to one on a black-diamond ski run and slams on his brakes. Snow was on her face and in her hair; she was cold and wet and sweaty and hot, all at once. One of the vampires got too close and nicked her knuckles with its teeth, so she was bleeding on top of all her other aches and pains.

The smell of blood and the presence of so many humans lent the walled-in compound the sense of a shark aquarium at feeding time; the vampires were in a frenzy. Some were clearly the more deranged sort, the newbies who dogged after blood no matter the dangers. Then there were cleverer ones, planning strategies and working together.

But nowhere did one particularly stand out as their leader.

As Lord Asano.

"Is he here?" India called to Jun. "The big cheese?"

Before he replied, he whipped around in a one-eighty and took out two vampires at once. Then he said, *"Nan desuka?"*

"Asano-*sama*," Kit called, as he punched a female vampire in the jaw, then in the stomach, then staked her. *"Imasuka?"*

"Ah. So," Jun replied, which was the Japanese language equivalent of "Hmm, let me see." He took inventory as he shot out a roundkick at a vampire attired in full medieval battle gear. The creature fought back hard, sending Jun sprawling.

"Jun!" India ran to him, bending down and grabbing the ankle of the vampire who loomed over him, and upended the demon. He landed hard on his back, stunned—*Can't exactly say he got the wind knocked out of him, since he doesn't breathe*—and India dashed to his side, raising her stake. With her patented India Cohen war cry, she plunged the stake into the vampire's chest and waited for the satisfying smell of dust in the nighttime.

She kept fighting with the others, putting a dent in the number of bad guys. At one point she realized how hungry she was; at another, how tired. She was also aware of how much blood there was on the snow, and of the fact that some of it was hers:

Her lip had been split open and blood was splashing from a head wound just behind her right ear. It was big and it hurt, but she had Slayer-strength regenerative powers, and she could already feel it beginning to heal. The other humans would not be so lucky, she knew; and as she stepped over the prone body of the girl with the crossbow, it took everything in her training not to abandon the fight to see if she could help her. But she knew about triage, and she knew that she, of all of them, had to keep fighting. If she didn't they could all die.

The moon scuttled behind clouds, scrimming the scene with flat gray light that sucked the contrast and depth out of India's surroundings. Her depth perception affected, she swung at another oncoming vamp . . . and missed.

Then Jun fought his way to her side and yelled, "Slayer-*sama*. I beg of you, sound the retreat!"

"Sound? . . ." She glanced around, realizing Jun was right. They needed to run the hell away, or they were all going to die.

"Let's go!" she shouted in English.

"*Ikimasho!*" Jun translated. He waved his sword above his head like a helicopter blade. "*Uchi de!*"

She had no idea what "*uchi de*" meant but "let's leave" in any other language would smell as sweet. She bellowed to Kit, "Let's clear the entrance!" and together, Watcher and Slayer began to fight their way from the interior of the square compound toward the open side, where they had come in.

"India!" Kit shouted; she looked up from slaying a very young female vampire to see a spindly, ratlike form leaping from gravestone to gravestone approximately twenty feet directly across from her. It crouched atop one of the obelisks, feet grasping the pointed top like a primitive animal, and shone blood-red, glowing eyes at her. It stared straight at her, knees wide open, bony white chest smeared with blood, and then it opened its maw and blood spilled out, staining long, sharp fangs as the creature smiled at her.

Her own blood chilled as more blood poured out from its mouth, the thing seemingly ignorant of it, or uncaring. Blood splashed on its skeletal fingers and down its chest, which was little more than yellowed layers of skin stretched over prominent ribs jutting from an emaciated torso. This creature was more . . . *everything* than its companions. More evil. More ancient.

Is it Lord Asano?

She was distracted long enough for the female she'd been about to stake to make an escape attempt. Brought back from her reverie, India took her out. Dust eddied in a stiff wind, then scattered.

The ratlike figure observed her from its perch, its smile growing until its face was nearly cut in two by the jagged extensions of its teeth. It threw back its head and might have been laughing; India couldn't tell, but its lack of caution at being so exposed to the battle infuriated her.

She took a step toward it, then remembered the primary objective—to make possible a retreat—and went back to kicking, punching, and staking as many vampires as came after her. Her arms and legs felt like gravestones themselves as she wearied. But still the vampires came, a seemingly endless stream of them.

"Retreat!" Kit yelled above the tumult; and India saw that yes, she had created a pocket of space through which the really swift members of the Living Clan might get the hell out of there. She felt like Moses parting the Red Sea—she couldn't hold the waters back forever—and she took up the chant.

"Retreat! Retreat!"

The humans finished out their battles. India watched one girl wailing on a vampire twice her size, all tricked out with martial arts postures and movements—and barreled through the safety zone India worked to keep clear of evilness.

"Hurry up!" she shouted at them as one by one, they fled the compound.

As she fought a wall of vampires, the spindly thing bounded from one grave top to another, and appeared ready to bound straight for her, when an elderly woman in burgundy robes, white hair streaming over her shoulders, appeared seemingly out of nowhere. Popping into this dimension beside her shimmered a Japanese *geisha*—a woman wearing heavy white makeup, a large lacquered hairdo, and large damascene pins and dingle-balls set into her hair. She wore a blue kimono emblazoned with a family crest on its sleeves and on either side of the V of the folds across her chest. Her obi was scarlet and gold, and in the vast field of blood and snow, she looked like the famous ghost fox woman of Japanese legend.

The elderly woman clapped her hands together and the spindly creature bounded off the obelisk and crabwalked toward her. India saw now that there was a collar around its neck. The beautiful *geisha* attached a leash to the collar and the three strolled away, as if none of the chaos around them was real.

Then, against the moon, they began to walk an invisible stair-case up and out of the compound, moving serenely to a height above the monuments. The *geisha* glided like a phantom, while the spindly creature loped ahead, losing purchase on the steps again and again. The older woman smacked it on the head, and it yelped like a chastened dog.

The wail of ancient Japanese music pierced the noise. Kit and Jun both looked up from their mop-up efforts, and the three vampire fighters observed the two women and the quasi-humanoid pet ascending the stairway. The music swelled for an instant as the spindly monster glanced over its shoulder at India.

Then the three hovered in the air as if they had reached a platform. The older woman spread out her hands and closed her eyes. Her lips moved.

At once, all the vampires in the compound disappeared.

India, Kit, and Jun, who had stayed behind with them while the others had escaped, gazed at the vast emptiness as wind lifted handfuls of bloody snow and smacked them against the stone graves and walls. Then they each ran to a fallen comrade.

There were five of them, and India's, a man about thirty years old, was dead. He stared straight at her, the life force drained out of him. With a sigh she left him, and ran to another.

It was Crossbow Girl. Planted facedown in the snow, she was crying and writhing from a deep gash in her upper biceps. Blood poured onto the snow at an alarming rate. India tore off a section of her black T-shirt and wrapped a field tourniquet in the arterial region.

As Kit approached she moved back to let him do his thing; he was far more knowledgeable about first aid. It was her job to cause injuries, not to fix them.

"She's badly wounded," he said quietly. "We should get her to a hospital."

Slayer and Watcher looked up as Jun ran over to them. Kit said to him, "We need to take her to a hospital."

"Hai-hai," he said, staring at his fallen comrade. "Two others," he added, then took a breath and asked, "Kochiro and Nabé?"

Kit cleared his throat. "I believe they are both dead," he said frankly. "I'm so sorry."

Jun held back tears. He averted his face and pressed both fists against his mouth, then leaned down and scooted Crossbow Girl into his arms. "We don't have time to be sad," he informed them. "We must get Michiko and Issai help soon." He looked at Kit. "I came by subway."

Kit replied, "We have a car."

"I'll stay here," India volunteered. "It'll be too crowded, and besides . . ."

She got up and loped toward the spot where the women had first appeared.

"No, wait!" Kit shouted after her. "We need to research what that was. Don't go near it!"

He has a point.

She slowed, admitting to herself that her sudden burst of heroics was for Jun—*I am the fearless leader, after all.*

"Well, then, I'll help you load the wounded," she suggested. "Jun should go with you. He speaks Japanese. I don't."

As Jun carried Crossbow Girl—Michiko—down the gravel path leading to the exit, he said politely, "Your Japanese is very good."

"Uh-huh. Thanks."

She trotted over to the wounded guy—Issai—and assessed his condition. His femur was broken and he had lost a lot of blood. Wishing she didn't have to move him, she carefully picked him up and laid him over her shoulder fireman style.

Kit gathered up all the loose weapons and retrieved India's satchel. He was loaded down but kept pace as Jun and India moved swiftly along the path.

Back past the looming statue, the stone cube, the lanterns. The guard gate. Despite the occasional passing car, no one took note of the transport of the wounded.

Then they were at Kit's vehicle, carefully laying down their unconscious burdens. There really was no room for India.

"I'll come back for you, unless you want to take a train home," Kit said. "Drop them off and come back for you. Good?"

"Good," she said.

They regarded one another. "Find a noodle shop, somewhere

to stay warm and rest. Check back at the temple every half hour. Don't go investigating," he ordered her. Her cheeks reddened. He narrowed his eyes. *"Don't."*

"Hai-hai, Watcher-*sama,"* she said finally.

He got behind the wheel. Jun rode shotgun.

India gave them both a thumbs-up and watched the car speed away. Jun stared out the window after her, his face a white oval against the night-darkened glass.

Miraculously, the racket from their battle had not caused anyone to investigate what was going on. Across the street, a purplish glow through a window signified that someone was watching TV.

There might have been some kind of magick damper in place, she thought. *Or else the locals around here have learned to stay away. . . .*

Cars drove through the slush, their wheel sounds like the surf. India wandered alone, thirsty, cold, and hungry. This section of Tokyo was very old, with tumble-down World War II–vintage cement block buildings next to wooden structures next to ultra-modern condos of glass and steel.

Eventually she found an open coffee house decorated like a place on the Left Bank in Paris, and wandered in, sitting down and ordering a cappuccino as she felt in the pocket of her jacket to make sure she had some *yen.* She did. There was a nice, sharp stake in there, too. A few, in fact. She was all set, so she got a pastry, too.

As she sipped and ate she wondered how they were doing at the hospital. She hoped her mother had not phoned. She'd be angry with India for not picking up, and especially not calling back. She'd have to lie—as usual—and say she'd gone to bed early.

She finished just as the polite but tired-looking *barista* began stacking the bistro chairs on the round black wood tables. No matter that the place was closing; it was time to check in at the temple anyway.

Thanking the *barista,* she pushed back outside. The wind had picked up, rearranging the snow drifts. She was halfway back to the temple entrance when something loped past her in the shadows.

It was the spindly creature.

"Hey!" India called after it, and gave chase.

It bounded ahead, sometimes raising itself backward in a semblance of running upright. It reminded her a little of a werewolf, only not so much. She had no idea what it was, or if she could—or should—kill it.

It was leading her back to the temple entrance, which, she being alone, was a good enough reason not to go there. She slowed her pace, shaking her head.

That was when she heard the scream. It came from the direction of the temple, and it was filled with terror.

"Great," she muttered. Putting on a burst of speed, she slid and slipped on the icy pavement but managed to half run, half slide in the right direction. Her breath came in steamy puffs like a speeding locomotive, and she kept thinking to herself, *This is a trap. A big fat trap.*

The thing was, that didn't matter very much if one was the Slayer. It was her job to risk her life if someone needed help. If she died in the process, oh well. Top priority was always someone else. That was the nature of the game . . . that she had never signed up to play.

There was another scream. No one in the neighborhood came out to investigate, which angered but did not surprise her.

She swung around the corner and reached the temple entrance. There she broke the lock on the guard gate and dashed on through, boots crunching on the gravel beneath the snow.

Then she stood still for a few moments, listening. There were no more screams.

Lack of screaming can mean a couple of things. One is the bad news and another is that the victim escaped.

She had no choice but to search for whomever had screamed; she moved forward cautiously, her Slayer reflexes on high alert, stake at the ready. She listened for furtive movements, scanned for the spindly creature and any number of vampires.

But she appeared to be alone.

Then she saw her.

About fifty yards ahead, turning in the snow, was the beautiful *geisha*. She was dancing to the solo accompaniment of a Japanese flute, a *shakuhachi*, which India knew about from Japanese culture class in school. Her beautiful robes of ice blue and white swirled around her. Her black hair was a stark contrast to the field of white on which she danced.

Her feet were not touching the ground. She was actually dancing a couple of inches above the snow. As she dipped and glided, incorporating movements of her ground-length sleeves, she glanced up coyly at India and smiled.

India felt the hair rise on the back of her neck. Definitely creepy.

Then she turned on her heel, showing her back to India, and opened her arms. The flute keened mournfully as she began to ascend invisible stairs, as before.

Then another scream rose above the flute. It was coming from above the *geisha*'s head, somewhere at the top of the invisible stairs.

For the Slayer, there was no decision to be made. She had to follow the ghost. She kept her wits about her and her stake close to her chest as she lifted her boot and put it down—on something that was solid but invisible. She did it again, and again, and soon she was halfway up the stairs.

Another scream shot through the melodious flute music like a cannonball. The ghost paid no attention, only continued her ascent. India did the same, fairly certain she was being set up. *Slayers rush in where others can opt out.*

At the top of the invisible stairway, the ghost disappeared as before. India took a breath and stepped onto the platform. The flute music rose and fell, sonorous and hypnotic.

As she listened to it, the space around her filled with the strong scent of incense such as is burned on the grounds of temples, before statues of Buddha and symbols of the divine. Incense smoke appeared about three feet away and wafted toward her, an undulating pair of arms appearing and disappearing inside the perfumed haze.

She stood her ground; then shapes moved and danced inside the incense; she saw court dancers moving and swaying, made out a deep jewel-toned *kimono,* silky hands waving elaborately painted fans in time to the flute's meanderings.

Those shadows blurred; then she was standing in a vast wood hallway, carpeted with fresh *tatami* straw mats and walled with rice paper. The screen doors were opened, and she was looking out on a rock garden. Smooth white sand had been raked into shapes resembling the ocean, with large boulders placed at random intervals.

Then the floorboards jingled and chimed like bells, and as India watched, a fierce, proud *samurai* in a blue kimono adorned with a family crest that resembled a yin-yang symbol strode toward her from the opposite side of the garden. He was broad-shouldered and extremely muscular beneath his robes. There was something extraordinary about his bearing; he walked like a god. His black hair was pulled away from his face into the famous *samurai* topknot. His twin swords, the *wakizashi* and the *katana,* hung at his side.

As she regarded him, he vamped. His features sharpened, hardened, into the grotesque expression of the vampire. His fangs were longer than any she'd ever seen. His eyes glowed like the sun at an eclipse.

On instinct, she inclined her head at the exact same time as the vampire did, so that they were a mirror image of each other.

"Slayer-*san,*" he intoned.

"Lord Asano," she replied. She was scared. No way was she going to let him know it.

His answering smile was proud and malicious. He put his hand on the hilt of his *katana,* the longer of his two *samurai* swords.

"You have brought weapons," he stated, glancing at her stake.

"I have."

"Then prepare yourself."

The words terrified her. She didn't move. Instead, she said, "You stepped up your activity to get me to come to Tokyo."

He raised a brow and grinned at her. "Something I shared with my descendant, Jun Asano, was that I was not sure if you were real," he freely admitted. "The old woman whose son gave me immortal life was certain that you were." He regally inclined his head.

The old woman and the spindly creature popped into existence beside India. She looked into the eyes of the creature and saw evil intelligence there.

"He's a vampire?" she asked.

"He has transcended that spiritual plane," his mother proudly informed her. "With my magick, I gave him a new shape. Now he is pure *kami,* pure demon."

India was not impressed; she certainly didn't think the new

demon was much of an improvement over the classic vampire model. Lord Asano looked twenty times better than this guy. Clearly, by her adoring glances, his mother thought he was pretty darn wonderful.

"I am Kohana," announced the beautiful specter as she reappeared at Lord Asano's side holding a lacquered tray. "I was this great lord's concubine in life, and this wise old woman put my soul into the world, so that I might continue to serve him after my death." She bowed low to the witch and said, "I am deeply grateful that you helped me learn how wonderful my lord had become."

Yuck, India thought.

Kohana added proudly, "Upon learning of her husband's transformation on the first anniversary of his death, his beautiful wife asked to be put to death. I gave her his death poem before I smothered her."

"You killed his wife?" India echoed, shocked.

"It was an honor. She was the lady of my lord, and she wished to conclude her life. I was not worthy to do it, but as she requested it, I fulfilled my obligation."

India was amazed, but said nothing.

"And then, I returned to my former life . . . until *he* came."

"Watch. See," the witch said to India. Then she tossed a handful of shining, snowlike crystals into the air, and through them, India saw:

Once Kira was killed, Kohana's former liaison with Lord Asano elevated her status, as his vassals had displayed their Bushido for all the world to see. Suitors vied for her company, and she owned an elegant home, which she maintained with beauty and grace in the center of the water world, another name for the pleasure district of Edo. She was happy, though she grieved for the handsome young lord whom she had allowed to become demonized.

Then, one fine spring night, when the rabbit on the moon pounded rice for sweet omochi cakes, a fine retinue approached her gates. Silk gleamed in the moonlight, and gold and silver; the hilts of katana and wakizashi gleamed with damascene. She was entranced by the splendor, and allowed the party to enter her compound.

She watched from her doorway as servants set down lacquerware boxes, presumably filled with presents for her from her mystery visitor. From a trio of curtained palanquins stepped the old witch, her vampire son, and Lord Asano himself. He wore the face she had known in his lifetime, and as she fell trembling to her knees, he glided toward her, put his hands around hers, and eased her to her feet. Her heart pulsed in her throat, and he leaned forward and kissed the vein without opening it. Her heart beat faster; she was consumed with both joy and fear at the sight of him.

"Do not . . . do not make me a vampire," she begged.

He shook his head. "Please, invite us in. Let us drink tea together. And then I will give you a different choice."

She bade them rest while she prepared an elaborate tea ceremony in her garden pagoda. They came in, her vampire lord and the witch who had transformed him.

They sat seiza in a hut lined with rice paper and one peony. They admired her simple tea articles; admired, too, the deft grace with which she prepared and served them tea and delicacies. They ate, and sipped, while the other creature, the vampire son, waited outside, having announced that he would guard them from intruders.

When the ceremony was concluded, Kohana rested her hands on her knees and bowed low. She was still frightened, but the sight of Asano in his human form had warmed her heart to him again, and she yearned for his touch.

"You love him," the old sorceress proclaimed, bringing the matter into the open. "I have heard your sighs throughout Edo. Your koto sings of missing him."

Kohana inclined her head. "That is true," she admitted, hiding her face behind the sleeve of her kimono.

She heard Asano's quick intake of breath and flicked her gaze toward him. His gaze was bright with ardor.

"I have missed you, as well," he said. "This witch can give you immortality, Child of Flowers. She can make you live for a very long time, as a ghost." His eyes glowed, but not with demonic power. With love. "She will capture your soul and put it back into your body. After you have committed ritual suicide, as I did."

Kohana paled beneath her white makeup. She was young, and the world loved her.

"The sooner you die, the more beautiful you will be," the witch informed her. "You will keep his heart throughout eternity."

"But you must choose," Asano told her. "I will not force this on you."

"So I chose," Kohana told India, who stirred from the vision as if she had fallen asleep. "I chose to spend endless nights with him." Kohana swept a deep bow, then smiled adoringly at the vampire. "It is a decision I have never regretted," she added. "Perhaps you have a choice as well, Slayer-*sama*."

She gestured to the tray. On it sat several objects, including two pottery bowls, what looked like an old-fashioned shaving brush, and some other stuff. India didn't take that long to look at it, preferring to keep her attention focused on Lord Asano.

"I invite you to a tea ceremony," the vampire lord announced, gesturing to the tray. "First we shall perform the ceremony, and then we shall do battle."

"No, thanks," India replied, trying to remain even. "I just spent the last hour drinking coffee."

"I insist." The vampire inclined his head. "Or I will send my *samurai* and my other followers down the stairway to the compound. From there they will fan out all over Tokyo, and murder as many human beings as they can. Eventually Jun and your Watcher will return, and they will be executed."

As he spoke, he waved his hand.

The hall filled with row upon row of vampires, all kneeling, but still at rigid attention. Four dozen of them were attired in blue Asano *kimonos*. They looked straight ahead, their eyes hard and unfeeling.

"So why?" India asked. "Why do you care about me?"

Despite his smile, his features took on an almost mad intensity. He said, "You are my enemy. After I was forced to commit *seppuku*, I swore that no enemy would live to harm me and mine."

India couldn't argue. She was his enemy. But she might have spent the time she would be in Japan under his radar, if Jun hadn't asked for her help.

"You stepped up your activity to force him to contact me," she guessed. "You wanted me to come here. To you."

He inclined his head. "You are wise, Slayer-*san*."

At the word, "Slayer," every vampire head in the room turned her way, glaring at her; some licked their lips as if in anticipation of the fine taste of Slayer's blood.

What was it some old rock-and-roll guy said? No one gets out of here alive?

"Let us enjoy the tea ceremony," the vampire urged.

Might as well, she thought, *while I figure out how to get out of this in one piece. Although "enjoy" is not the word that comes to mind. Endure? Survive? Those work better.*

"You will be the chief guest," the vampire told her grandly. "Since of course you are the only guest."

India had not yet been to a Japanese tea ceremony. Her father had told her they would be going to one when he came back into port. Her mother said they were boring.

Guess I'll find out.

"Please remove your shoes," he said.

"Sorry. Not happening," she shot back.

The vampire laughed. "I should have realized you would not share my sense of decorum."

"Guess not." She fought to keep her voice steady. She was out of her element, and she started to feeling panicky. But she had to keep it together . . . even if Kit was not here to remind her how.

Kohana placed the lacquered tray on the floor. A man in a long black silk *kimono* trailed after her, with another tray of ceremonial objects for the tea.

Her boots firmly laced up, India walked around the rock garden on the straw mats. Kohana was taking the things off the male servant's tray and arranging them just so.

"First, we must wash our hands to purify them," Asano told her.

The servant left, then reappeared with a wooden dipper and a simple bowl. India shook her head.

"Putting down my weapons also isn't happening," India told him.

"My *samurai* came to me willingly," Asano said, observing. Then he gestured to his vassals. "They each accepted the gift of the Change, then returned to lives in the world of men until I gave the word. They converged on my enemy, Lord Kira. Breaking into two formations, one attacked the rear of his castle, while the other broke down the entry gates. Within minutes they had slaughtered all his guards. They cut off his head, and put it on my grave. And then we feasted."

"On his head?" India blurted out, disgusted.

Kohana tittered, then looked away. Asano chuckled. "I like you, young Slayer. What a pity . . ." He trailed off meaningfully.

India let his comment pass. Making sure he saw her stake, she lowered herself to the floor Japanese style, her legs underneath her, her bottom resting on the backs of her feet. *Seiza.* She was limber, and the position didn't bother her, but Kit complained endlessly whenever he had to sit that way for any length of time.

"It makes my legs fall asleep," he'd complain.

Asano lowered himself to the mat, sitting across from her less than two feet away. If he made any sudden moves, she might not be able to defend herself.

I'm still awfully new at this; coming up against a killer who's survived for three centuries is not something that fills me with joy. Plus, he's got more than a few of his friends with him.

The ghostly Kohana offered a pristine white towel to India, who wiped her hands and put it back on the lacquered tray the *geisha* held out to her. Lord Asano gestured to the tray and said, "That piece of cloth is identical to the ones that *samurai* use to tie their thighs together prior to committing suicide. It helps them preserve their dignity."

"Neat," India murmured, her panic level rising a notch.

"It is a very interesting ritual. Do you know anything about it?" he continued.

"No, but here's something I'm even more curious about: Why do I understand you? Are all of you speaking English to me or are we using some kind of universal translation magick?"

"We have been alive—or in Kohana's case, present on this plane—for three centuries. We speak many languages, including French, Chinese, and Spanish. It helps to pass the time."

She nodded, taking that in. "You must have a lot of time to read, too."

"A lot of time to plot and plan," he told her. "I have decided that it's time for us to push beyond our island home of Japan. There's a large world out there. We have been making inroads.

Hawaii. Korea." The places where the Living Clan members had been killed. His glowing eyes seemed to soften a bit, if that were actually possible. "In our day, we were very insular. We wanted to have nothing to do with the rest of the world."

He carefully scooped brownish-green powder into the two simple bowls, then held back his sleeve as he reached for an iron kettle. Slowly, deliberately, he poured hot water over the powder. It began to eddy and swirl. As India watched it, a wave of fear churned inside her.

Lord Asano bowed to her, and she to him; then he picked up the tea bowl with both hands and handed it to her. She accepted it, accidentally brushing her fingers against his. His skin was as cold as the Tokyo snow.

"You do me honor, Slayer-*san*," he said, as she touched the teacup to her mouth. She didn't actually drink it. For all she knew, it was pure poison.

"You deserve this moment, before I kill you." He bowed again. Then he leaned forward and said, "You do accept that this night will be your last, yes?"

She picked up his bowl of tea and handed it to him, improvising, but figuring she was close to conforming to the ceremony's pattern when he accepted it and answered her bow.

"Not really," she told him, wrinkling her nose. "No offense."

"I would be very disappointed if you had said yes." He lifted his teacup toward her. "I admire courage."

"That's nice." She made sure her stake was in her grip.

"And loyalty." He swept his hand at the rows of *samurai*. "They will not interfere while we fight, Slayer. Not even if you gain the upper hand. They would not want me to lose face by helping me." He chuckled as if the idea was lunacy.

"That's a little hard to believe," she told him, her voice quavering. "No offense again."

"Ah, you are so young." He looked a little pensive. "This won't be the night their obedience to the code of the *samurai* is tested. For you will surely die, Slayer." He regarded her teacup. "Let me recite my death poem for you. If you like, you may adopt it as your own."

On cue, the court music played again. India jerked, startled by the sound, and spilled tea all over the *tatami* mat. A collective gasp went through the room as Asano's *samurai* retainers noted what she had done.

Lord Asano looked vexed, but said nothing for a moment. Then he rose to his feet in a graceful movement reminiscent of Kohana's dancing above the snow.

"Dead spring blossoms fall,
Winter snow in the fortress,
Blood on white petals."

Then, unsheathing his *katana* sword, he grabbed his cup and tossed it in the air. As it tumbled end over end, spilling tea, he arced his sword behind his head and sliced the cup in two.

Then he assumed an offensive posture and said to her, "We begin our dance."

India leaped to her feet and took a similar offensive stance with her stake.

I can do this. I can.

The music soared, blaring so loudly she could barely hear the roar of blood in her head. A drum sounded once, twice, as melancholy as any death march.

The vampire *samurai* turned on their knees to watch. Kohana, the witch, and her son also fell to their knees, facing the combatants. Their faces were grave, but relaxed.

They think he's going to win.

So do I.

Before this night is over, there may be a new Slayer in town . . . or rather, in the world. Potential, do you hear me? If I go down . . . good luck!

The drum banged again, then faster, faster, as Asano bellowed and rushed her, flashing his sword on either side of his body so that he was a blur of blue and steel; her depth perception couldn't handle the overload and she could no longer see him.

She jumped aside, rolling, her stake held straight out from her chest. She got to one knee, planting her other foot on the ground so that she could pivot and duck; once she realized where he was, she lowered her shoulder and executed a perfect *aikido* roll, coming back up on her feet.

Asano looked mildly surprised, as if he hadn't thought she'd last even one move. He took a step back, dipping his sword in front of himself, as if in respect, then pushed it through the *tatami* mat, using it as a lever as he flipped forward over it, slamming into India with both feet as his body followed through on the momentum.

She fell back, hard, and then he was on her, straddling her as he opened his mouth, exposing his fangs, and leering at her. Adrenaline ripped through her. She pulled her right wrist free and she slashed forward with the stake as he tried to grab it again. Though she grazed his chest, he was able to push himself backward out of her reach, then rolled onto his side and up again.

She didn't give him time to plan his next move. She hustled toward him, extending her stake.

He swept his foot in her path, and she went sprawling.

The vampire leaped on her back . . .

. . . and then someone was pulling him off, shouting, "Oh, no, you don't!"

It was Kit, his head and shoulders dusted with snow. There was blood on his cheek. He had on his gloves and his coat, and he fished in the pockets while the vampire whirled around, his sword above his head.

Her heart leaped. *Kit! He's back! He's here!*

And then she was very afraid for him, and she blurted out, "What are you doing here?" as she rolled onto her back, then made a bridge of her body and propelled herself back onto her feet.

Asano was hissing. Kit had a bottle of water in his fist—*holy water,* India assumed—and he had flung some of the contents on the vampire to keep him down while India regained her footing.

"Dishonorable man!" Asano thundered. "This battle is between the Slayer and me!"

"Did she agree to those terms?" Jun asked, dashing through the rock garden with a crossbow in his hands. His hair was also disheveled and he looked wan and sad. India wondered if one of the wounded hadn't made it to the hospital.

"Three against one is not fair," Kohana asserted indignantly. It was clear she wasn't very worried that the addition of two more human opponents would tip the outcome of the fight. "Crossbows are not allowed."

"Did she agree to those terms?" Jun repeated, gazing at the great and terrible Lord Asano. When his vampiric ancestor did not respond, he said, "Then they do not apply to her. Or to us."

"Nonsense," Asano said. "She knew she was coming to Tokyo to fight me."

"She did not agree to those terms," Kit insisted.

"She drank tea with me," Asano said. He looked to his *samurai,* who were still all vamped out. They gazed stonily back.

Then the duel resumed.

Asano cut India out of the trio, going at her, his sword flashing, his mouth pulled back in a rictus of fury. She could almost feel the anger emanating off him in waves. He truly disliked the fact they weren't playing by his rules.

"This is not a fair fight!" Kohana insisted.

Then, the *kami* that had once been the witch's son scrabbled toward Kit, pulled back its grotesque arm, and slammed it into his temple.

The Watcher went down.

"No!" India cried. "Kit!"

Jun paled, maneuvering around the monster to stand by India. He put his back against hers and said, "Circle slowly, India-*san*. This will give us two points of defense."

What about offense? she wanted to ask him, but she said nothing. She couldn't even afford the luxury of looking at Kit to see how he was. His body was a shadow in her peripheral vision.

Then Asano attacked again, racing at them both.

"Good luck!" Jun cried, as he wheeled around to face the vampire and let go a crossbow bolt.

It went wide, despite the proximity of Jun's target. As the vampire lunged for him, attempting to thwart a reload, India jammed her stake into his arm and quickly grabbed another from beneath her jacket.

Enraged, the vampire backhanded her. She was sent flying across the room, crashing through the rice paper wall into another room. By the time she got to her feet, there was a horrible scream, followed by the sound of a sword entering flesh.

She dashed back through the tattered wall, and came up short at what she saw.

The vampire stood over the inert body of Jun Asano, his *samurai* sword dripping with blood as he raised it into the air. Kohana knelt before him with one of the white towels; he lowered the sword toward her and she carefully wiped the blade clean of Jun's blood.

"No!" India cried, fury rising to a nearly uncontrollable pitch. "You *monster!*"

And as she launched into the air, sailing toward Lord Asano, she actually saw her entire life flash before her eyes. In the instant it took to reach him, she saw herself as a baby, then her first day of school, a Christmas pageant, all the fights between her parents, the many times they had left her behind—

The drinking—

And she found herself thinking, *In a way, dying would be a relief.*

The music crescendoed, reaching an apex.

I hope dying doesn't hurt, she thought.

She half flew, half tumbled through the air, watching as if in slow motion while he hefted the sword and aimed it at her, eyes burning with hatred and evil. Emotion boiled up inside her. She would miss Kit so badly. . . .

Take care, my Kit. I love—

He held the sword over his shoulder, as if he were preparing to lop off her head.

And in that moment, Jun scrabbled toward him, threw his hands around Lord Asano's ankle, and yanked hard.

The vampire slammed to the mats.

And India made contact . . . point to heart.

She pressed home her advantage.

The great feudal lord, Asano, burst into dust.

It showered her, the ashes of his bones, muscles, and sinews.

The ashes of his former soul.

It took her as long as one deep breath to comprehend the enormity of her action: She had killed the enemy.

She had prevailed.

Kohana's head fell back as she began to wail with grief. It was clear that she had not expected her lover to die.

Raising herself on one elbow in the ash, India followed the trail of Jun's hands to his face . . . and saw that his eyes were glassy and open. He was dead.

Then, as one, all the vampires in the room rose from their knees and faced her. India's eyes went wide and she sat upright.

"Kit," she murmured.

"Here," he whispered back.

She glanced toward him. He was half sitting up, rubbing his face. He looked terrible. But he was alive.

There were so many of them . . . all coming for her.

"They converged on the castle of Lord Kira," Kohana hissed savagely. Tears spilled down her chalk white cheeks. "They showed no mercy to my lord's enemy." She clapped her hands. "Kill her! Kill her Watcher!" she yelled to the *samurai*.

The first row of vampire warriors reached India. Kit fumbled in his jacket for a stake, groaning as he half fell back down. But India sat tall, and waited for death to come.

She had no more stakes.

"I am Oishi," said one of the vampires, the tallest in the row. He was incredibly ugly, even by vampire standards. His features were almost batlike, and he had a face not even a mother could love. "It is my statue that greets you on the temple grounds. I was Lord Asano's chief retainer."

India said nothing, only eyed the stake that Kit had dropped. It was about ten feet away. The vampire was no more than three feet away.

"You have killed my master," he continued.

Then, before India could say or do anything, he darted forward with supernatural speed and grabbed up Kit's stake. He held the stake firmly in his right hand and moved forward. India braced herself, terrified that she was about to watch the vampire kill the man she loved.

"Revenge!" Kohana screamed over the reedy, bold music. "Take revenge, for his honor!"

"You are the Slayer," Oishi continued, bowing low. "But you are a young girl. You did not consent to this duel." He cast his gaze down. "That was unworthy of him. The way he fought . . . also unworthy."

He moved toward India and held the stake toward her.

"I cannot live with this shame," he said bitterly. Tears formed and he looked completely and totally undone. "Please, allow me to retain my honor."

She stared first at the stake, and then at him. He gestured impatiently to the stake, shaking his fist at it, then slamming that fist against his chest.

"It was unworthy of him, and I am his vassal," Oishi pressed. "Therefore, I strive to retain my honor through ritual suicide, known as *seppuku*."

"More crudely, *hara-kiri*," Kit gasped out.

"Yes," the vampire said.

"No! No!" Kohana cried. She raced toward India.

"Yes," the witch said. She gestured to her son. The spindly creature dashed at Kohana, picked her up, and carried her bodily toward the entrance to the room.

They both immediately disappeared.

"Yes, Oishi-*sama* is correct," the witch said. "There was shame in what Asano-*sama* did." She took a breath. "He is right in desiring to end his existence."

India blinked as the vampire turned the stake around so that the handle end was to her. Slowly she took it from him.

He dropped to his knees before her and yanked open the top half of his *kimono*. His chest was exposed to her.

He closed his eyes and waited.

India hesitated.

After a moment, Kit said, "For God's sake, do it, India."

She did.

It took them a while to kill all the *samurai* vampires. Those not as old and seasoned took flight out of the room, ostensibly back down the stairway to Tokyo.

When it was done, the once pristine room was heaped with dust, and India's arm ached.

Kit was smudged with dust and blood, and as the last, youngest follower of Asano died, he and she stared wonderingly at each other. Exhausted, she let the stake fall out of her grasp, and began to weep.

Kit rushed to her and put his arms around her. He held her tightly and she closed her eyes, listening to his wonderful heartbeat. Feeling his warmth.

Oh, Kit, we're alive. . . .

"Come," he urged.

They went back through the entrance, and down the invisible stairs; back into the compound where Jun's much-diminished Living Clan had reassembled. By the stakes in their hands, India assumed they had dusted the vampires who had fled the killing scene in the sky.

They had also collected the bodies of their two fallen comrades, which were now covered with jackets. A number of the Living Clan shivered now in sweaters and sweatshirts, having given up their comfort for the honor of the dead.

As they saw Kit and India descend, one of the guys—it was Dragon Boy—hurried toward them and demanded, "Where is Jun?"

India swallowed hard and raised her chin. "In a better place than Lord Asano."

Dragon Boy's mouth dropped open. As he gaped at India, he visibly staggered backward, so stunned was he by the news.

"He is . . . he is *dead*?"

She took a breath. *"Hai-hai."* She put her hands to her temples to force herself to remain composed. *To lie well.* "He died killing Lord Asano. They battled. He managed to kill the vampire, although he died from his own wounds."

"He died with honor," Kit asserted.

"Then karma is served well," Dragon Boy murmured sadly.

Slayer and Watcher bowed low to him, and to all the members of the Living Clan.

Behind them, there was a great cracking sound; the stairway, which apparently had been made of ice, shattered, and brittle shards of ice rained down on the shoulders of the living and into the snow. India and the others dodged the downpour, watching as the stairway was destroyed. It took less than thirty seconds; it was as sharp and swift as a Tokyo earthquake.

For a moment the witch's face showed atop the platform; she looked terrorized, screamed once, and then darkness swallowed her up.

"Michiko is in hospital," Kit said. "Issai . . . didn't survive the trip there. We'll take you to her."

Dragon Boy turned to the others and spoke in Japanese. Several began to cry. Others, to move toward Kit and India.

Everyone walked toward the open quadrant of the compound, across the gravel toward the entrance to the temple grounds. The surviving members of the Living Clan appeared to be in shock.

They're finished, India thought. *Off the hook. Mission accomplished, and now they can have lives.*

They walked, murmuring to one another in Japanese. Then Kit came up beside India and took her hand in his. Warm skin on skin, a comforting gesture, but it meant the world to her. More than the world.

"Let's let them have this little legend of Jun Asano," he whispered to her. "There's no use in telling what really happened, unless you want the glory."

"There's no glory in it," India said, her voice breaking.

"I won't even tell it properly in my diary, to protect them from the slightest chance that anyone would ruin it for these people."

"Of course," she said.

"And I suppose the original story of *Chushingura* will remain intact," he continued.

"I suppose."

"The devout will continue to pray to these . . . fiends." He sighed heavily.

In the distance, as if from a dream, murmured the plaintive wail of a *shakuhachi,* a Japanese flute, sad and keening and filled with grief.

She turned her head, to see the spindly creature and the ghost of Kohana dancing slowly above the snow, at a great distance away. The moonlight gleamed on their heads, and they moved as if they were not quite there . . . as if they were becoming nothing more than memories.

India glanced at Kit.

"As soon as I can learn the proper magicks, I'll dispatch them," he promised, speaking beneath his breath. "In the meantime, perhaps we can find a way to keep Jun's friends and family out of here."

India nodded. Then she turned to the new leader—at least, that was how he bore himself—and said, "Let's go to Harajuku next Sunday. We can have a band. We can dance."

Dragon Boy smiled plaintively. "Jun-*san* would have liked

that. He loved rock and roll." Then, after a pause, he added, "I like it as well."

You're going to have a future, India thought, envying him.

The *shakuhachi* grieved and mourned, and India Cohen, the Vampire Slayer, led the Living Clan away from the Temple of Sengaku-ji, ancestral home of legends . . . and lies.

About the Authors

Yvonne Navarro spent her youth (which is ongoing) making up stuff. When she "grew up" she started writing more and more, and now she's had seventy-some stories and over a dozen books published, and she's even managed to get a few cool awards (most recently the Bram Stoker for *Buffy the Vampire Slayer: The Willow Files, Vol. 2*). She has no spare time, that stuff having been stolen away by various evil entities in her life. She recently got married, and finally moved to southern Arizona. Alas, even Arizona isn't hot enough for her. Yvonne maintains a big old Web site at www.yvonnenavarro.com with all kinds of fun stuff on it. She's also the owner of Dusty Stacks Bookstore (www.dustystacks.com). Come visit!

Mel Odom lives in Moore, Oklahoma, with his family. A frequent contributor to all things Buffy, he's written novels about Buffy the Vampire Slayer and Angel as well as the first *Tales of the Slayer* collection. His fantasy novel *The Rover* won an Alex Award and has spawned several sequels, the first of which will be out next year. His historical thriller about a whaling ship stalked by a sea monster, *Hunters of the Dark Sea,* is on bookshelves now. He's currently working on the first book of his original series Hunter's League for Simon Pulse. Please visit him at www.melodom.net.

Christopher Golden is the award-winning, *L.A. Times* best-selling author of such novels as *The Ferryman, Strangewood, The Gathering Dark, Of Saints and Shadows,* and the Body of Evidence series of teen thrillers. Working with actress/writer/director Amber Benson, he cocreated and cowrote *Ghosts of Albion,* an animated supernatural drama for BBC online.

Golden has also written or cowritten a great many books and comic books related to the TV series *Buffy the Vampire Slayer* and *Angel,* as well as the scripts for two *Buffy the Vampire Slayer* video games. His recent comic book work includes the creator-owned *Nevermore* and DC Comics' *Doctor Fate: The Curse.*

As a pop culture journalist, he was the editor of the Bram Stoker Award–winning book of criticism *CUT!: Horror Writers on Horror Film,* and coauthor of both *Buffy the Vampire Slayer: The Watcher's Guide, Vol. 1* and *The Stephen King Universe.*

Golden was born and raised in Massachusetts, where he still lives with his family. He graduated from Tufts University. There are more than eight million copies of his books in print. Please visit him at www.christophergolden.com

Nancy Holder's work in the Buffyverse has appeared on the *L.A. Times* best-seller list, and she has received numerous awards, including four Bram Stokers and a very nice plaque from Amazon.com. Together with Debbie Viguié, she has created the Wicked saga for Simon Pulse, and all four titles, *Witch, Curse, Legacy,* and *Spellbound,* are available in stores now. She teaches creative writing classes at the University of California at San Diego Extension, the Maui Writers Conference d Writers Retreat, and in private seminars with writing guru zabeth Engstrom. She lives in San Diego with a dog, two cats, d her daughter, seven-year-old Belle, who is the head of an international spy ring and in her spare time is studying to be an entomologist. Please visit Nancy at www.nancyholder.com.

Everyone s got his demons....

ANGEL™

If it takes an eternity, he will make amends.

Original stories based
on the TV show
Created by Joss Whedon
& David Greenwalt

Available from Simon Pulse
Published by Simon & Schuster

AN AGELESS VENDETTA, AN ETERNAL
LOVE, AND A DEADLY POWER . . .

"I m living in a new town with a new family, and
suddenly I m discovering new powers, having
new experiences, and meeting all sorts of new
people. Including Jer. So why does it feel like
I ve known him forever? Even before I was born?
It s almost like . . . magic."

Aaron Corbet isn't a bad kid—he's just a little different.

On the eve of his eighteenth birthday, Aaron is dreaming of a darkly violent landscape. He can hear the sounds of weapons clanging, the screams of the stricken, and another sound that he cannot quite decipher. But as he gazes upward to the sky, he suddenly understands. It is the sound of great wings beating the air unmercifully as hundreds of armored warriors descend on the battlefield.

The flapping of angels' wings.

Orphaned since birth, Aaron is suddenly discovering newfound—and sometimes supernatural—talents. But not until he is approached by two men does he learn the truth about his destiny—and his own role as a liason between angels, mortals, and Powers both good and evil—some of whom are bent on his own destruction....

the fallen

a new series by Thomas E. Sniegoski
Book One available March 2003
From Simon Pulse
Published by Simon & Schuster